It All Comes Back to You

Beth Duke

This is a work of fiction. Names, characters, places, and incidents are either products of the author's imagination or used fictionally.

ISBN: 978-0-578-44883-1

For the best man I know, Jay Duke
There's a bit of you in every hero I write.

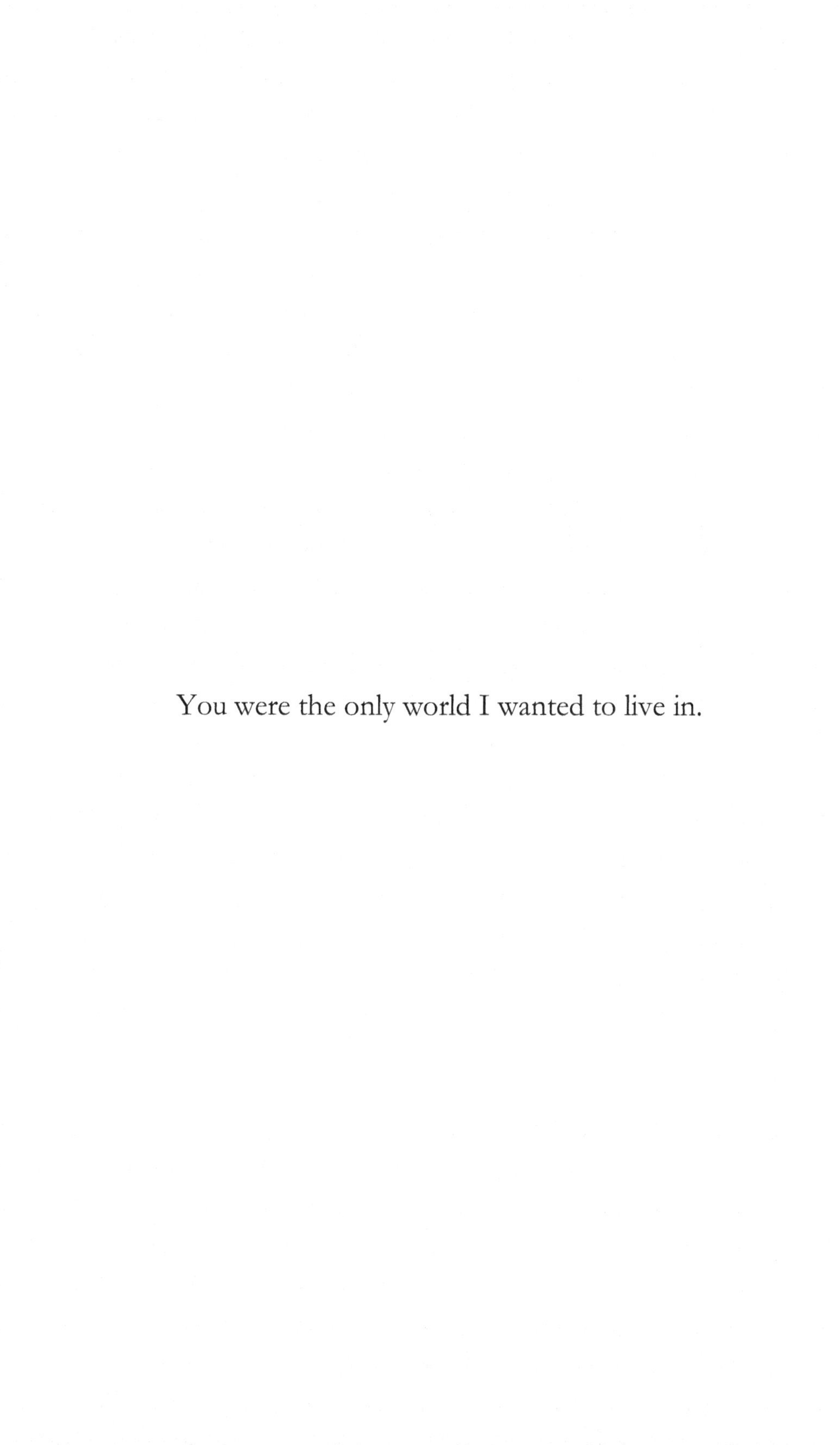

You were the only world I wanted to live in.

One

RONNI

Audrey Marie Haynes Ledbetter was pitching a full blown, deep fried Southern hissy fit. She squirmed back and forth in her wheelchair yelling, "There are vines in my vaginny! Vines in my vaginny!" She struggled valiantly to stand.

I eased her albino cricket body back down gently. "I'm sure there aren't, Mrs. Ledbetter. That's not possible. We would notice."

She narrowed her eyes and shot me a look designed to fork-pierce my jugular. "You nurses don't notice anything! There are vines. VINES, I'm telling you." Audrey paused for a wheezy breath and added in a conspiratorial hiss, "In my vaginny."

Donna, our director of nursing, poked her head into the hall. "Ronni, before you leave, schedule a gyno with Dr. Aronson."

"Really, Donna? She's been going on about this for over a month."

"We can't have her waking up with morning glory twisted around her legs, can we?" Donna nodded at Audrey and smiled. It was easy to be indulgent when you spent your days in a rose-scented office eating chocolate.

Audrey Marie Haynes Ledbetter calmed immediately and flitted onto a new subject, asking Kait sweetly, "How soon is lunch?"

My shift partner Kait blew her blonde bangs upward, ignoring the question. She muttered, "We could just call in a gardener. Or maybe a shot of Round-Up?"

Kait has the only sense of humor at Fairfield Springs more wicked than mine. It's necessary for preserving sanity in the workplace.

"Mrs. Ledbetter, we'll get the doctor to see you." I patted her hand, noting her fingernails would soon qualify as deadly weapons.

"It's about time," she snapped. "The Haynes family will shut this place down if you ignore my medical needs, you know. The vines are terrible, just terrible." She never missed an opportunity to note her glorious lineage. Audrey was descended from an Alabama peanut and cotton dynasty, and I wondered if her vine fixation might have something to do with peanut flashbacks. Maybe she had gynecological kudzu nightmares.

Kait snickered and whispered something to me about pruning shears. I had twenty minutes to go today, and my love/hate relationship with my job was running about 20/80. I felt my pocket for the lavender envelope Donna handed me earlier, my name etched on front in Violet's scrolly chicken-on-valium handwriting. I wanted some privacy to open it, because thoughts of Violet made my heart feel like freshly furrowed earth. I waved to Kait to signal she was in charge of the daily lunch debacle and headed off to sit on hold with Dr. Aronson's office.

Hours later Halle Berry, my black Persian cat, greeted me and threaded my legs enthusiastically in hopes of tuna. I sank into a worn kitchen chair and she leaped into my lap to decorate my white scrubs with fur. My hands shook as I pulled Violet's letter out and unfolded it.

Dearest Ronni,

How best to thank you? The care you gave me and the loves of my life was the best anyone could ask, and you deserve to be rewarded. My attorney, Melvin Sobel, will be in touch with you soon about that. I set aside a nice sum for you; enough to help launch your writing career and maybe get you out of that uniform and Fairfield Springs.

You have talent, darling. Use it. You're free now to tell the stories I shared with you, and the letters. I'm gone and the world can know everything—no more secrets. When you get the book written, send it to Jennifer Meyer at Bravissimo Books. Jennifer is Mel's niece, and he will furnish you her contact information. She will be waiting to read your manuscript. I have no doubt you'll have a best seller on your hands.

Take care of yourself with the same tenderness you showed me.

With love,

Violet

It was hard to see through the waterfall, much less process what I'd read. Violet had changed my world in so many ways throughout the past five years, and she was still doing it a week after her funeral. Halle licked a tear from my face and jumped to the floor, utterly unconcerned with anything but her food bowl.

"We're starting a new life again, cat, in true Violet fashion." I reached for the can opener. "This one may be the best yet."

Violet Louise Thompson was beautiful and elegant at eighty-two and so scandalous in the manner she passed away Fairfield Springs was being sued for negligence. I alone knew why Violet was where she was when her heart stopped beating. With her permission, the world would soon find out.

She planted the seed of my writing career when I was a newly licensed practical nurse and had worked in the assisted living facility/nursing home for two months. Violet was relentlessly inquisitive; all it took was a few literary references from me in casual conversation.

"You love to read, don't you? I'll bet you dream of writing, too."

I'd secretly been penning sappy poetry since the age of seven and changing song lyrics in my head to suit every situation. My tenth grade English teacher, Mrs. Herold, insisted I had enormous talent and imagination. My short story on mothers and daughters made her cry. Of *course* I dreamed of holding my own book in my hands.

"Doesn't everyone, Violet?"

"Maybe," she smiled, "but they actually pursue it. You're spending your days tending to God's waiting room."

"I love my job."

"Yes, but you have a knack for painting pictures with words. You're obliged to use it. That short story you showed me was as good as anything Flannery O'Connor wrote."

She'd been an aspiring novelist in her younger days and encouraged me every chance she got. "Encouraged" is too mild a word. She pushed me with the subtlety of a tsunami.

"Honey," she said, watching me dab sweet potato casserole from Mr. Hardy's chin, "have you started writing a novel yet?" She swept her chin-length hair back, lustrous and snow-white but immersed in a pale field of lavender before Kelly Osbourne even thought of it. Her brown eyes sparkled at the men who joined her in the dining room every day at the elderly equivalent of the Cool Kids' Table. Johnny was always seated beside Violet, though Sam was obviously highly favored, too. James, Clifton and Harvey joined in the daily adoration.

"Not yet, Violet. I'm still trying to imagine the story I'll tell."

"You don't need to imagine a thing," she nodded and gave my hand a fluttery pat. "My life would make a pretty interesting novel." She turned her gaze to Mr. Raintree, who smiled shyly and regarded his lime jello. The other men exchanged knowing smiles.

She had no family or visitors save one nephew through marriage who trotted in occasionally bearing a pot of (predictable) African violets. She accepted them with a gracious smile but walked them over to our long-term care patients as soon as Herb left. "He thinks he's in the will," she said, shaking her head at her nephew's retreating form, strutting in tight jeans and a shrunken black tee shirt. "Herb's a fawning fake. Look at him...thinks he's Simon Cowell. His hair is dyed the color of burnt toast. I swear, Ronni, he tried out a British accent on me today. Called me his favorite Aaauhnt-eee Vee." Violet laughed and whispered into my ear, "Fairfield Springs is getting a lot of my money. Y'all are going to need a new entertainment room when I'm gone."

"We sure will, Violet," I told her. "You are the life in this place."

This was undeniably true. Homecoming queen at seventeen and Fairest of Fairfield at seventy-seven, Violet wore her beauty effortlessly. The old ladies generally despised her, but the men—every single one—took in her smiles and laughter like parched ground drinks spring rain.

Fairfield employed a man named Emory who piloted an ancient white Lincoln Town Car for its residents. Violet referred to him as "my driver." His Friday afternoons were spent waiting outside The Coiffure & Couture while she got her hair done, then dropping her off at the grocery store for fancy cheese and crackers. Violet's last stop was Duffy's Liquor Store, where she sauntered in and purchased the same fifth of bourbon, sugar cubes and maraschino cherries each week. Five o'clock every day she enjoyed a cocktail or two in her apartment. I was extended an open invitation but usually had to work through six-thirty unless I was working night shift, which made a visit impossible. By that point, Violet was entertaining gleefully in the dining room, sneaking salt onto tasteless chicken.

She didn't need assistance of any kind, at least not for the first few years of her stay. Violet was there for love, pure and simple. The man she'd adored for more than fifty years—her biggest secret—was in extended care at Fairfield. Having Johnny, Sam, James, Clifton and Harvey by her side was icing on her social cake.

The facility surprised every visitor with its beauty. Fairfield drew a moneyed crowd from all parts of Alabama, especially the upper crust families in surrounding counties. There was nothing remotely comparable in the state, and it wasn't unusual for people who'd played teenaged tennis together at area country clubs to find themselves reunited as they strolled around the gardens and lake.

The lobby, library, sitting room and administrative offices were housed in a renovated Queen Anne Victorian. Wings on the east side were for independent living. On the west was an extended care complex where I worked. Residents and workers met in a posh dining room and common area behind the lobby. That's where Violet shared her first stories with me, sitting in her favorite wingback chair and transporting me to post-WWII Alabama.

The memories nibbled at my heart like minnows. Violet was my surrogate grandmother, my closest confidante, and the source of what little understanding of life's mysteries I had. As soon as Halle finished licking her bowl, I took four legal pads of notes, the cardboard box holding her countless letters and my laptop to the bedroom to contemplate writing her story.

Violet had chosen the title for my work, though she gave me permission to brainstorm an alternative. "Everybody Loved Her" was the epitaph she'd chosen for her headstone and her (typically) modest suggestion for the novel based on her life. I pored over my notes, staring at the first sentences she'd told me to write down.

"A love story can be described, but it's truly known to only two people. They share the first accidental brush of fingertips, every sigh and private joke. They dance to the same music in their hearts for a lifetime."

I wiped away fresh tears and read her note for the tenth time. No matter what inheritance she'd arranged, I couldn't simply walk away from my job. Fairfield had been very good to me, and besides, there was no guarantee of my producing a book, much less having success with it. The bad part of Violet's wonderful news was having no one to tell. My family was gone and friends at work would be less than thrilled to hear I'd inherited money from a resident.

Halle jumped to my side and began pawing legal pads left and right. I swatted her toward my feet and she curled up, content to let me read until her stomach beckoned for service. I sighed at the five pound box of letters and journals. I hadn't looked at a single one, and knew I should start.

It was overwhelming to contemplate a beginning and middle to Violet's story. I knew the ending all too well. Fifty three old people in an overheated funeral home, the women dabbing their eyes dramatically over the loss of one they'd considered a rival. Her nephew and his family shaking hands solemnly as we filed out after the brief service; Herb glancing at his watch. I wouldn't have been surprised to find a Porsche brochure in his suit pocket.

I'd spent a lot of my childhood in Violet's hometown of Anniston. I despised it, but it was the cradle of all that was dear to her. As soon as she found out I had a car and some Saturdays off, she asked me to drive her around and reminisce.

I'd rather have reminisced about my first root canal.

Violet looked at the few landmarks that remained from her youth and described a Frank Capra movie unfolding before her eyes. "Stop, Ronni! This is the house where Johnny lived. See that bright yellow ginkgo tree? Dr. Perkins planted it for his wife after seeing one in Georgia, at Emory Hospital. He adored that woman." She sighed and shook her head. "Anyway, it was just a tiny twig and he forbade us to go near it. He even built a protective wire fence. I don't remember the thing ever growing past two feet. Johnny accidentally hit the tree with a basketball once and nearly died of worry." Her eyes were wide and teary. "Now it towers over everything." She bit her lip. "I wonder if Johnny's been back here. He would love seeing it." The tree was magnificent, at least thirty feet tall and blazing yellow. "They only stay like this for a few days. The yard will be carpeted in golden leaves soon."

The house was a two story brick rectangle with ivy climbing its side. The white front door opened and a woman my age with a ponytail and yoga pants maneuvered a running stroller onto the small landing. "Hurry," Violet said, "Get us out of here." I started the car, smiling and nodding at the mom, who was now staring at us. Violet had her face in her hands.

"Are you okay?" I asked her.

"Yes," she nodded. "That was just a big jolt into the present, seeing that strange girl there." She patted her knees. "Let's see some of your favorite places."

"I don't have any," I shook my head firmly. "Nothing good

happened to me here."

"Well, at least show me where you lived."

"What about where you lived, Violet?"

"They knocked down my childhood home and built a pediatrician's office. It would only make me sad. Show me yours."

I managed to locate the rundown house on Knox Avenue. There were tricycles and neon orange plastic toys strewn across the scraggly front yard. "That's it," I announced. "The mimosa tree on the left is my reverse equivalent of your ginkgo. It seemed much larger years ago. I used to climb up and hide in there to read."

"What sorts of books did you like?"

"Anything I could get my hands on. My first book-love was "They Loved to Laugh" by Kathryn Worth."

"Oh," Violet said, "I remember that book. It's a wonderful story."

"And I read lots of successful woman biographies, daydreaming about the important life I'd have someday." I laughed. "Maybe I was a feminist in my early years. Or maybe I just wanted revenge."

Violet offered her sage smile. "You didn't want revenge, honey. That's ugly. You wanted what you have: a career you enjoy and the opportunity to help people."

"I'm not nearly as noble as you think, Violet." I drummed my fingers on the steering wheel. "Hey, you went to Anniston High School, didn't you?"

"Yes, but they've torn it down, too."

I smiled and made a right turn onto Quintard Avenue.

"This isn't where the school was, Ronni." Violet was gazing at the pizza joints and supermarkets lining the street, shaking her head. "It used to be lined with elegant Victorian homes. They're all gone, replaced by this mess."

"Look toward the center, Violet." The wide median was populated by huge leafy oaks and azaleas in full bloom.

"Yes, at least that part's still beautiful," she allowed.

"Now look ahead on your right." I nodded.

"Oh, my gosh! Is that what I think it is? The arches. We have to stop."

"We will." I parked the car and led her to the preserved entrance from Violet's old school, tall brick and concrete arches towering near one of Anniston's many war memorials. She placed her hands on their worn surface and closed her eyes.

"This was one of the happiest places in my life," Violet said. "Right here, under this entryway, Johnny and I held hands as we walked in and out every day. It was so perfect in our world, Ronni. We had everything, absolutely everything." She swiped at a tear rolling down her cheek. "I can't believe they saved this."

"I'm sure it means a lot to many people." I smiled as she touched her lips and planted a hand-kiss on the inside of the arch.

"I can practically see Johnny and Sam and Katie Ruth and Johnette and Mary Nell...God, I'm the only girl left in that group. We were all so close, once upon a time. Katie Ruth died last August. You would have loved her."

"I'm sure I would have. Here, let me take your picture." I held up my phone as Violet struck a very sixteen-year-old pose, one arm extended up a row of bricks, the opposite arm and leg playfully extended like she was preparing to cartwheel. Her pleated ivory skirt and jacket were perfect.

"Adorable. You need saddle shoes."

"Darling," she came to examine the pic and nodded, "I never wore saddle shoes. That's pretty cute. Will you print it out for me?"

"Of course."

"Thank you for bringing me here. So many good memories." Violet gazed at the arches one last time.

"You are most welcome. Where to now?"

"If you know any decent restaurants, let's get a non-institutional meal. I'm buying."

I drove to an upscale place called Classic On Noble, all chandeliers and fancy salads for ladies who lunch.

"This used to be Woolworth's!" Violet blinked at the crystal sparkling in the windows. "Imagine that. From soda fountain to chic. I love it." She swung her car door open and walked her ballerina walk to the waiting doorman as I schlepped behind her, feeling like I should be carrying her train.

That was the thing about Violet: she entered any room like a queen and inspired train-carrying impulses. "You should always walk like you have a crown on your head, Ronni. You are beautiful when you radiate confidence. Remember that."

So, where would I begin to write the story of a woman who inspired me so? I picked up the many scribbles I'd made about conversations with her, trying to write a decent opening sentence:

"Violet Glenn was born in 1930, during the Great Depression, as God's gift to cheer the world." No. Sappy and stupid.

"Violet Glenn rode her bicycle down the sidewalk to the home of her first love, Johnny Perkins. She was ten years old and lived in the perfect place at the perfect time. Her parents doted on her and so did Johnny, even before he realized it." No, too boring.

"Everybody loved Violet. Let me tell you why." Who would turn that page? No.

I glanced at my phone, surprised to find I'd passed two hours navigating a sea of confusing notes. The day was sunny and I'd had enough reading. In two minutes I had my faded tank suit on, covered by a huge white Birmingham Barons t-shirt. I fixed a sloppy peanut butter and banana sandwich, barbecue potato chip and Diet Coke feast to enjoy poolside. Halle stared after me at the living room window, no doubt cursing my freedom and food. The pool area was usually deserted this time of day. I was banking on complete privacy. No one wants to see the pale chubby girl basking in a lounge chair with banana and peanut butter smudged on her chin. I'd start my diet tomorrow.

As I licked my fingers clean—it occurred to me I was turning into my fat, lazy cat's white twin—I heard a door close and approaching footsteps. Jake Hodges came into view, strutting in A&F swim trunks and no shirt to cover his perfect pecs. Jake ran the complex's gym and worked as a personal trainer to the few who could afford it. Suddenly I was on an episode of The Biggest

Loser, longing to melt into oblivion, a humiliated peanut butter and banana puddle left to sizzle on the cement.

"Hi, Ronni," he grinned. "Haven't seen you in the gym lately."

I squinted up at him. "No, I've been working most of the time. I'll be back soon." I gathered my used napkin and Diet Coke can, hoping the napkin conveyed freshly consumed celery and carrot sticks. As I tugged my shirt into place I found the inevitable Jif mark where I'd dripped. It could have passed as baby poop, which I'd consider less embarrassing.

"I'll come by for a workout soon, Jake." I stood awkwardly and headed to the safety of my apartment for a nap.

"Good." He caught his reflection in the pool and our conversation was complete. I wondered if he'd drown retrieving a mirror tossed in the deep end.

I trudged home and inspected myself in the bathroom for signs of sun exposure. There were none, not even my usual brilliant pink hue. My reflection revealed a large, very white girl, likely descended from Irish mole people who would never tan. I took my hair out of its ponytail and shook it loose to fall in a series of droopy blond curls down my back. My eyes were dark blue and slightly red from the sun. I blinked several times and tried to imagine myself with a smooth, sleek bob with bangs like Kait's. My face would look like a vanilla Moon Pie.

I heard Violet's voice in my head: "Ronni, you are so pretty. You should see yourself the way I see you." I never believed her, mainly because any boy who'd ever gotten close enough to see the real me had disappeared. I responded every time by growing a protective layer of fat. It was very effective.

I went and plopped on the bed, swept my writing paraphernalia aside, and wiggled my toes for Halle to attack. She obliged and I rested my head on the pillow, where I must have fallen deep into a sleep abyss. I woke to find her paws gripping the side of the mattress, staring me awake at six a.m. The clock screamed at me to hurry. Halle obliged by running to the kitchen and prying open the louvered doors concealing cat food and Pop Tarts.

I arrived at work five minutes late wearing one Reebok and one Nike, wondering if I should be allowed to dress old people when I rarely managed to do the job properly for myself. At least both shoes were white. I took a little consolation in that.

"Ronni," Donna waved me into her office, "a Mr. Sobel's office in Birmingham called this morning, looking for you. I told them you'd return their call on your break. Is this about Herb Andrews' lawsuit?"

"Um, I don't know, Donna. I don't think so."

She looked deeply concerned. Donna was always deeply concerned when litigation loomed, and it often did at nursing homes. Attorneys practically perched like vultures in the oaks by the driveway, though Fairfield had never been found guilty of negligence.

"How did she get in that room, Ronni? You're going to be deposed, you know, and I need to hear the truth. We have to take this very seriously."

I opted for semi-honesty. "She got there all by herself, Donna."

Donna offered her most skeptical look but relented into a nod. "Okay, then. Call this number and let me know what Mr. Sobel wants if it's work-related."

"I will, Donna." I put the scrap of paper in my pocket and went to pull charts. Kait caught my eye and waved as she adjusted Mrs. Nealy's glasses for the first of a thousand times for the day. A minute later she joined me.

"Nothing much going on," she informed me, "other than Aronson's office moved Mrs. Ledbetter's exam up to eight fifteen this morning."

"Well, at least that will shut her up."

"Not if she needs pruning," Kait said.

"I think she's pruning quite well on her own."

"That she is, Ronni." Kait grinned and handed me a tray of meds. "Let's hand out goodies and offer cheerful encouragement."

"You're chipper this morning, Kait." I eyed her up and down, looking for clues. "Did you see Kyle last night?"

"Saw him, did him, said bye this morning."

"You're such a delicate flower."

"Freshly pollinated, too," she smirked. "We need to find you a boyfriend."

"No we don't. My heart belongs to Mr. Woodson." I nodded at him, gnarled hands in pockets and leering as usual.

"Well, don't let him touch anything else."

We worked side by side handling the usual calls for assistance with everything from bored penises (ignored) to drinks of water. A bit after eight Kait was summoned to help Dr. Aronson.

"This should be good," she rolled her eyes. "At least I can count on having no appetite for lunch. Or possibly ever again."

I glanced up from a chart. "Give me a full report free of imagery as soon as you're done."

Ten minutes later she rushed up to the station, sparks practically flying from her heels. "You're not going to believe this," Kait gushed, "She had a *potato* in there. She told Dr. Aronson she put it in because it would make her "feel better." He says she has a prolapsed uterus. She really did have vines!"

I tried valiantly to wrap my head around this information. "Jeez Louise! Where the hell did she get a potato in the first place?"

"From one of the World Travelers."

That was our term for the assisted living residents in the adjacent wing who boarded a mini-bus each Tuesday morning for their grocery store outing. The bus was white and painted in Fairfield's Caribbean blues and greens, sporting cheery little heliotrope daisies between each window. The windows were unfortunately positioned, so passing motorists saw a load of drooping shoulders and white hair. Kait said it looked like a hotel shuttle for a wizened wizard convention. Smart shoppers vacated the store when our bus rolled up and began dislodging its passengers. If caught mid-aisle, they hurried to check out before the inevitable coupon files emerged and single-penny-counting payments commenced.

"She had someone buy her a single potato? To treat abdominal pain?"

"Yes," Kait responded. "She doesn't remember who or when. She'd forgotten the potato, actually. Dr. Aronson was only slightly more surprised than Mrs. Ledbetter."

"I take it he's not encountered tuber therapy before."

"Nope," Kait grinned. "God, I love this place." She began her incident report. "At least we caught it before a blight occurred."

"That's nasty." I laughed, though.

"Nasty? You should have been in the room. I've *seen* things, Ronni. Things no one should see. Or smell. As a matter of fact, I've definitely eaten my last french fry, chip or hash brown."

"How about a loaded baked potato for lunch?" I asked.

"You're gross."

"Oh, yeah...*I'm* gross."

Kait clutched her stomach and headed to the staff ladies' room. I decided to avoid the topic until she was less green. There was enough to clean up already.

When Kait returned—still woozy but pinker in the face—we began dispensing meds, tandem-pulling the huge cart up and down the halls. This was followed by calls for more water and Mrs. Delaney's usual request for a candy bar. Mrs. Delaney's blood sugar level never allowed for a Three Musketeers, but she tried valiantly anyway.

After that it was time to round our wards up for the dining room. It was a symphony of cream, taupe, gold, and chandeliers, used by all residents regardless of their level of care. I'd spent much of my time with Violet here, listening and jotting notes as she regaled me with her experiences.

My eyes landed on The Cool Kids' Table. It had been decimated over the past year. Now a fresh group of octogenarians had colonized it like cocky high school jocks, walkers and canes notwithstanding.

I shot Kait an evil grin. "I smell mashed potatoes and gravy."

She turned without a word and began rolling our charges up to tables, shaking napkins and dropping them onto laps as though we were in a Parisian brasserie. The serving crew delivered salads and ice water.

"Girl! Girl!" Mrs. Ledbetter had gotten her wheelchair stuck, and was employing her tender pet name for me. "Girl! I need help!"

I crossed to her side. "Yes, Mrs. Ledbetter?"

"I need a push. Put me over there with Mr. Willis."

"Certainly." I began propelling her. "I heard you saw the doctor."

"Yes. I'm not pregnant."

"Well, that's a relief." I positioned her next to the unfortunate Mr. Willis, whose eyes begged me silently to join the table and save him from Audrey and her terrorizing flirtation. Mr. Willis had a lovely wife who visited regularly, sometimes finding Audrey Marie Haynes Ledbetter attempting to climb into her husband's lap. I dutifully sat down next to him and attempted to make conversation. Audrey rolled a cherry tomato toward Mr. Willis.

"I know you like these, darling," she cooed.

"No, I don't," he grunted.

"You two be nice, now. I have to see about some other folks." I excused myself and rounded the room opposite Kait, looking for spilled food and signs of choking. Lunch passed blissfully uneventfully, and we headed back for an afternoon of disgusting bodily fluids and solids.

I called Mr. Sobel's office on my break.

"Please hold one moment," his secretary said. "He's been expecting your call."

Melvin Sobel sounded like a Southern Baptist preacher on the phone, drawling friendliness and comfort. "Hello, Miz Johnson. I know you were real close with Violet, and I'm sorry for your loss. She was a great lady. I'll miss her, too." He paused. "Anyway, there are some things we need to discuss and I'm wondering if you could come to my office soon. We're in downtown Birmingham."

"I could come tomorrow afternoon," I offered. It was my day off and I couldn't wait to hear what he had to tell me.

"Tomorrow at three o'clock, if that works for you?"

"I'll be there." I hung up and went to find Kait, wondering what Violet might have considered a "nice sum."

two

VIOLET

Anniston, Alabama 1947

Johnny pulled his daddy's shiny black DeSoto to the curb in front of Violet's house. After a quick scan for neighbors and, most importantly, Violet's mother, he leaned over and dug his fingers into her soft blonde curls, pulling her face to his and brushing her lips tentatively. She responded with the kind of kiss she usually reserved for the Ritz Theater's back row. Johnny heard himself groan.

Violet pulled his hands from her hair and laced her fingers palm-to-palm with his, gently pushing him away. She knew she'd gone too far for three o'clock in the afternoon in broad daylight, but Johnny smelled like peppermints and movie star cologne. She wanted to try out the back seat and finally do the things Darlene Coffey talked about at slumber parties. She wanted to follow Johnny to The University of Alabama and leave Anniston behind. She could clean and cook while he attended class. Surely Dr. Perkins could afford an apartment for the two of them instead of a stinky dorm room.

"I love you," she told him. "I'll see you tonight."

"I can't wait, doll. Tonight is going to be special." He smoothed his black hair in the rear view mirror. "We're going to show this car things it's never dreamed of." Dr. Perkins had bought a new

Cadillac three weeks ago and given Johnny full-time use of the DeSoto as long as he kept his grades up and ran the occasional errand for his parents.

Violet giggled. She was on top of the world, seventeen and beautiful, with the most wonderful boy in love with her. Life could not get any better. She knew the *Hourglass* would have a page dedicated to her as homecoming queen, and expected she and Johnny would be named Best Looking or Most Popular. She smoothed the skirt of her cherry print dress and adjusted the cap sleeves. Johnny came around to help her out and hand her books over.

"Don't walk me to the door. She knows we're out here by now, and I'd just want to kiss you goodbye again." She touched a fingertip to Johnny's lips. "Tonight." Violet offered him her most alluring smile and turned to sashay up the walk, noticing he didn't even start the car until she'd closed the front door.

She dropped her books on the kitchen table and heard Mama calling. "Honey? Betty needs you to babysit tonight. She said you should be there by six."

"Can't she get someone else?" Violet wailed up the stairs. "I have plans."

"You're not running off with some boy, Violet," she answered as she brushed by with a load of towels for the kitchen. "Your father and I think you're spending too much time with That Johnny."

"*That Johnny* is a nice guy, Mama. He's going to college this fall. I want to be with him as often as I can."

"Violet, I've been knowing Johnny since he started bringing his frog collections over here at the age of seven. I know he's nice. Give me a hand with this laundry, please." She handed over the stack of dishcloths and headed back up to her room. "You can see him tomorrow night. Betty really needs you."

Violet sighed in defeat. Mama ruled the Glenn household with raised eyebrows and exasperated sighs, controlling her husband and daughter with field marshal precision. There was no arguing with her. She'd be stuck with Chet and his snot-nosed sister

CeeCee for hours tonight instead of exploring mysteries with Johnny on the plush leather back seat. Violet put the towels away and trudged to the telephone in the hall.

"Number, please?" she recognized Mabel Tilley's soft voice. Violet grew up thinking Mabel connected every phone call in the world until she and Mama visited New York City when she was nine. She'd picked up the telephone in the hotel and heard a nasal, clipped "Operator" that shook her so hard she'd hung up.

"375," she responded, hoping Johnny's mother didn't answer. Mrs. Perkins didn't think her precious son should be talking to Violet or any other girl in Anniston, Alabama, preferring to imagine him selecting from the wealthy and cultured coed crop at the university in September.

"Hello?" Johnny sounded out of breath.

"Hi, it's me. I have to cancel tonight. I'm sorry. Babysitting duty."

"Again?"

She could feel and share his disappointment from head to toe.

"I'm so sorry, Johnny. I have tomorrow night free."

"I don't, Violet. I have practice all day and then I'm supposed to take Kimmie back to Tuscaloosa."

Kimmie was Johnny's older sister, who was studying Home Economics and stationed at the University of Alabama to steer her brother toward marriage prospects Mrs. Perkins might approve. Violet remembered the shiny black DeSoto had been offered partly in exchange for Johnny's transportation services.

"Maybe we can see each other Sunday," she offered.

"Maybe." Feigned indifference.

Violet rolled her eyes and twirled the phone cord. "I'll call you after church."

"Okay. I think I'll see what Jennie Holcomb's doing tonight."

"Go right ahead, Johnny." She chuckled at the thought. "Jennie would be thrilled to ride in your daddy's car. Maybe she'll," she checked to see if Mama was lurking and eavesdropping, "stuff her bra for you."

"Very funny, Violet. I'm miserable and you know it. I'm going to call Red and take him over to the gym to shoot some baskets for a while." Red was Johnny's best friend and point guard, also known as Sam Davidson or "the Jewish boy." They'd all been introduced to the wonders of bar mitzvah through Sam, and she and most of her friends had wanted to convert to his much-more-fun religion at twelve. His hair was a darker version of Alabama clay, and he was the most hilarious person she'd ever met.

"Good," she replied. "That will cheer you up."

A long pause. "Not like my original plan for tonight. I love you."

"I love you, too, with all my heart. Bye."

At six o'clock sharp Violet raised her hand to knock on the Wilsons' weathered door, but Chet swung it open before she made knuckle contact.

"Hi, Violet!" he yelled. "Mom, Violet's here!" Chet smoothed his long dark hair back with one hand and pulled her inside with the other. His huge brown eyes sparkled with excitement, and Violet noticed he was standing ramrod straight to maximize his ten-year-old height. "Mom will be ready in a minute, Violet. Would you like a Coke?"

So suave, he was. Violet knew Mrs. Wilson didn't have money for a barber shop, but wondered why she couldn't at least trim the poor kid's hair. She'd do it herself, but was afraid she'd look out her bedroom window late one night to find Betty Wilson hovering on a broom, casting an evil spell on her.

She adored Chet, but CeeCee was another matter. She followed her mother into the hall, clutching a clay-stained muslin doll and staring at her with openly declared hatred.

"No, thank you, Chet. I'm not thirsty."

Mrs. Wilson darted her heavily mascaraed eyes at Chet. "We don't have any Co-colas, Chet."

"I could go get her one." He rubbed his bare foot on the dirty boards of their cheap floor.

"No, you cain't. Now go on back and play. Violet, Mr. Wilson will be home about ten or so. They don't get anything for supper other than the peas and mashed potatoes on the stove." She waved her hand at the children. "Y'all go on to the back yard. Now."

When they were out of earshot she confided, "My husband should have the money to pay you. If he don't, I'll bring it over tomorrow. I'm goin' to visit my Cousin Dewey and his wife. Make 'em behave." She was gone before Violet could respond, trailing orange blossom cologne and a touch of whiskey.

Chet was instantly back by her side, tugging her hand. "Come and sit out back, Violet. I'll show you how high I can jump from."

"No, you won't," she replied. "I need you and your sister to stay in one piece."

He shrugged and thrust his hands into tattered jean pockets.

"I brought you a present. Do not tell CeeCee." Chet brightened immediately when Violet produced the Baby Ruth from her handbag.

"I'm goin' to hide and eat this. Will you go out back with my sister?" He eyed the kitchen door anxiously.

"Yes, I have some homework to do, so I'll sit out there and watch her. See you in a minute." She winked at him, but he missed it as he raced off.

"Homework" consisted of writing "Mrs. Johnny Perkins" and "Violet Perkins" over and over on the last page of her biology notebook. Violet added tiny hearts and the wedding date she wanted: July 30, 1947. He would ask—she was more certain of this than anything in her life.

Chet appeared and yelled for Violet to watch him imitate a fighter pilot, shooting his sister and other targets of choice as he ran around the yard. He took a break to squat on the ground next to her chair. "So," he began, "you still datin' that skinny basketball player?"

Violet swatted a mosquito and stifled a laugh. "Yes, I am. He's not that skinny."

"Looks wormy to me." He squinted at CeeCee, who was producing a giant mound of dirt with a small shovel. "I think you need someone more manly. Maybe a guy who fought, like my

Uncle Chunk."

"Uncle Chunk" was his father's younger brother, well known for killing "thousands" of Krauts and Chet's role model. He'd settled back into town after the war and started a car repair business on Leighton Avenue using his preferred name, Wally Wilson.

"I bet your uncle has lots of girlfriends already. Besides, he's a bit old for me."

"No, he is not. You need a full grown man, Violet, not some high school kid." He stood and announced, "I'm really hungry. Could you fix supper for us?"

"Yes," she smiled. "I'll call y'all in a few minutes."

"Thank you, Violet. You're the best." He seated himself in her chair, carefully placing the notebook in his lap.

When the skimpy meals were on the kitchen table, Violet opened the door to find Chet and CeeCee on the step. He handed her the biology binder with a flourish. "I'm goin' to take CeeCee to wash her hands."

For some reason, Violet thought she should look inside. There it was, on the next to last page:

You are pretty.

She smiled at his sweetness and put her notebook with her handbag. If she ever had a son, she hoped he'd be like dirt-smudged, smelly, lovable Chet Wilson.

Chet and CeeCee seated themselves and ate like they hadn't seen food in a week. Violet wondered if that were true. The little girl was characteristically quiet, listening to her brother ramble on about guns and airplanes. She never made eye contact with Violet unless absolutely necessary.

Chet helped with the dishes as CeeCee threw her doll around the living room. Violet persuaded her to get into the tub by promising jellybeans on her next visit. She read the only children's book in the house to the little girl, a beaten copy of "Cinderella" she'd delivered months ago. CeeCee listened wordlessly and began snoring softly after five pages.

Chet wanted to turn on the radio, but Violet persuaded him to sit on the front porch and talk. She sipped water as he outlined his school problems one by one: the meanest bully in class wanted to fight him after school. Mrs. Dothard got onto him every single day for talking too much. Math was boring. Finally, in the most casual manner possible, "I never have lunch or lunch money, and everybody makes fun of me."

Violet reacted by fetching her purse and extracting fifty cents. "Hide this in your room. You should be set for a week."

Chet pretended to swipe a bug from his cheek, but she knew it was a tear. He hugged his scabby knees and laid his head on them. "Are you going to see Johnny tonight? Tomorrow night?"

"That's none of your business, Chet." She shook her head at him with a smile. "But no. He's busy and I won't be with him again until Sunday afternoon."

Chet nodded. "I was just wonderin'." He stared out at the street for a minute. "I'm tired, Violet. I think I'll go on to bed."

She was completely surprised; bedtime was usually a major battle. "Okay, honey. Sweet dreams." She grabbed his hand and squeezed it. "I'll wait out here for your dad." Violet watched the sky and wondered where Johnny might be. Was he thinking of her?

At nine thirty Mr. Wilson walked up the street, exhausted by hundreds of impatient travelers at his train station ticket window. He greeted Violet with a wave. "Everything okay?" he asked.

"Yes, sir, they were angels."

"I kinda doubt that." He pushed his wire-rimmed glasses up his nose and reached into his pocket, handing over twenty-five cents more than Violet had secretly given his son. "Will this be enough?"

"Yes, thank you, Mr. Wilson. I'll just get my things."

He held the door for her and followed, collapsing onto the couch and closing his eyes. "Did Mrs. Wilson say when she might get home?"

"No, sir. I'm sorry, she didn't."

He sighed and put a pillow behind his head. "No matter. I'll wait up for her."

Violet thought the poor man deserved so much better than his conniving wife offered. She gave him her brightest smile and said, "Your children are very nice, Mr. Wilson. You should be proud."

"Oh, I am. I'll see you next time."

She hurried out the door and began walking the three blocks to home. She heard nothing but distant traffic downtown, and a cool breeze tipped her dress upward every few steps. Most houses she passed had already turned out their lights for the evening. As she turned onto her street, Johnny pulled up in his dad's car. He reached over and lowered the window. "Get in, baby. It's early."

"Oh, Johnny, I really should..."

"...get into the car with your boyfriend," he finished.

Violet dutifully climbed in, wondering if he was taking her home or elsewhere. She got her answer when he turned, heading up the mountain road. Excitement scampered along her spine. What would Mama say? *Mama would never know.*

Johnny found a spot overlooking the city lights and turned the radio on. Nat King Cole crooned "I love you for sentimental reasons...I love you and you alone were meant for me, please give your loving heart to me, and say we'll never part" Violet turned her face to Johnny's and whispered, "Let's move to the back."

"If you say so," he grinned. He reached for her hand, his face suddenly still and solemn. "Are you sure?"

"Yes, I'm sure. It's been over a year, Johnny. I don't want to wait any more."

Violet laid across the seat and pulled his body to hers. She explored his mouth with her tongue, teasing and probing. He unbuttoned her dress and eased it off along with her white lace bra, then lowered his head to her nipples, kissing and licking each one until she moaned. "Please..." she said.

"Please what?" he sounded choked.

"Make love to me, Johnny."

Afterward, she tried to decide what all the fuss was about. It took only a minute and hurt more than she'd imagined. She wondered if sex ever felt good, and if practicing made it better. Johnny had collapsed on top of her with a groan. She stroked his sweaty back, grazing it with her fingernails. "I love you, Johnny."

"And I love you. I'm going to marry you, Violet."

She giggled and raised herself to rest on her elbows. "When?"

"Soon. I need to talk to my folks about a few things. And I'll want to ask your dad for permission."

She pulled her dress up and began fastening buttons, gazing at him in the moonlight. Violet told him, "I'll love you forever, Johnny, but I won't wait forever. I want to be your wife when you start college."

He nodded. "Of course. That's part of the plan, baby." He pulled her close for a long time, his head buried in her hair. "Now let's get you home before your folks start wondering where you are." He climbed out and helped her to the front seat. "Smoke, smoke smoke that cigarette," Tex Williams chanted at them. Violet thought that sounded like a good idea, but hadn't ever smoked around Johnny. He was too concerned with having good wind on the basketball court.

Johnny eased the car down the mountain as Violet smiled at a thousand diamonds glittering in her hometown below. Johnny said, "If they see the car, I gave you a ride home from the Wilsons'. That's all."

Violet glanced at her house, reading the lights and realizing her parents were still awake.

"I'm not an idiot, Johnny. Except where you're concerned." Violet regarded her clasped hands and suddenly felt like a tearful little girl. "I love you."

"I love you, Future Mrs. Perkins." He jumped out and swept her door open, then kissed her for only a second. "I'll see you Sunday."

She nodded. "Sunday. Good night." Violet realized she had no idea of the time. Johnny's tail lights disappeared as she opened the front door. Her mother sat on the sofa, knitting.

"How was babysitting?" she asked.

"Wonderful, Mama, wonderful." Violet noticed Mama's odd smile.

"Was he there to help you?"

"Oh, Mama, he picked me up as I was walking home." The family's golden retriever, Blondie, lifted her head and ambled over to sniff Violet.

"I see. Well, I'm going to bed, and you should, too. Good night."

"Good night, Mama."

Violet closed her bedroom door, removed her clothes and studied herself in the mirror. Same small breasts. Same everything. Nothing looked different or changed on the outside, though she thought her face looked more mature. She pulled on her white chenille robe and went down the hall to take a long bath.

She returned smelling of White Shoulders and shampoo. Blondie was asleep at the foot of her bed as usual. Violet patted her gently and whispered, "Tonight I am a woman, Blondie." The dog snorted and rolled over.

Violet took out her diary and wrote, "Finally." She placed it back beneath her underwear and turned out the light, hoping to dream of Johnny.

Early Saturday morning her mother woke her to help Corinna with housework. Corinna was a short, sturdy woman who never seemed to tire of washing and ironing the Glenns' clothes or scrubbing their floors. Her mahogany face was broad and perpetually smiling. Violet loved her nearly as much as Mama. They hummed spirituals as they worked, exchanging only a few words. When Corinna sat down with her afternoon coffee, Violet joined her.

"You drinkin' coffee, baby girl? You feelin' all growed up?"

"Actually, Corinna, I am."

"You all lit up like a bonfire of sparklers and mirrors. Somethin' to do with young Johnny Perkins?"

"Well, I did see him last night. I think I'm going to marry him someday, Corinna."

"Is that right? Well, I s'pose you could do worse. He a good boy from a good family, though his mama be one grumpy, spoilt woman. Spoilt as year old milk."

Violet laughed. Corinna had worked for Mrs. Perkins for one week before informing her she had too many other houses to clean.

Corinna finished her coffee and began preparing supper. While she fried chicken, Violet swept the downstairs floors. The phone rang and she dropped her broom with a clatter.

"Hello?"

"Hey, doll. Just wanted to hear your voice. I have to get back to the basketball court and teach these jokers how to play in a minute." She heard Red's laugh in the background and wondered how Johnny had gotten into the school's office.

"I'm helping Corinna clean, and then I'm doing nothing interesting at all while you run off to Tuscaloosa."

"You could ride with us. I'm spending the night over there, though."

"You know my parents would never go for that." Violet bit her lip. "You'll be back for lunch after church, right?"

"Yes, I promise. Coach is yelling. I have to go."

"I love you, Johnny."

"You, too." Red must still be listening. She hung up and put the broom back into lazy motion. Soon Mama and Daddy would be home from shopping and she'd join them for supper and television. Theirs was the first house in town with a set, and it was a special point of pride for Doug Glenn. His family loved watching together. "Mark my words," he'd say, "this television thing is going to be big. Someday nearly every house will have a set."

When they arrived, however, Doug and Alice Glenn were arguing heatedly over something. Violet swept the back porch and listened as they stomped up to their room and closed the door, then resumed yelling. She decided she'd had enough Cinderella time and wandered into the kitchen to pester Corinna for a piece of chicken and some iced tea. It was on the table with a note: "Here, sweet girl. Love, Corinna"

She knew Violet very well.

Mama and Daddy wandered downstairs a half hour later, looking calm and determined to coexist. She set the table and the family ate in companionable silence, pausing only to ask for more potato salad or rolls. Violet did the dishes as her father fiddled with the television antenna so they could watch The Kraft Television Theatre. After that, Violet excused herself to read in her room, though she used the time to update her diary in greater detail about the wonders of sex.

Violet woke to sunlight streaming through her windows and Blondie's nose in her face. She stretched and greeted the day by brushing her teeth and hair, then made her way to the kitchen for Adult Coffee with Mama and Daddy. They shared Corinna's pecan muffins and talked about the baptism scheduled for Mrs. Edwards' twins that morning. Mr. Glenn was on his way upstairs to dress when the telephone rang. Violet and her mother listened intently, but couldn't make out his end of the conversation. He returned to the kitchen a few minutes later, his face the color of Elmer's glue.

"Violet," he began, then glanced at her mother. "Violet, there has been an accident, honey."

"Okay, Daddy. Is everyone all right?" She wondered if their preacher had hit something on his way to church and it might be canceled. It was worth hoping.

He moved to her side. "It's Johnny, honey."

"No, Daddy," she replied. "Johnny took Kimmie to Tuscaloosa last night. I'm sure he's back by now. We're seeing each other for lunch."

"Violet, he's in the hospital in Birmingham. He went off the road somehow between there and Tuscaloosa and into a ravine." He paused. "Violet, Kimmie didn't make it."

"Oh my God! I have to get to the hospital!" she screamed, jumping to her feet. "He's okay, isn't he? Daddy, he's okay?" Violet was hysterical and sobbing. Her mother grabbed her and forced her to sit, then looked to her husband for answers. There were none. Violet's parents told her to collect her things. They'd drive her to Johnny.

It took two hours to reach the hospital. Violet found Dr. Perkins in the dull green concrete hallway outside his son's room. "Mrs. Perkins has been admitted and sedated, Violet," he told her. "Johnny is not doing well. You can't see him right now." He grabbed her upper arms and met her wildly darting eyes. "Violet, he's suffered a spinal injury. They're watching him closely. He's not conscious yet, and wouldn't even know you're in the room."

"He...he doesn't know about Kimmie?" She immediately regretted her question. Dr. Perkins began to cry, horrifying her.

"No, Violet. He doesn't. We won't tell him until he's stronger. His doctor is not sure he'll pull through, Violet. Please understand what we're dealing with here." He turned to Violet's mother. "I have to go and check on Edna. Please wait here."

She nodded and forced Violet onto a hard metal chair. "We'll be right here, Dr. Perkins. Praying."

"Thank you." Violet saw her father place his arm around the older man's shoulders. They walked away together.

three

RONNI

The drive to Birmingham gave me lots of time to think. I was very nervous about Mr. Sobel's news and the impact it would have on my life. The worst part would be having no one to share it with.

My mother, Jocelyn Edwards, had a passionate affair with whiskey and bars. She never met a pill she didn't adore, either. Her greatest talent was for disappearing; it approached genius level. I have almost no memories of her and the ones that remain hurt. I try to keep them locked away.

I'm five. Someone is banging on the door very hard. Mama is asleep in her room and I am not supposed to wake her up. I pick up Mrs. Noodle, my only doll, and carry her to the door. I stand there very quietly. "Open up, Joss!" a man yells. I go to Mama's bed and shake her arm. "Go away, Ronni," she mumbles. "I'll get you something to eat later." She rolls over and starts to snore. The door sounds like thunder now, and I'm afraid it will break.

I go back to Mama and shake her again. This time, she grabs me and throws me toward the wall. I start to cry and hug Mrs. Noodle. "Please, Mama. The man is yelling."

This seems to wake her up. "What man?" She rubs her eyes and jumps up to put pants on. She doesn't have a shirt, but I'm afraid to tell her. She goes to open the door and the man walks in. "Where is it?" he asks.

"I don't have anything, Mose," she tells the man.

"I'll tear this place apart, Joss. You know I will."

I hide in the closet behind some boxes. The man is throwing things all over our apartment and screaming. He is going to kill my mother, so I put Mrs. Noodle behind the boxes and walk out to save her.

"What the hell?" The man yells. "You have a fucking kid? You lying bitch." He slaps Mama hard and she falls on the floor and looks down. She puts her hands over her chest.

"Ronni, I have to go somewhere," Mama says. She runs her fingers through her hair and smiles at the man, flashing her teeth. She tells the man, "I'll be right back."

The man looks at me like I am a bug or snake. He pulls a cigarette from behind his ear and lights it, squinching up his eyes. "What's your name?" He blows a cloud of smoke at me.

"Ronni." I go to Mama's room to help her but she already has her shirt on.

"When will you be back??" I ask. "I'm hungry, Mama."

"You and Mrs. Noodle stay in my room and don't open the door, Ronni. I'll bring you a burger or something."

And she was gone. I went to get Mrs. Noodle from the closet and curled up on Mama's bed.

She came back and woke me up the next day, smelling like she had been in a forest fire. She'd brought me cold french fries in a greasy napkin for breakfast.

The state's Child Protective Services removed me from my squalid little life when I was six years old and placed me in foster care. Jocelyn was the only child of older parents who'd died years earlier after retiring to the Mobile area, so there was no alternative. My father was an unknown quantity, though I was sure he'd been an addict, too. Let's just say my family crest would've featured bottles.

I had no memories of my first foster home, but the second was too present in my mind. I lived with the Randalls and their five other revolving fosters from the age of six until I was ten. They had two biological children as well, daughters named Heather and Danielle who were dark-haired beauties; tall, popular, skinny and highly favored over the rest of us. We were there to generate a monthly check for the Randall Family Foster Farm. I learned not to get too close to the ever-changing roster of kids who came and went. I prayed a lot for the day I'd go.

Heather was sixteen and in another world altogether, but Danielle was my age. She and I were usually in the same classes in school and she did everything possible to avoid me. Heather and Danielle got their clothes from the mall while mine mostly came from Mrs. Randall's Goodwill forages.

The Randalls were very involved in their Baptist church. We attended services Sunday morning and evening as well as Wednesday night. Mr. Randall believed strongly in discipline, usually carried out via willow switch on bare legs. Cursing might get you a whipping, but taking the lord's name in vain made one a certainty. I learned early on to substitute the "Jesus!" I'd learned from my mother with Danielle's slightly less punishable "Jeez Louise." To this day I might say a really nasty word here and there, but Jeez Louise is usually my reflexive response to surprise or disgust.

When we were eight, Mrs. Randall decided we should join a local Girl Scout troop. She even accompanied us to sell cookies in front of the grocery store to fund a summer trip to camp. It was the first time I felt included in any fun family activity and I sold more than my share of Thin Mints. Danielle treated me nicely in front of her mother, of course, and other girls from our troop did, too. When we were alone, I was shunned.

I dreamed about Camp Juliette from the minute I heard of it. There would be crafts, hikes in the woods, swimming in the lake and "beach" volleyball, our troop leader, Mrs. Levant, announced with twinkling eyes. All of this awaited on June sixteenth, the day I was sure would begin a better chapter in my life.

Danielle immediately sought out the popular girls when we arrived at Camp Juliette. I soon noticed her whispering to them and glancing my way. It didn't take long for me to realize I wouldn't be making new friends, no matter what their campfire songs said.

The first time we played volleyball I missed a lot of returns.

Rachel Tomkins, with long blond hair and green eyes, the prettiest attendee of Camp Juliet's glorious summer, pronounced me "spastic" in front of our entire team. I began to sit out anything I could, claiming headaches and vague stomach troubles. At night I cried silently in my bunk bed and hoped things would get better. I fell asleep listening to Danielle and her friends giggling about boys and clothes.

I wasn't hated or ridiculed anymore; it was much worse. I ceased to exist.

My final camp trauma came when a water moccasin was captured and displayed on the sandy shores of Lake Juliette. We were assured over and over it was safe to swim afterward and forced to enter the water. I never, ever got over my fear of snakes.

Danielle and I shared a small bedroom. She said much more to me, but the only thing I recall clearly is four years of, "Leave my stuff alone." She collected things, mostly figurines of horses and troll dolls.

My sixth grade teacher, Mrs. Whitley, was ancient by our standards. Her white hair and sensible shoes made her seem a hundred or so, but she was probably more like sixty. For once, Danielle and I were in different classes and I didn't have to wither in her poisonous shadow. And God bless her, Mrs. Whitley seemed to know everything about me before I opened my mouth the first day of school. She asked me to stay after class.

"Ronni, I've heard good things about you. I'm hoping you can help me with some things in the classroom this year. Would you like that?"

I nodded, mute with wonder about the "things" she might want.

"Also, I think that like I do, you love to read. I brought a book for you from my own collection. It's old and worn, but I think you might enjoy the story." She handed me "They Loved to Laugh" by Kathryn Worth.

"When you finish this book, Ronni, I want to know what you think of it." She saw the immediate anxiety on my face and chuckled softly. "No, honey, not in a book report way. I want to know if you like it, that's all." She patted my arm. "When I need notes delivered to the office or papers collected, I may call on you to help. Would you mind?"

"No, ma'am. Thank you." I clutched the book to my chest and hurried to the car line before Mrs. Randall sent a search party.

Two days later I tried to return the book to Mrs. Whitley. "I loved it so much," I told her. "It's the best book I've ever read. Honestly, it made me cry, Mrs. Whitley." I pushed the book across her desk and smiled. "I feel like every word was meant for me."

"I thought you might," she said. "I'm so glad you enjoyed it, Ronni. Now, I want you to keep this copy and promise me you'll read it to your children someday."

It's still one of my favorite novels.

She introduced me to Miss Sasso, the school librarian, and explained my "book tastes." Miss Sasso hurried up one aisle after another, gathering the stories that would spark a lifetime love of reading.

I started collecting something of my own: words. Whenever I found a new and intriguing one, I'd look it up on the school's computers or in the Randalls' fat dictionary. Each was written with its definition in a red spiral notebook I kept under my mattress. Danielle had her horses and trolls, but I had "prevaricator" and "rendezvous" and "ephemeral."

One Saturday in December Danielle and I had our thousandth argument over private space in our small room. I stood firm on the imaginary center line as she screamed I was on her side. She lunged past me and grabbed my red notebook. I chased her down the hall and watched in horror as she flung it into the fireplace. All that work—my entire collection—disappeared in seconds. Danielle stood glaring at me, arms crossed in defiance. Then slowly, little by little, she started to smile.

I ran back to our room and grabbed her new pink sequined sweater from the Gap and her favorite purple-haired troll. I threw them into the flames before she could stop me, mainly because she didn't think I'd actually do it. The next thing I knew, Danielle was hitting my face and I grabbed her long, lovely hair and shoved her to the floor. I sat atop her and hit as hard as I could. Mr. Randall pulled me off and sent Danielle to her room.

I was in trouble, but it was the most fortunate trouble ever. I was removed from Danielle Hell within two days and sent to live with Mr. and Mrs. Jimmy Brooks, where I was the only foster child in a warm, comfortable home. They were young and childless and all of their attention centered on me. Best of all, I could stay in school with my wonderful Mrs. Whitley for the remainder of the year.

Mrs. Brooks was a large, bosomy woman who loved to cook. Her response to any bad day was cookies, cake or biscuits. Her response to any good day was cookies, cake or biscuits.

We read and watched TV together, snacking in happy silence. She funded every Scholastic Book Order I'd ever dreamed of. We took trips to the mall in her tiny Toyota, gradually replacing my wardrobe with pieces I wasn't ashamed to wear.

I was happier than I'd been in my life.

Two years later I came home from school to discover "Ma Brooks" slumped in her chair in front of Days of Our Lives. She'd suffered a massive stroke. I called 911 and screamed for help, hysterical in my belief she could be saved if the ambulance would hurry.

She couldn't.

I stood in Jimmy Brooks' arms and cried in the hospital's waiting room, knowing he could never care for me on his own.

I came to Fred and Lena Johnson in Birmingham through their church. They were a kindly couple already in their late sixties as I struggled through adolescence, and they treated me as the daughter they'd always wanted and taught me the lessons they'd learned over a lifetime. Mom and Dad filled my head with a fragile sense of self-worth and possibility; my battered heart with unconditional love. They legally adopted me on my sixteenth birthday—the proudest day I'd ever known.

Mom volunteered at the nearby nursing home twice a week

and insisted I help. It was there, watching her hold the hand of an elderly stranger as she read to him, I decided to become a nurse. The kindness, the wisdom, the sheer friendliness and gratitude of those old people brought tears to my eyes.

Much more importantly, they made me feel needed.

I told Mom about my decision. "You have so much goodness in you, Ronni. I knew it from the minute I met you. I'm thrilled you're going to share it with those who are thirsty for the smallest kindness."

We had far too few years as a family. Both Mom and Dad had battled cancer throughout mid-life, and they died within weeks of each other while I was in nursing school. I found myself alone again at twenty-one. Selling our house paid for my degree and a shiny maroon '06 Honda Accord I nicknamed Ruby. She was taking me to Birmingham now.

I never heard a word from Jocelyn, nor did I want to try to locate her. My mystery father had no idea I existed. I used to daydream about him, and had assigned him Robert Downey Jr.'s face and voice years earlier. He probably looked more like Nick Nolte's mug shot.

Friends from high school had all moved on and away. I was grateful for Kait and a few others at Fairfield, though we rarely found time to socialize.

My first job out of nursing school was juggling bedpans in Nashville, where I'd followed a boy who believed he was the next Kenny Chesney. Looking back, my main attractive quality was Ruby's ability to transport us and our few belongings to a squalid apartment he'd rented, as far from Music Row as Siberia and about as appealing. He called himself Dakota Pine and carried a guitar when he went to the bathroom. I had known him in high school as Pete Turner, acne-plagued and awkward. Dakota was much smoother and managed to find a barmaid/singer/songwriter/whore named Daisy to replace me while I was working the night shift. I headed back to Birmingham, crappy lyrics ringing in my ears, and began to plot my next escape to a better place. The following day, though, I found an online ad hiring for Fairfield Springs. It was nursing home heaven.

On the other hand, my love life was pathetic. I had an awkward relationship with a guy named Kenny throughout high school, a military nut with testosterone to match. His jealousy and possessiveness drove my parents crazy. I'm sure they celebrated when he managed to get through Army basic training and boarded a flight to Iraq two years after graduation.

My five months with Dakota/Pete was followed by a series of interchangeable domineering males and older men—father figure, anyone?—none of whom lasted very long. My most recent dating experience was a short-lived fling with a musclebound egomaniac named Todd. Kait fixed me up with him in a fit of desperation over my endless whiny complaints of loneliness. He stopped calling or texting me after two weeks of romantic splendor (that's sarcasm), and was now obsessed with a redhead he'd met at his gym named Ashlee, sleek as a seal with large, incongruous boobs that looked like a coconut bra on a skinny tree.

I didn't meet a lot of men through work under the age of eighty. I had my choice of great-grandfather figures any day of the week.

I double-checked the address as I pulled up to the building. Mr. Sobel must be a fancy lawyer indeed; the converted mansion serving as his office reeked of courtroom conquest. It was framed by leafy magnolias and azalea banks. I checked my face and hair, then patted Ruby's dashboard for luck.

The reception room was hunter green and burgundy, suitable for British hunting lodges and moneyed clients. An elegant black woman rose to greet me behind an antique cherry desk, offering her manicured hand. "You must be Ronni," she said. I took in her gray silk suit and Jimmy Choos, feeling frumpy and ridiculous in my TJ Maxx sundress and cropped sweater.

I cleared my throat. "Yes, I'm Veronica Johnson. Your office is lovely."

"Thanks, I'm Laura. Did you have any trouble finding us?" She waved at an armchair upholstered in pheasants, indicating I should sit.

"No, not at all. I used to live in The Magic City," I smiled. "I haven't been back in a while, though."

"You live in Harrison, right?"

"You've heard of it?"

"Well, I've seen correspondence from Mrs. Thompson and references to you in her paperwork."

Of course. I was feeling more idiotic and out of place by the second. "Oh yes, Violet. Did you ever meet her?"

"Once or twice, some years ago. She was one of Mr. Sobel's favorite clients. A beautiful and elegant lady."

I wondered if Laura was trying to imagine how a creature like Violet had anything to do with me. If I were in her place, I certainly would. "Yes, she was." I shifted in my seat and tried to smooth the wrinkles set in my dress.

"Mr. Sobel will be with you in a minute. He had a meeting in Homewood and is running a bit behind. May I offer you something to drink?"

"No, thank you," I answered. "Well, maybe a glass of water would be nice."

"Coming right up." She crossed to an impressive wet bar with an array of crystal glasses. I wondered if I should've asked for scotch or bourbon.

"Ronni?" A man nearly my height poked his head out from behind a polished oak door. He had short, curly red hair and eyes the color of cornflowers. I liked him instantly. "I'm Mel Sobel. Please come in."

Laura followed, delivering my ice water on a linen napkin and setting it on a mahogany table next to an overstuffed chocolate velvet chair. I sat and sipped, watching Mr. Sobel shuffle through papers on his desk. His office was all muted browns and beiges. A host of framed diplomas and awards decorated the walls. I spotted a photo of him with the governor.

He looked up and smiled at me. "First things first. You know Violet left you a sum of money, and we're issuing part of it to you today. She had me place most of it in a trust for you."

I nodded.

"The trust is valued at about two hundred and sixty thousand dollars at present."

I coughed and managed to spill water on my lap.

"The amount you'll receive today is fifty thousand dollars. One hundred thousand more will be disbursed upon completion of the manuscript. You can't touch the rest until," he paused and glanced at his notes, "you'll turn thirty in four years, right?"

"Yes, sir." I swiped at my lap with the napkin.

"There is a condition of inheritance, Ronni, and Violet was adamant about it. Her will stipulates you must complete the book based on her life within one year of her passing. You are to share absolutely no information she furnished you with anyone during the process. If there's an issue, you can tell me—*only* me. You cannot seek help to write it."

He glanced up and saw my frown.

"But, Mr. Sobel, I've never tried to write a book. Violet believed I could, but..."

He nodded and continued without expressing an opinion. "When your manuscript is finished, it's to be submitted to my niece for consideration. There is no guarantee it will be published. Violet told you about this, right?"

"Yes," I nodded, trying not to embarrass myself further. My brain was already shrieking *How can you write an entire book? You don't know the first thing about it!* "But, Mr. Sobel, what if I don't get it done in time?" I asked.

"She insisted the one-year timetable was vital for a number of reasons. If you don't submit the completed manuscript within that period, your inheritance is limited to the amount we issue today." He paused and smiled at me. "She really wanted you to realize your dream of becoming a writer, and she knew a thing or two about unfinished projects."

"Yes, she told me about that," I said. "I understand."

"Violet selected charities to benefit in the event the book isn't submitted for publication." He shrugged his shoulders. "She left most of the remainder of her estate to Fairfield Springs. Her bequest is earmarked for a new entertainment room for the residents. It should be quite a nice one."

"She mentioned that idea to me," I answered. "Does Fairfield Springs know about this yet?"

"No, I wanted to talk with you first. Do you plan to continue working there?"

"I'd thought so, at least for a while."

"There's no need for you to stop. The money Violet left you is completely confidential. No one there need know."

"What about Herb?" I asked.

He drummed his fingers. "Yes, Herb. Violet provided for him. I spoke with him yesterday." Mr. Sobel cleared his throat. "He is disappointed in the amount she left him, but can't contest the will. He does not know about her provisions for you, Ronni, and there's no reason for him to find out. He's under the impression the nursing home is receiving what he considers 'his' money. Again, the will cannot be contested."

"You know he's filed suit against Fairfield for negligence?" I met his eyes.

"Yes, I'm aware of that. I can't see how he has much of a case, but that's between Herb and his attorney."

"There's something else, Mr. Sobel."

"Yes?"

"Are you aware Violet had a daughter when she was a teenager?"

Shock skittered across his features, but he recovered quickly. "Are you sure about that?"

"Yes, she told me all about it. She gave the baby up for adoption and believed her to be living in Florida. Violet said the records are sealed. She was never able to locate her daughter, and her daughter didn't try to find Violet."

"I see. Well, the daughter and her family would have no claim."

"I feel awful knowing there's a daughter out there, probably grandchildren and great-grandchildren, and I'm supposed to inherit all this money." I studied the woven carpet and waited for him to reply.

"Ronni, there's no need for you to feel guilty. Obviously you meant a very great deal to Violet. She considered you like a granddaughter. She loved you."

"I know. I loved her, too." I was horrified to find myself bawling in the plush office. Mr. Sobel stood and handed me a tissue. "It's just..."

"Again, Ronni, these were her wishes. Violet knew she had a daughter out there. She chose to help you in the best way she could." He offered me a smile designed to calm and reassure. I offered him one designed to convey sanity.

"Here is a check, Ronni," he stood and reached across the desk again. "Take it to your bank. I'd advise you to tell as few people as possible about your sudden good fortune."

"That won't be a problem." I stared at the piece of paper with all its zeroes. It was issued in the name of Mr. Sobel's practice. "What will they think at my bank? I usually deposit one hundred dollars in a panic when I'm down to twenty."

"You don't have to explain anything, Ronni. Let them think you won a lawsuit. Let them think whatever they want. Do you have a financial adviser?"

For my previous net worth of two hundred and three dollars? "No, I don't. I guess I should talk to someone about investing this."

"That's a good idea." He rose to shake my hand and placed a business card in its palm. "Please verify your address and phone number with Laura on the way out, and update us with any changes."

"Yes, I will. Thank you, Mr. Sobel."

"Call me Mel. I look forward to sending your manuscript to Jennifer. Let me know when you're ready, and I'll take it from there."

I gathered my purse and glass, wiping Mr. Sobel's nice table with the napkin.

"Ronni? Ronni, Laura will get that."

"Sorry, force of habit. Thank you, again, Mr...Mel."

Laura smiled sweetly and wished me a nice evening on my way out. I made it all the way to Ruby before bursting into tears all over again. I looked at the Birmingham summer sky, golden rays framing bunches of deep purple clouds. "Thank you, Violet. I love you." My strappy black sandal's heel caught on the worn floor mat as I started the car, and I had to smile.

On our third Saturday adventure, Violet had insisted we go to Dillard's at the mall in Anniston and get my make-up done. "Honey, you're a Southern woman. We don't go to the mailbox without our face and hair fixed up. And while you're beautiful just as you are, it wouldn't hurt to try a little enhancement."

"I'm no good with that stuff, Violet. I never have been."

"And that's why we're getting you some help. I know the girl at the Clinique counter and she will bring out your lovely blue eyes. Then we have an appointment with my stylist Summer. She's going to shape your hair a tiny bit."

I was shaking my head no. "I appreciate it, but I love my hair as it is."

"And you should. A few layers will make it thicker and fuller. Summer is a hair genius, Ronni. She's not going to change it, just enhance it."

"So today is Enhance Ronni Day? What are you going to do?"

"I'm going to watch you bloom, honey. And pay for everything, of course." She glanced at my Nike-clad foot on the accelerator. "Maybe we'll look at some shoes, too."

"I'm a nurse. I wear comfortable shoes."

"Only while you're nursing, Ronni. The rest of the time your shoes should make a feminine statement." She extended a leg to show off her kitten-heeled pink pumps on the floorboard. "Oooh, and a pedicure would be fun, too. We'll do that together this afternoon. I know a great place. The chairs even massage you." She smiled brightly.

"I hate massages. I hate people touching my feet."

"Then, for today only, pretend you like it. For my sake. If you want to scrub your mascara away later and rip the polish off your toes and put your hair back into that ponytail, you can. Let me do this for you."

Of course I gave in. I couldn't say no to her. The make-up lady was kind and had a light touch, though she managed to sell Violet over a hundred and fifty dollars' worth of concoctions to "enhance" me. She wrote detailed instructions for me to take home. We crammed my feet into strappy black heels Violet insisted I'd need for a new dress we'd find (we didn't, but I'd worn them to Mr. Sobel's). Summer touched up Violet's lavender hair and transformed mine into a style that framed my face and showed off my suddenly-huge, sparkling eyes. We laughed all day, especially as we tried to decode the Vietnamese chatter during our pedicures. Violet translated much of it in a running commentary that included, "The blonde one never shave her legs" and "Woman with purple hair is a goddess."

And she was. I got into the habit of wearing make-up and carefully styling my hair every day for that goddess, and she beamed blessings and approval at me.

I missed her so much.

four

VIOLET

Alice Glenn sat across from Johnny's hospital room door, watching her daughter run down the corridor to greet Sam Davidson. He folded Violet into a hug and allowed her to sob into his plaid shirt, patting her back gently. Alice caught his eyes and tried to look reassuring for the two young people, clasping the purse in her lap to quell the shaking in her hands. She didn't believe Johnny would live, and tried to imagine how she'd get Violet through the nightmare to come. There were more months of classes ahead and she was a practical woman who considered her daughter's finishing senior year at Anniston High School first and foremost. It was good that Violet had the support of friends—she'd encourage them to help one another through this cruel passage. She gave her daughter another minute, then went to say hello to Sam.

"Mama, you know Red," Violet palmed tears from her face.

"I got here as soon as I could, Mrs. Glenn," he said. "Violet told me Johnny's not awake yet." The boy looked like he'd walked the sixty miles to the hospital.

Alice patted the wood bench for Red to sit, placing herself between the young man and her daughter. "Are you hungry or thirsty? I could get you something."

"No, ma'am," Red replied. "Thank you, though."

Violet began the litany she'd been repeating to her mother for Red. "I can't believe this happened. Johnny's a careful driver. He wouldn't have been speeding or anything. Something must have jumped in front of the car. It doesn't make sense." She shook her head and bit a fingernail. "Red, his heart is going to shatter when he finds out about Kimmie. How am I going to tell him?"

"You're not going to tell him, Violet," her mother interjected. "His father is the one to do that. It's not your place."

Violet stiffened and slapped hands to her knees, looking to the ceiling for patience. "I don't think you realize what my relationship with Johnny is like, Mama."

Alice Glenn's heart slammed into an iceberg and began its descent. She turned to look Violet straight on. "I don't think *you* realize you're seventeen years old."

Violet smoothed her skirt. "Red and I are going to walk around for a while, Mama. We won't be long." Red looked as though he'd been collared and leashed, regarding Mrs. Glenn with an embarrassed glance as he stood.

The nurses at the station desk watched Violet and Red pass without offering a word. They looked down quickly and busied themselves with paperwork. There was nothing to say to these kids.

Violet sniffed. "Red, he's going to be fine. Johnny's in great shape. You've seen him play. He can beat this as well as he beats every team that comes to our gym. It might take him some time, but he'll be playing again before you know it."

Red searched for a light remark, a joke to untie the knot gripping his stomach. He found nothing and chose to say, "I know he will, Violet. Have you seen him yet?"

"Dr. Perkins didn't want us in his room, so we've been sitting on that bench outside the door for an hour and a half. Mrs. Perkins is on a different floor. We're waiting for my daddy and Dr. Perkins to get back from seeing about her."

"Have you talked to Johnny's doctor?"

"No, we haven't met him. The nurses go in and out of the room without telling us anything, other than he's asleep." She spotted an exit and said, "Let's sit outside for a few minutes."

They settled under a mimosa tree laden with fluffy pink

blossoms. Violet said, "I hate her sometimes, Red. She thinks I'm a stupid little girl and she doesn't understand what it's like with Johnny and me. We're going to get married."

"You don't hate her, Violet. Don't say that." Red plucked pink mimosa fuzz from Violet's hair. "So you and Johnny are getting married, huh? When did this happen?" Another question danced in his eyes, and Violet wondered if Johnny had told Red about Friday night. Surely he wouldn't. She blushed and turned away.

"It's not official yet, but we talked about it. I love him and he loves me."

"We'll get Johnny through this," he said, looking up into the tree. "Deborah wanted to come with me," he added casually, "but I told her it would be best to wait until later in the week to visit him."

Violet recalled a dark-haired girl from nearby Oxford. Nice clothes, and a handbag she'd envied. "Did y'all go to church together this morning?"

Red chuckled. "I believe we've discussed this, Violet. My mother brings fresh flowers in Friday afternoons and spends hours decorating every room in the house, including mine. She lights candles Friday evening and we have a special meal. We go to temple Friday night or Saturday morning. Then my dad hides from my mother on the golf course or in his darkroom, and she uses the time to interrogate me about my week."

"Your mother does talk a lot."

Red laughed. "I'll tell you a joke my dad told me. A boy comes home excited about getting a role in the school play. His father asks what role he's assigned, and the kid says he's portraying a Jewish husband. The father pats his shoulder and says I'm sorry, son. I was hoping you'd get a speaking part."

Violet giggled at Red, her eyes lit with mischief. She loved his sense of humor, and was glad he'd come to lighten the day.

Red hailed a group of prim old ladies walking by. "Shalom, y'all!"

They exchanged puzzled looks and walked a bit faster, rushing into the hospital.

"Guess they're in a hurry," he grinned.

"Guess they think you're crazy. It's too hot out here," Violet announced. "I'm melting. Let's go back in."

A tall man in a suit stood talking with Dr. Perkins and her parents. Violet heard her mother say, "Well, we should take her home, then."

"I'm not going home yet, Mama," Violet dismissed the idea with a wave. "I have to be here when he wakes up."

The tall man extended his hand. "You must be Violet. I'm Dr. Deason. I'll be taking care of Johnny." He ignored Red.

"How soon is he going to wake up?" Violet asked. The man didn't look old enough to be a doctor. Doctors were supposed to have gray hair and wrinkles like Dr. Perkins, who tended to every man, woman and child she knew.

"I believe he'll be conscious soon, Violet. There's no harm in talking to him, and it might help. Would you like to go in and keep him company?"

Dr. Perkins sighed and sank onto the bench in defeat. "Violet, I won't stop you...but not a word to my son about Kimmie or his mother. Mrs. Perkins' health is fragile right now, too."

"I understand, Dr. Perkins," she responded. She followed Dr. Deason into Johnny's room and stifled a scream. Every part of him that wasn't bandaged was the color of eggplant. A tube snaked from the narrow white bed to a bag filled with urine. Violet felt her stomach lurch.

Dr. Deason listened to Johnny's heart and smiled at Violet. He wound his stethoscope around his neck as he told her, "You can hold his hand. Talk to him about things you've done together."

Violet searched for an appropriate memory to recite in front of Dr. Deason. She settled on a night they'd gone for ice cream after a basketball victory, then segued into Johnny's love of the game and how strong he'd always been. She told him, "You have to wake up. We all need you, Johnny."

Dr. Deason nodded approvingly. "I'll be in the hospital for a few more hours today. Have one of the nurses find me when he opens his eyes." Violet liked that he didn't say "if." She gave him her brightest smile, determined to be cheerful for Johnny and the rest of the world.

Violet waited for three hours while Johnny never twitched a finger. Nurses came and went without saying much. They offered her encouraging smiles and drinks of water. Her mother wandered in and out of the room, her lips pursed into a thin line. Red stared from the bench when the door opened, but did not join her. Violet knew her parents wouldn't wait much longer to go home. She stood and whispered into his bandaged ear, "I'll be back soon, and you'll be feeling much better. I love you, Johnny Perkins." She found a patch of exposed forehead to kiss.

Mr. and Mrs. Glenn exchanged weary glances when their daughter emerged from Johnny's room. "We'll try to get back here soon, honey," her daddy said.

"Not soon, Daddy," Violet insisted. "Tomorrow."

Alice shot her husband a look that combined 'I told you so' with 'keep your mouth shut.' "No, Violet, we live far from the hospital. You have school to attend and responsibilities at home. We'll bring you back later this week."

Violet noticed Red was gone, and decided to shift the conversation. "When did he leave?"

"About an hour ago," her father said. "Come on, honey, we all need to eat and rest. Dr. Perkins has promised to telephone us if there's any change."

Violet laid down in the back seat of Daddy's Chevrolet and fell asleep immediately. Her mother shook her shoulder gently and said, "Violet, we're home. Come help me with supper."

"Mama, I feel really sick. I'm going to my room. You can manage without me, can't you?"

"All right, honey. I'll check on you in a while."

Violet closed her bedroom door and ran her hand through Blondie's fur. The dog rolled onto her back for a belly rub, paws to heaven. She drew her diary from its secret place and began to write about the horrors of the day. She finished with, "God, please help him." Her biology book sat waiting for her homework assignment. She ignored it, preferring to brainstorm a way to get to the hospital tomorrow. Her mother could be handled; Violet had years of experience in getting her way. She thought long and hard, glancing at the biology book. An idea began to form in a dark corner of her mind.

When Alice knocked an hour later, Violet told her she was still nauseated. Her mother opened the door. "Do you need castor oil?" she asked.

Violet cringed. "No, Mama, I'm sure I'll feel better in the morning. I'm going to sleep."

"Did you do your biology homework?"

"Yes, ma'am," she lied.

"All right, then. I'll see you in the morning." Mama looked exhausted. Violet heard her murmuring to Daddy, something about gray hair.

Samuel "Red" Davidson had driven home in his '38 Plymouth Coupe, partially a gift from his parents and the rest paid for with years of toil in his father's department stores. He thought about Johnny and wiped a few tears, then pounded the steering wheel. His best friend in the world might not live, or might not walk again. Red tried to decide which would be worse.

When he walked into the parlor his parents were reading, though his mother asked fifteen questions before he could escape to his bedroom. He opened a dresser drawer and removed an envelope. The best part of being yearbook photographer was keeping certain pictures for his own. He looked at Violet, beaming at a school dance. She'd worn white satin and pearls, every inch the princess. Johnny was in the background, laughing and waving at Red's camera. He replaced the envelope and collapsed onto his bed.

The following morning Violet waited until she heard her father's car exit the driveway. She straightened her clothes, applied lipstick carefully, and went downstairs. Her mother sipped coffee at the kitchen table. Violet sat opposite her and began, "Mama, there's something you should know. Johnny is more than my boyfriend. He's the father of my baby."

Alice set her cup down carefully. "What are you talking about?"

"The reason I have to be by his side right now. Johnny and I have been...acting like husband and wife for months now. I'm pregnant."

"What in the world?" her mother dropped her forehead into her hands. "I can't talk to you about this right now. Go to school and we'll discuss it this afternoon."

"I'll be going to the hospital after school."

"Exactly how are you planning to get there, Violet?" Alice spoke to the table.

"I have friends at school with cars, Mama. One of them will give me a ride."

five

RONNI

My throat was scratchy Friday night, so I spent the evening looking over my Violet notes and occasionally taking Mr. Sobel's check out to examine. It didn't look any more real than Monopoly money, and made me nervous. I moved it to three different "safe places" before settling on my underwear drawer. Victoria's Secret, overused Spanx, granny panties, unmatched socks, faded bras and my future mingled.

Work was boring and uneventful Saturday and Sunday. Kait asked me three times where my head was, as I drifted off in thought and presented looks slightly blanker than our patients'. I told her I wasn't feeling well, and it was entirely true. By the time I got home Sunday night, my throat was inflamed and the lymph nodes in my neck felt like ripe cherries.

You don't go to work in a nursing home with a cough, sore throat and temperature of 101.9 degrees. Half the population can be decimated in your wake. I called Donna Monday morning, still Nyquilly, and squawked, "I can't come in today."

"You sound awful," she said. "I'll arrange coverage for your shifts until you're better. Don't come anywhere near this place, Ronni. Do you have chicken soup?"

"I'll pick some up."

"Let us know if you need anything. I have to run. Mrs. Ledbetter is screaming, and Darlene is ignoring her."

Better Darlene than me. I was in no mood for Audrey Marie's

antics today. I fed Halle and located my keys. The drugstore offered soup, frozen pizzas, ice cream and more Nyquil. I'm a firm believer in feeding a cold.

I began typing ideas on my old laptop between naps—okay, food comas—and realized I could afford new writing equipment. This led to an hour of research on the latest technology, followed by an agonizing online book-formatting guideline quest. Information overload and confusion made me close the computer and eat as much pizza as my throat allowed. I closed my eyes and hoped to wake in a few hours with fresh ways to transform the legal pad scribbles into something people might want to read.

Halle licked my face awake and abandoned me when I coughed into her ear. I grabbed the laptop, deciding to begin with Violet at seventeen, the year when her life "truly became interesting." I lost myself in her story, crying over Johnny the way she had when she remembered his accident and the months that followed. By midnight I'd typed thirty pages of *Everybody Loved Her* or whatever the title would be; I went over them and made a million corrections. It was good, I thought. *I'd* buy and read it.

Halle and I watched sitcom reruns and MTV until two a.m., when I drugged myself back to sleep with soup, vanilla ice cream and everything I could locate in the medicine cabinet.

Tuesday morning I felt like a cement truck had emptied into my sinuses. Still, I dressed and went to the bank. I parked my old Honda out of the staff's sight, straightened my skirt and walked into their cool lobby trying to project confidence and wealth instead of phlegm. Was it too much to hope for tellers who didn't handle my tiny transactions every week? I glanced toward the glass-fronted offices where officers usually ignored my beelines to the counter.

A pretty woman with sleek black hair and ocean-blue eyes rose to greet me. "Hello, I'm Kristin. Welcome to First National." She took my hand and shook it. I hoped I hadn't transmitted my germs to her. "How may we help you today?"

"I want to open an account. Well, I have a checking account with y'all but I want to put most of this in a different one." I extracted the check from my purse and handed it to her, wondering if she'd raise an eyebrow. Maybe she'd call the police. What was someone like me doing with that much money?

Kristin waved me to a chair at her desk without any indication of shock. "You're Veronica Johnson?" she asked. She was already pulling up my information on her computer.

"Yes. Please call me Ronni."

"All right, Ronni." She smiled and produced a sheath of papers. "Do you need to access the funds in this account?"

I offered one of my blanker recent looks.

"Do you need to write checks on the new account?"

"Oh, no. I want to deposit ten thousand in my checking account, and put the rest in a secure place where I can't spend it. I mean, I don't want to be able to access it for about a year. I read online about CDs?"

She smiled and nodded. "We can upgrade you to an interest-bearing checking account and put the rest in a certificate of deposit for a year. The interest rate is only about one percent right now, but your money will be safely invested and you can't withdraw it without a penalty. Give me a few minutes and we'll have you all set. I'll need your driver's license."

I handed it over, stifling a cough. "Um, Kristin? I know it sounds stupid, but would you make a copy of the check for me?"

Kristin smiled. "Not stupid at all. I'll be right back." She wandered off to the copy machine and I looked at the photos on her desk. A great-looking guy held a huge fish, grinning ear to ear on a weathered dock—a big golden dog eyed the fish. A formal portrait of a handsome businessman, the husband, no doubt. My favorite was a close-up of an orchid silhouetted against a brilliant sunset. She saw me staring as she sat down.

"Your family?" I asked.

"Yes, that's my son Chase, our dog Riley, and my husband, Bob. The orchid is one I took a few weeks ago. Plants are a hobby, but I really love photography."

"You're very good," I told her. "Maybe you should go pro."

"I just might someday. It's a dream of mine."

"My dream is to publish a book. I'm working on one."

"What's it about?" Kristin leaned back in her chair and touched the pearls at her neck.

"The life of a lady I knew. She was wonderful and amazing." I looked at my cheap sandals and added silently: my guardian angel, and the reason I'm not digging for quarters to go to the grocery store.

"Well, I'm sure your book will be, too. Let me know when it comes out, and I'll be one of your first customers. I'm always looking for a good read."

We signed enough papers to charter a small country. "Thanks for everything," I told her and caught an image from the corner of my eye. Oh lord—Donna was strolling up to a teller window. I slid down in the wingback chair and asked Kristin, "Where did you get that dress? It's really pretty."

She glanced at her navy linen sheath. "A boutique in Birmingham." I knew she was wondering why her newest customer appeared intent on hanging around all afternoon. "Your skirt is lovely."

My size twelve floral skirt from TJ Maxx, designed to make me feel summery, but more accurately rendering me a life-sized replica of someone's grandmother's sofa from the waist down. I really needed to start working out. Maybe when the cold was gone. "Thank you. I'd prefer it were three sizes smaller. You're one of those naturally thin people, aren't you?" Donna was talking to the teller. I needed three more minutes of chit chat before I could get up.

Kristin regarded me with a tight smile. "I have to exercise, just like everyone else. Particularly if I want to keep these on my desk all day." She handed me a crystal bowl of M&Ms. I scooped up ten or so, hoping the hand sanitizer had worked. *Finish up and leave, dammit, Donna.*

Kristin couldn't miss my fifth sneaky glance at the teller window. "Friend of yours?"

"My boss. I called in sick. I have a cold, and can't spread it around Fairfield Springs."

"Oh." Kristin nodded in Donna's direction. "I'm sure she'd understand. My great-aunt is at Fairfield. Her name's Audrey Ledbetter."

"Audrey? She's, um, something else. A nice lady." I hoped I sounded sincere. "It's not so much that I'm sick and running around when I should be home. I don't want her to know I'm a customer here." The thought of Donna discovering my Violet money made my stomach clench.

If that puzzled Kristin, she didn't show it. "Aunt Audrey is a pill," she said. "All of us would visit more often if she'd stop complaining as soon as we arrive." She looked Donna's way, and we both realized she was about to pass us on her way out, fifteen feet across the lobby. I pretended to drop something and ducked to the floor, wondering if Kristin had heard about Audrey's vines.

"You can sit up now. She's gone. And don't worry—you have banker/client confidentiality. I promise to be discreet if you promise me chicken soup if I get your cold." She grinned and opened her desk drawer, pulling out a package of B-12 supplements with echinacea. "Here, take two of these. I swear by them. Haven't been sick in three years."

"Wow, thanks. I'll be going now." I stood and knocked her crystal bowl to the floor, scattering M&Ms for miles. Every head in the place turned to gape. Kristin jumped up, her hand a stop sign.

"No, I'll get them! Have a great day, Ronni. This is for you, with our thanks." She held out a green tote bag filled with First National souvenirs; a purse mirror, several pens, a travel mug and the pile of paperwork.

I stepped into the sunshine and rounded the corner to find a man standing next to Ruby, shaking his head.

He was gorgeous—liquid chocolate eyes, thick brown hair and a good six inches taller than me. Looked like he spent lots of time in the sun; the tan was nice. I guessed he was somewhere between thirty-five and forty, a good bit older than anyone I'd dated. Mystery Man smiled, revealing perfect teeth and, I supposed, a personal trail of broken hearts.

"Is this your car?" he asked. "Somebody hit you and drove off. I got a partial plate."

Ruby was injured? I came up beside him. There was a massive scrape of yellow paint down her fender.

"Oh, great," I sighed. "I really didn't need this today."

"Aww, it could be worse." I pegged his drawl to the more rural portions of the state. "Don't you worry. There's a crappy little Toyota with a glass pack fixin' to be pulled by a sheriff's deputy a mile or two from here."

"You're a cop?"

"Yep, name's Rick O'Shea." He shook my germy hand.

"Ricochet? That's..."

"Don't even start," he said. "My parents have a wicked sense of humor, and believe me, I've heard every possible joke. You can imagine what shooting practice was like at the academy." Rick raised his eyebrows. "Hey, Ricochet...see if you can hit three with one shot!" He deepened his voice and intoned sternly, "A Ricochet is deadly on the firing range," then shook his head. "Yeah, such wit in my class."

I sneezed three times and wished for a tissue. I couldn't possibly swipe my nose on my shirt in front of him. Fortunately, his cell phone started playing the "Cops" theme...*bad boys, bad boys, whatcha gonna do*. I laughed and he grinned, turning away. Finally, a chance to temporarily stop my nasal river.

"O'Shea." He listened for a full minute. "Good," he said. "Thanks, Craig. Bring him back here." He shoved his phone into a jean pocket. "Your culprit is a very frightened sixteen year old. You're lucky, though—daddy bought him insurance." Rick leaned against my sad little car, crossing his arms. "You didn't tell me your name."

"I'm Ronni Johnson. Thank you for helping me."

"Oh, I have a weakness for damsels in distress. Speed Racer took off as you exited the bank, so I tried to get a good look at his car. The kid was driving like he'd just robbed the place, but his maroon-accented bumper led me to examine your Honda." He paused and glanced at his watch. "I have to get into the bank to work, but Deputy Simmons will be here with a teenager in serious need of an underwear change shortly. Nice meeting you, Ronni." He didn't move, though. His eyes were locked on mine and I'm sure he was enjoying melting me with them.

"You work here?" I blurted.

"Security. Helps pay for my vices."

I wondered what those were. "You're not in a uniform. Do you change inside?"

"They like me plainclothes and undercover. I mostly sit around and steal candy from the desks," he replied.

"Thank you again, Rick. I'm very grateful." I was getting tired of holding my stomach in. He was in great shape, and I kind of hated him for it. Did everyone but me work out constantly?

He saluted and gave me the smile he must reserve for accident victims with severe snot problems. It was beautiful and my heart thudded. I have never known how to flirt—it's not in my repertoire—but I heard myself say, "If I can thank you properly by buying you and Mrs. O'Shea dinner, I'd like to."

"There's no Mrs. O'Shea. Just me and Kitty O'Shea."

"Kitty?"

"Kitty's my bulldog. I have my parents' sense of humor. You like ribs?"

I despise them. "Yes, love 'em."

He offered me a business card. "Call me, Veronica Jean Johnson. Pretty ladies don't usually offer to take me out. I'd like that very much." That smile again. I leaned against Ruby and tried to smooth my hair. It was two days overdue for shampoo.

"Wait a minute. How do you know my full name?"

"Darlin', I'm a state trooper. I know more about you than you'd imagine." He nodded at my license plate. "Talk to you soon."

I waited until he'd gone into the bank to look at his card. Lt. Richard O'Shea, Alabama Highway Patrol. His cell number was written neatly on the back, like he'd planned to give it to me all along.

I swallowed the B-12 with a warm swig of Dr. Pepper from my

car as the sheriff's cruiser arrived. The back seat held a small, scruffy boy who looked about thirteen. His hair was cropped close and bleached to near-white; his eyes were pale gray surrounded by red roadmaps. They were accented by painful-looking acne. I felt sorry for him despite myself.

Deputy Simmons stepped out, clearly a man who relished his job. His uniform was freshly starched and I thought he was smiling more than the occasion warranted. "Hello," he greeted me, then opened the back door and released his passenger. "Jeffrey, this is Miz Johnson. I believe you have something to say to her."

He willed himself to look at me. "I'm sorry, ma'am."

"Me too, Jeffrey. I wish I were meeting you under better circumstances."

"Yes, ma'am." He turned to Deputy Simmons. "Can we go now?"

"In a minute, Jeffrey." He opened the back door and reinserted the kid, clamping his head in a huge paw. After slamming the door for effect, he told me, "He has no priors. We're on the way to the office to meet his father." He made a few notes on an accident report, then handed it to me to sign along with a piece of paper bearing Jeffrey's insurance information. "Give them a call and report this as soon as possible. They'll get you fixed right up." He regarded my car's fender. "Doesn't look too awful. You have a nice day now."

"Thank you, officer." I started Ruby up and headed home for fresh Nyquil and a nap.

six

VIOLET

Violet sat on a concrete bench waiting for her friends to arrive at school. Katie Ruth came first, wrapping her in a hug and then holding Violet at a distance to search her tired face.

Katie Ruth said, "He's going to be fine. We all just know it."

Violet nodded, choking back tears. "Thank you, Katie Ruth. I hope you're right."

Johnette, Mary Nell, Patsy, Evie Lou and Frances joined them; they cried delicately and pried every detail they could about Johnny's condition. Violet responded to their questions in a polite whisper, searching the crowd of students over their shoulders for Red. When she spotted him she excused herself quietly, leaving her court to update classmates about the queen and her injured king.

"Hi, Vi." He looked exhausted. Violet experienced a brief glimmer of guilt for what she was about to ask.

"Red, I was wondering if you could take me to the hospital after school."

He blinked at her. "Violet, I wish I could, but I have to put in an hour in the stockroom for my dad..."

She jumped in, "...and I'll come help you. We can finish in half the time. Please, Red?" Violet turned her wide-eyed gaze on him, knowing it never failed to affect Sam Davidson.

"I guess I..."

"Great! I'll meet you right here. Thank you, Red." She pecked his cheek. "You're a sweetheart."

Violet hurried to catch her friends before the first bell rang. They escorted her into the school's entrance, shielding her from curious looks and murmurs. Her homeroom teacher, Mr. Boshell, led the class in a prayer for Johnny and his family after the Pledge of Allegiance. She was consoled, pitied and comforted everywhere she went; several people offered cards to deliver to the hospital. Miss Gerrity allowed her an extra day to turn in her biology homework. Violet smiled and assured everyone Johnny would be back soon. Anything else was unthinkable.

Red was waiting for her after school, arms crossed and impatient. "We really need to get going, Violet. I'm probably going to be in big trouble for driving to Birmingham, and if Dad finds out I let you in the stockroom, I'll be killed."

She tilted her chin down and made her eyes as big as possible, gazing into his. "I would never do anything to get you in trouble, Red. Maybe I can find someone else to take me." Her lower lip quivered slightly. "My parents are mad at me, Johnny needs me, I'm terribly behind in my schoolwork...I just don't know what to do." A fat tear traced her cheek, and Red reached to swipe it with his thumb.

"Come on," he said, sweeping the car door open for her, "no need for tears. Everything's all right. Please don't cry." He hated the effect Violet's emotional displays had on him, hated the mental image of himself as a fish hopelessly hooked. Not even a sporting fish with fight...a weakened minnow.

The drive down Quintard Avenue was short. Violet smiled at the beautiful azaleas and graceful oak trees; the spectacular Victorian homes lining the street. She adored her town, and couldn't imagine living anywhere else.

Red parked his car out of sight at Davidson's Department Store and hurried to open Violet's door. "Are you sure you want to come in and help?" he asked. "You could wander around downtown."

"No, it'll go much faster if I pitch in." Violet noted Red's eyes scanning the path to the stockroom. "No one will see us, silly." She beamed at him and straightened her skirt, then rolled up her shirtsleeves. "Let's get to work."

She thinks she's Rosie the Riveter, Red decided. He wondered how she'd react to the dusty, dank stockroom with its occasional scampering mice. Violet was accustomed to plusher environments and little in the way of physical work. He'd let her price the shipment of handbags—easy and probably amusing for a female.

He swung the door open and nodded Violet ahead, waiting for her delicate sneeze or other expression of distaste.

She smiled and asked, "Where do I begin?"

Red pointed to the stacked boxes of handbags and the wood chair next to them. "Price sheet's in each box along with tags you tie to the handles." He demonstrated by attaching a tag. "Make sure you check the style number inside each one and match it to the correct price." Violet immediately began scanning the price sheet and pulling out purses, focused as Da Vinci sketching the Mona Lisa.

Thirty minutes later he was finished with the clothing racks and returned to check on her. Violet stood and swept her elegant hand at the boxes. "All done. Every one has its tag."

"Great," he told her. "We'll leave as soon as I speak to the store manager for a minute." Red opened the door to a flood of bright sunshine and announced, "You should wait in the car. I'll be right there."

The drive to the hospital was much too long for Red, even with Violet all to himself. He was not used to Birmingham traffic and got lost twice, cursing softly and banging his hand on the steering wheel. Violet alternated between forced cheerful chattiness and tears. She checked her face in a compact mirror and reapplied lipstick three times on the way, but still required a five minute beauty break in the restroom before visiting Johnny.

She stopped Red in the hall, saying, "Please let me have a minute alone with him first."

"Of course. I'll join you in a little while." Red sank back onto the bench he'd suffered on yesterday. When Violet entered

Johnny's room, he saw there were no other visitors. He hoped Dr. Perkins was occupied with his wife; he didn't think he could make small talk with anyone.

Violet was thrilled to see Johnny's eyes open, and to find him alone. She sat next to the bed and reached for his hand.

He moved it away. "Get out," he spat. "I don't want to see you or anyone else."

Violet plastered a smile to her face. "Johnny, I know you're going through a horrible time, but..."

"A horrible time?" Johnny turned his eyes to the ceiling. "Yeah, Vi, it's kind of difficult. I killed my sister. My mother is upstairs having a nervous breakdown. My body is broken into pieces, and nothing—are you listening, Violet?—works from the waist down." He offered her a grimacing smile.

"We're all praying for you, Johnny."

"Save your prayers. God has already decided how to punish me. I'll never walk again. I'll never *stand up* again. All I want to do is die, and I promise you, I will find a way." He closed his eyes. "Get out, Violet. I am no longer your boyfriend. Find someone else."

"This is nonsense, Johnny. You are going to be fine. The doctors will help you..." Violet twisted her hands in desperation. Johnny was shaking his head violently back and forth.

"I am begging you: get out of this room and don't come back, Violet. If you have someone with you, tell them I don't want to see them. I want to be alone. Do you understand?"

Violet patted the stack of cards in her lap. "People at school sent these for you," she sobbed. "I'll leave them on your bed."

"Take the goddamn cards with you. Leave, Violet. Please." He slapped the bedsheets. Violet saw tears streaming to the bandages on his head.

"I love you, Johnny. I'll always love you. I can help you..."

"I don't want your help. Unless you can help me die right here and now, there is no reason for you to be here."

"You'll feel better..."

"When? When they bring my wheelchair? When I roll into

Kimmie's funeral? Do you know why I wrecked that damned car, Violet? I was hurrying to get her to Tuscaloosa so I could get back Saturday night and see you. I ditched practice and left early."

Violet palmed the tears from her face. "Please let me try to help you through this. We can be happy together. We'll find a way."

"Violet," he glared at her, "I want nothing to do with you. Nothing."

She placed the cards next to his leg and Johnny swept them to the floor. He threw his arm over his eyes. Violet yanked the door open and ran to the only place she could: Red's arms. He jumped from the bench to enfold her.

"What's wrong? Violet, honey..." Red threaded his hand into her hair and pushed her head harder into his shoulder, wondering what Johnny had said or done to reduce her to choking sobs. She stayed there for at least a minute. The nurses at the station watched silently. As Red and Violet walked away, one started out for Johnny Perkins' room.

"Miss?" she said to Violet. "Give him time. He needs to adjust to all this. Dr. Deason has arranged for a psychiatrist to see him tomorrow morning."

"But he will walk again, won't he?" Violet asked. "He can get better with therapy, right?"

Nurse Meador shook her head. "No, there is no possibility. I'm sorry."

Red stared at the scuffed linoleum floor and fought down his emotions. He turned to Violet. "Would he talk to me?"

"No. He doesn't want to see any of us."

Nurse Meador patted Violet on the shoulder. "He's young and strong. He will find his way. Pray for him." She went down the hall, silent as Red's tears.

"I don't want to go home," Violet told him outside. She took a deep, raggedy breath. "Could we get a cup of coffee? I don't think I could eat anything. The truth is, I could use a cigarette."

Red produced a pack and shook one out for her, then cupped her hand to light it.

"I didn't know you smoked," she said. "You basketball guys

are always too concerned about your breathing."

"Johnny's a true basketball guy." Red cringed. "I'm only out there because it's fun." He lit a Marlboro and exhaled slowly, contributing to Birmingham's early evening smog. The western sky was awash in brilliant vermillion and gold. His parents told him "The Magic City" got its name from these exotic sunsets produced by industrial haze. He took Violet by the arm. "Let's walk. I know a place nearby."

She attempted a smile for him. "Red, you are the sweetest thing."

"Would you do something for me, Violet? Something no one but my family will do?"

"Yes." She cocked her head, puzzled.

"Call me Sam. I hate being called Red."

Violet gave a weak laugh. "Sam it is. What a pair we sound like, anyway: Violet and Red. That's bad poetry."

"Yes, I know." He wished he could tell her how many times he'd considered that very thing.

Violet snapped him back to reality. "I have to figure out what to do for Johnny."

"Like the nurse said, we pray for him. Johnny has to make up his mind to get better, Vi. The shrink will help him with that tomorrow." They started down concrete steps toward the city street, Sam's hand reflexively grasping Violet's elbow.

"The little diner near here has excellent pie," Sam offered. "My parents like to go there."

"You eat pie. I'm too fat already." Violet tugged at her narrow belt.

Sam raised his eyebrows. "Yep, you're a tub of lard. That must be why you were Homecoming Queen. Alabamians love girls who look like prize heifers."

"Thanks, Re...Sam. You're too good to me."

No, Violet, he thought. *You're* too good *for me*. "Let's have coffee and get back on the road soon," he said. "I have a feeling your parents and mine are not going to be pleased with us."

They weren't. Violet's mother met Sam's car at the curb, thanking him for delivering her daughter safely. She ushered Violet inside without a word and nodded toward the sofa. A teary Chet Wilson jumped up and ran to Violet, wrapping his arms around her waist.

"Chet? Honey? What is it? What's wrong?" Violet looked to her mother for an answer.

"He's been waiting for you since school let out," she said. "Mrs. Wilson has moved away and taken CeeCee with her."

Chet turned his dirt and tear streaked face up to Violet's. "She left Daddy a note. She didn't want me, Violet, just CeeCee. She said she could only take one of us." He broke into fresh sobs. "Daddy says I have to go live with my Aunt Junie. I don't want to leave here. Can't I stay here with you?"

Alice Glenn said, "Chet, we can't do that. Your father knows what's best for you." Her gaze told Violet she'd better add to that message.

"Chet, my mom's right. I'm sure your Aunt Junie will love having you with her. It's probably only for a little while, until your dad can work things out. I'm sure you'll be back soon."

Chet responded by clutching Violet harder. "I don't want to go."

Mrs. Glenn cleared her throat. "Violet, Mr. Wilson is waiting for Chet to come home. I've telephoned him twice while we were waiting for you. You walk him home and don't forget this." She held out a paper sack of cookies. "They're chocolate chip, Chet—your favorite."

Chet allowed himself to be hugged and gently released, swiping at his face. He took the cookies and held his hand out to Violet, head bowed low. As soon as they reached the sidewalk, he stopped and tugged her around to look at him. "You can't make me go, Violet, please. I belong here with you. Can't you see?"

"Chet, you know I care about you, but there's no place for you to stay here, honey. Your dad knows what's best for you. I'm sure we'll see each other again soon. You'll come to visit."

He clung to her hand and kept his eyes on the ground the rest of the way, without another word.

Mr. Wilson was sitting on his front steps. He had aged ten years since Violet had seen him a few days ago. Violet felt everyone had.

He stood slowly and brushed the knees of his trousers. "Chet, wait for me inside."

Violet's heart broke for the boy. He clung to her and allowed himself to cry for another minute before facing his father, then trudged into the house.

"I'm so sorry, Mr. Wilson."

"Me too, Violet. Me too." He shook his head. "But he's in trouble and I can't take care of him by myself."

"Chet's in trouble?" She glanced at the house and saw a living room curtain move back into place.

"He's suspended from school for the second time this year. The first was for fighting, and hell, I understood that." He shook his head and adjusted his glasses with a sigh. "This one, though, is for a full two weeks because he stole lunch money from three other students in his class. One little girl says he threatened to hurt her if she told."

"Lunch money," Violet said, thinking of all the change she'd slipped Chet. "I hate to hear that, Mr. Wilson." She placed a sympathetic hand on his arm and squeezed. "I'm sorry for all you're going through." She glanced at the house once more and saw Chet peering out a different window. "I'd better get home now."

Mr Wilson hesitated and then blurted, "His mama has never done right by him. He needs a woman to take care of him. My sister can do that. He deserves a good mother."

"I'm sure he'll be fine," Violet smiled and walked away, hoping it was true.

Alice Glenn was again waiting for her daughter at the door. She waved Violet in and crossed to the sofa. "We need to talk. Sit down with me."

Violet would rather have been anywhere but under Alice's steely stare. She folded her hands in her lap and crossed her ankles in Southern lady fashion, a perfect imitation of her mother's posture.

"Violet, we are going to have to speak to your father about your condition."

Too many things were twirling through Violet's mind. It took her a moment to realize she'd informed her mother she was pregnant. Now what? She decided to tell a version of the truth. "Mama, I lied to you. I am so sorry. I knew you and Daddy would try to keep me from Johnny's side, and I thought the only way you'd take me seriously was if I was carrying his baby. I'm not. We've never," here she paused and looked down, "never done anything like that. I'm sorry, Mama."

Alice found she'd been holding her breath and released it slowly, in little relieved gasps. She threw her head back and said a brief prayer for patience. "Are you sure, Violet? You must tell me the truth."

"Yes, ma'am. I'm sorry for worrying you. It was a stupid thing to do." She reached for her mother and began crying for the twentieth time that day. "Red took me there after school. It's terrible, Mama. Johnny is never going to walk again. He doesn't want anything to do with me. I don't think he loves me anymore."

Alice held her daughter at arms' length and forced her to meet her eyes. "Dr. Perkins called earlier, Violet. He wanted to tell you about Johnny's emotional state and ask you to wait several days before visiting the hospital." She bit her lower lip. "Violet, they need time to grieve. To heal. Your father and I knew that. You'd do well to listen to us, honey. We usually know what we're talking about."

"Have you ever been through anything like this?" Violet had trouble believing her parents had experienced much of anything prior to her birth.

"Of course we have. Everyone on this earth has been through pain and loss, Violet. Please try to see beyond the tip of your nose for a minute and start considering other people's feelings."

"You make me sound like a terrible person, Mama."

"No, I think you're one of the finest people I've ever known, Violet. You are warm and caring and kind. I'm only trying to point out that you often act without considering the consequences. For instance, scaring your mother to death with a lie about pregnancy." Alice rubbed her forehead. "I'm going upstairs to lie down. Your father will be home soon. There are leftovers in the icebox if you're hungry."

"I love you, Mama."

"I love you, too. Do your biology homework."

Violet wondered—not for the first time—if her mother had spies following her.

Two mornings later Violet opened the Glenns' front door to find Chet waiting on their front porch, rocking in her dad's favorite chair and seemingly unaware he was at the wrong house. He grinned at her and patted the seat next to him. "I only want to talk to you for a minute. My train leaves in two hours."

Violet sat and offered him her prettiest smile. "Are you excited?"

"To be going to Aunt Junie's? No." Chet shook his head and reached into his pocket. "I came to give you this." He placed a small gold nugget in Violet's hand. "It's not real. It's Pyrite."

Violet suppressed a grin and said, "It's beautiful, Chet, thank you."

"I bought it on a field trip we had to Noccalula Falls last week."

"It must have been expensive," Violet turned the rock over in her hands, thinking about what Mr. Wilson had told her.

"I saved up lunch money." He shrugged his shoulders." It's to remind you how much I care about you, Violet." He turned his gaze to the street. "I know you don't understand, but I was just born too late to be with you now. Someday, though..."

"Chet, you'll find someone who is perfect for you. Wait and see. In the meantime, I'll cherish this gift and hope to see you when you visit your dad." Violet stood and held out her arms.

"Give me a hug before you leave."

He held on for a long time, then looked up at her, biting his bottom lip. "Promise me you'll think about me."

"Promise me you'll behave for your Aunt Junie," Violet responded.

Chet shook his head like a freshly bathed Labrador Retriever. "I doubt that's gonna happen. See you, Violet."

She watched until he turned the corner, where he looked back one last time with a wave.

seven

RONNI

The photo on the newspaper's website was five years old. He stood next to a smiling blonde goddess with thoroughbred legs—she wore a cream lace dress the size of my ankle socks. The caption read, "Sargent Richard O'Shea named Alabama's Trooper of the Year after heroic rescue." The accompanying story identified her as his wife, Victoria. Sargent O'Shea had risked his life to pull a three-year-old boy from a burning wreck on I-20. When I reached the part about his two young sons, I closed the laptop and cried for twenty minutes.

I spent a snotty, phlegm-y week writing Violet's story. I missed her every day, and wondered what she'd have said about Rick O'Shea.

Returning to work saved me. I was grateful to be focused on something other than writing about Violet's glorious love life and pondering my own, dismal one. I had missed my patients, who greeted me with kindergarteners' enthusiasm.

Kait was happy to see me, too. We were mired in incident reports and trying to figure out why Mrs. Meyers kept hearing a cat in her room in the middle of each night. She'd risen to feed it and fallen twice. Her alarm did no good, as it only went off after it was too late. Her face was covered in bruises. No amount of reassurance could convince her there was no cat, and the bedrails didn't slow her down at all.

Kait and I stood in her room.

"Mrs. Meyers," I began, "we've checked everywhere and there is no cat. Maybe you're hearing one outside the building."

"It's not outside," she said stubbornly. "My hearing is very good and I'm telling you, the cat is in my room. I can't just ignore it."

"Do you hear it in the daytime?"

"Not usually. It's only in the middle of the night. You have to find it. I know it needs food."

Kait made a big show of looking under the bed and in the closet. "There is no cat, Mrs. Meyers."

"But it meows very loudly. It's hiding from you. Cats are good at that."

Kait sighed and left me to deal with an increasingly agitated Ruth Meyers.

"Did you look in the bathroom?" she asked. She shared a small toilet and shower with Mrs. Harrigan in the next room. "Go search in there." She turned her gaze to the door.

I did. I swept the shower curtain aside. I opened the cabinet under the sink. I swung open the door on Mrs. Harrigan's side, and discovered the key to our feline mystery. The spring was old, and creaked a loud, wailing meow sound when the door moved.

"Guess what, Mrs. Meyers?" I patted her bony leg under the blanket. "I know what you're hearing, and it does sound exactly like a cat. We need to fix Mrs. Harrigan's door and you won't hear it again."

"There's no cat?" She was crestfallen.

"No, ma'am. Just a silly door imitating one very well. I'll call maintenance and you won't hear it any more." I made a mental note: Mrs. Harrigan is going to the bathroom in the middle of the night. A lot.

"Can I get a cat?"

"No, Mrs. Meyers, we can't have cats in here. Too many people are allergic."

"I hate this place." She closed her eyes and sank into the pillows. "We need cats."

"I'm sorry, Mrs. Meyers. We do our best." I closed her door

and decided to pick up a stuffed animal at Target for Mrs. Meyers soon. I smiled and went to tell Kait what I'd found before we had to start wound care rounds, every nurse's least favorite part of the day.

Our first stop was poor Mr. Ridley, who was covered in bedsores and required more ointment than we could ever supply. We tried to be gentle but he cried silently as Kait and I tended to him. We noted charts and examined lacerations, looking for signs of infection in each patient.

Kait returned from her break and announced, "There's a good-looking man in uniform here to see you." She nodded toward the lobby and took the gauze I was using on Mr. Herman from my hand. "Go. I've got this."

I couldn't believe Rick would show up at Fairfield Springs unannounced. Though I was impressed (and more than a little intimidated) by his heroism, the thought he had a beautiful ex-wife and two children made my stomach hurt. I'd put off calling him for a week, then decided too much time had passed and abandoned the idea altogether. By the time my nose stopped running I'd gained six pounds and lost my nerve. I dashed in the ladies' room to check my hair and swiped a mystery stain from my scrubs, cursing the fluorescent lighting.

The man in the lobby was not good-looking, and considerably shorter than Rick O'Shea. He wore a drab brown sheriff's deputy windbreaker and khakis. "Veronica Johnson?" he asked, his expression flat and bored.

"Yes, that's me," I said.

"This is for you." He handed me an envelope and waved. "Have a good day."

It was a subpoena from William Ratliff, attorney at law. I recognized the name from the endless commercials on the Birmingham channels, all of which insisted William was "*for* the people." By this, he meant he'd be happy to sue anyone over anything for the possibility of a juicy settlement. I'd always thought of him as "BillRat." BillRat wanted to question me about the circumstances surrounding Violet's death. I took a deep breath and went to Donna's office.

"I got one too," she said, barely glancing up at me. "Frankly, Ronni, I have no damned idea what to tell him."

"It's better that way, Donna," I replied. "I'll be the one to explain. You just show up and tell him you weren't here, nor were you aware of the situation."

She leaned her forehead into her palm and scratched her hairline with long red nails. I'd known Donna long enough to know what came next.

"Ronni, my career is on the line here. You do realize the man was married, do you not?"

I nodded, "Yes, I do. His family's not involved in the suit, though, are they?"

"No, they want to forget Fairfield Springs and the whole mess it represents in their lives. His wife and son told me this place 'sickens' them. They don't want a lawsuit and they don't want money." She paused to close her eyes and sigh, exhaling her frustration. "They'd simply like for us to disappear, and I can't say I blame them. Their husband and father was admitted here in a fragile condition. Losing him like that..."

"Donna, there is so much more to this story," I interrupted. "Violet was in love with him, and he with her."

"You're delusional, Ronni. He was a devoted family man. His wife said dementia led him to believe he'd known Violet in a past life or something."

"Then she's the delusional one. I'm sorry, Donna, but the truth is the truth." I placed my palms on her desk and leaned forward to look her in the eyes. "Violet wanted me to wait until they were both gone, then tell the world their story. That's what I intend to do."

"What the hell are you talking about?"

"I'm writing a book based on Violet's life."

"No you're not. Not with information you gained by working here. There are confidentiality issues, Ronni." She glared at me. "Get back to work and forget your book idea if you want to keep your job."

I fought back tears. Donna could be moody, but had never spoken to me harshly. I closed her door and went back to trying to concentrate on my patients. I'd become immersed in Violet's teenaged world over the past week and written thousands of words. I couldn't stop thinking about the chapters I'd finished and those waiting for me. No matter what Donna said or thought, I would not stop. The book had taken on a life of its own, waking me with ideas to be jotted down each morning.

By the time five o'clock arrived I was more than ready to leave Fairfield Springs. I said goodbye to Kait in the parking lot and spotted Ruby, still sporting her sad dent. I needed to get her to the body shop soon. There was a folded slip of official-looking yellow paper under the windshield wiper. This was perfect—a subpoena *and* a traffic citation in one day. I unfolded it carefully.

Dear Ronni,

I couldn't help but notice how many times you haven't called me. I'm still hoping for that rib dinner. Hell, I'll eat some prissy kind of chicken if I have to. I'd really like to see you.

Rick

My hands started to shake, my knees felt like jelly, and I smiled bigger than I had in years. I drove home watching for highway patrol cars, at least fifteen miles per hour over the speed limit.

eight

VIOLET

Violet's diary reflected more sadness than joy through the rest of senior year. Graduation was two weeks off. She'd barely managed to pass Biology and Algebra, but would be crossing the stage with her classmates. When she consulted her mirror—and she did often—an eighteen-year-old woman returned her gaze.

Johnny had not returned to school. His parents hired a series of tutors to ensure he'd graduate. It was rumored he'd accept his diploma in a wheelchair.

Violet hadn't heard a word from him. The one time she worked up the nerve to ask the operator to ring the Perkins' number, his father said Johnny was not accepting calls.

She attended the Spring Formal, resplendent in pink and without an escort. The boys at Anniston High seemed to be demonstrating their respect for Johnny by leaving her alone. She rarely saw Sam; their class schedules didn't correspond and he worked immediately after the school day ended.

Chet Wilson mailed a postcard from Birmingham; it featured the Vulcan statue on Red Mountain and he'd painstakingly printed, "I miss you. Love, Chet."

When the *Hour Glass* was distributed, she'd turned its pages to find she and Johnny had been named "Best Looking." The yearbook featured too many photos of Johnny on the basketball court to number. Pictures of the two of them at Homecoming, walking through the halls and eating lunch together were scattered throughout. Violet couldn't look through it without tears.

Two months after Johnny was released from the hospital, she accepted a Friday night date with Hugh Parker, a lineman for the Bulldogs destined for a life of hard work in his father's auto repair shop. Hugh was a gentle giant, a fumbling mess of a clay-stained man-boy off the football field. Conversation was limited to sports and cars; Violet struggled not to yawn all night. He held her clumsily after a showing of *The Treasure of the Sierra Madre* at the Calhoun Theater, trying to steal an awkward kiss. When Hugh suggested a stop at their classmate Jerry Payne's party, she jumped at the chance to socialize with her friends.

Hugh immediately set out to fetch beer for the two of them. The first person she recognized in the Paynes' darkened living room was Sam Davidson. He was sitting with Deborah but spotted Violet across the small crowd of slow dancers and made his way to her side.

"I heard you were going out with Hugh. He's a nice guy."

Violet nodded. "Not as nice as you. Much smarter, though," she teased, smiling across the room and waving her fingers at an obviously distracted Hugh, laughing with a fellow football player. He either didn't see her or chose to ignore her. She rolled her eyes and clasped them shut, wishing she'd stayed home. "Have you seen Johnny?"

"No. I tried, but his dad answered the door and sent me away. You?"

"I called him but he won't talk to me, either." Violet scanned the room for her girlfriends, finding none. She wondered if her mother might pick her up from the party. It was a long walk home.

Sam wore an amused expression. "So, I didn't get a chance to tell you, but my dad summoned me to his office regarding twelve handbags I'd priced below wholesale."

"The ones I did?" Violet was appalled.

Sam laughed. "The very ones. I told him I'd been in a hurry that day."

"I am so sorry."

"You owe me thirty-six dollars," Sam added. "You can cancel the debt by going to Atlanta with me next Friday. We have the day off school, so my father is sending me to a clothing factory as his emissary."

"What about Deborah?" Violet glanced in her direction and found Deborah engrossed in conversation with Hugh, apparently sipping her own missing beer.

"Deborah doesn't have to know. There's wine on the back porch. Care to join me?"

"Yes, I'd like that."

The moon peeked at them behind a wispy cloud. Sam poured wine into a juice glass for Violet. She felt his fingers draw across hers slowly and deliberately as he placed it in her hand, trailing tiny electric tingles. She looked up at him, surprised.

Sam was not looking at her. He leaned forward across the porch rail; the sky had his attention. "I wish I could get a shot of those stars with my camera," he said. "It's beautiful tonight."

"You and that camera. You did a great job for the yearbook, Sam."

"Did you happen to notice who appears in more photos than anyone else?" he asked. He turned back to Violet and poured his own wine. He clinked his glass to hers with a map of lights reflected in his eyes. "Here's to my favorite subject."

"If you mean me, that's very sweet. You took way too many of me." Violet was shy and confused around a boy for the first time in her life. It was a feeling as foreign as if she'd awakened atop a sand dune or iceberg. She put a hand on his arm. "We should probably get back inside. Deborah and Hugh will think we're up to something out here." She tried to make it sound light and funny.

Sam grinned. "Have a sip of wine. We are up to something."

"What is that?"

"We are working out details of our secret trip to Atlanta. After my factory visit, the day is ours. There's a lot we could do and see."

"I don't know if I can get away, Sam. Mama makes me clean our house every time I'm out of school." Violet stared at her beloved platform sandals and winced. "These heels are killing me."

"Take 'em off. I'll carry them."

"Carry them where?"

"To the other side of that tree." He pointed to a massive oak, its canopy covering a third of Jerry Payne's back yard.

Violet slipped her shoes of agony off, darting a look into the kitchen window to see if anyone might be watching. In one swift move, Sam dangled her sandals from his left hand, cradled his juice glass next to them, inserted a large stolen lawn chair cushion under his left arm and grabbed Violet's free hand with his right.

She giggled. "That's quite a talent."

"Basketball hands. Come on."

The soft grass felt wonderful under Violet's feet. Sam threw the cushion to the ground on the far side of the tree. He plopped down on it and pulled Violet with him. "This is better," he announced.

"Better than what?" she smirked.

"Better than making small talk with a roomful of people while waiting for you to get here. I suggested to Hugh you might want to come to the party tonight."

"I should have known." Violet took a large swig of deliciously sweet wine. Sam reached over and took her glass, setting it next to his. "I don't want you to have too much of this," he explained.

"Why not?" she pouted.

"Because I want you to remember every detail of our first kiss."

She shook her head in exasperation. "Sam, you're here with Deborah. You've been together for years. I have no intention of kissing you. Walking me into the darkness to make out was a big mistake." Violet glared at him and stood, preparing to go back to the living room.

He focused on a distant light atop a downtown building, one that glowed green if there had been no traffic fatalities within the past twenty-four hours. Sam felt like Violet's kick to his heart should cause it to turn red at any moment.

"Vi, I am not in love with Deborah. My parents are, and her parents are in love with me. She and I are more like a forced dating experiment." He hugged his knees to his chest and rested his head, mumbling, "I'm not happy with her—never have been." He looked up, eyes glittering moist, and reached for her hand. "Please sit back down, just for a few more minutes."

"Won't she be looking for you?" Violet sighed and eased herself to his side.

"I told her I needed to talk to you about Johnny, and we'd be gone for twenty or thirty minutes."

"Then talk to me about Johnny. Go ahead."

"I'm so sorry about all he's been through, Violet. He'll never be the same; none of us will. He was my best friend. But..."

"Yes?"

Sam pulled a clump of grass and scattered it, stalling.

"What is it, Sam? But what?"

"I have loved you, Violet Glenn, since sixth grade. I've stood in Johnny's shadow and watched you adore him, even when he didn't deserve it. I've taken photograph after photograph of your face, none of which came close to capturing the beauty I see every time I look at you. Your smile is the first thing on my mind when I wake and the last before I sleep. Your laugh makes me want to sing with happiness." He paused and laughed softly, eyes on the ground. "I know I sound like an idiot, or the most repulsive poet of all time. I had an early start with the wine."

Violet touched his cheek, surprised to find it damp with tears. She turned his face to hers with a finger. "Then kiss me."

Sam swept Violet's hair back, tracing her jawline with his thumbs. His hands grasped the back of her head and tilted it to the stars. He leaned his forehead to hers and paused, breathing deeply. Then he pressed his lips to hers, offering nothing but a light, slow, wet caress of her mouth. He held her head in place a few more seconds and sucked her bottom lip gently before releasing her to fall back on his arm. He leaned away to look into her eyes and whispered, "Well?"

Violet could not answer. The tiny electric tingles were now racing all through her body. She scrambled to her knees and threw her arms around his neck, offering the kiss Sam Davidson had been imagining for as long as he could remember, the one from her heart and soul.

Minutes later, when they paused for breath, Sam asked, "Am I dreaming?"

"Yes, you are. So am I. Don't wake me up."

"Will you go with me to Atlanta?"

"Only if you let me kiss you again sometime." Violet nuzzled his neck and inhaled deeply behind Sam's left ear. He smelled like a curious mixture of soap and of manly sweat—like the place she wanted to be forever. Like home was in Sam Davidson's strong arms.

"Hey," Sam whispered. "We have to go back and rejoin the party."

"I know, but I want to stay right here." Violet was dizzy with wine and her newfound feelings for Sam. She knew they had to walk into Jerry's living room without looking like they'd discovered a pot of gold and three unicorns in the back yard. She smiled to herself and kissed Sam's forehead lightly. The moonlight reflected traces of her pink lipstick there and on his mouth, so she swiped at them the best she could and laughed. "Let's go," she said, standing and extending her hand to him. "I'll tell Hugh I'm not feeling well and ask him to drive me home."

Sam considered this for only a second. "No," he said. "I know Hugh Parker too well to allow that. I'll drive you and Deborah. We'll drop her off first."

Violet's stomach lurched, offering a taste of wine and guilt.

nine

RONNI

As soon as Halle was crunching her food I called Rick from my bed/office, all messy sheets, cracker crumbs, legal pads and laptop. I glanced at the drugstore foundation and mascara streaks on the pillowcases, vowing once again to improve my nighttime facial routine and devotion to household laundry.

"Hey," he answered. "Took you long enough."

"I've been busy," I said. "Work and my social life leave me with about four hours to sleep if I'm lucky. Life's good." Great—like he wouldn't see through my lonely, desperate, fake-cheerful routine. "How have you been?"

"Busy chasing assholes in Porsches, drug mules, idiots with no taillights and eating bank candy. We did have a chicken truck burst into flames the other day and that was exciting. Almost called KFC to pick up the whole barbecue before the fire guys showed up."

"That's horrible, Rick."

"Actually, the fire was out before one feather was singed. I even talked softly to the chickens to calm them down."

"You are my hero." I paused. "I had no idea you were Trooper of the Year and all that stuff."

"It was a slow year with no other likely candidates. I did what any Boy Scout would've done, and a reporter happened to see it. Good PR for the Patrol. You been Googling me?" I was pretty sure I heard a smug laugh.

"Just my usual is-this-guy-an-ax-murderer research. Girl's gotta be careful."

"Especially one as beautiful as you," he answered. "So, are you buying me a rib dinner or not? I know a fantastic place in Oxford, and it's on the way to something I'd like to show you. Saturday, about five, maybe? Wear jeans and bring extra clothes."

"Are the ribs that messy?"

"No, we're going on a small adventure. I want you to be prepared." I could practically see him grinning through the phone. "You don't work Sundays, right?"

"Are you stalking me?"

"Only in the most professional manner. I'll pick you up at your apartment Saturday at five. I have to run. Be good." *Be good*? He hung up before I could say another word.

I had three days to lose five pounds, get my hair highlighted, de-pimple my chin, clean the apartment, and find some cute jeans. Somehow I'd fit in a chapter or two of Violet's book, which was truly starting to intrigue me. I had read and re-read what I'd written and found it as appealing as most novels I checked out of the library. Research had shown me the odds of getting it published were about like getting struck by lightning while standing in a basement thirty miles from a thunderstorm, but maybe Mr. Sobel's niece would show me first-time-writer mercy and offer advice.

Saturday at 4:58 p.m. I was peeking through the living room blinds when a shiny black BMW pulled up next to Ruby. "Jeez Louise. Flashy car for a cop," I told Halle. "Maybe Rick takes bribes from drug dealers. Maybe this is a huge mistake." I swiped my sweaty palms on the overpriced jeans I'd squeezed into as the cat sensed a stranger and darted off to hide under the bed. Rick's knock on the door matched the thudding of my heart.

He was wearing a dark brown button-down oxford shirt to match his eyes with the sleeves casually rolled up, jeans that looked like he'd ironed them, and he smelled like fresh-cut grass and a hint of lime. Heavenly.

"Hi, you," he flashed the knee-melting smile and held out a bouquet of sunflowers. "You look great. Let's put these," he edged by me toward the kitchen, "into a vase and get going. I'm starving."

"They're so pretty, Rick, thank you. I love sunflowers, but you probably knew that. You seem to know more about me than you should."

"Sunflower sticker on your car's rear window. Keen police brain," he replied, tapping his temple with an index finger.

"Very impressive." I took out a clear plastic pitcher. "This is the best vase I have for those."

"Perfect. Vases are too fussy for sunflowers, anyway." He was looking around the apartment, and I was wishing I'd rounded up a few more dust bunnies.

I put the flowers on my little kitchen table and turned to him, surprised by how much he towered over me. Tall, dark, handsome, funny...a grown-up man with history. He was gorgeous. What was he doing with me on a Saturday night?

"Something wrong?" He cocked one eyebrow.

"Oh, no. I was just wondering..."

"I'm turning forty next month." He leaned back against my kitchen counter and crossed his arms. "I have an ex-wife and two sons. They live in Tuscaloosa with their stepdaddy, a big, fat sloppy professor at Alabama. She found him 'sophisticated'," Rick spat the words. "Left me for all the *sophistication* in his bank account two and a half years ago. He's an overpaid professional noxious gasbag with a constant assortment of condiment stains on his baggy shirts." He fired a finger gun at the ceiling. "War Damn Eagle." He was quiet for a minute, then added, "I was born in Birmingham and grew up in Gadsden. Joined the Marines at eighteen. Got out as soon as I could and chose the patrol because I like to drive fast. I love Jesus but I like beer a lot. I'm a neat freak. I have a weakness for old dogs, children..."

"...and watermelon wine," I finished. "I've heard that old song. My mom and dad were classic country music fans. Some of it's not bad."

"French wine, actually, but I'm glad you have good musical taste. Still want to go out with me, Miss Johnson?" He held out his arm. "I promise you won't have to help me across the street or wipe my chin."

"Very funny. You are a newborn babe compared to the people I spend time with every day."

"That's what I was hoping you'd think. Contrast can be helpful to my cause."

"Your cause?"

"To win your heart, Ronni. I've been focused on that since I saw you walking in the bank's parking lot. Would've dented your Honda myself if that kid hadn't done it."

I took his arm in mine and loved how he immediately tugged me closer. Rick felt solid—the most solid person I'd ever met.

He opened the door of his fancy car for me. I noticed it looked like it had been detailed with a toothbrush. The radio blared a 70's song I didn't recognize, and I hoped there wouldn't be an oldies music quiz.

"Here," he said. "Let me switch that." We were instantly saturated in satellite radio top twenty; something with heavy bass by Jay Z. I wondered if Rick's ears were bleeding from his attempt to entertain me. I reached over and turned the volume down.

"Let's talk," I said. "Did you serve overseas in the Marine Corps?"

He nodded. "Operation Desert Storm. I helped hang on to some oil wells. Not my favorite subject." Rick grasped the steering wheel hard and sped up to ninety on the interstate. We'd be in Oxford within ten minutes at this rate.

I checked my seat belt and activated my imaginary brake pedal.

He laughed. "Don't worry. I'm a professional."

"Do you have a blue light for this thing?"

"If we need one. I'm going kinda slow for it right now."

"Uh huh." He seemed to want to race every car we pulled aside, expertly weaving around traffic. I was trying very hard to appear nonchalant. Please God, I prayed silently, just get us to the restaurant.

By the time we arrived I was nauseated, shaky and grateful the menu offered a sandwich I could nibble while Rick devoured ribs caveman-style. He had a Coors Light and I managed to gulp three glasses of cheap barbecue-house wine to settle my nerves. They were worth every penny. Our eighty-year-old waitress, Cora, handed the check to Rick. He promptly presented it to me.

"Y'all must be married," Cora said. She placed her hands on her ample hips.

"No, ma'am," I answered. "I'm taking him out to dinner to thank him for a favor."

Rick grinned at Cora. "I helped her catch an evil teenaged villain who hit her car."

"Oh, it's you," she replied, squinting through thick glasses. "Didn't recognize you out of uniform. Tell you what, honey," she grabbed the check from my hand, "this one's on the house." She winked at Rick.

I had the feeling Rick ate a lot of free meals along the I-20 corridor. When we were back in the car I said, "Friend of yours?"

"Cora broke down on her way to work last year. I changed a tire in the rain so she could make it in time for her shift."

I began singing Abba's 'Super Trouper' as he started the car.

"Yep, that's me. Now for the fun part of the evening. Ever been to Lake Wedowee?"

"No, I haven't."

"Well, hold on tight. I'll have us there before you know it."

"I believe you, Rick. Don't you ever get a ticket? Cops can get speeding tickets, right?"

He laughed and floored the accelerator. "No, I don't, and yes, they can." I closed my eyes and tried to pretend I was skydiving, bungee jumping or on Six Flags' fastest roller coaster. Those were less nerve-wracking than his driving.

Rick steered into the marina's gravel parking lot carefully—mustn't get dust on the BMW—and parked far from the array of pickup trucks and boat trailers. He opened my door and asked, "You have your extra clothes?"

"Yes, but why do I . . .?"

"Just bring them. Trust me." He extended his hand and pulled me out, dragging my purse and shopping bag along. "You do trust me, don't you?" He leaned over and kissed my forehead, then tilted my face up to his. The late-day sun glowed around his head like a halo. I resisted the urge to tell him.

We walked hand in hand to a dock with several boats tied up. Rick waved his hand at a sleek, bronze-y metallic speedboat with 'Catch Me, Copper' emblazoned in white on its stern.

"Seriously?"

"Well, it's copper colored, and I drive it fast, and I *am*..."

"A cop. I get it, Rick O'Shea. Nice boat."

He helped me clamber aboard. "You're probably going to get a bit wet. I'll store your extra clothes under here." He shoved my bag and purse under the dashboard and cranked up what sounded like a jet engine. "Hold on," he said.

Like I hadn't figured that part out. Rick untied the ropes and threw them on the dock. We exited the marina slowly, so I stopped white-knuckling the seat. That was a mistake. My head was snapped back as soon as he hit open water, and I found myself laughing and screaming 'faster!' as the boat shot across the lake. I didn't even mind the spray ruining my carefully arranged hair. This was pure joy.

We arrived at a dock in front of an a-frame house on stilts, surrounded by pine forest. A huge black Labrador Retriever sat wagging its tail on the dock. Rick threw the bow rope to the dog, obviously trained to assist with boat parking.

"Hey, Darby," he yelled. "Thanks." The dog pulled mightily on the rope, digging in her paws and backing up until we were in position. She sat and thumped her tail on the dock, looking like she was grinning in triumph with the rope between her teeth.

"Is that your dog?" I asked.

"No, Darby belongs to the neighbors. She always hears the boat and waits for me." He reached in his pocket and extracted a napkin full of barbecue scraps. "Good girl." He tossed the treat to Darby, who ignored it until Rick took the rope to tie the boat. I climbed out as gracefully as I could and patted Darby, who had swallowed the meat whole and was looking hopefully at Rick.

"Is this your house?"

"It belongs to my family," he said. "My dad built it when we were kids. My brother and I share it, trading off weekends. Mom and Dad hardly ever come out here anymore."

Darby continued to stare soulfully at Rick, who shrugged and told her, "That's all, girl. You can visit later." The dog turned obediently and trotted off into the woods. Rick reached into the boat for my clothes. "Here," he handed my purse and bag to me, "you can freshen up in the downstairs bedroom. It's all set up and ready."

"You think I'm spending the night with you?"

"Only if you want to. There are two bedrooms. I'll be sleeping upstairs unless you want company." He tossed a ring of keys to me. "I have to finish up with the boat. The door's around back and the key with a red top fits it. Make yourself at home."

I walked carefully, scanning for rattlesnakes. I'm not an outdoorsy girl. The door opened into a small kitchen of harvest gold and avocado green, prompting me to look around for The Brady Bunch. I crossed into a large living room with a stone fireplace and tall windows overlooking the lake. Rick was pacing back and forth on the dock with his cell phone to an ear, laughing and shaking his head.

I found a tiny apology of a guest bedroom downstairs. It had enough space for a twin bed, a small dresser and a thinner person to turn around. A chocolate brown quilted spread held light blue decorative pillows, and there were old family photos covering one wall. I had an easy time recognizing Rick's grin in each of them, most of which featured freshly-caught fish. I was thrilled to find a private bathroom. I peeled off my wet clothes and regarded myself in the mirror. I needed makeup and hair styling immediately. Thirty minutes later I emerged in more comfortable jeans and a pink Alabama sweatshirt to find Rick slouched in a chair on the deck, feet up on the railing. The sun was dipping into a pool of pale coral and evening had fallen like coal dust on the treeline across the shore. He'd lit tiki torches at each corner and sat next to a plastic table with one beer, a plate of cheese and crackers, a wine glass and an open bottle of chardonnay. My chair was to its left. It took three tugs of the sliding glass door to make my entrance.

"Sorry," he said. "That door sticks. Come sit and catch the last of the sunset. The bugs aren't bad tonight."

I poured myself a large glass of wine. "Cheers," I said, clinking his Coors Light can. "This is beautiful."

"Yeah, it's a nice view. Quiet tonight. Most people are away this weekend."

"Any special reason?" I tried to remember if there was a race at Talladega or other state holiday.

"No, I had all the neighbors arrested so we'd have the place to ourselves."

"I'm still catching onto your police humor," I replied.

He chuckled. "Yeah, humor. There really is a roadblock near here tonight. It's probably slowing folks down a bit."

"You think of everything, don't you?"

"I try. Have you decided whether you're staying until morning? I need to know if I can open three or four more beers." He raised his beer can, swishing it from side to side.

"I guess so, as long as I have my own room. Halle has plenty of food and water."

"Halle?"

"My cat's name is Halle Berry."

"How cute. I'm thinking Kitty O'Shea would consider her a tasty appetizer."

"I forgot about your bulldog. I'm a cat person."

"And I am not, but I am cat tolerant when necessary. By the way, we need to leave here around ten tomorrow morning. Would you like to go mini-golfing in Tuscaloosa?"

I decided not to feign enthusiasm for mini-golf. "No, thank you. I can go home and write. I'm in the middle of a chapter."

"You're a writer? I thought you were a professional angel to old people."

"That's my day job, and I'll need to keep it. I'm writing a book with little hope of publication."

"I see. What's it about?"

I considered my wine glass for a minute before answering, "The life of a wonderful woman named Violet. She was kind of an adoptive grandmother to me. The only grandmother I've ever known."

"Your parents live in Birmingham, right?"

"My parents passed away a few years ago. It's just me. No brothers or sisters." I gulped wine, stressed as always by any discussion of my childhood.

"I'm sorry. They must have been very young."

"Actually, they had me late in life." My practiced line. Not, *they adopted me after I was passed around by three foster families.*

"Well, I'm sure they were wonderful people. I want you to meet my folks soon. I think you'd like them."

"I'm sure I would. Are you mini-golfing alone tomorrow?"

"No, I had a call from my son Josh earlier. He and his younger brother are mini-golf enthusiasts. Want to see a picture?" He held out his phone, revealing two blonde, smiling little boys. "Josh is eight and Jeremy is seven."

"They're adorable," I said. "It must be hard, being away from them."

"It kills me, to be honest with you." Rick stared at a bird flying low across the lake, tracing its path. "I want to tell you a story," he said.

"Okay." I wondered why he wouldn't look at me. I was probably in for thirty minutes of how wonderful his kids are.

"A few months ago, I was standing in a corner of the bank, hidden like they want me. Maybe peeking through a fern. High-level surveillance near the end of a Friday shift." He took a sip of beer. "In walks this girl. She's wearing ripped jeans and a faded black t-shirt, so I know she's not too concerned with impressing anyone. Gets halfway to the counter before remembering to take off her sunglasses. I caught a glimpse of her eyes as she said hello to the teller and they reminded me of a late-afternoon winter sky.

She smiled as she slid a piece of paper through the window and laughed at some joke she made. In that moment...God, she was pretty."

He paused, still looking at the lake.

"Anyway, the girl cashes a check and turns to leave. She notices this old couple fifteen feet away, trying to open the door. She sprints over and swings it wide and holds it for them. The old lady is leaning on the man, so she takes the lady's arm and helps them all the way to the counter. Then she waits, introducing herself and talking quietly to the woman, while her husband finishes his business. A full three or four minutes. She takes the lady's arm again and slowly walks them all the way to their ancient Buick, then stands and watches to make sure they pull out into traffic okay before walking to her own car." Another sip, and he turned to smile at me. "A maroon Honda."

I bit my lip and looked up at him. "And?"

"And I called a buddy to run your plate. Because your eyes are beautiful and you wear awkward ripped jeans and I loved the part of your heart I saw that day. And no, I didn't stalk you, outside of a quick Facebook and Twitter search that didn't tell me much. But I sure watched for you to come back into the bank."

"You could have..."

"I could have placed myself in your path a hundred different times, but it felt wrong. Then that kid did me the enormous favor of scraping off a bunch of your car's fender. Kinda felt like I was in that place and time for a reason."

"But you waited for *me* to ask *you* out."

He laughed. "Yeah, I loved that part. If the conversation had gone differently, though, I probably would've found a way." He took my hand in his and squeezed it before letting go. "Anyway, I want you to know I've been thinking about you for a long time, Veronica Jean. And after that bold confession, I'm going for more beer. You need anything?"

"No, thank you." I smiled up at him. "Maybe a first kiss at sunset on this pretty lake after you've been all romantical..."

"That's not a word," he said.

"Believe me, I know."

Rick pulled me out of the chair and wrapped his arms around me, then kissed me long and slow. I responded like a teenager full of pent-up Friday night hormones. He swept my legs around his waist and carried me to a picnic table at the end of the deck, sitting on top with his feet on the bench and situating me on his lap.

I pulled away and said, "I don't usually do this, Rick. I mean..."

"Neither do I," he interrupted, shaking his head. He laughed softly. "Let's try it and see if it's fun." He kissed me softly, barely touching his lips to mine. Every molecule in my body answered.

I was oblivious to the world until I heard the stupid "Cops" theme droning on. For a second I thought the neighbors had turned on a TV. Rick smiled apologetically as he drew his cell from a back pocket. "I gotta change that ringtone, huh?"

I nodded and looked at the phone. It displayed a flying monkey from The Wizard of Oz and the name Victoria. "I'm sorry, Ronni. This will just take a minute." I tried to get off his lap but he held me fast with his free arm.

"Yes?" he said, rolling his eyes upward. "Victoria, that's not fair. I'm at the lake. It's going to take me an extra hour to get there. Why the hell didn't you tell me before?" He sat and listened, screwing his face into a scowl. "Okay, ten o'clock. Bye."

I managed to pull free and stand. "Well, that was a mood killer."

"I'm sorry. She and Sir Humphrey Knowsalot need to take the boys to a faculty birthday party tomorrow at three, so I have to get to Tuscaloosa two hours earlier. Victoria loves to dress them like little bookish nerds and parade them around the university. Probably puts bow ties on them. If she thinks I'm having fun tonight, she likely made the whole thing up. She's a conniving bitch who directs my life from Revenge Hell."

"Revenge? I thought she left you."

"I was not a model husband, Ronni. I was and am, however, a model dad. Josh and Jeremy are my world."

"I'm not even sure I want kids." The words left my mouth

before I tasted them.

"You don't know that. You're too young to make decisions so huge."

I sighed and stood up, glorious makeout session forgotten.

He shook his head and held out his arms. "Where were we?"

"It was a good stopping point," I replied. "We're moving too fast here." I returned to my chair and picked up my wine.

He nodded cheerfully. "I agree. I didn't bring you here to hook up tonight, Ronni. I never bring women to the lakehouse on a first date. This place is special to me, and I just wanted to sit and talk—get to know you— in the moonlight, I swear." He looked into my eyes. "I'm going for that beer now. When I get back I want your life story, Ronni Johnson."

I wondered if there was enough chardonnay in the world, and figured I might as well find out. I was halfway through the bottle when Rick returned. He set a small cooler of beer next to his chair and looked at me expectantly.

"There's not much to tell, Rick. I did not have a happy childhood. I'd like to leave it at that and talk about movies or music or global warming. Any other subject you'd care to name."

"Have another glass of wine." He reached over and filled my glass helpfully. "I want to know all about you, Ronni. Please."

No one in my current life knew about my past. I'd opened up to Violet, of course, crying with her on more than one occasion. I took a deep breath and drained half the wine. "Okay," I began, closing my eyes, "it may not be what you want to hear."

"Try me."

"My mother spent my early years pursuing whiskey and pills instead of paying attention to me. I was removed to foster care at five. I don't know who my father is. I was passed around from family to family and never knew what a stable home looked like until the Johnsons adopted me. I was a teenager by then."

"So Johnson is not your real last name?"

I glared at him. "It's real to me."

"What's on your birth certificate?"

"Veronica Jean Edwards."

"How old was your mother when you were born?"

"Sixteen."

"And you have no idea where she is?"

"I don't want to know, Rick. She is dead to me."

"One more question: what is her first name?"

"Jocelyn."

He stood and leaned over the railing, rubbing his head and looking across the water. "I thought you looked like her," he said quietly.

I swallowed something sharp and felt it lodge in my throat.

Rick came over and placed his hand on mine. "She was living near Heflin four years ago. I arrested her twice for DUI and she fought the charges both times. Her boyfriend owned used car lots and hired a sleazy defense attorney for her. The first time she lost her license and got probation. The second...well, she's been living in the Tutwiler Prison for Women in Wetumpka. She may be out now."

I crossed to the railing and retched a barbecue sandwich and wine onto the grass below.

ten

VIOLET

Violet sat in Sam's car, powdering her nose and watching the entrance to the pants factory. She'd been waiting for twenty minutes. Sam had left the car running so she could listen to the radio, and she drummed her fingernails impatiently on the dashboard in time with Peggy Lee's "Golden Earrings", eager to get to Atlanta for the surprises he'd promised. The parking lot was surrounded by dogwoods in bloom. She tried to focus on the birds flitting from tree to tree.

Ten minutes later he emerged, grinning and shaking the hand of a white-haired man in a business suit. Sam was carrying a briefcase—Violet thought he looked like a successful young tycoon.

He threw the case into the back seat and announced, "Sam Davidson, ma'am, Negotiator Extraordinaire and Oozer of Charm, at your service. Dad's going to be very pleased with the fall selection and inspired to offer me a raise. Maybe he'll sign the company over to me."

"He should," she replied, watching him shed his jacket and lay it carefully across the back seat. He loosened and threw his tie atop it, then jumped behind the steering wheel and slammed the door heavily.

Sam pecked Violet's cheek perfunctorily and started the car. "Now for the fun part. Mr. Taylor almost made us late. I know way too much about his irritable colon and low fiber diet." He shook his head. "Anything you'd like to know about the human digestive system?"

"No, thank you. Mine could use lunch, though."

"You'll love the restaurant. It's a nice little place. Then we're going to the Loew's Grand for a movie."

"Oh my gosh," Violet replied. "The one where Gone With The Wind premiered?"

"The one and only. We're taking in a matinee this afternoon before we go sightseeing."

An hour later Sam parked on a side street in downtown Atlanta and opened Violet's door. He led her to a colorful trolley car and helped her aboard, arm tight around her shoulders. The other passengers looked bored and ignored the sights Sam was busily pointing out. Violet decided they must be heading to or from work, and used to Atlanta's splendor. Her mouth hung open at the buildings, signs and bustling streets.

"That's Ponce de Leon Park, where the Atlanta Crackers baseball team plays. We'll walk over there later," he said. "There's an amazing feature in the outfield."

"I can't imagine anything related to baseball I'd find amazing," Violet answered as she kissed his cheek. "You've been to Atlanta a lot, haven't you?"

"Yes, I have relatives over here. You'll meet some of them later."

Violet raised her eyebrows and said nothing. Sam hadn't once taken her to spend time with his parents.

Sam jumped up and grabbed Violet's hand to exit in front of Mary Mac's Tea Room, promising her the best lunch she'd ever experience. A large woman with red hair in a messy bun greeted him at the door. She hugged Sam and extended her hand to Violet. "I'm Regina, honey. Welcome to Mary Mac's." She led them to a table near the front window.

Sam fluttered his napkin across his lap and announced, "I'm trying to fatten her up, Regina. We'll have chicken and dressing, mashed potatoes, green beans and cheese grits."

"Well, sugar, I'm bringing y'all fresh peach cobbler for dessert, too. That ought to help," she answered. "She's very pretty, Sam."

Violet regarded Regina with a smile. "How long have you known Sam?" she asked.

"Since he was in short pants and spilling everything I brought to the table. His family's been comin' here long as I can remember." She patted Sam's back affectionately. "How's your daddy and mama?"

"They're doing very well, Regina. I told them I'd say hello and give you this." He held out a small package wrapped in pink.

"White Shoulders? I was almost out!" she exclaimed. "Thank you, Sam. That is so nice of y'all."

"You know I wouldn't show up here without a present for you, Regina." He glanced at his watch. "We need to hurry up so we can make a movie time at Loew's."

"Lunch is comin' right up. I'll bring some sweet tea to get y'all started." Regina hurried off and returned almost instantly with sweet tea and a huge platter of food. The chicken and dressing—Violet's favorite dish—was heaven on a plate. She stuffed herself as Sam watched with an amused smile.

"Are you going to have room for peach cobbler?" His eyes were wide.

"Can we come back for that later?" Violet suppressed a burp. "I think I need to walk for a while before I eat another bite."

They hugged Regina goodbye, promising to return after the movie.

Violet blinked at the afternoon sunshine and clutched her stomach. "I'm probably going to fall asleep during the movie," she told Sam.

He grinned and swung her to the opposite direction on the sidewalk, narrowly missing a woman pushing a baby stroller. "Then I have a better idea! I promise you'll stay awake. First, though, we're sneaking into the ballpark." Sam grinned at Violet's open mouth and pressed a finger there to shush her. "I've done it plenty of times." He pulled Violet along to a narrow opening in the fence, hidden from the street. "Sideways," he commanded, "squeeze." Violet followed, compressing lunch as much as she could.

"There," Sam pointed. "Have you ever seen that in a baseball stadium?"

Violet laughed. "Well, no. How do they play around it?" There was a stately, blooming magnolia tree in the back of center field.

"Balls that go into the tree are still in play. It makes for some interesting games." Sam tugged her hand and they walked to the tree, which was much larger than Violet had thought. Sam pulled a pocketknife out and began to carve "VG + SD" into the bark.

"Sam, that's silly," she giggled, secretly pleased at the gesture.

"It will be here forever. At least, until they tear this place down to build something bigger." He finished and put the knife away, then kissed her. "Maybe we'll get married here."

"Uh huh. Our parents would be delighted with that choice."

"Who says they have to come?" Sam kicked at a dirt clod. "Come on. Our next stop is a better surprise."

Violet eyed the huge building before they reached it and planted her feet on the cement. "No, Sam. I've never skated in my life. I'll break a leg or wrist..."

"Aww, come on, Vi. The Rollerdrome is fantastic, and I'll hang onto you real tight." He pulled her close. "Trust me," he whispered.

"You keep saying that." She glanced at the entrance and back at him. "If I skate like a newborn giraffe, we'll leave. Deal?"

"Deal."

Sam carried the heavy skates and spent two minutes lacing his own, then ten minutes on Violet's. He tugged and adjusted, lingering happily as he contemplated Violet's lovely calves. He darted his eyes to the counter. The clerk was busy, so he slid his hand up her right thigh. She leaned to kiss him as she started to stand, promptly wheeling herself onto her backside with a resounding thump.

"I *told* you I can't do this!" Violet started tearing at Sam's careful lacing. He knelt down next to her and stilled her hand.

"Trust me," he repeated, pulling her upright. "I won't let you get hurt." He steered Violet like a mannequin and helped her onto the rink. There were only two other skaters, a white-haired man and his grandchild circling effortlessly.

Violet tried to concentrate on the music. The Pied Pipers were singing "Open The Door, Richard." It was a singularly stupid song in her mind, but the beat helped her move along, imitating the broad sweeps Sam made with his legs. Every time she stumbled she'd bend over in nervous laughter. Sam's arms were strong, and he kept her upright.

"You really are clumsy, darling, but I love you." Sam patted Violet's head for a second, not daring to release his grip any longer. By their seventh trip around the oval Violet was feeling secure enough to demand he let her go. Sam shook his head. "You're not quite ready."

"I am, too." He released her slowly, astonished to see her skate ahead. She picked up speed, then panicked as a curve loomed ahead. "How do I slow down?" she screamed. Violet's deep blue skirt billowed behind her; a storm cloud giving chase. He reached her in time to catch her in a dramatic dip for a kiss.

"You couldn't do that again in a million years, Sam Davidson," Violet laughed as she opened her eyes. "Nice move."

"Yeah, well, no more skating off by yourself. Let's work on our couple's routine today, shall we?" Sam pulled Violet's waist close, watching the glee on her face as they sailed faster and faster. He let go long enough to speed up and face her. He grabbed her hands and skated backward, smiling as Eddy Arnold sang "I'll Hold You in My Heart."

"Sam..." Violet said.

"Shh. Just be quiet and enjoy this. I know what I'm doing."

"But!"

"Violet, be quiet. Listen to the music." He gazed soulfully into her eyes and clutched her hands tighter. "I could get a gold medal in backward skating."

Violet jerked her hands away and grabbed the railing as Sam slammed into the grandfather, knocking him to the floor. His granddaughter screamed and skated across the rink. Violet watched in horror as the old man allowed Sam to help him to his knees, begging his forgiveness.

"I'm all right," the stranger told him. "Why don't you find another way to show off for your girlfriend for a bit while Katie and I finish skating? We'll be here for another few minutes, then you can pretend you're Sonja Henie on wheels all you want." He nodded at Violet. "That all right with you, miss?"

"Yes, sir. I'm very sorry," Violet answered. The little girl scowled at her and took her grandfather's hand.

"Your lipstick is all smeared," she announced to Violet and the world. "Maybe you should go fix it while Papa and I skate."

Violet stood silent as they took off. She arched her eyebrows exactly as Alice Glenn did to chastise her family, and Sam heard every unspoken word. He helped her off the rink and removed her skates, terrified to speak.

As soon as she'd replaced her shoes, Violet was out the door and stalking away. Sam ran to her side and matched her pace. His jaw was clenched tightly, and Violet noticed a vein throbbing in his neck. Neither spoke a word until they reached the car. Sam opened the passenger door as Violet handed him her heels, declaring, "My feet are killing me. Let's just go home."

"Not until we visit my cousin and his wife. They're dying to meet you, and I promised."

Violet sighed. "I guess I have no choice." She settled into the seat and pouted, refusing to look at Sam.

An hour later they rolled up in front of a compact house surrounded by oak trees. A red-haired toddler was furiously pedaling a miniature Pontiac on the sidewalk leading to the front porch. He jumped out and ran to scream into the screen door, "Mom! They're here!"

Sam helped her out and into a hug from a beautiful young woman with a drooling baby on her hip. "I'm Katie," she said. "We've heard so much about you, Violet. Welcome." She shifted the baby and grabbed his starfish hand to wave it. "This is Melvin, and the wild boy circling the yard is little Samuel. He's named after his handsome cousin." She pecked Sam on the cheek. "Y'all come in. Mel's in the kitchen, where a good husband belongs."

Violet followed her, charmed by the baby grinning over Katie's shoulder. They settled on a couch as Sam went in search of Mel, leaving them to "girl talk."

"So," Katie began, "Sam seems pretty crazy about you." Melvin stared at Violet with huge blue eyes.

"Maybe until today. We had a little spat, and I think he's mad at me," Violet answered. She smoothed her skirt and smiled at Melvin, who responded with giggly spit bubbles. "He's adorable," she told Katie. "Sometimes I want a baby of my own so bad."

"I'll let you spend some time with my little monsters. That'll cure you." Katie glanced out the window. "For instance, my older child is trying to dismantle Sam's car." She handed the baby to Violet and ran to the screen door, screaming. "Samuel Patrick Sobel! Stop that right now!" The boy rose and held up the tire valve cover he'd removed, grinning ear to ear. "Put it back!" Katie yelled. She settled back on the couch and ran her fingers through long red hair. "They're a mess," she told Violet.

Violet hesitated a second, then blurted, "Patrick isn't a Jewish name, is it?"

Katie laughed. "Not in the least. My maiden name is O'Connor. I converted to marry Mel." She nodded at Violet's gaping mouth. "I was raised Southern Baptist in Atlanta. My parents have never met their grandchildren—you'd think I married Duke Ellington. Mel's folks are even worse. They'd be happier if he'd run off with Gypsy Rose Lee."

Melvin began to squirm in Violet's arms and reached for his mother as the men entered the room. Violet forgot Southern lady protocol and jumped up to greet Mel, who shook her hand heartily. He was a tall, handsome man with dark brown eyes and hair; Violet thought he resembled a very young Clark Gable. Mel looked about twenty years old.

"Welcome, Violet," he said. "We're happy to meet you."

Katie chimed in, "Don't let him fool you, Violet. He's thirty-three, but keeps a portrait in his office to do his aging like Dorian Gray. I married an older man."

"That painting depicts an ancestor of mine, Judah P. Benjamin.

He was the first lawyer in the family, and my mother presented me with the portrait when I passed the bar. He holds no magic, I assure you. I'm just naturally young and good-looking."

"Judah P. Benjamin, Secretary of State for the Confederacy?" Violet asked.

"Ah, so you're a history buff," Mel answered.

"No, I hate history. That's the only thing I remember from Miss Forrestal's class," she said.

"Well, old Judah was some sort of great uncle or cousin on Mother's side. If the Jews had saints, he'd have been one in my childhood household. These days he gazes upon my desk with disapproval."

"Stop it, Mel," Katie ordered. "Violet, I need to feed the baby. Why don't you come back to our bedroom with me? Excuse us, gentlemen." She stood and flipped Melvin onto her shoulder.

Katie and Mel's bedroom was a riot of pink and green. It featured what Violet guessed had to have been Katie's childhood bed—an elaborate white four poster with canopy. Katie settled the baby at her breast and announced, "Yes, it's not the best thing for his masculinity...but I make him sleep here."

"What was that remark about his ancestor gazing on his desk with disapproval?" Violet asked.

Katie sighed. "Mel's lost a lot of clients since he married a shiksa." She saw Violet's blank look and added, "Non-Jewish girl." Violet nodded, patting the fluffy pink chenille bedspread. "Have you met Sam's parents?" she continued.

"No," Violet said, "I've never even seen them up close."

Katie switched the baby to the other side, biting her lower lip. "Look, Violet...it's probably not my place...but you should know they chose Deborah to marry Sam years ago. The families are very close. Sam and Deborah grew up together."

"So did Sam and I," Violet answered, indignant.

"Not in temple, you didn't." She shook her head. "I shouldn't have mentioned it. You and Sam seem very happy together."

"We are." Melvin blinked at Violet and grinned little milk bubbles before Katie lifted him to burp.

"Well then," Katie said, "You've seen living proof today that biscuits and bagels can mix well. I wish y'all the best."

Sam waited until they were nearly to the Alabama state line to say, "I'm sorry about the Rollerdrome. I shouldn't have been showing off." He reached for Violet's hand and kissed her palm. "Forgive me?"

"Of course," she replied. "I love you, Mr. Davidson. Your cousin and his wife are very nice. Katie and I had an interesting talk."

"Did she tell you Jewish men are the best lovers?" Sam's smile glowed in the dashboard light.

"That's what she told me. I said I'd need proof."

Sam drummed his fingers on the steering wheel. "Soon after our graduation, my parents are going to New York. Maybe you'd like to come over?"

"Maybe I would."

On graduation day, she and Sam had held hands and watched Johnny roll across the auditorium stage in a wheelchair to accept his diploma. Violet's friends cheered loudly when her name was called. She looked into the audience and waved brightly, spotting Johnny and his parents in the back of the room. He wheeled himself out without a glance.

Mr. and Mrs. Davidson were standing with Violet's family in front of the school. Violet was thrilled to see Sam's mother pat Alice Glenn on the arm and share a laugh over something as she and Sam approached.

"Mother, Dad, this is Violet," Sam announced.

"At long last we meet you," Esther Davidson said, extending her plump hand to Violet's. "Such a pretty girl."

"Thank you, Mrs. Davidson."

Philip Davidson shook her hand and said, "Sam talks about you all the time."

Violet beamed at Sam, who cleared his throat and said, "We have to get to the party at Ralph's. We'll see y'all later." They were ushered off in a round of congratulatory hugs.

Sam's parents were leaving on an unseasonably cool Alabama May morning.

"We're staying at the Waldorf," his mother said. "Mrs. Turley will be here to clean Monday, so you'll have to come straight home after work to give her a ride home. There will be no parties, and no guests in this house. Do you understand?"

"Yes, Mother." Sam watched his father struggle to drag suitcases out the front door. "Let me help, Dad." When they were loading the car, he asked the question he'd been pondering for days. "Why are you taking Mom along on a New York buying trip?"

"Oh, well, you see, Sam..." Philip Davidson began what seemed a practiced speech. "She's coming along to visit some friends of ours. You remember the Greenbergs. She and Eve are planning to shop while I'm in meetings. Dave and I are going to talk a little business, too." He smiled broadly at his son and clasped his shoulder. "It will be good for your mother to be away for a few days, Sam. She worries so about you."

"There's no need for her to worry," Sam answered. "I'm happy, healthy, and recently graduated twenty-ninth in my class of thirty-eight. What mother wouldn't be proud?"

Philip laughed and hugged his son. "You're a blessing, Sam. Not so much to your teachers, but you're a blessing." He looked toward the front door and yelled for his wife, who emerged swathed in fur—a compact Yiddish teddy bear smearing red lipstick on her son's cheek—and they were gone.

Eight hours later Sam led Violet into his bedroom—decorated, she pointed out with a giggle, in Early Sports Team. She sat on the bed, an awkward smile frozen on her face. He offered her a glass of wine and put a record on the phonograph. Violet recognized "There, I've Said It Again" by Vaughan Monroe.

Sam sat next to her and stroked her hair. "I do, you know," he whispered into her ear. "I love you to the end. Forever. I want to marry you, Violet." He turned her face to his and kissed her, soft as rose petals. Violet closed her eyes and listened to the music as he undressed her and eased her back onto the pillows. When she opened them Sam was straddling her body, fully clothed. He stared at her in the soft light.

"You are the most beautiful woman in the world, Vi. And I am the luckiest guy. Everybody loves you, but you're mine." He started a line of kisses between her breasts and down to her belly button. Violet grabbed his hair, confused. Sam laughed gently. "Close your eyes, Violet. Relax."

She felt his tongue licking her and gasped. Sam pinned her hands down, twining his fingers in hers and holding tight. The entire world was Sam's mouth, urging her toward a place she'd never imagined existed. Violet's hips began to move. She arched her back and screamed, breaking her hands free and clutching Sam's ears. She lay very still for a minute, then opened her eyes to find him smiling down at her.

"I..."

"Shh," he told her. Sam threw his clothes across the room and lowered his body to hers. He was inside her in one smooth motion and started moving slowly. "Look at me," he demanded. "I want to watch your face."

She locked her eyes on his and wrapped her legs around his waist. And Violet understood, for the very first time, what the fuss was all about.

Violet woke up in late July feeling nauseated. She didn't blame the previous night's spaghetti because she'd suspected she might be pregnant for a month or so. She patted her belly, happy to know she and Sam would be starting their family right away. She imagined his smile when she told him her news. Poor Sam had been locked in his father's store for days doing inventory, and she knew he'd been focused on this day to get him through. Now she had a wonderful surprise to add to their adventure.

They were meeting at the train station tonight at seven o'clock to elope. It wouldn't be the big wedding she'd dreamed about, but she didn't care. Sam had assured her it was best, and a more romantic beginning for them. She hid her packed suitcase in the closet and went to greet her mother for the last time as a single woman.

"Pancakes, honey?" Alice asked.

"No thanks, Mom. I'm not very hungry."

Alice regarded her daughter with a long gaze, eyebrows arched in question. "You're not sick, are you? Let me feel your temperature." She pressed a velvety hand to Violet's forehead, then patted her cheek with a smile. "Come help me strip the beds before Corinna gets here. Then we can get ready to cook lunch."

Violet stifled a sigh and trudged after her mother, vowing silently to keep her life with Sam more interesting than housework and meal preparation.

That evening Katie Ruth smuggled luggage out as Violet distracted her parents, kissing them goodnight as she left for a fictional pajama party. Violet smiled at her best friend's tears when they arrived at the station.

"I can't believe you and Sam are getting married, Vi. I wish I could be with y'all."

"I do too," Violet answered. "You know you'd be my maid of honor. We'll get together as soon as we're back from New Orleans." She pecked Katie Ruth's cheek and wiped a pink lipstick smudge and a tear track with her thumb. "Don't cry, silly. This is the happiest day of my life. I'll bring you a fabulous souvenir."

Katie Ruth brightened and started the car as Violet exited to get her bags from the trunk. "I love anything with pecans or diamonds," she yelled. Violet laughed and closed the car door, rapping a quick goodbye with her knuckles on the windshield.

eleven

RONNI

My mother's face loomed over me, her index finger doing that bumblebee-tickle thing parents try when nothing else amuses their toddler. I must have been around two years old, because we were living in a beaten Oldsmobile she'd told me was magical. How many people's homes can take them directly to a Happy Meal?

I blinked away the memory and returned to charting meds. It had been over a week since I'd quietly asked Rick to take me home from the lakehouse. He walked me to my apartment at two o'clock in the morning, and we stood in the awkward silence of strangers sharing a horrible secret. He bent to kiss me. I turned my face and mumbled something about both of us needing sleep, hurrying to unlock my door. I hadn't seen or heard from him since.

I knew two things: I missed him desperately, and he was done with the junkie whore's daughter. I was Relationship Poison, the Girl Best Left Alone, Most Likely to Be Avoided, Miss Greet with Congeniality Only and Run Fast. We were ahead of my usual three week schedule, but the rest was a familiar story. I'd known from the minute he'd starting paying attention to me in the bank's parking lot he would stop soon.

Kait interrupted my thoughts by throwing a cracker at my face. "Some people are crack addicts and some are cracker addicts. I think you have a serious saltine and Goldfish problem, Ronni."

She began reading ingredients on the side of the box, shaking her head. "You are what you eat, and you're mostly salt."

"And preservatives. They're important, too. Look around you." I handed her a memo about flu season and hand washing, because corporate thought we nurses needed constant reminders we were germ-infested Trojan horses. Prophylactic hand sanitation was logical. I pointed at the Activities Schedule. "Gird yourself. This afternoon is Pat's Pets."

"Oh, goodie," Kait replied. "I hope she brings the ferret today. It's always fun to hear Mrs. Andrews scream for someone to kill the rat."

Leola Hartness—tall and elegant, with carefully coiffed white hair and perfect makeup—approached the nurse's station wearing a vibrant orange floral sweater and striped mint green pajama pants. "Excuse me," she smiled graciously, "where am I?"

"You're in Fairfield Springs," I told her.

"Oh." She considered that for a second. "How long have I been here?"

"Two years."

"Oh, dear," she answered. "Where is my room?"

I nodded at 185, with her name printed on a large placard next to the number. "It's right there, number 185."

"Thank you, honey." She walked gracefully to the doorway and waved, disappearing inside. One minute later, she walked out and asked, "Excuse me—where am I?"

"Fairfield Springs, Mrs. Hartness."

"How long have I been here?"

"Two years. Why don't you rest for a little while? Lunch will be coming up soon. Maybe you'd like to put on your tan slacks."

She patted her hair. "Yes, I will. Thank you."

She would return soon in a heartbreaking loop of inquiry about her location. There were no visitors for Mrs. Hartness, and I tried to spend time each day helping her reminisce. She'd been a corporate secretary and mother of two sons, both of whom had died years ago.

Kait and I pushed the med cart out and fired up the tablet

computer to begin our way down the hall to dispense. We'd check blood sugar levels, heart rates, pulses, bedsores, bruises, temperatures, and many other things along the way, plus field requests for additional pain medication. I knew before reaching Mrs. Henderson's room that her sugar would be sky high—and that she'd ask me to fetch her three candy bars to scarf down before we gave her insulin. My pocket held a crossword puzzle, which I'd produce in Miss Shelton's room and ask for her help. Miss Shelton was an English teacher whose vocabulary rivaled Merriam-Webster's, but her vision was almost gone. I carried a photo of an Irish landscape for Mr. Neely, plus a rhinestone collar for Mrs. Meyers' stuffed cat. She cradled and petted "Fluffy" all day long.

Audrey Marie Haynes Ledbetter—who no longer required pruning—was wheeling herself toward us. "You two need to hurry up," she declared. "You're running late, and I can feel my blood pressure rising."

"You can *feel* it?" Kait responded.

"Yes I can, smart girl," Mrs. Ledbetter snarled. "While you dawdle in the hall, I'm getting closer and closer to a stroke. I'm going to wait right here for my pills. My room smells like a latrine in the middle of an old cow pasture surrounded by dead fish..."

"We get the idea, Mrs. Ledbetter," I interrupted.

"...thanks to Helen," she finished.

Kait scrunched her nose. "Is Baylee on today?" she asked me.

I nodded.

"I'll page her to clean Helen up."

She pressed a button on the wall as we both said silent thanks for our advanced nursing degrees.

"Someone will be in your room to help Helen in a minute, Mrs. Ledbetter," Kait said. "Let me get your medication for you." She pulled up the chart and rifled through the cart's drawers, then handed over a paper cup of water and six pills. "And by the way," she added as Audrey handed back her crumpled cup, "you look very nice today."

Mrs. Ledbetter glared at her and rolled off toward the activity room.

"Why did you do that?" I asked. "You know politeness and kindness are two of her biggest pet peeves."

"I'm hoping she'll put me in her will," Kait answered, grinning.

My heart skidded to a stop. Kait couldn't possibly know about my inheritance from Violet. I'd been very careful. "Good luck with that," I said nonchalantly. "Audrey is more likely to leave it all to The Society for Advancement of Cruelty to Nurses."

"Yeah...speaking of that," Kait giggled, "I was thinking maybe we could dress up Audrey's room while she's sleeping. Put some polished wood slats all around the bed, bring in candles and big floral arrangements...we could play some hymns real softly in the background..."

"You are pure evil," I laughed. "Oooh—we could put satin all around her on the bed..."

I hadn't noticed Donna coming toward us, frowning with more ferocity than usual. "Shouldn't y'all be done with meds? You're at least ten minutes behind." She locked her gaze on Kait. "You finish alone. Ronni and I need to discuss some things in my office." She spun on her chunky Payless heel and headed off without another word.

Donna closed the door behind me more forcefully than necessary. I cringed and waited for her latest heart-seeking missile.

"Ronni, your deposition tomorrow is right before mine. I presume you're not going to tell Mr. Ratliff anything that could render us liable in Violet's death?"

"There's nothing I could tell him that would show any negligence, Donna. Violet went to that room on her own. She died of natural causes. I'm sure the suit will be dropped after our depositions, because Herb has no legal grounds to come after Fairfield."

She tapped her bright red fingernails on the desk. "So you're an attorney now?" Donna leaned back and crossed her arms under an ample bosom straining against navy polyester knit. She exhaled slowly, staring at a space in the distance.

"No, but it's obvious we did nothing wrong." I offered my brightest smile, and she returned it with the warmth and sincerity of a low-level driver's license office employee two minutes before lunchtime.

Donna leaned forward, punishing her desk chair into a series of loud squeaks. "You're not still writing that book, are you?"

Of course I was. Trying to work on it and keep up with my job was stressing me beyond anything I'd ever known. "It's a hobby, Donna. Just a hobby. I enjoy writing."

"A book about one of our residents might get you fired, Ronni, and you could find yourself on the receiving end of a lawsuit of your own."

"I'll take my chances," I announced. Donna's face fell like she'd been hit by a giant Botox dart. "I'm not doing anything wrong," I continued, "and you know I'm the hardest working nurse on your staff. There's no reason to threaten me."

"How about this?" Donna held up her hands in mock surrender. "You show me what you're writing, and we'll decide if you should continue."

"I can't do that."

"Why the hell not?"

"I can't say. Trust me, though, I can't show it to you or anyone."

She shook her head. "This hobby of yours is going to cost you everything, Ronni."

If she only knew. I was losing my sanity to meet an impossible deadline in order to inherit money and garner attention I wasn't sure I deserved or even wanted. Trying not to tear my hair out was my real hobby.

I was out of words and energy for this conversational swordfight. "I need to get back to work, okay? I'll meet you at Mr. Ratliff's office tomorrow." I stood to leave.

She pressed her fuchsia-stained lips together and cleared her throat. "Ronni, I'm concerned your attention isn't on your job. You're past due on reports and clocking in late every other day.

Frankly, you look tired."

Touché, Donna. I'm staying awake early into every morning trying to write a book, and I have no idea if I'm doing it right. I'm worried sick about losing the nicest man I've ever met. I recently found out my long lost mother is in jail. My apartment looks like I invited a few hoarder families to move in.

"I'll try to do better," I said. *And Donna, your dress looks like it's from the Sears Polyester Doubleknit I've Officially Given Up Collection.*

twelve

VIOLET

The lobby was deserted except for an old man reading a newspaper in the corner. Violet saw Mr. Wilson at the ticket window's desk and turned her back to him, praying he wouldn't recognize her.

Violet sighed, wishing her future husband were as punctual as he was handsome. Their train was scheduled to depart in fifteen minutes and there was no sign of him. She watched the seconds tick away on a huge wall clock as she fanned herself with a movie magazine against the stifling heat. A family with three children arrived on the 7:20 from Atlanta and stumbled wearily through the station to embrace the old man, who suddenly came to life and jumped to greet them, sweeping a tiny girl into his arms. Violet tracked them from behind her magazine as they made their way to a battered DeSoto and piled in.

She leapt to her feet as Sam's car pulled into the lot, then sank onto the bench when she saw Mr. Davidson heading for the station door. He spotted her and crossed the lobby to sit down, clasping his hands as if in prayer.

"Hello, Violet," he began.

"What has happened to Sam? Where is he?" Violet tried to shove her thudding heart back down into its cage.

Philip Davidson sighed, exhaling days of exhaustion and worry. "Sam's mother and I have arranged for a career for him in

New York City, Violet. We're opening a flagship store there soon, and he's going to run it. An excellent opportunity for Sam and our family's business." He paused for breath and met her eyes for the first time. "Sam left with Deborah and her parents last night."

"No. No, you can't..."

Mr. Davidson was shaking his head. "Violet, you won't be able to contact Samuel. He is staying with friends of ours for a few weeks. There will be no telephone. We thought that would be best."

Violet was trembling and couldn't seem to stop. It took a minute for her to find her voice and form words. "Mr. Davidson, there's something you should know."

"Nothing you can tell me will make a difference, Violet. I'm sorry. I know you care about Sam ..."

"It's much more than that, Mr. Davidson. I..."

He held up his hands. "No more, please, Violet. The two of you will be much better off this way. Deborah and Sam are getting married and beginning a life in New York. Wish them well."

"But I'm almost sure," she stammered through tears. "I'm almost sure I'm carrying your grandchild." She watched new lines etch themselves into Philip Davidson's face. He bowed his head for a minute, then stood and reached into his pocket.

"Here is some money to help with expenses, Violet. Go somewhere and stay for a year or so. The baby—if there is one—well, it can be adopted. Surely you have family to help with your ...situation." He glanced around to see if anyone was witnessing their conversation and spotted a wide-eyed boy peering from a doorway near the ticket window. Violet was curled into an apostrophe of sadness, rocking and clutching her stomach. Worse, his wife was emerging from their car. Esther would do nothing but make an even worse scene.

He hurried to finish. "I warn you, Violet, you must tell no one. And under no circumstances should you try to find Sam. His future is settled, and you can't be a part of it. My son has no child with you. Do you understand?" He straightened his back and walked away from the stunned girl on the bench.

Violet felt a hand on her shoulder and turned to find Chet Wilson smiling down at her. He was a foot taller than the last time she'd seen him. She shook her head gently, trying to focus on how she could explain her presence in the station. It seemed easier to ask him the question instead. "What in the world are you doing here, Chet? Have you come back to live with your dad?"

"I'm just visiting. My aunt let me ride the train here yesterday, and I have to go back tomorrow." He sat beside her and searched her eyes. "What happened, Violet? Who was that man?"

"Oh...he's my friend's father. She and I were supposed to go on a trip together, but she got sick at the last minute. He came to tell me and," she noticed the roll of bills in her hand, "bring the money I was going to use for our fares and expenses. We'll just reschedule." Violet stood and started to reach for her luggage, but Chet grabbed it.

Chet glanced at his father manning the window. Mr. Wilson waved at the two of them, and Violet desperately hoped Sam had purchased their tickets from someone else.

"You've been crying," Chet said. "I'm sorry you're so disappointed. Where were y'all going?"

"New Orleans," Violet replied. She struggled to smile. "Will you carry my luggage, Chet? I need to ask your dad if I can use his telephone."

thirteen

RONNI

As it turned out, Rick didn't leave me. I left him, though it took me a while to realize it.

He'd placed single flowers under my windshield wiper twice while I worked. Once there was only a small note saying, "I miss you, beautiful."

"Ronni," Rick said two nights before, "when you're finished with your project, let me know. I'm not asking you out again until I have a decent chance you'll say yes."

I didn't blame him. Most of the time I felt too pressured to write to spend time on anything else. Rick and I had been out to dinners and a couple of movies, always with my eye on the clock, wondering if I could work on the book for an hour or two when I got home. I'd gotten into the habit of stalling for time whenever he suggested we go out.

"Soon, I promise, soon," I'd say. "Just let me finish another two chapters."

The last time I'd seen him, we'd been to an elaborate restaurant where everyone, once more, seemed to know his name. Our table held a candle in an antique silver filigree holder, surrounded by a cluster of roses and baby's breath. Rick's smile, in that candlelight, was the most beautiful thing I'd ever seen. We held hands between courses and walked out with our arms around each other, Rick clutching a box with a complimentary chocolate cake slice. We'd walked two blocks when he suddenly stopped, set the box down on a brick planter, and kissed me until I lost all consciousness of the world around us. He gently lifted me to sit next to the cake and there I was on a deserted city street at eleven o'clock, making out with the most exciting man I'd ever met and trying to ignore an incessant nagging thought about two sentences I needed to change before I forgot.

The manuscript was driving me crazy.

I'd gone backward instead of making progress, deleting every other sentence and agonizing over how to replace it. Online research on writing only confused me. So did the books I'd ordered. I briefly considered trying to contact Jennifer, Mr. Sobel's niece, for help—but it seemed too desperate; too pitiful, too amateurish. I pictured her holding a phone, rolling her eyes at the injustice of being saddled with an author writing in crayon. Besides, Violet had insisted I show it to no one until it was finished.

It felt like someone had handed me a knife and fork and demanded I perform brain surgery.

I longed to throw my hands up in surrender; to be with Rick without feeling I should hurry back to the keyboard. Most of all, I wanted to stop thinking about the book every waking moment. Violet's good intentions were ruining my life, not blessing it. No amount of money was worth the stress I was feeling.

I looked forward to my shifts at Fairfield. Donna had become friendlier and less critical after the depositions with BillRat were done and our attorney said the lawsuit would likely be dropped. Work was my refuge; the only place I laughed anymore. Writing had become agony.

So I quit. One afternoon I came home from work, gnawed my way through the writing straightjacket's straps and threw my laptop into the closet. I felt giddy with freedom. *Violet, I love you and would like to have lots of money...but no thanks. Maybe someone else can pen your book someday. Not me.*

I called Rick and babbled a voice message, "I've given up on writing. It's not my thing. Nursing is my thing. *You* are my thing. Please come over and we'll celebrate. Umm, this is Ronni. Call me."

Two hours later he knocked on the door. He wrapped his arms around me and said, "So I'm your thing, huh? Very poetic."

"Just kiss me."

I did, feeling electricity shoot through my body. Rick was the best kisser I'd ever known, starting out soft and slow and building to something that made me ache for him. "You're too good at this," I whispered, struggling for breath.

"That's the idea. Let me show you how I feel about you, Ronni." He was melting me with those chocolate brown eyes. They were locked onto mine and not letting go.

"Okay," I said. "Show me."

He threw his trooper hat across the room, picked me up, and carried me to the bedroom.

I lay with my head on his beefy right biceps, stroking the hair on his chest. Rick opened one eye and gazed at me. "So," he said, "You're giving up on your book?"

I plucked a chest hair and he winced. "I don't want to talk about it."

"It's just that, you know, it seemed so important to you. My keen police brain tells me there's more to the story. Talk to me, Ronni."

"Okay. I was asked to write a novel based on the life of a woman I knew at Fairfield Springs. I thought I could do it. I can't. End of story." I jumped up with the sheet wrapped around me. "I'm going to feed Halle. You want anything?"

"Nope. Hurry back." He offered me one of his melt-your-knees smiles and patted the bed.

I brought him a brown sugar cinnamon Pop Tart to share, along with a Diet Coke.

Rick laughed and drawled, "Do you know how much this means to me after years with various versions of Miss Bean Sprout Tofu Kale?"

"I'll feed you all the junk food you want if you promise to pay me in hot monkey policeman love."

Rick grabbed my sheet-toga and pulled me on top of him, locking his eyes on mine. "This," he announced, "is what you get for half a Pop Tart."

I made a mental note to pick up a box.

The next morning I woke to find him removing his neatly-hung uniform from my closet. I wondered if I could coexist with someone so creased, polished and organized.

"I'm late," he said, pausing to kiss me as he buttoned his shirt. "I'll pick you up at six for dinner. Fancy. Dress up. Champagne." He reached for his shoes and said, "Whoa, what's this?"

Rick held up a battered, dirty doll with short gray curly hair and fake wire-rimmed eyeglasses.

"That," I answered, "is Mrs. Noodle. Closest thing to a mother I had as a child."

"You kept her all these years." He sank onto the bed and placed the doll beside me. "I guess you two went through a lot together."

I was horrified to find I was crying. Rick wrapped me in his arms. "You know, Ronni," he said, "She'll be getting out soon. Are you sure you don't want to meet with her?"

I swiped at my eyes. "I'm positive. I'll never forgive what she did to me. Even the idea of seeing Jocelyn makes me feel sick. I was an unwanted, unworthy, disposable child. I hate myself when I think how little I meant to her, Rick. I tried," I sobbed, "I tried so hard to take care of her..."

"Take a deep breath, Ronni," Rick held me at arm's length and searched my eyes. "You don't have to see her."

"That's good, because I think I would split wide open."

He kissed the top of my head and slid his bear-paw hands down my arms to grasp and squeeze mine. "See you at six."

"Be safe!" I yelled at his back.

"Always," he answered.

The restaurant was full of chandeliers and floral arrangements that could comfortably host entire flocks of birds. Rick seemed right at home, ordering some kind of fancy appetizer and champagne as soon as we sat down.

"About the book, Ronni," he began. "I've been thinking. You might not be able to show it to me, but we could discuss the things you're trying to put into words, right? Surely Violet allowed for pillow talk."

I stared at him.

"I'm a big reader," he continued. "Mostly crime and spy stuff like James Patterson and Nelson DeMille, but I know a good story when I see one. Or hear one."

"I told you I'm giving up."

"Yes, you did. Right before you told me how your mother made you feel worthless. I'm wondering if the two are related."

"Jeez Louise, Rick, you're not my shrink. Let it go."

He covered my hand with his. "I'm trying to do what's best for you. Giving up on something you've worked so hard to do ...well, I think you'll regret it. I want to help. I can take some time off work, and so can you. We could stay at the lake and shut out everything. You, me and a laptop."

I smiled. "And case of Pop Tarts."

"And, of course," Rick added, "a bulldog and an antisocial cat. But we can keep Kitty and kitty separated. Come on, Ronni, say yes."

Across the restaurant, an elderly couple held hands and smiled at us. Maybe they thought Rick had just proposed.

"All right," I said. "I'll talk to Donna Monday about taking a couple of weeks."

fourteen

VIOLET

Bradenton Beach, Florida, 1948

No one told Violet the baby would flutter and kick and grab fistfuls of her heart. No one told her she'd feel so nauseated, either. Tourists traveled from everywhere to see the Gulf of Mexico caress the sugary beach, and most days she was sick in it before her morning walk ended.

Violet swore she'd never return to Florida.

She opened her eyes and gazed out the window. The beach was deserted this time of morning, so she felt free to waddle out for a little exercise. Her belly was too enormous to appear in a bathing suit. Aunt Jean would be gone to work, expecting Violet to join her in an hour.

She'd had no idea where to turn after Katie Ruth picked her up at the train station. They'd cried together for hours, finally deciding Violet had to call and beg her mother's younger sister in Florida for help.

Aunt Jean had listened to Violet explain her situation without interruption or judgment. She telephoned her sister Alice the next day and explained she'd like Violet to come work in her ice cream shop. She would send money for a bus ticket and meet her niece in Tampa.

A few months later, she'd asked if Violet could stay and help with her business, explaining Violet had become so skilled at serving cones and sundaes to tourists, Jean couldn't do without her.

This was far from the truth. Violet consumed any profits she might have generated each day in the form of Coke floats. She found it hard to tolerate most of the tourists. Jean constantly reminded her niece she had to smile and be courteous, even if a customer was railing about the price of extra caramel or insisting ice cream—and everything else—was better up north.

Violet felt sure her mother didn't suspect any reason for the trip other than her daughter's heartbreak over Sam's move to New York. She'd asked Jean to introduce her daughter to "some nice Florida boys."

No one, Aunt Jean assured her, would ever know about the baby. She had a lawyer friend in St. Pete who had arranged an adoption. Violet's monthly visits to Dr. Southerland and the hospital stay would be covered. And because she'd been hysterical at the thought of handing her baby to a stranger, she was promised she didn't even have to see her child's new parents. Everything was arranged, planned, set into motion, going forward, and rushing to rip Violet apart.

The baby was due in one month. Violet ran her hands across her stomach and cried salt back into the Gulf of Mexico.

fifteen

RONNI

I had come to believe Rick was right about everything. He seemed to know exactly what any given situation required, have an answer to every problem, and never waver when he'd made a decision. It was one of the things I adored about him.

Our days at the lake were set in a pattern: I'd blink my eyes about seven each morning and find Rick staring at me, smiling me awake. He'd cook breakfast—usually waffles or scrambled eggs—and bring it to me in bed with a cup of strong coffee. We'd eat while discussing Violet's latest chapter. Then he'd kiss the tip of my nose, take the dishes, and disappear.

I spent the next four hours with the door closed, clutching the laptop and writing while Rick roamed the woods and water with Kitty. I'd written more in six days at the lake house than all the months before. The lack of distractions was nice, but I knew the book was flowing freely because I discussed ideas with Rick. Violet, I'd decided, did not expressly prohibit general discussion with my boyfriend. It wasn't like I was talking to Kait or Donna about it; surely this was okay.

Sometimes I clutched the laptop and didn't write. I deleted sentences and added them back. My word count had expanded to eighteen thousand, and I'd told most of what I knew about Violet's youth from my written notes and her teenage diary. I found myself trying to remember our more casual conversations, hoping for revelations.

And about sixty thousand more words.

On one of those days I got exasperated and joined Rick on the dock, where he'd been fishing for an hour. He heard me walking up and patted the space next to him, mouthing "shh" and pointing to the water.

After a few minutes he announced, "I'm giving up. Not accomplishing anything here. I think we're having hot dogs for supper."

"I'm not, either. I deleted everything I wrote this morning. There was this long scene about Violet at a dance with Johnny, where she'd gotten jealous of another girl. She went on and on about it in her diary. I decided it was boring and took it back out. I've been going back and looking for new Johnny and Sam stories I might've missed." I thought for a minute. "Johnny was a great guy, and Violet's first love, but Sam is more my type. He was funny and smart and had some amazing lady-pleasing skills."

Rick laughed. "How do I compete with that?"

"Very well, sir." I ran my fingernails up and down his back. "I'd choose you. Anyway, he was deeply in love with her. Violet found out he'd been collecting photos of her for a long time…"

"That's creepy," Rick interrupted.

"Stop thinking like a cop." I punched his arm. "He was the yearbook photographer. He took lots of candids of Violet she never knew about plus the usual yearbook stuff. He kept copies at home."

"More romantic and less creepy, I guess. If you say so. Let me ask you something," Rick said. "Why do you think Violet wanted you to write her story?"

"I don't know." I looked across the lake at a little boat putting along. "I think she saw her life as fascinating. She was the center of attention in any room. She felt loved and adored by men. She lost her daughter and survived that pain, then I came into her life and she doted on me in her place. So many things came full circle for her at Fairfield Springs. You have to admit it was remarkable."

"Can you think of any other reasons?" He raised his eyebrows.

"She wanted me to prove to myself I could accomplish it. I told her more than once I didn't know how I'd even begin."

"Is that everything?"

"Well, she wanted the world to know what she'd been through. She'd had to keep a lot of secrets. And Violet was the type of person who craved attention..."

"...even after she was gone," Rick finished.

"And the book will immortalize her. Hmmm. I never thought about that. You're right. Violet would have loved the idea of living on as a character for millions of people."

"And why do you think she set this one year time limit for you?"

"Believe me, I've wondered. Mr. Sobel didn't have an answer for me. I think it has to do with Violet's own writing experience. She worked on stories but never finished them. She told me one time it was because no one pushed her. So she left me a carrot and stick to make sure I'd follow through."

"A very effective one." Rick smiled. "I hope to be the center of attention in your rooms again someday." He began packing up his gear. "I think I'll run into town and buy some fish. That's extremely damaging to my ego, but necessary." He kissed my forehead. "And I have an assignment for you."

"That's great. As long as it's not writing."

"It's not. First of all, Google how to make hollandaise sauce and print it out for me. I'm pretty sure I know what to buy. Leave the recipe on the kitchen counter and then go back to your laptop and type out the first conversation with Violet that comes into your mind, no matter what or when it was. Something you didn't write down, something she didn't intend for your book."

"I could stay here and catch some fish instead."

"Not a chance. And if you did, I'd be all hurt. Go on now. I'll see you in an hour or two."

I printed Rick's recipe and delivered it to the kitchen, wondering for the hundredth time why anyone ever found avocado green suitable for appliances. Then I plopped onto the bed beside Halle, closed my eyes and fell asleep. When I woke up, it was fresh in my mind:

I found Violet sitting in Fairfield's library one day. I'd finished an overnight shift and was exhausted, but something about the way she was hunched over a book drew me in.

"Hey, are you okay?"

She slapped the book shut and placed her hand over its cover, barely concealing the flowing Fabio hair on its hero. "Hi, Ronni. Yes, I'm fine." She saw me grinning at the book. "Oh, all right, I'm reading a stupid clichéd romance novel."

"Look, if you want to read As the Bosom Heaves it's fine with me." I reached over and turned the cover toward me. "Hmm. This one looks very romance-y and heave-y and throbby."

"It's a stupid book, but I began thinking about the men in my life and wondering how they measured up."

I laughed.

"Oh, stop it. Not like that and not really, anyway. I've never read a bodice ripper and I was curious."

"Are you going to finish it?"

"I haven't even started. I'm skimming it for declarations of undying love and pondering the whole thing. Sometimes I think romantic love is only real half of the time. The rest is a chemical reaction."

"Well, that's depressing. How do I know if I just have magnificent pheromones?"

"That's the question, isn't it? I'm starting to wonder how any of us know. Maybe you should call my book The Magnificent Pheromones of Violet."

"Not catchy. I don't like Everybody Smelled Her, either."

Violet collapsed into laughter. "I do love you, Ronni."

"I love you, too. Any particular reason this is on your mind?"

She sat back and crossed her arms. "Today is the anniversary of my wedding to the only man in my life who didn't love me. I used to wonder why that happened." She brushed at her skirt. "It's a long story I'll tell you someday. Right now you look exhausted and I'm not in the mood to talk about it."

"Okay. I'll see you tomorrow. I've been on for ten hours and I need some sleep."

"Get some rest, honey." She opened the book and began searching for her place as I walked away.

I closed the laptop and heard Rick come in a few minutes later. He poked his head into the room. "Thanks for the recipe. Did you think of anything?"

"Yes, I did, and it's made me curious about her marriage. She never did say much of anything about Tolly, and I still haven't read the journals in the bottom of the box, which should be about those years."

"Why not?"

"Because I have to break this into small pieces, Rick. If I read it all, I'll get overwhelmed. I was trying to finish The Early Years with Johnny and Sam before piecing together her marriage."

He'd nodded and said, "You're the writer. You know what you're doing." I heaved an exasperated sigh at him. "But," he added, "You can always come back to the earlier stuff. Might be a good idea."

"Okay. But for now I'm helping you cook and we're using lots of wine."

He laughed. "Way ahead of you. There's a glass on the counter."

I should've been writing the next morning, but I found myself daydreaming about ways to spend the inheritance money. Every one of those fantasies included Rick, whether I willed it or not. I saw us together in exotic places; kissing in front of the Eiffel Tower, walking through the streets of Vienna at Christmas time, gazing at the chandeliers sparkling overhead. Neither of us had jobs anymore, of course.

Then I remembered that I was twenty-six, and while Violet had promised a huge amount of money for the book's completion it wasn't nearly enough to contemplate complete freedom. There were increments as I aged, but I didn't know how much and when. It occurred to me I'd failed to ask Mr. Sobel a lot of important questions about the will.

Mr. Sobel.

Did he know about his cousin Sam's relationship with Violet? Since I'd read her diary and reconstructed her day with Sam in Atlanta, I knew how she'd chosen her attorney years later. I was almost positive, though, that she'd never told Melvin Sobel about her relationship with his cousin—or that she'd visited him at his home when he was a baby.

Did no one in his family ever mention Violet? Considering her exit, it was possible. Mr. Sobel certainly hadn't known Violet was pregnant at the time.

I shook my head to stop wandering through cobwebs and took Rick's advice. I dug out a beautiful purple journal with *Violet* engraved in gold script on the front cover. Today I would allow myself to read it. I pulled Halle onto my lap and turned to the first page, practically purring along in anticipation.

Part Two

sixteen

VIOLET

Birmingham, Alabama 1960

Violet consulted her Cartier watch and patted the pearls at her neck nervously. The Junior League's placement committee would be meeting here in thirty minutes. She ran through a mental checklist: crackers, cheese ball, crab dip, mixed nuts, fruit salad, chicken salad, potato salad, deviled eggs, yeast rolls, centerpiece, napkins, plates, forks, crystal, sweet tea, wine, Cokes and Tabs...dessert. Oh lord—had Beatrice remembered the lemon icebox pies? She raced to the kitchen, heels clicking a frantic tattoo on the polished wood floor. Yes, thank goodness, the pies were on the top shelf.

Now, if Tolly would just stay at the club until nine or so. He hated these "home invasions," preferring to write an enormous check to The Country Club of Birmingham or a restaurant when it was Violet's turn to host.

Tolliver Burnette "Tolly" Thompson was known to almost everyone in his insular world as Dr. Thompson. He allowed the use of his nickname by his wife, in-laws, sister, and three or four colleagues. Not only was Tolly a well-respected surgeon; he was married to a beauty twenty years his junior. He had a handicap of seven on the golf course, a mansion in Mountain Brook, and a bourbon addiction that beckoned with gentle, cradling arms every afternoon. If he had to stay at St. Vincent's to monitor a patient, there was a monogrammed leather flask in his pocket. By mutual agreement, emergency surgeries were assigned to partners on call after twelve o'clock each day—no exceptions. Doctors Lacefield and Healy took up the slack because it was worth it to have Tolly's name on the practice.

At fifty, his hands were still steady. Tolly believed his afternoons and evenings in the company of Jack Daniels were one reason his mornings in surgery were such a success. A man needed and deserved a sip or two to relax as the day wore on. Surgery was a demanding and high-pressure discipline.

As Violet prepared for her meeting, he marched the corridors at St. Vincent's like he was in a parade, waving at nurses and nodding benevolently at visitors. His post-op patients were in various stages of recovery and monitored by staff he trusted well. Tolly decided to have a drink or two with a smoke on the hospital's roof.

Stewart Mattison began to show signs of internal bleeding as Tolly lit his first Kool. Mr. Mattison had surrendered his gallbladder in a simple procedure. He wasn't being watched too closely. No one noticed, not even the two nurses trading gossip over coffee at the station down the hall. No one saw Stewart try to blink his eyes open and tell his wife something was wrong. No one saw Stewart Mattison dying until he was dead.

By the time Tolly wandered down to the third floor for his final round of the day, Marie Mattison was sobbing outside her husband's room. A nurse stood in the doorway, shaking her head solemnly at him.

Tolly dug fingernails deep into his palm inside his lab coat pocket. He assumed the concerned face with detached demeanor he'd perfected over the years, and hoped the spearmint gum he was chewing would do its job.

Violet checked her lipstick in the powder room and smoothed her ruby red shift. She'd placed the record player's needle at the beginning of Mozart's piano sonatas twice already. She closed her eyes and inhaled the music, just as she had as a little girl in her parents' living room. The doorbell blasted her out of her reverie. Genevieve had arrived to help her set up, though there was nothing left to do.

Genevieve Carroll was a Mississippi beauty queen married to Birmingham's premier jeweler. She wore a simple black shirtwaist accented, Violet thought, by everything DeBeers had dug up in the past six months. Violet watched Genny smooth her auburn hair over and over, flashing the five carat anniversary gift on her right hand.

Tolly didn't believe in buying jewelry. Violet glanced at her modest wedding ring set, summoned her inner gracious hostess and said, "Oh, Genny, is that ring new? It's so beautiful!"

Genny held her right arm straight and waggled her fingers. "Edward is great with the diamonds. If I could get him to add European vacations to his repertoire, he'd be damn near perfect." She surveyed the dining room table. "Looks like we're all set. Let's have a glass of something."

"Isn't it kind of early to start?" Violet eyed the wine chilling in a silver bucket.

"Not if you live with three children under the age of five, Violet. I'd have a chardonnay IV if I could figure out how to drag it around." She handed Violet a full wineglass and clinked hers to it. "Here's to the placement committee. May they select chairmen naive enough to be flattered and smart enough to accomplish great things next year. You look gorgeous, by the way. Red is great on you."

Tolly sat in the bar at his club, watching people come and go as he nursed his fourth bourbon. He spotted Pete Hughes, a cardiologist and sometime golf buddy. Pete inclined his head slightly at Tolly and followed his wife into the dining room.

Had word spread through the hospital already? Tolly raised his glass to signal for a fresh drink, cursing the Birmingham Junior League. He was going to make Violet resign from The Do Good While Dressed Expensively Club. The thought made him smile for the first time today.

Bourbon relaxed Tolly temporarily, but soon it would cause him to pick at the thread that would unravel his life.

Violet had agreed to host placement interviews this year because she loved opening her home to big groups and it was an easy meeting for the hostess. All she had to do was keep refreshments set up as the women came and went, occasionally helping someone find her placement advisor. She viewed her expansive living room from a fainting couch that had belonged to Tolly's grandmother. Antiques galore, none of them connected to her.

The house, she thought, was a monument to ostentation. She knew the neighbors resented the way it towered over their roofs. She also knew they called it "Tolly's Folly." Twelve thousand square feet of Tudor splendor, but her husband insisted they couldn't afford to take a vacation. She sipped her wine and waved at Genevieve as she ushered a young woman toward the library. One hundred and sixty women would walk through her house tonight to carefully plan their upcoming year of Junior League commitments. Family obligations would be discussed. Pregnancies, ailing parents, demanding husbands...and for a few, work schedules...would be factored.

She closed her eyes. Our lives, she considered, were so frighteningly *unplanned.* Everything came before or after certain moments; huge rocks that sent rivers of expectation and hope spilling into new directions, never to return.

April 3, 1948 divided her life forever. A nurse handed Violet a tiny bundle of sleeping baby girl to kiss goodbye. What she remembered best were her eyelashes, so long and delicate on those creamy cheeks. The little fists clenched under the hospital blanket. The way her head smelled.

She'd named her Alicia, even though they'd told her not to give her a name. When they carried her away, Violet knew that all the joy and light in her had passed into her daughter. She was a dark, empty shell.

She tried to get up and follow. She needed to tell them it was a mistake. She screamed at a nurse, who gave Violet medicine to make her sleep.

Later, she curled into a ball on her bed at Aunt Jean's and refused to eat or drink. She wanted to die, so her body obliged.

Aunt Jean took her to the doctor's office for a postpartum check a week after Violet came home. Her temperature was 103.6 degrees. They readmitted her to the hospital immediately and gave her antibiotics for puerperal fever. And Violet lost two more things: the opportunity to die and the ability to conceive children.

By 1949, she was back living in her parents' house and working as a hostess in a nice restaurant downtown. Alice Glenn never suspected what her daughter endured in Florida. It simply would not have dared to enter her mind. Violet used her only job qualification—homecoming queen skills—to charm customers each evening at The Annistonian. She flirted without intention, smiled without happiness, and extended the politeness and hospitality that were her birthright. On Saturday nights after work, she'd sometimes go to a movie with Harvey Hughes, an Army lieutenant stationed at nearby Fort McClellan. He was from Indiana, three years older than Violet, and called her "my beautiful Southern belle." He told her over and over he wanted to marry her and settle in Alabama permanently. Violet would laugh and shake her head each time. She said, "The novelty will wear off, Harvey. You'll forget me when you're transferred."

He never did, even after Violet left him for Tolly.

She'd been so ready to try to begin a new life; to try to put the horrible Florida memories behind her. Tolly was handsome, successful, and wealthy. He impressed her parents, reached for her hand, placed a ring upon it and arranged a wedding before Violet could object.

She heard Bitsy Cunningham and Theresa Wiley discussing their children, sharing school photos and attempting to top each other with stories of good grades, mischief, Sunday School attendance and vegetable rejection. She felt tears welling and closed her eyes, trying to block the thoughts she could never escape.

What would she look like now? Did she have her father's red hair and easy laugh? Did she do well in school? *Had they told her she was adopted?*

A month after they met, Tolly mentioned casually that he didn't want children—in the manner others might state an aversion to cats or parakeets. She'd looked into Tolly's dark blue eyes and summoned the courage to tell him all about her baby daughter. She sobbed as she told her story, ending with the fever that left her barren. He held her close until she quieted. Then he lifted her chin with an index finger and said, "Please marry me."

Violet had been asking herself if she could marry anyone her own age, knowing she could never offer him children. She decided God had given her an opportunity to be Mrs. Tolliver Thompson instead. She would start over. She would be the wife of a wealthy doctor, spending her days by the country club pool and shopping at the fanciest stores.

How far out of the lines she'd colored *that* picture.

Violet shook her head and checked her watch. Genny caught her gaze and held up a bottle of chardonnay and her eyebrows, hurrying over with a refill in response to Violet's smile. She settled next to her in a red velvet chair, collapsing elegantly and folding her ankles.

"You're really sweet to host this, Violet. It's a lot to take on."

"Not really. Besides, I was promised my pick of placement in return. I'm going to see if there's a Napping Committee."

"I'll join you if there is." Genny surveyed the room. "They're almost done. Bitsy apologized for running behind, though it's only about ten minutes."

"Bitsy apologizes if someone bumps into *her.* She apologizes for her *hair color*, for heaven's sake."

Genny shook her head. "That's just Bitsy. Her husband has convinced her she's responsible for all that's wrong in the world. It's sad."

Violet said, "Yes, it is." She wondered what time Tolly would get home. "Let's see if we can help wrap things up." She clinked her glass to Genny's and rose to begin hinting at the crowd around the refreshment table. "Melanie," she said, "Won't you take some of this cake home to your family?"

Fifteen minutes later she and Genny had graciously dismissed everyone with hugs and food packages. They were clearing the table when Violet heard Tolly's car enter the garage. She told Genny, "I'll finish this—there's practically nothing to do. Thank you for all your help." She handed her friend a small, gift-wrapped box she'd hidden earlier. "Don't get too excited. It's just chocolates."

Genny laughed and hugged her. "Chocolates no one knows about but me. Do you know what a rare and precious gift this is? Better than diamonds and gold and a sable bedspread, Vi. I love you." She made a tiny finger waggle and gathered her purse, tucking the present inside. Violet smiled, then closed her eyes and prayed Genny would be out the front door quickly.

She carried a stack of dishes to the kitchen and began washing them, one eye on the hallway to the garage door. As her husband rounded the corner she sucked in her stomach and plastered a smile onto her face.

Tolly looked happy, she thought. She exhaled a little as he pecked her cheek.

"I'm starving," he announced.

"You didn't eat at the club?" It was a silly question. Tolly had no doubt been sitting in the bar all night. He was swaying slightly.

"No, I wasn't hungry earlier. How did your meeting go?" He fixed his stare on the serving platters and bowls stacked on the counter, then swiped a finger through some chocolate frosting. He licked it off and gathered more, which he dragged down her left cheek.

"Tolly..."

"What, dear? I'm just being playful. You always say I'm too ser-ee-ous." He slapped her butt hard enough to sting. "I'm going to change clothes. Will you cook me a steak and baked potato?"

"That will take a while, Tolly. Wouldn't you rather have a nice chicken salad sandwich?"

Genny swung the kitchen door open. "Oh, gosh, I'm so sorry. I can't find my keys. Hi, umm, Tolliver, nice to see you, oh there they are next to the refrigerator, goodnight y'all." Genny was backing out of the room.

"Don't be so quick to leave, Genevieve," Tolly said, eyes glittering. "Come tell me what you and my lovely wife did tonight. Explain the mysteries of your cult to me."

"Tolly, please, Genny needs to get home to her kids." Violet dried her hands and swiped the frosting off her face. She moved to walk Genny out, but Tolly halted her with a hand to her abdomen.

"Oh," Genny said, "It's all pretty boring stuff. Just girl talk and nibbling on snacks."

"Then you all can have your goddam meetings in someone else's house. I thought y'all were doing something *worthwhile*." Tolly made an exaggerated shrug and laughed, adding, "Not really." He sneered at Genny and headed toward the staircase.

Violet waited until he was out of sight and walked to Genny's side. "I'm so sorry," she said. "He's had a rough day."

Genny was crying. "Violet, you don't have to stay here. Come with me."

"Don't be silly." Violet opened the massive oak door. "He's fine. I'm fine. Don't worry about me." Genny walked into the night with a backward glance, promising to telephone in the morning. Violet stood stock-still, too embarrassed to move. "Drive safely," she called, closing and locking the door.

She selected a frying pan for the steak and placed a large potato in the sink to scrub. She was turning on the oven when Tolly entered the kitchen. He leaned against a far wall, arms folded, and watched her work.

Violet said, "How was the hospital today?"

"One of my patients bled out. It was swell." Tolly rubbed his eyes with his palms. "Can't trust the nurses to do their fucking jobs."

"Oh, Tolly," Violet struggled for the right words. "I am so sorry. I'm sure you did everything you could."

"You are truly stupid, Violet. Of course I did everything I could in the OR. This was post-op. If the nurses had been watching him closely, the outcome might've been different." Tolly crossed to the pantry to retrieve the bourbon he kept behind a flour canister.

"Where were you?"

"What the hell do you mean, where was I? Was I supposed to sit with him and his wife?"

"No, Tolly, of course not," Violet searched the refrigerator for the sirloin steak. "I just wondered..." She didn't hear him approaching. Something slammed into her side, and she toppled to the floor. She looked up at Tolly, the potato gripped in his hand. He pulled her up and said, "You should know better than to accuse me."

"I'm not accusing you of anything, Tolly, nothing at all. I didn't mean to imply...to make you mad...please, Tolly, calm down."

He answered by beating her in all the perfect, well-hidden, non-fatal places on her body with the potato, then throwing it at her head as he left the room. "I'm not hungry anymore," he said.

seventeen

RONNI

I was packing my clothes and watching Rick on the dock with Kitty and Darby, the neighbor's black Lab. The dogs leaped into the water after pieces of kibble Rick threw. Darby looked like a sleek seal flying through the air, while Kitty O'Shea thumped into the lake on her little sagging bulldog belly every time, swimming frantically to the dock for Rick's assistance upward.

I took a deep breath and smiled, looking around my writing sanctuary. The past two weeks had been the best of my life. I would put finishing touches on my manuscript back at the apartment, but the hard work was mostly done. I'd meet my deadline, even if the book were never published. *I've done my best, Violet. I can't help it if the current market demands nothing but teen vampires, werewolves, wizards, and hormonal adolescent post-apocalyptic warriors.* I'd told Rick last night, "I think I'll title it *Fifty Shades of Twilight: Harry Potter's Hunger Games*. Then I might have a fighting chance."

I wasn't sure how I'd feel about coming to the end of my writing journey and turning over countless hours of work to a stranger. I tried to remember what I'd done to fill my free time before Violet had settled into every waking moment.

I think I was mostly eating and hoping for a boyfriend. Now I had him and food didn't mean much more than fuel to me.

And one more thing: I finally believed Violet. I was pretty. Maybe it was because I smiled at the girl in the mirror. I really liked her.

I'd be back at Fairfield after one last weekend at the lake. I missed my patients and the feeling of competence I had at work. I missed thinking up wicked jokes with Kait.

Being surrounded by people who were in their final years—sometimes final moments—could tear a person to pieces. Laughter was the only way we could cope. It was like the momentum needed to keep going forward on a bicycle. The humor propelled us down the halls.

Work would be fine, but I was worried if Rick and I would get along as beautifully outside the sanctuary of the lakehouse. He'd told me last night, "I want you to meet my boys. Let's go to Tuscaloosa soon."

The thought of his sons, freed from the locked room in my brain, made me start to shake. *Please, God, let them be crazy about me.* I would Google every possible area of interest for eight-year-old males, study them like Goodall and chimps. They would love me. I would *make* them love me.

I had smiled and answered, "Sure, that would be great," even as my insides liquified and boiled in terror. "I can't wait to meet Joshua and Jeremy. I'll just need some time to get caught up at home and work."

Liar.

I couldn't tell Rick that in my most recent fantasies I was already married to him and pregnant with our first child. I saw him fussing over me the same way he had at the lakehouse; breakfast in bed; the occasional bouquet of flowers, rubbing my tired feet. We'd shop for adorable tiny clothing and paint the nursery together. No, Rick wouldn't let me paint. Too risky for the baby. I'd bake cookies instead, filling our new house with wonderful smells.

When the baby arrived I'd use my huge check from Violet and stay home to be a full-time mom. I nuzzled the cheek of my baby girl—it was always a girl—and patted her back as I carried her across the nursery. It was tastefully furnished in pastel blues and greens. I laid her on the changing table, which Rick had built of mahogany with his own hands. The baby smiled and gurgled happily, stuffing a tiny fist into her drooling mouth.

I held those thoughts for a minute or two before my brain slapped my heart: Rick already had a family, and was fourteen years older than I was. He'd never given me any indication he was interested in more children—it was a subject we'd both felt sitting in a corner staring at us, shaking its head and holding a finger to its lips. I always avoided any mention of marriage or children, preferring to circle a minefield that could blow us apart forever.

I scolded myself for worrying. We loved each other. It would work out. *Jeez Louise, Ronni, quit looking for trouble.*

I returned to the window. Rick and the dogs had disappeared from the dock. I listened for the door, smiling to myself, waiting to throw my arms around him. Nothing. Ten minutes later I abandoned the suitcases and headed outside. The boat was gone. How had he slithered noiselessly into the lake? *Catch Me, Copper* sounded like the Blue Angels were barnstorming every time Rick started the engine. It wasn't like Mr. Military Precision to leave without checking in with me.

I started to worry after an hour went by. I'd packed everything I could until time to leave. I called Rick's cell and got voicemail. I texted him twice. There was no answer.

I grabbed a glass of water and went to the dock to wait. Darby joined me, tail thumping the wood slats as she scanned the water. Fish jumped, birds screeched, mosquitoes buzzed my ears, and Darby panted in the heat.

"Come on, girl, I'll get you a treat. Our favorite man has apparently deserted us for a while." I was almost back to the house when Darby began barking frantically. I heard the boat long before I saw it. When I did, I struggled to breathe and construct a welcoming smile.

Rick was waving at me, two little boys at his side pretending to help steer.

eighteen

VIOLET

He shook her shoulder very gently. Violet knew Tolly wouldn't leave for work until she spoke to him, no matter how repulsive she found it. She opened her eyes to find him bent over her, tears streaming down his face.

"My darling, I am so very sorry. I can't believe I hurt you. Please forgive me, Violet. It will never happen again." He ran a hand through his hair, and Violet noticed the gray for the first time. She shrank as he reached out to touch her face. "Please, Violet. I beg you. Give me a chance to make this up to you."

"There is nothing you can do, Tolly." She buried her face in the pillow. "I'll be gone when you come home tonight."

There was no response. Tolly left the bedroom, quietly closing the door. Violet turned over, every muscle in her body shrieking in pain, and went back to sleep.

She woke to the ringing telephone a little after ten o'clock. She answered on the third ring and heard Tolly's voice. "Yes, she's asleep upstairs, Genny. Violet's running a slight fever and coughing. She's likely coming down with a nasty cold or maybe flu." He sounded so relaxed and confident. Violet recognized Doctor Mode.

Genny didn't seem convinced. "I'm so sorry to hear that. Will you ask her to call me later? Maybe I'll stop by with some chicken soup."

"If her voice allows it, she'll call. I've told her not to talk unless absolutely necessary. Her throat is inflamed. At any rate, her mother is coming to stay with her. No need to bring soup, though that's very kind of you. Alice will start cooking the minute she arrives, no doubt."

Violet was dumbstruck at the boldness of this lie. Tolly would do everything in his power to keep her from her mother.

"Oh," Genny said, "I'm glad she'll have her mom to fuss over her. There's no substitute for that. Please tell Violet I called, and to let me know if she needs anything at all."

"I surely will, Genny. You're such a good friend to my wife, and I appreciate it. Goodbye."

Another lie. Tolly wanted Violet to have no friends, no family, no contact with the world unless he was at her side. She couldn't smile at anyone more than a few seconds, male or female, without inviting a scathing comment from him. She willed herself out of bed and went downstairs. He was sitting in the den, sipping coffee.

"I called Beatrice and told her to come in late so you could rest," he began.

"You really think no one's going to find out this time?" she asked him. "I'm going to a lawyer, Tolly. We're getting a divorce. You will never touch me again." Violet clasped her hands to keep them from shaking. Tolly regarded her from behind his coffee cup with a tiny smile. He turned to the window and waved a hand at the manicured garden.

"Lovely flowers. They're all so fragile, though. I need to remind Herman to water the roses more often." He met her eyes. "You won't go to a lawyer, Violet. Divorce is not in my vocabulary. You and I took vows, and we will honor them." He sighed. "You made me so angry, Violet. I lost control. I told you I'm sorry."

"You won't stop me, Tolly," Violet said. "You also won't convince me that the monster in you is caged and released by me. I don't believe your lies. I'm not the innocent girl you married."

Tolly looked like he was stifling a laugh. "Let's not talk about your level of innocence when we met, Violet." He paused and stared at the pattern in the carpet, as though inspiration waited there. "Did you ever wonder why I was almost forty years old before I decided to marry?"

"You probably beat every woman you encountered. It's not hard to understand why they weren't eager to shop for dresses and veils, Tolly."

"You're wrong. Until you came into my life, I never knew the kind of love that could make a man lose his mind. I love you so much, Violet." He looked like he was going to cry again. Violet turned to leave.

"Wait, Violet. You need to hear this. You will never leave me. You will never betray the secrets in our marriage to anyone, certainly not to an attorney or the police. I promise you, you won't."

"Why? Are you going to kill me, Tolly? I'm already dead inside. That threat doesn't discourage me, honestly."

Tolly sighed and closed his eyes. "Do you ever think of your little girl in Florida, Violet? She'd be, what...about twelve years old now?" He reached to cradle Violet's face in his hands and locked his eyes on hers. She struggled not to flinch. "I can locate her, you know."

Violet knew this was his version of a veiled threat, and he would quickly lift the veil if she showed fear. She forced her face to remain smooth and calm, a summer lake on a quiet day. "Those records are sealed. I can't find out where she is, and neither can you."

Tolly conjured a condescending surgeon smile. "I have connections and access to records you'll never have, Violet. But I love you, my darling. Please don't make me hurt you ever again. Not in any way." He used his thumbs to stroke her temples and kissed her forehead, then gazed into her eyes for another few seconds and walked away, jingling the keys in his pocket. "I'm going to the hospital. Please tell Beatrice I'd like fried chicken for supper."

She watched Tolly pull his car into the street as she tried to slow her galloping heart. He'd never threatened her daughter, though he'd once said he'd kill Violet rather than live without her. Violet watched the car's taillights as Tolly braked at the corner and realized she'd been waiting to exhale.

She was twenty-two the first time he'd hit her, and Tolly had literally begged on his knees for forgiveness. He pleaded with her to stay and swore he'd never hurt her again. She had believed him with all her heart.

Violet believed him the second time a year later, when he brought her a dozen roses and swore he couldn't bear a moment without her as his wife. He would never raise a hand to her in anger one more time. He'd sobbed like a small child, and she'd been naïve enough to hold and comfort him.

He was true to his word for months, until she forced herself to believe his apology and promises the morning after he'd had too much to drink at a hospital Christmas party. He lost his temper on the drive home because she screamed when he hit a stray dog crossing the road. The same Tolly who'd just viciously slapped her face stopped the car and gently picked up the dog, clearly less than a year old. He treated the puppy with heartbreaking care and tenderness, keeping it alive until the veterinarian's office opened the next day. He called as soon as he learned the puppy would recover, offering to bring it home to be Violet's pet.

Violet said no.

She shook off the memory and walked to the library, drawing a line with her finger down a row of Tolly's classics collection. Violet unlocked a hidden drawer in her writing desk and removed two black leather journals. One was her diary, the other a novel she was writing about a foundling. Angelica was a tiny baby girl in a red boat washed onto a Florida beach. She'd been discovered by an elderly couple as she waved her dimpled arms toward the sun. At this point in the book Angelica was five years old; Violet hadn't been able to imagine beyond that chapter.

Violet took the journals to her room and collapsed on the bed. She was surrounded by gold silk moiré wallpaper, plush ivory satin-covered furniture, paintings from Birmingham's finest galleries, and exquisite antiques from Atlanta. Tolly would walk into the house in a few hours and kiss her cheek as though nothing had happened at all. In a few nights they'd have dinner at the club, sure to parade Violet from table to table so their friends and associates could see she looked well and beautiful as ever. Her husband's fingers would dig into her arm if she betrayed the slightest hint of anything other than adoration for him.

She closed her eyes and tried to remember one true thing in her life.

nineteen

RONNI

Kait hugged me for the longest time. "Do not ever, ever again leave me here to deal with the madness alone for two weeks. I will hunt you down and deposit Audrey Marie Haynes Ledbetter in your bed. Much more effective than a horse head."

I looked toward Audrey's room. "Why isn't she rolling the halls?"

"Says her arthritis is bothering her. Hasn't been harassing anyone for three days. I'm sure she'll summon the strength to emerge for an afternoon reign of terror, though. She's missed you."

"Well, I *am* special.' Girl' has an extra sweet inflection when she uses it to summon me." I nodded at two old men huddled in the corner of the sitting room. Both wore plaid pajama tops and baggy jeans. "Mr. Leland and Mr. Daugherty still singing The Song of the Old Man?"

"Every verse, every afternoon." Kait answered. "'The world has gone to hell, the world has gone to hell, it was perfect when I was a kid, the world has gone to hell.' Catchy, huh?"

"It's certainly number one with a bullet around here."

Kait cocked her head and studied me with soft blue eyes. "Ronni, I heard a rumor." She glanced around before adding, "That you are writing a book."

"Where did you hear that?" Damn Donna.

"Lisa, on the night shift. She said you're writing a novel about

Fairfield Springs, only with a different title."

"That," I harrumphed, "is not true."

"So you're not writing a book?" Kait was still pinning me in place with her stare.

I love Kait, and she's my only real girlfriend in the world. So I changed the subject. "All I'm thinking about right now is Rick. He brought his sons to meet me at the lakehouse, which was wonderful and flattering until I realized they truly hate me. The little turds did everything but gather villagers and come after me with torches."

"Oh, I'm sure they like you, Ronni. You're always so hard on yourself."

"Joshua and Jeremy waited until their father took a nap, sent me outside on a fake errand and locked all the doors. I stood in the heat for over an hour because I didn't want to wake Rick up and get them in trouble."

"Well," Kait began.

I threw up a hand. "Oh, that was just the beginning. They let me 'overhear' a loud discussion about how they'd never have a 'stepmonster' because their daddy still loves their mom. The grand finale was spitting cherry Kool Aid on my back as we sat down in the boat."

"And Rick's oblivious, of course."

"Like a deaf and blind man wrapped in a cocoon of divorce-guilt. Poor babies said they accidentally squirted my white shirt with those tricky drink boxes. They apologized and the younger one did a convincing audition for 'kid who just shot Old Yeller' for their dad. As soon as he turned his back they smiled at me and plotted how to throw me under the jet props. At least, that's what I suspect they were thinking."

Kait considered all this as we loaded the med cart. "I'm sorry, Ronni. You know how kids are, They'll come around."

"Not these kids. They are hell-bent on getting rid of me. They're probably harboring fantasies of Mommy and Daddy reuniting after they kill off the stepfather. They look like they need an exorcist to me."

We were ready to roll down the hall. I poked my head into Mr. Gravely's room, and he held up his arms for a hug. It was hard not to cry a few happy tears. I unfolded my crossword puzzle for Miss Shelton on our last stop, where Kait and I had an arrangement allowing me to stay for twenty minutes or so.

"Today's puzzle really has me stumped," I began, "and if you could help me out, I'd appreciate it."

Miss Shelton sat up straighter and smiled. "What do we have? Is there a theme to this one?"

"No, that's why it's frustrating me. Okay, one across, four letters: Streisand to friends."

It took her two seconds. "Babs."

"Forty-six across, six letters: Serengeti scavengers."

"Hyenas."

"Ten down, four letters: bassoon's kin."

"Oboe."

We completed the entire puzzle in record time and I hugged Miss Shelton and thanked her before leaving. "I'll see you tomorrow. You have everything you need?"

"I sure do. I love you, Ronni."

"I love you, too."

Kait grinned at me across the nurse's station. "That is so sweet of you, Ronni, especially since I know you can do those things in pen. In the dark. With your toes."

"It makes me as happy as it does her," I answered. "It's good to be back."

I had to make the weekly trudge through Walmart on the way home, the only choice for discerning shoppers who need cat food, soft socks, a heavy-duty staple gun, fabric, popsicles, lettuce and toilet paper. Rick and I were going to re-upholster my kitchen chairs on Saturday, after much discussion and a few YouTube tutorials.

I was sidetracked by a baffling array of canned black beans when a cute guy, dressed in camouflage pants and hat, approached me—presumably straight from a duck blind or deer stand. "Excuse me," he said, "Is your name Sherrie?"

"No, it's not." I smiled and shook my head.

"Oh, my bad, my bad. I'm sorry." He waved his arms and backed away with a grin.

Five minutes later he turned up in the frozen food aisle. "Excuse me, but is your name Laurel?"

I laughed softly. "No, it's not."

"Oh, I'm so sorry." He grinned sheepishly and walked off.

And there he was again in the checkout line.

"Excuse me..."

"Are you still trying to guess my name?"

"No." He paused and looked into my eyes. "I was just wondering if you'd go out with me sometime."

"I have a boyfriend. But thanks." I began unloading my cart and looked back up as he said, "It's just you're so beautiful. Of course you have a boyfriend. I'm sorry. You don't see women like you in Walmart. I had to ask."

"Yeah, well, I may be a Walmart nine but I'm a Neiman Marcus five." I winked at him.

"A nee-who?"

"Never mind." I laughed and felt him watching me sashay out to the parking lot, getting my Violet on for the first time in my life.

twenty

VIOLET

1963

Violet struggled to open her eyes. The left one finally cooperated, allowing a glimpse of Tolly across the bed. He had his back to her, the phone pressed to an ear.

"Alice," he said, "Violet is fine, but she's been in a car accident. She's bruised all over her upper body and face. Thank God, no broken bones."

She watched him stiffen his spine and forge ahead. "It's my fault. I should never have let her drive my new Corvette. It's far too powerful for a woman." Tolly tapped his foot as he listened. "No, she didn't need to go to the hospital; she's just a little banged up. I'm taking good care of her here. She can't rest and recover very well at the house, though, because her friends keep calling and Beatrice makes all sorts of noise. When she is up for the trip, we were wondering if she might stay with you for a bit." He paused. "That would be perfect, Alice. Thank you." He turned to sweep his eyes over Violet's body. "No, she's sleeping right now, but I'll give her your love. I'll drive her over in a few days. Goodbye, now."

Violet was trying to swim to the surface through a mixture of oil and cotton. There was no pain, but she couldn't summon the energy to hold her eyelid in place. It fell like a curtain before she could remember what Tolly had said.

Her husband carried a tray into their bedroom, smiling as if he were delivering diamonds to her instead of chicken broth and water. "I'm so glad you're awake, honey. Sit up and let's get some nourishment into you."

Violet tried to shake her head and found her neck wouldn't cooperate. *What had he given her this time?*

"Oh," Tolly said, "That will wear off soon. You're still slightly groggy, but it will pass." He pulled her eyelids up and shined a light into her pupils. "I'll bring the tray back later, and you'll want to eat then." He set it on a table by the door and walked to the bed. "We're taking you to your parents' house in a few days, when the bruising has healed some."

She struggled to form the words. "You're insane. They'll know you did this."

Tolly seated himself and leaned forward until he loomed over her. "Now, darling, you have to let your parents believe you wrecked my car. They can't know about our argument." He ran his hands through his hair and closed his eyes. "Have you forgotten your mother's heart condition? I've examined Alice, and I doubt she'd survive such a shock. You might as well pull a gun on her, Violet." Tolly looked out the window thoughtfully. "If you were to run to your mother with your secrets, you'd need to tell *all* of them. She certainly couldn't handle finding out she has a grandchild born when you were nineteen and presumed virginal. I'd hate to have to tell your parents about that. Plus your little girl is out there somewhere, vulnerable and probably willing to trust a stranger, maybe more than ever at the age of fifteen."

Violet willed herself to stay still, not to respond, to give him no sign of the terror she felt. It had been over a year since her latest attempt to locate her daughter. The clerk in the records bureau had been blunt: "If she wants to contact you, ma'am, your daughter can initiate the process. There's nothing we can do for you."

Tolly continued, "You won't tell them, Violet, because you'd destroy the one thing you care about in the process." He rose and walked to the door. "The truth is, honey, I scared myself this time. I lost all control of my emotions and truly hurt you, and I'm so sorry. I've decided to quit drinking, because I can't bear the thought of anything like this happening again."

"I hate you, Tolly. I can't feel any other way about you."

"You'll see, Violet. We'll be happy again. Take a couple of weeks at your folks' house, and when you come home things will be fine. I promise you."

"They'll be fine until they're not fine." Violet turned onto her side, dismissing him.

"Violet," he said quietly, "I cannot live without you. If you ever leave me, I'll kill you and then myself." He closed the door.

The next morning Violet woke with every nerve ending in her upper body screaming for relief. Tolly was sitting in a chair across the room. He walked over and handed her two tablets and a small glass of water.

She sat up slowly and swallowed them. "I want to know why you're sending me to my parents' house. I would think they're the last people you'd want to see me this way."

Tolly frowned. "You can't stay in Birmingham, Violet. No one here knows anything of a car accident. My Corvette is in pristine condition in the garage. You have bruises on your face and arms, and Beatrice is bound to see sooner or later. It's also hard to explain where you are to our friends and associates. Better you should rest and recuperate during a visit back home."

Violet said, "Would you bring me a piece of toast and some ice water, Tolly? I should eat something."

"Of course, darling." She noticed for the first time that Tolly locked the door on his way out. Violet wondered what he was telling Beatrice.

She slid out of bed and wobbled to her antique French vanity table, collapsing heavily on the gold velvet seat cushion. The mirror was a gilded Baroque affair that made Violet want to don a towering white wig every time she saw it. This morning, she regarded her reflection in the soft light filtering through the curtains and decided Tolly had done well; the right side of her face had a narrow trail of deep purple from the outer eye to her chin. It could easily have come from a steering wheel.

Alice Glenn gasped and grabbed her daughter's face, then jerked her hands away. "Oh, honey, did I hurt you? I'm so sorry."

"No, it's okay," Violet said. "The bruises have mostly healed. They just look awful." She lifted her hand to her right cheek, now a widening abstract watercolor of green, yellow and maroon. "I have some make-up that helps. I just didn't apply it yet today." She shot a triumphant look at her husband, who smiled tightly and hugged his mother-in-law.

"Oh, honey, what were you *thinking*, driving that car? I barely trust myself to operate the Buick. I'm so grateful you weren't injured worse than you were."

"Well, it won't happen again," Violet said quietly. "I've learned my lesson."

"Y'all come on to the kitchen. Lunch is already on the table, and your dad's in there."

Tolly said, "I'll put Violet's suitcase away and freshen up a bit. Don't wait for me. I'm going to have to wolf down my food and run to the hospital. I have a surgery at three o'clock."

"I thought you only operated in the morning," Alice said.

"I used to. I've made some changes lately." He offered Alice his charming doctor face, accented by his hand on her forearm and a soft pat or two.

Violet made her way to her father and hugged his neck from behind. "I've missed you, Daddy."

Doug Glenn had become an old man since retiring five years ago. Violet watched the lines on his face grow deeper as he looked at her bruises, both of them embarrassed by the tears in his eyes. Doug cleared his throat and patted the chair next to his. "Have a seat, honey. Your mom's been cooking for hours." He grazed her cheek softly with the back of his fingers. "I'm so sorry you're hurting. Thank God it wasn't worse."

"Yes, thank God," Violet mumbled.

Her mother was piling dish after dish onto the table: fried chicken, mashed potatoes, biscuits, gravy, corn, sliced tomatoes, and green beans. Tolly walked in and immediately began helping her arrange them, the dutiful and helpful son-in-law. He pulled Alice's chair out for her.

Violet waited for her father to finish saying the blessing. "Mama," she said, "this looks wonderful. Your cooking is just what I need." Tolly reached for her hand, and she managed not to jerk it away.

"My wife," he said, "is almost as good a chef as her mother. Of course, Beatrice cooks every day, so I'm rarely treated to her creations anymore."

Violet translated for her husband, "Tolly is trying to tell you I'm spoiled and pampered, afforded every luxury." She locked eyes with him. "That's true. My life is filled with things I never dreamed of. It's a constant adventure." Her mother beamed at Tolly, clearly missing her meaning.

The family ate in silence for a few minutes. Violet listened to the kitchen clock tick away the seconds with Tolly in the house, willing him to leave. She studied her parents. Daddy's hair was fully white now. Her mother had streaks of gray and creases around her mouth and eyes. Tolly was right. She couldn't tell her parents the truth without risking their health. She chewed Mama's fried chicken slowly, trying not to aggravate the split in her lower lip.

"This is delicious, Mom," Tolly said.

Violet cringed at the blasphemy. He had no right to call her that. She didn't know how much longer she could sit next to her husband and keep from exploding. She closed her eyes and tasted something metallic, then realized her mouth was bleeding. Nausea rose like a flooding spring creek. She tried to think of anything but the truth she was keeping from her parents, from the world. The taste was overwhelming her.

This is the taste of secrets, she thought. Be quiet and let it linger on the tongue: the sickening cost of preserving the world for those I love, who can't know I have a daughter in Florida; who can't know my shining example of a husband is a drunk who beats me.

Violet set her fork down and turned to see Tolly rising from the table to peck her mother's cheek and shake Glenn's hand.

"I know you'll take good care of our girl," he said. "Goodbye, darling. I'll see you soon." She fought the urge to cry as he bent to kiss her.

"Bye, Tolly," they chorused.

Violet scooted her chair out as soon as the front door closed. "If y'all don't mind, I'm going to lie down."

Her parents exchanged worried glances. "Of course, honey," Alice said. "Get some rest." She switched the light over the sink on and off, over and over. Nothing happened. She sighed in exasperation. "Doug, we have to get an electrician here. Please call somebody."

"I'm goin' to check the fusebox," he muttered. "Probably blew another one."

Alice rolled her eyes at Violet as she left the kitchen, a universal "See what I put up with?" among women.

If you only knew, Mama. Violet took the stairs slowly and collapsed on her childhood bed, inhaling the scents of home: Pine Sol from the hall bathroom, her mother's Chanel No. 5, and Lemon Pledge. Her stomach lurched. She hurried to the bathroom down the hall, closing the door and leaning against it, trying to breathe.

Later she found the basket of freshly-baked chocolate chip cookies on her dresser. "Welcome home, baby girl," the note read. "Love you, Corinna"

She hoped she'd get to see Corinna before she left for Florida. Violet had two thousand dollars she'd saved up and the name of an investigator in Tampa. She knew the way to the bus station. She'd figure the rest out later.

twenty-one

RONNI

I had been staring at my laptop's email screen for an hour, clicking on messages about a missing teenager in Idaho, Groupon deals for deep sea diving excursions, invitations to chat with live singles in the area (highly preferable to the dead ones), and the latest Publishers Clearing House sweepstakes. Anything to keep from releasing my book into cyberspace and the hands of Jennifer Meyer, who would hate it and laugh at me in the posh break room of her snooty publishing office. "Look what came from Alabama, *y'all*!" Jennifer would wave the printed manuscript at her New York colleagues, all of them Harvard summa cum smugness grads and swathed in Versace. "A kudzu-covered pile of steaming manure."

"Not another one," they'd chorus, yawning into their twenty dollar lattes.

Mr. Sobel had said, "All you have to do is email the file. Jennifer will get back to you within six weeks." I was having a hard time letting go.

The stomach-grinding clock would start ticking as soon as I hit "Send." I jumped up to pace the bedroom, kicking a stray Nike out of my way. *I have to be at work in forty minutes. This is silly. I've read and re-read my manuscript a thousand times. I've done my best.* I reached over and pushed my literary baby from its nest. *Message sent successfully.*

Blood, sweat and tears converted to bits and bytes.

Halle wove back and forth through my legs and bleated in Felinese, "I haven't had Fancy Feast in hours." I wasn't moving toward the kitchen, so she bit my foot and hid under the bed. "Fine, cat," I told her. "I'll feed you tonight, when you'll appreciate your server properly."

I wondered if Violet would be angry that I hadn't used "Everybody Loved Her" as the title. I took out the letter I'd found taped at the end of the purple journal.

Dear Ronni,

By the time you find this you'll have discovered a darker side of my life I didn't discuss, with you or with anyone. I wanted to, on a couple of occasions, but I was afraid you'd have thought less of me for staying with my husband. I didn't want you to see the woman I saw in the mirror back then. She was weak and it took me years to forgive her. It was a different time, though, and Tolly got away with things no man would these days.

One reason I wanted you to write my story was to show you that a person can survive the most difficult experiences and go on to lead a joyful life. I did, and you will, despite what your mother and others did to you.

I see so much strength and beauty in you, Ronni. I love your humor. I love your spirit. You're smart and funny and loving. You're everything I imagine my daughter to be, and I can only hope and pray she grew up with the love and attention every child deserves.

I believe everyone comes into our lives for a reason. You came to show me my life with a daughter, the most precious gift imaginable. I hope you always remember how much I love you.

Violet

P.S.—The envelope taped below has the picture you took of me at the school entrance and one Sam took of Johnny and me in our junior year. We were supposed to look like we were jitterbugging. There's also a costume jewelry bracelet with little angels I wore in high school, and I hope you'll wear it and think of me. All my "good" jewelry was sold and the proceeds donated to a women's shelter in Birmingham.

I'd slid the photos out first. Violet's pose for me was exactly as it had been all those years before, only with Johnny opposite her and their hands and feet stretched to meet in the middle of the archway. They were laughing. I could practically feel the joy radiating from the image Sam captured of two beautiful people in love and on top of the world.

The bracelet was silver with tiny angel charms dangling between lavender and clear crystal beads. It was delicate and I could imagine it on Violet's dainty wrist as she waved to her friends. I was wrapping it in tissue for my jewelry box when I'd noticed one angel was missing. That made it perfect to me.

I took the bracelet out the next day as I dressed for work but decided against wearing it. I was a little teary-eyed as I gathered my purse and keys, both because I missed Violet and because she'd suffered so much and never told me.

I spotted construction trucks all over the back parking lot at Fairfield Springs. This could mean only one thing—Violet's entertainment room was being built at last. The detailed plans had been posted on a bulletin board for us to ogle for a month.

She had designed a place I personally hoped to experience as an eighty-year-old. Only Violet could have envisioned it: a huge area for Wii and X-Box games like bowling and golf, a mock corner "cafe" with low lighting and four plush booths for romance (there is a lot of swooning in Fairfield Springs; precious few places to swoon effectively), and a fifties-style soda fountain where we'd distribute ice cream several times a week. There would be a jukebox stocked with songs she'd personally selected. *She's created a place for residents to date. How very Violet.*

I put my stuff in a locker and straightened my new scrubs in the mirror with a grin. They were two sizes smaller than usual and featured tiny police badges. Rick found them on eBay and made me promise to wear them at least twice a week. I texted a quick "I love you" and walked to the desk, where Kait was reassuring Mrs. Hartness that she did indeed live in Fairfield Springs, fetching Tylenol for Mr. Quattlebaum, and listening to Audrey condemn her mattress as "some sort of medieval torture device."

She smiled sweetly and muttered, "Well, Mrs. Haynes, we were trying to replicate the era when you grew up."

Audrey held a hand to her ear. "What's that, girl?"

"I said I'll send maintenance to take a look." Kait waved goodbye to Audrey in a futile attempt to get her to leave. "How are you, Miss Eternally-Free-of-Speeding-Tickets? Those scrubs are pretty cute."

"Wonderful, fabulous, in love with the man of my dreams, waiting for his children to murder me in my sleep."

"Have they been back to visit?"

"No, but Rick says they're taking karate lessons and can't wait to show us what they've learned. I'm taking that as a veiled threat."

Kait laughed and swatted my butt. "Come on. It's almost time for bingo, and you need to help Mrs. Hughes find her lucky pink pants. I'll go set up."

Bingo always exhausted our patients, who were either euphoric with their ten dollar jackpots or trudging off angrily in defeat. Kait and I were settling people into their rooms for meds before lunch when Tina walked up and said Donna sent her to relieve me. "There's a lady waiting to see you in the lobby," she announced. "Says she's Violet Thompson's daughter."

I hid behind a pillar and studied her, holding my breath. She was on the short side, you could clearly see that even as she sat and clutched her handbag. Probably early to mid sixties. A decent but inexpensive black knit dress with a bright floral scarf around her neck. A bit chunky, with dark hair and huge sunglasses. Sensible shoes. This person looked nothing like Violet from a distance.

She was glancing around and swiping at her eyes.

Donna crept up beside me. "Her name's Deanna Henderson."

"Where's she from?"

"Palmetto, Florida. She found out a few weeks ago she was adopted. Can you imagine?" Donna shook her head. "Her parents have been dead for years, and an aunt decided to tell her at the age of sixty-three that she was adopted."

"So she tracked down her birth mother, and it was Violet?"

"And I had to tell her," Donna sighed, "that she's ten months too late. I feel so sorry for the poor woman. She asked if anyone here might have known her mother especially well." Donna patted my shoulder and pushed me a little. "Go talk to her."

Deanna stood and took off her glasses as I came closer. I saw her shining brown eyes, the same eyes I'd smiled into a million times. I bypassed the hand she extended and hugged her for a few seconds, inhaling a scent both familiar and new. Then she spoke in Violet's voice: "You must be Ronni. The nursing director said you knew my mother."

"I did know Violet, yes," I began cautiously. *Slow down, Ronni. Why should you believe this is really Violet's daughter?*

She held out a shaking piece of paper. "It's my birth certificate. My aunt gave it to me when she told me I'd been adopted. My parents sure did a great job of hiding it, and I've tried to figure out how," she sighed heavily. "You didn't need one to get a driver's license when I was growing up, and my mom made some excuse about needing to locate it when my husband applied for our marriage license. She delivered it to the courthouse while we were both at work."

I examined it closely. There was Violet's name, the date and place were perfect, and the father was listed as "Unknown." I nodded at Deanna to go on.

"Would you please tell me about her past? Where did she grow up? Did she have brothers or sisters?"

"She grew up in Anniston, Alabama, and had no brothers or sisters."

"Oh," she said, "I was hoping to find someone who might know who my biological father is. The birth certificate said "Unknown."

I took a deep breath. "His name was Sam Davidson, and he also lived here, until he passed away a few years ago."

Deanna blinked. "You knew *him,* too?"

"Not like I knew Violet." I was desperately searching for the right way to introduce this woman to her past gently. "The thing is...well, Sam and his family never knew about you. He was married and living in New York when you were born. He spent most of his life there."

"New York? How did he end up in this place?" She waved her hand at the Fairfield Springs logo stenciled on the lobby wall.

"Sam's parents insisted he marry a girl—her name was Deborah—and go to New York with her and her family. They arranged a career for Sam running a large department store. That was the family business, and a sort of deal was struck..."

"Wait," she interrupted. "They *made* him go to New York? I don't understand."

"Well, I don't entirely, either, except it was 1947, and I think Sam knew they'd never accept Violet. His parents may have threatened to disown him if he married her." Deanna was staring at me, puzzled and impatient. "Sam was Jewish. Violet was a Southern Baptist girl."

"So? If they loved each other...did they love each other?"

"Yes, they did, very much. But like I said, it was a different time, and Sam never knew Violet was pregnant."

"And he came back to Alabama? Why was he here?"

"After his wife passed away he returned to Alabama. His health began to fail within a year or two and he ended up in assisted living here. He used to sit next to Violet at lunch. I called it The Cool Kids' Table."

Deanna paused to allow me a tight, fleeting smile, but her words came faster and faster. "She never told him? He never knew he had a daughter in Florida?"

I shook my head. "You need to understand, Violet tried to find you for years. She was told that unless *you* inquired about your records no information could be released. In addition, she wasn't sure you knew you'd been adopted. She didn't want to shatter your world." I reached for her hand and squeezed. "She didn't want to burden Sam, either. He was a frail old man when he came to Fairfield."

"I might have half-brothers and sisters in New York," Deanna said. She wrung her hands in her lap and began tapping her foot nervously. The nurse in me was worried about her blood pressure.

"Yes, that's true," I said.

Deanna looked at my face and read it quickly. "But they have absolutely no idea I exist. After a lifetime, I just show up and ..." She shook her head and collapsed into sobs, just as her mother had in a train station over sixty years ago, in a world neither of us knew or understood.

You are always on my mind, no matter where I go or what I do.

The thought of you brings light into the darkest day.

twenty-two

VIOLET

She woke in the middle of the night and stared at the unfamiliar shadows dancing on the wall. A glance from her bedroom window revealed a new streetlight silhouetting the limbs of an oak tree she'd climbed as a child; now thirty feet tall and swaying gently in a pre-dawn breeze. A thin branch tapped the side of the house.

Violet turned toward the darkness of her closet and tried to conjure the dream she'd been having: she was slow dancing in Johnny Perkins' arms, her head on his shoulder. She nuzzled his neck, inhaling his spicy Seaforth cologne and the faint odors of fresh shampoo and soap. The music was familiar, something about forever love, and Johnny was softly singing along. They glided as one body across the polished wood floor, pure joy and peace. Suddenly there was a jolt and Johnny stumbled; he'd been shoved to the floor and lay in a heap at her feet. Violet turned to see who'd attacked Johnny; no one was in the room but the two of them. Then, off in the distance, she saw Johnny's limp body carried away by a group of people. She chased them, screaming, until she collided with a closed metal door. She'd been pounding it with her fists when she woke.

She wondered if she ever crossed Johnny's mind, if he closed his eyes and found himself dancing with her.

Violet knew when the seed of this dream was planted: Katie

Ruth telephoned one afternoon last week. Her husband, Roger, was a big, hairy army sergeant from Kentucky who'd been stationed at Fort McClellan during their whirlwind courtship; Violet and Tolly had attended their wedding in a chapel on base eight years ago. Roger was a likable guy who adored his three children and fussed over Katie Ruth like a movie star when he was home; cooking, cleaning and changing diapers more often than his wife did. She was struggling while he was away for three months of battle training and called Violet at least twice a week. After a long session of reading excerpts from his letters—during which Violet painted her nails and made appropriate noises—she said, "Oh, and there's one more thing. I saw Johnny having lunch with Dr. and Mrs. Perkins downtown. He's married and working as an attorney in Montgomery, at a big firm that does a lot of state government stuff. He has a daughter named Caroline who's about four. She and the kids played together on the floor while the adults caught up." She paused to see if Violet had any comment, then blathered on, "His wife is pretty; not as pretty as you, of course, but she kinda looks like you. He met her at the University of Alabama. I think she's a teacher. Anyway, I thought he couldn't have children?"

"Apparently," Violet answered, "he can." She waited a beat to see if Johnny had asked about her, but Katie Ruth filled the silence with a lengthy monologue about *My Favorite Martian*, urging her friend to watch, then yelling at her five year old and explaining she'd have to hang up.

"Wait," Violet had said. "What's her name?"

"Johnny's wife? It's Rose. That's weird, huh, a flower like you? I have to go fix supper. I'll call you soon."

She rolled over and stared at the ceiling, knowing she'd never get back to sleep without help. Violet reached for the pills Tolly gave her for pain. It didn't really matter if it was her battered face or her battered heart, did it?

Violet woke at ten o'clock, her mind blessedly blank. She heard her mother and Corinna talking downstairs, lots of shh-ing and shushing, voices lowered and then raised for her to hear what they deemed appropriate. "Oh, wait until you see her," Alice exclaimed, "the wreck bruised her a bit, but she's beautiful as ever."

She selected a dainty dress, knowing her mother would love the pink rosebuds embroidered on white cotton. Violet took extra care with her make-up and smiled at the result: it would be hard to see the marks on her face, and the long sleeves covered her arm damage. She swept her hair into a ponytail and hurried to hug Corinna and thank her for the cookies.

Coffee and fresh-baked biscuits lured her nose to the kitchen, where her mother and Corinna were busy slicing apples for a pie. Corinna dropped her knife and walked to Violet with a huge smile, arms wide open to enclose Violet in warmth and security. She was six years old again whenever Corinna hugged her; she always would be.

"Law, you too thin to see in the mirror, missy. Sit down and eat a few biscuits, and tell me all that's goin' on in your fancy life these days." Corinna swept her eyes up and down Violet's body. "Then you can tell me what foolishness caused you to think you need to drive a fast sports car."

"Well, you know me, Corinna, I'm gonna do what I want to do." Violet sat at the table and hurried to steer the conversation as far from the Corvette story as possible. "How are Edward and the boys?"

"Fine, fine. They all say hello." Corinna wiped counters as her mother piled apple slices into a big pot, then placed a plate of biscuits and a cup of coffee in front of Violet. A few seconds later Alice and Corinna were seated across from her, firing questions about everything from her experiences as a Junior Leaguer to the cuisine at the country club. Everything except whether her wonderful husband ever beat his wife.

She would've lied, anyway. Somewhere deep inside Violet a voice had grown louder and more insistent over the years: It's your fault. No man hits a woman who doesn't deserve it somehow.

Violet was sprawled across her bed reading a novel late that afternoon when she heard a group of men laughing downstairs. She strained to listen, trying to determine if a Bible study or a poker game was on—either would be typical of Doug Glenn.

"Violet," her father yelled. "Someone here wants to see you!"

She checked her makeup and hair, slipped on some heels and performed her best beauty queen walk down the steps to hug one of Daddy's old friends...probably Mr. Aderholdt, who'd been a partner in Doug's firm and one of her favorite "uncles."

The group had moved into the kitchen, Daddy leading three uniformed men preparing to examine the faulty wiring Alice complained hourly was dangerous and on the verge of burning the house down. The backs of their shirts read "Superior Electric" in bold blue letters. Two followed her father down into the basement but the tallest stopped and leaned back against the sink, arms crossed.

Violet studied him from the hall. This man was good-looking, and he knew it. You could tell by the way he stood, a faint smile on his face. His longish dark hair reminded her of that Elvis Presley guy her friends obsessed over.

He glanced toward her and grinned, revealing a dimple in his left cheek deep enough to dive into and swim. He held his arms wide and Violet walked straight into them, allowed herself to be enclosed, breathing deeply just behind his right ear. She felt something she'd never felt in her adult life.

Home. She felt home.

She pulled herself away, which was hard to do. It was as if he were gravity itself.

"You work for," she read the patch on his shirt, "Superior Electric?"

"I own it. We're about to open a second location in Gadsden."

"I am so proud of you, Chet. That's wonderful."

"Found something I like to do, and people pay me for it." he said with a shrug. "I've been lucky, and I have a great mentor, old Mr. Harris. Bought the business from him when he retired two years ago." Chet looked at the floor. "He's like the father I never had."

"You have a father, Chet."

"I'm sorry. I know that sounds awful. My dad was never there for me, Violet. He was physically present sometimes, but so broken by my mother I don't think he could stand to look at me. She died last year, you know."

"I'm sorry, Chet."

"Don't be. My aunt raised me, and she's the only mother I need. I'm just glad CeeCee got grown before Betty's overworked liver finally blew up."

"How is CeeCee?"

"She's going to college. Can you believe it?" He grinned down at her, the proud brother.

"No, actually." Violet tried to imagine a CeeCee beyond the tiny, dirt-smeared urchin she'd known. "What about you, Chet? Is there anyone special in your life?"

He looked out the kitchen window and nodded. "I'm married. My wife's maiden name is Harris. I guess you can figure out the rest." He nudged the floor with the toe of his shoe, embarrassed.

Violet placed a hand on his arm. "I'm very happy for you."

"Well, I'm not real proud of the way it all happened," Chet continued, "but I have a son who means the world to me. Loretta and I get along pretty well most of the time." He produced a wallet and showed Violet a studio portrait of a grinning, drooling toddler boy clutching a ball. "That's Eric. He'll be two next month." He flipped to the next photo. "This is Loretta."

Violet said, "Oh, she's lovely," though she had to work to sound sincere. Loretta was a mouse of a girl with a tiny, clenched mouth and sharp nose. Violet tried to imagine her with a smile and failed.

Chet said, "And what about you? Are you still hurting from the accident?" He ran his thumb gently across her cheek, and Violet shivered. "You're bruised pretty bad, Vi. I bet the car was nearly totaled."

She nodded. "Yes, there was a lot of damage."

"I've never seen a Corvette after a wreck. What did the body look like?"

"Just, you know, crumpled metal. Like any other car." *Why was he focusing on the car?*

Chet smiled gently and stared at her. "You did have a wreck, right? That's what your dad said."

Violet touched her face absently. "Yes, of course. I should've known better than to try to drive Tolly's car."

"Well, I'm sorry," Chet said. "A beautiful face like yours should never have a bruise. You'll be fine in a few days, though, and you can forget this make-up." He swiped at her cheek again, a tiny bit harder, then rubbed his finger and thumb together. "You don't need it. You never have." He turned his gaze to the window again and said softly, "I was there, you know. The day you married him."

Violet felt a tiny collision in her chest. "How? Why didn't I see you?"

"I made my aunt let me take the train home. I wasn't going to miss it. Spent the entire time against the back wall of the church, then I sneaked away." He took her hand. "Dr. Thompson is a lucky man."

"I can't believe you were there. Why didn't you tell me?"

"I was a kid, Violet. Nobody cared if I was there." Chet met her eyes and smiled. "Anyway, there's not much in your life I haven't heard about. I keep up."

She opened her mouth to speak, but couldn't form the words. Violet swallowed hard. The taste was back, coppery and biting.

Alice Glenn cleared her throat at the kitchen entrance, arms crossed in front of her patchwork apron. "Hello, Chet," she said. "Shouldn't you go on down and help your men in the basement now? Violet and I need to start thinking about cooking supper."

twenty-three

RONNI

Deanna and I spent as many hours together as we could during her time in Alabama. Rick was working multiple shifts and I barely heard from him. I heard a *lot* from Deanna over late night glasses of wine, though.

We were curled up on the couch, Halle purring between us. I'd made it into a makeshift bed and invited her to stay the night. Deanna stroked the cat absently and asked, "How did you come to be so close to my mother?"

I took a deep breath. "I was drawn to Violet for so many reasons. She was beautiful and smart and so alive. When she walked into a room all eyes were on her. She asked me questions about my past, my likes and dislikes, my boyfriends, my hopes and dreams." I paused to picture the Cool Kids' Table. "Violet seemed to know I needed her friendship. I think she tried to help build me up. I don't know." I set my wine glass down, embarrassed. "I loved her very much, Deanna. She knew I wanted to be a writer. I've found out even more about your mother because I've spent most of the past year writing a book about her. Before I say another word, you should know she tried very hard to find you. She was told it was impossible to obtain your records, and you'd be better off if she'd give up trying, anyway. An investigator convinced Violet she could cause a lot of hurt by contacting you—that you might not know you were adopted."

"I didn't," Deanna replied. "It's still hard for me to believe my parents never told me. If Aunt Anne hadn't, I'd never have known." She frowned. "I don't understand why you'd be writing a book about her. Can I see it?"

"I'm sorry, Deanna, I can't show it to anyone yet. I promised. I can fill in a lot of blanks for you, though. Violet had a very full life, and she thought it would make an interesting novel."

Deanna looked puzzled. "But, she wasn't any sort of celebrity, I know that much. So, why?"

I laughed a little. "She was a celebrity at Fairfield, I promise you. Look, it's probably never going to be published, but I've sent it off and I'm waiting to hear. If it's not, I'll show you everything I've typed. The truth is, you've had to process a lot very quickly." I patted her hand. "Let's take this one step at a time. You should hear, rather than read, about your mother."

Deanna shook her head yes and then, exasperated, no. "I can't describe what all this feels like. I mean, at first I was angry. Just really angry. I loved my mom and dad, and would never have suspected they were keeping so huge a secret from me. Anne says Mom could never decide when the time was right to tell me. Can you imagine? I'm practically an old lady, and I woke up one day to find I'm not who I thought I was." She twirled her wine glass. "And that my mother didn't want me. I look at my granddaughter, that precious rosebud mouth and those eyes shining with trust and love—the most beautiful creature I've ever seen—and ask myself how any mother could walk away from that. You have no idea how hard it is to accept and understand."

"Actually, I do."

She turned to stare. "You were given up for adoption?"

"I was given up for Jack Daniels, amphetamines, and whatever other pharmaceuticals tapped my mother on the shoulder. Spent a lot of years in the foster care system." Deanna, fresh from her lesser tale of woe, now considered me pitiful—I could see it in her eyes, and wished I'd kept my secrets to myself.

"I'm sorry, Ronni," she said. "Your mother is a sick woman. So is my daughter. That's why I pretty much raised my grandchildren, Kevin and Charlotte. Their mother, Sarah, was in and out of rehab from the age of sixteen, but she's been sober for three years now." Deanna swept the room with her eyes. "My marriage ended in 2008, mostly because my husband couldn't handle it. He coped by marrying his hairstylist. She's thirty-two years younger than Jack, and they have a six-year-old." She laughed softly. "The thing is, Sarah always fought to get her children back, even when she clearly couldn't take care of them. And I believe the biggest reason she's stayed sober is her baby, Lacey. She's the most adorable six-month-old on the planet."

"Every situation is different, Deanna. Violet was only a teenager, at a time when unwed mothers were shunned. Her fiance—your father—had moved far away to marry another woman. She couldn't even contact him."

"She carried around a lot of secrets, didn't she?" Deanna sipped her wine and set it down carefully. "There's so much I need to know."

"I'll try to help. Your parents," I saw Deanna's frown and rephrased, "Your biological parents loved each other. They just couldn't be together."

"Why? If they loved each other like you keep saying, I can't understand."

Why, indeed. I took a long gulp of cheap moscato, closing my eyes. I had a sudden inspiration. "You know what? I am taking you to lunch day after tomorrow, and I'm hoping you'll get to meet your cousin Mel." I glanced at my phone and saw it was after midnight. I stood and took our empty glasses to the kitchen, yawning. "I'm going to do a little research on my laptop. But first, I have something I should've given you already." I went into my bedroom and placed Violet's small stack of photographs atop her senior yearbook. It hurt my heart to think of parting with them, but they belonged with Deanna.

"Here," I handed them to her, "I'll tell you what I know about each one tomorrow."

"Oh my gosh," she said. "This is the most precious gift. Thank you, Ronni. For everything." She began sorting through the pictures. "She was gorgeous!"

"Yes, she was. Gorgeous, glamorous and fascinating. Violet was unlike anyone I've ever known." As I turned to go to my room, Deanna looked up and asked, "How are things with you and your mother now?"

"There are no things. I haven't seen her since I was a little girl. She's been in prison, but supposedly she's out and living in Heflin. I have no desire to have anything to do with her."

"Oh, I see," Deanna said. "I'm so sorry. Goodnight, honey. Sleep well and I'll see you in the morning." She returned her attention to the photos.

"Good night."

twenty-four

VIOLET

Chet found excuses to stop by the Glenn home almost every afternoon: replacement wiring, electrical outlets that mysteriously failed, estimates for Doug to look over—one day he pleaded truck trouble and asked to use the telephone. None of this was lost on a wary Alice Glenn, but she didn't know what to do about it. No one could miss the way Violet's eyes locked on Chet the moment he arrived, or the way they always ended up on the porch swing talking and laughing before he left, sitting too close for propriety.

"What in the world are y'all talking about?" she'd asked Violet.

"Everything, Mama. We like the same movies and books. Did you know Chet's seen 'To Kill a Mockingbird' three times? He liked the book better, the same as me. He wants to see 'Cleopatra' when it comes out. He thinks Vivien Leigh is prettier than Elizabeth Taylor, though."

"Everyone in the South thinks Vivien Leigh is prettier than anyone, Violet." Alice rolled her eyes.

Yeah, except Chet thinks I'm more beautiful than she ever was, Mama. Imagine that, Violet thought. "That's the truth. And all the women, including you, still have crushes on Clark Gable."

"A woman could do worse." Alice smiled. "You look good, Violet."

"Thank you, Mama. I feel good." Violet pecked her mother on the cheek and went upstairs.

Almost too good, Alice thought. Maybe she would telephone Tolly and invite him to supper on Sunday night. Surely he'd take his wife home to her rightful place and Chet Wilson would stop pestering her daughter.

Violet didn't care about anything but Chet's next visit. She'd delayed her escape to Florida, reasoning she could travel from Birmingham as easily as Anniston. She would enjoy the small amount of time they had and return to what she regarded as the Mountain Brook Theater: she'd resume her role as Dr. Thompson's happy wife. She felt she could do it with renewed enthusiasm because she knew she now had the strength to leave Tolly and find her daughter. This time away from him—especially with the attention Chet had lavished on her—built Violet back up.

As soon as she lulled Tolly into believing she'd settled back into their life, she'd work out her exit. He would be on his best behavior for at least a month or two, affectionate and reliable, carefully scheduling patients and avoiding liquor. Slipping away while he was in surgery would be easy. She would hire an investigator in St. Pete; she would disappear into the crowd of tourists. Even if she only saw her daughter from a distance it would be enough. It had to be.

Violet wished she could tell Chet what he'd done, how he'd brought her back to life after years of deadening herself to survive with Tolly.

She remembered the night she'd realized she was starting to fall in love with Chet Wilson. He'd stopped by after supper to drop off paperwork for her dad, and she'd followed him onto the porch to say goodbye. Her mother's gardenias and white roses glowed in the moonlight as they sat on the steps between them.

Chet was unusually quiet, staring at the street. She studied his profile, memorizing every line and plane. She was searching for conversation, any conversation, to keep him there for another minute or two. "What are you thinking about?" she asked.

He continued to look straight ahead. "You. Always you." He

shook his head slowly. "You've been the light in my life for as long as I can remember, Violet." He picked up a stick and began dragging it along the step in front of him, then threw it into the yard. "Did you think it was lost on me? All you did for me back then? I hope not." He wiped a single tear from his face and Violet reached for his hand before she could stop herself. "Don't," he pulled his hand away. "Don't feel sorry for the kid you knew. He's long gone."

"I wasn't feeling sorry for you, Chet. I was only going to tell you how good it is to see the wonderful man you've become." She hesitated. "And that you've made my time here at home something I'll never forget. You've made me feel special again."

He turned to face her, his eyes on hers for the first time that night. "You *are* special. When other people look at you they see a gorgeous woman, but there's so much more. When I look at you, I see kindness and joy and laughter and grace and every other beautiful thing I could ever imagine. I see *you*. And it takes my breath away." He smiled, revealing the dimples she couldn't resist. "I can't hide how I feel, either. I'm sure no one can miss it. Your mother doesn't. She's going to run me off with a broom soon."

Violet laughed softly.

"I also see the way you look at *me,* Violet. It makes me the happiest and saddest man on earth." He stood and glanced at the house. "I'll be back as soon as I can. Now, go in there and just try to think of anyone or anything but me." He walked to his truck without another word. As he opened the door, he looked into her eyes and said, "Anyone but me."

He knew she couldn't. She did, too.

Violet kissed her parents good night and went up to her room, claiming she was going to read. She substituted a legal pad for a diary and made a list like she would've as a teenager: Chet was great-looking, strong, tender, warm, funny, smart, successful, confident, the perfect height for her, his eyes were the darkest brown and full of sparkles, his dimples made her want to lick his face, when his fingers brushed against hers it sent a riot of sensation all over her body, he adored her, he made her feel safe and protected, and he would never hit her. She told herself it was pathetic to put that on a list of a man's good points, and tore the paper into tiny pieces. She knew it all by heart, anyway.

And she'd have to forget it soon.

Two days later, as her parents ran errands in town, Chet appeared at the front door. "Hey. I was wondering if you could go for a ride with me." He stood there awkwardly, hands in pockets, his eyes pleading.

Violet looked around the neighborhood. Mrs. Sweeney was sweeping her porch. The Tanner children rode bicycles by and waved.

"I can't, Chet. I'm sorry."

"Then let me come in. The truck's here in the open. I'm working on a circuit breaker or something." He glanced over his shoulder. "Your folks are downtown, and I saw them walking into Jimmy Gardner's Cafeteria. They'll be at least another hour getting home."

She knew she shouldn't, but her hand swept the door back of its own accord. Violet closed it quickly and took a look out the window beside it. "Five minutes. Then you'll have to go, Chet."

He sat in her father's recliner and leaned his elbows on his knees as Violet settled onto the couch three feet away. She clasped her hands to hide their shaking.

"Five minutes, huh? Is that long enough to kiss me? One kiss, Violet, that's all I want. I'll never ask you for another thing." He leaned forward, lacing his fingers into the back of her hair and sweeping his thumb along her jawline softly. "You're shaking." He smiled with a touch of concern, but mostly satisfaction.

Violet reached to pull his hand away and planted it on the arm of his chair, pressing it into place. "Stop it, Chet. You know that's something I won't do. I can't."

He leaned back, grinning at her. "But you want to. I know you so well, Violet Louise Glenn. And I'm not the boy with a crush anymore. I don't need a picture of you, I don't need a note from you to take out and read, I don't need you to promise me anything, and this house hasn't needed electrical work for a week."

Violet laughed. "You'd better give my dad a great deal on all these service calls."

"I've been telling him everything's under warranty." He patted the sides of the recliner and looked around the room, settling on her eyes. "What's between us is always going to be there, Violet, whether you admit it or not. You're not happy with your husband..."

"You don't know the first thing about my marriage, Chet," she interrupted.

"I know what I see in your eyes. I know how the light goes out of them when he's mentioned." Chet leaned forward. "Is he good to you, Violet? Does he treat you like you deserve to be treated?"

She forced a smile. "Yes. Tolly's good to me."

"Has he ever hurt you?"

"No. I don't know why you'd even say that."

"The bruises from your accident didn't look like they were caused by a steering wheel, Violet. And the front of a wrecked Corvette is crumpled fiberglass, not metal. You can easily see the difference." He crossed his arms and leaned back.

Violet felt the actress in her take over. "He's a wonderful husband. And I don't know anything about cars. I was too shaken up to notice what the damned car looked like."

He nodded slowly. "All right, then. You know you can always call me, right? Call the office. They can track me down."

Violet looked out the picture window nervously. "I appreciate that, Chet. You should go now."

He stood and leaned over to whisper into her ear. Violet closed her eyes and held her breath as he lingered there. "You'll give me that kiss someday." He brushed his lips on her cheek and walked out the front door, leaving Violet with one hand to her face, staring after him.

Last night he'd telephoned after her parents had gone to bed.

Violet stood in the kitchen, whispering and watching the staircase.

"You looked so beautiful yesterday," he said. "It's gonna kill me when you go back to Birmingham. Even though we can't be together, Vi, you know how I feel about you. It's not going to change."

"I wish things were different, Chet." She wouldn't let herself say more than that.

There was a full thirty seconds of silence before he spoke. "I know you're not happy with him. You can lie to me all you want, but I can see right through you. I've known you forever, Vi. I know you tell people you like rock and roll but you'd really rather listen to classical music. You like the color red and you have a weakness for graham crackers and you're a terrible dancer and you dream of writing a best-selling novel and you bite your bottom lip when you're nervous. You're doing it right now." *Dear lord, she was.*

He paused, and Violet imagined him looking over his shoulder to be sure he was alone. "Everything about you is mapped on my heart. I love you, Violet. I always have."

"Chet, I've loved being with you these two weeks, but..."

"Don't say it, Violet," he broke in. "Don't try to tell me you don't feel the same way about me. I know you do. We laugh together, we never run out of things to say, and you look forward to seeing me the whole time I'm not there. Admit it. You sat there thinking about that little brush on your cheek until your parents got home, didn't you? "

"No." *Yes. They'd opened the door to find her in a daze, glued to the couch with her eyes closed.*

"You're as drawn to me as I am to you. I can't stand in the same room without shaking all over, trying to resist the pull you have on me. Please, before you go, just let me kiss you one time. I'll never ask again. Meet me somewhere, Violet. Name a place and I'll be there."

She shook her head. This had to end. "It doesn't matter what I feel. I'm a married woman and you're a married man. I'm going home to my husband soon." *And one kiss would be the end of life as I know it. There would be no turning back, no stopping my body's response, no end in sight. There would be no way to stop Tolly from ...she shuddered to think what he'd do.*

"You won't forget me. You won't forget any of this."

"No, I won't, Chet. Good night." Violet hung up the phone in her parents' kitchen and slid her back down the wall to sit on the worn green and cream linoleum squares. She closed her eyes and saw nothing but Chet's face; heard him saying *You're as drawn to me as I am to you. I can't stand in the same room without shaking all over, trying to resist the pull you have on me.* She wondered if he knew he'd put her own thoughts into words.

She had to get out of here, and she had to do it fast. She'd call Tolly tomorrow.

Chet didn't return to the Glenns' once. Violet found herself staring out the windows, listening for his truck, but he was gone. She sat on her bed and recounted every word, every look, every time their eyes had met. She let that warmth settle into her bones and promised herself she'd keep it there. It was hers alone, something Tolly could never take from her.

Tolly came on Sunday and seemed so happy to see her it hurt her heart. She kissed her mother and father goodbye and smiled at her husband as he closed her heavy car door with a thud. His Coupe DeVille was annoyingly perfect inside, not a speck on the bright red and white leather. Violet fought the urge to smear lipstick in a hidden patch and lost. She swiped a pinkie tip full of Revlon's Spring Tulip and smeared it along the bottom of her seat.

When Tolly slid in beside her he said, "You look radiant, Violet. It's done you so much good to be with your folks. I've missed you, but I'm glad you had this time with them." He pecked her cheek and shifted the car into drive. Violet noted he smelled of some new cologne, one without the slightest hint of bourbon.

She looked out the window at the flowering trees and pink azaleas on Quintard Avenue, marveling at the beauty of her hometown. She smiled at the majestic Parker Memorial Baptist Church where she'd married Tolly. In a parking lot on her right, Chet leaned against his truck and stared at Violet as they passed.

He didn't smile. He didn't wave. He said more to her with his eyes than a thousand letters could have; more than if he'd been driving the car and holding her hand, talking all the way to Birmingham.

twenty-five

RONNI

Deanna and I stood in the reception area of Mary Mac's Tea Room. It was eleven o'clock, and the place was already filling with a steady stream of Atlanta regulars and tourists. Melvin Sobel arrived in the middle of a big group of Red Hat Society ladies, swept along in a wave of chunky, middle-aged women. He spotted me and parted the red-and-purple sea to walk over.

"Mr. Sobel," I said, "Meet your cousin, Deanna Henderson."

"Please, both of you, call me Mel." He was about Deanna's height and gave her a side hug.

She hugged back, her eyes glued to Mel's face. She was studying him, I knew, for genes she recognized. I wondered if Sam was in Mel's craggy, lined features anywhere.

I waved at the hostess, who flashed a brilliant smile and beckoned us with three menus. She led us by framed photos of celebrity diners ranging from the Dalai Lama to Alan Jackson. A large sign proclaimed Mary Mac's was declared "Atlanta's Dining Room" by the Georgia House of Representatives. I eased into a seat at our table under a huge, colorful landscape painting.

Deanna did not sit, and was clearly struggling not to cry. "I'll be right back," she muttered.

Mel patted her hand gently and smiled encouragement. He looked around the room as Deanna walked away. "Funny you chose Mary Mac's. My family loves the food so much we drive over every couple of months. My daughter used to want to live here when she was little." He waved at a black lady with gray hair in cornrows and her hands on her hips. "That's Marietta. She's been working here since the seventies." Marietta practically ran to our table.

"How you doin', Mr. Mel?" She cocked a hip and wagged her finger at me. "This your first time?" she asked.

"Yes," I said, wondering what difference that could make.

"We have a guest who's new here, too," Mel told her.

"All right."

What kind of initiation was coming? A Mary Mac's hazing?

I know what you're drinking, Mr. Mel." A wink. "How about you, ma'am?"

Mel pointed to the Georgia Peach Martini on the menu. "Oooh," I said, "I'll have that and a glass of ice water, please."

Marietta's smile crinkled her eyes and radiated sweetness. I felt like we were visiting her house, not a restaurant. "You're gonna want two of those, wait and see. What about your guest?"

I shrugged. "I have no idea. Let's start her with ice water."

She nodded and disappeared.

Mel showed me the order form and pencil supplied to give Marietta our choices of entrees, side dishes and desserts. "Only place I've ever seen that does this," he said. "It's a great idea. Take a look at your menu, because I promise you'll have a hard time choosing."

He was right. I wanted every single bit of Southern comfort food listed: fried chicken, turkey and dressing, baked chicken and gravy, country fried steak, chicken and dumplings, roast pork, honey-glazed ham—the entrees were endless—and every side dish, too. I wondered if cheese grits and macaroni and cheese might be overdoing it.

Marietta placed the world's tiniest cup of collard greens and a mini corn muffin in front of me and left some for Deanna, too.

"It's tradition," she said. "Complimentary taste of heaven. And the good food you'll get today."

Deanna slid back into her seat, hair and makeup freshly fixed and smiling. She picked at her tiny collards with a fork and asked Mel, "Please tell me about my mother."

He looked at the table. "Well, for starters, she was good with secrets. I never had any idea she had a relationship with my cousin Sam, much less a daughter. And I talked to Violet a lot. I was her friend as well as her attorney." He played with the salt shaker, frowning. "Honestly, she was a good bit older, but I always had a crush on her. Everybody loved her."

"That's true, Deanna. She wanted it to be the title of a book her book," I chimed in. I caught Mel searching her face along with me. Her eyes were Violet's deep brown and she'd inherited her mother's skin. Anyone would think she was at least fifteen years younger if they didn't know better. If she had Sam's and Mel's red hair, it had been transformed by a pro into a light shade of brunette.

"We have a lot to talk about," I patted Deanna's arm. "Let's get through lunch and then we'll take a little walk."

Mel glanced at his watch. "I won't have time to join you after we eat. I have a three o'clock."

"Can you call and reschedule, Mel? Just one hour later?" I asked. "I want to show y'all something." I smiled at Deanna, who eyed my martini as Marietta set it down.

"I'll have one of those, too," she told her. I was surprised; I had her down as a sweet tea person.

"I'm starving." I waved my pencil and order form in the air at Mel. "Let's fill these out quick before I change my mind. I'm trying to make a firm commitment to turkey and dressing. Or maybe chicken and dumplings."

"You won't be sorry either way," Marietta said. "I'll be back in a minute with your drink, and take y'all's orders."

Mel excused himself to call his secretary.

Deanna followed him with her eyes. "Not what I expected. I know it's stupid, but I'd imagined him younger than me."

"You have cousins younger than you, Deanna. I'm sure Mel will help you get in touch."

Deanna looked at the drink that appeared before her. "Thank

you," she said. "I need this." She took a long swallow.

Marietta gathered our order sheets and waved, sensing we were in the middle of discussing something serious.

"Ladies," Mel announced, "I'm yours for the rest of the afternoon. Mrs. Detweiler can wait until tomorrow to discuss her case for increased alimony. Cheers." He clinked his glass to ours.

The turkey and dressing was better than any I'd ever had, and I'm a connoisseur. I'd rounded out my carb festival with cheese grits and—yes—macaroni and cheese. Deanna seemed to savor her country fried steak, and Mel clearly relished every morsel of fried chicken.

There was no way we could hold dessert. Mel reached for the check, and I didn't try very hard to stop him. He was probably amused by my feeble protest.

"All right," I announced, "If y'all will please get into my car, we're going to take a little ride." Mel volunteered to sit in back, so Deanna could see Atlanta. "She's not going to see too much," I laughed. "We're only going a few miles."

When I pulled into the parking lot they looked at each other and frowned.

"Ronni, why are we at Whole Foods?" Mel asked.

"Just bear with me. Y'all come on, it's not too far from here."

"What's not too far?" Deanna removed a shoe and rubbed her heel. "You could at least tell us."

"I'd rather show you." I led them to the edge of the parking lot, then around back past the array of dumpsters and loading docks. Both wore looks of utter boredom with a thin layer of determined politeness. "Here," I waved a hand at the huge magnolia tree, "this is what you came to see."

"Well, it's lovely, Ronni, but..." Deanna was looking around as though she expected to be mugged or worse.

"Look, please, both of you," I stood on my tiptoes and pointed at a spot several feet above us. "This tree was once in the outfield of Ponce de Leon Park, where a team called the Atlanta Crackers played baseball." Deanna was shaking her head, confused. "And one bright spring day, two young lovers visited it and the boy carved their initials into its trunk. Do you see?"

They squinted and finally focused where I'd pointed at the faint VG + SD. Deanna released a tiny gasp and started to cry. I did, too.

Mel put his arm around his cousin, her head on his shoulder. "I wish I'd known him better," he said.

"So do I," she answered.

I was about to leave for work the next morning when Deanna came into the kitchen, perfectly made up and patting her hair, sporty in a dark rose velvet tracksuit. She looked like a Florida grandmother postcard.

"Ronni," she asked me, "would you mind if I stayed here a few more days? I hate to impose, but there's something important I'd like to do before I leave."

"Sure, I love having you here." I gave her a quick hug. "I have to run or I'll be late. See you tonight."

"Thank you. I'll try to earn my keep by doing some housecleaning and cooking for you."

"Oh, good," I said. "I am extremely fond of having other people do both of those. Ooops, I forgot. Rick is supposed to come over for dinner. Would you mind if he joins us?"

"Don't be silly," she answered. "I'm the one who should be asking that. But I'd love to meet him, and I promise I'll put together a nice meal for all of us."

"Anything will be better than the usual salad for me and pizza delivery for him," I grinned at her. "Thanks."

Rick charmed Deanna with Really Funny Stories of the Highway Patrol while I sipped wine and watched them laugh. I'd heard them all before and was waiting for the grand finale in which a driver with an expired license says, "Do you mean my remit done collapsed?"

I gathered the dishes, shushing Deanna's protests and carrying them to the kitchen. She'd cooked a delicious chicken casserole. I slipped Halle a plate to lick and began washing up, straining to hear as the conversation in the other room turned somber and much quieter. I wondered if she was telling Rick about her past.

By the time I returned the two of them were laughing again.

"Well," Rick said, "it's getting kinda late for me. I have an early shift tomorrow." He grabbed Deanna's hand and kissed it. I swear she blushed.

I walked him to his car. "Ronni, I need to tell you something," he began, leaning on the driver's door. He reached out and held my shoulders. "You know I love you. And I want what's best for you."

My stomach flipped like an Olympic gymnast. "And?"

"Well, I'm not sure what's going to happen, but Victoria has left Professor Gasbag." He looked at the asphalt, then the sky, anywhere but at me. "Apparently he was accused of improper behavior with a student."

I stared at him, quietly waiting.

"She brought the boys and moved into the lakehouse. It's only for a little while. She's going to have to decide what to do about school and all."

"When did this happen?" I asked.

He looked like a man with his privates in a vise. "A little over a week ago."

"So this is why I haven't heard from you."

"Ronni, please, I didn't know how to tell you."

"Have you been there with them?"

"A few times. I had to help move some stuff, make sure they were settled in. I'm not living there, Ronni."

"You should have told me."

"I didn't because I knew you'd act like this." He reached for my hand and I jerked it away.

"*Act like this*? Seriously? How should I act, Rick? Did you not think I deserved to know your ex and kids had come running home to you?"

"They didn't Ronni, that's not what happened. I'm just helping her out..."

"Don't talk to me until this is settled, Rick. I am not going to be in the middle of it." I turned and hurried back inside so he wouldn't see me cry.

Deanna jumped up from the couch when she saw me. "Oh, honey, what's wrong?"

I tried to force words out through my sobbing, but gave up and laid my head on her shoulder. When I could take a breath, I leaned back and said, "Rick's ex-wife—the beautiful, exotic mother of his children who can have any man she wants—left her husband and has moved into Rick's lakehouse. It's only a matter of time before they're back together. And I'd be a horrible person not to want those boys back with their dad, wouldn't I?" I broke down all over again. Deanna dragged me to sit next to her.

"Ronni, I am sure Rick loves you. No matter what happens, remember that."

"Oh, jeez, he told you, didn't he?" I was horrified. "That's what you were talking about while I washed dishes."

Deanna's semi-circular eyebrows knitted together. "No, not at all. I had no idea, I promise you. But talking to him assured me of his feelings for you."

"I don't understand."

She drew a breath and took my hand. "I asked him how to find your mother. Rick and I both think you should meet with her."

I buried my face in my hands and shook my head. "I don't need to meet with her, Deanna, it's a horrible idea. I've avoided her for so many years, and she certainly hasn't reached out to me. Why should I do anything to help or comfort her? She doesn't deserve one minute of my time."

"But you deserve as many minutes of *her* time as you need, Ronni. This is for you, not her." She hugged me. "Do this for your own peace of mind, sweet girl."

"Peace of mind is not a concept I can relate to right now, Deanna. I can't promise you I'll go through with it."

She smiled and yawned. "My brain is on Florida time and I'm exhausted. I'm going to sleep now unless you want to watch television."

"Oh, no, I'll go to my room and read."

"Good night, Ronni. Everything will be fine. Fine for you and Rick and fine for you in general. Wait and see."

"I hope so."

I closed the bedroom door. I re-read the same six paragraphs of a stupid dystopian romance novel Kait had loaned me before I gave up on it. Then I spent two hours trying not to think, wishing Deanna wasn't sleeping between me and the half-bottle of wine in the kitchen.

twenty-six

VIOLET

The mirror reflected a beautiful woman in a very expensive cream silk dress and pearls. Violet had never dared spend money the way she was spending it lately. It felt daring and powerful to hand Tolly's credit card over in Rich's and Parisian.

He was being so patient, so unbearably tolerant, it almost drove her insane. And she was pushing him, pressing on every sensitive place as hard as she could, toward...toward what? Violet needed to know if her reformed, teetotaler husband was capable of holding his fists in check.

"Dinner's not ready. I gave Beatrice the day off. Let's go to the club tonight."

"Your shirt is wrinkled? I'm sorry. Why don't you drop your shirts off at the dry cleaner's to be pressed? Genny's husband does."

"I drove the Cadillac while you were golfing, and I opened the door into a wall and chipped the paint. Sorry."

Best of all: "I have a headache, Tolly, go to sleep." For as long as she'd been back home.

He smiled vaguely in response to her bait so often Violet was sure he was taking tranquilizers. She certainly didn't want to be hit, but Tolly was fading into a wispy translucence; an insubstantial man with a placid facial expression she didn't recognize.

Then she found out tranquilizers had nothing to do with it.

Violet invited Genny and three other women to join her at the club for lunch, something she'd only been allowed on the special occasions Tolly felt warranted the expense. She ordered champagne and toasted the afternoon of shopping they'd planned.

Juliet Horne, Junior League President, took a sip and told Violet, "You look more beautiful than ever. I don't know quite what it is, but you're lit up like a thousand dollar chandelier." She eyed Violet carefully. "Oh my gosh, you're not pregnant, are you?"

Genny shifted uncomfortably, aware that Violet couldn't have children but unsure what to say.

"No," Violet answered. "I'm just happy." She smiled and emptied half her glass. *No, but I have a daughter somewhere, just like you, Juliet. And I'm going to find her. Oh, and did I mention there's a great-looking younger man who's crazy about me? And my husband's not beating me anymore. I'm pretty happy right now.*

"Well, if you're not pregnant I want the name of your face cream," Juliet answered. "Now, let's talk about shoes." The women smiled and followed Juliet's lead into more comfortable conversation.

After an hour of picking at salads and competitive dessert refusal, Violet wrote Tolly's membership number on the check. Each woman thanked her graciously. Violet knew some of them would write thank you notes and mail them as well.

Genny had once whispered to her, "Know why Junior Leaguers don't go to orgies? Too many thank you notes to write."

She told Genny she'd meet the rest of them at Parisian; she was going to stop in the ladies' room. Genny kissed Violet's cheek and walked out behind Juliet, carrying her imaginary train.

When Violet emerged ten minutes later she spotted Tolly's white Corvette across the parking lot, as far from other vehicles as possible. He was terrified of real damage to the car she'd supposedly wrecked. *Maybe he cleared his schedule to play golf.* She sighed and climbed into the plush leather of the Cadillac, hoping he wasn't making love to a glass of bourbon in the bar. Violet turned the ignition key and looked up to see her husband emerge from the woods, holding the hand of a woman she didn't recognize. She was wearing a sleeveless pink golf shirt and capris, laughing and running her fingers through her long auburn hair. The woman stopped and tugged on Tolly's hand to halt him. Violet saw him look around for people, then cradle her head and kiss her for what seemed to be three or four minutes. She stared in disbelief until the truth dawned into a smile on her face. Tolly had just handed her grounds for divorce. She could be rid of him and financially independent, too. Violet waited until they were seated in the Corvette and facing away. She shifted the car into drive and headed to join her friends and exercise Tolly's BankAmericard until it was exhausted and begging to go home.

Violet heard Tolly drive into the garage and tried to remember exactly what she'd planned to say. She greeted him by pointing to a suitcase and a bag full of his toiletries on the polished wood floor. "I know about your affair, Tolly. I saw you at the club with that woman. All I ask is that you take your things and leave. I can't have you here in this house."

He gave her an incredulous look. "I don't know what you think you saw, Violet, but there is no woman and no affair, and there is no way in hell I'm leaving my own home."

"You were *kissing* her. I saw you with my own two eyes." He made no response, just studied her face impassively. "What's her name, Tolly? How long have you been with her?"

Tolly continued to stare. "I don't know what you're talking about, Violet. You're acting crazier than usual, and that's saying a lot."

She watched his jaw clench, saw the vein throbbing in his neck. Still, she pressed on. "Get out, Tolly. You can't expect me to ignore another woman."

"There is no other woman." He started toward the liquor cabinet and Violet felt fear crawling up her back for the first time. If he was going to drink, she'd have to get upstairs, lock the door, and leave this until he sobered up tomorrow. She was relieved when he seemed to reconsider and walk back to her.

Violet extended her palm to his chest. "I don't want you near me." It took all her focus to keep her voice steady.

Tolly came closer and closer until his face was inches from hers. He shook his head and backed away. She allowed herself to close her eyes and exhale slowly. She didn't even feel the pain in her cheek when his fist landed, not for several seconds. By then he had hit her stomach twice.

Violet did not open her eyes again.

The next morning there was no remorse, no begging for forgiveness, just Tolly's undivided medical attention. He checked her vital signs and satisfied himself he'd caused no significant internal damage. He loomed over Violet's face and said, "I fired Beatrice this morning. You neither need nor deserve help with this house."

She watched him gather his things and close the bedroom draperies. "Get some sleep, Violet. I injected you with some medication to help. I'll be home early."

She lay in their bed for four days, heavily medicated and rising only to accept soup and water from Tolly or make her way to the bathroom. On the fifth day she woke to find him seated at her vanity, watching.

"You should have a clearer head now. I backed off the morphine."

She nodded.

"Good. I left you a pill next to the bed with some water. You can take that if you need it for pain." Tolly shrugged into his jacket. "I wish I hadn't had to hit you, Violet. I think we both know I've worked hard to control my temper at every provocation from you. You became so outrageous I couldn't ignore it." He waved at the window. "There is no other woman out there. She lives only in your twisted, jealous imagination." Her husband bent to kiss her forehead as though it wouldn't thoroughly repulse her. "You're all the woman I need. Enough trouble for one man, surely."

Violet listened as he made his way out and started the Corvette. Then she let herself cry for poor Beatrice, and for her own complete loss of hope. How could she have forgotten that Tolly always won?

twenty-seven

RONNI

I clutched my stomach and shook my head at Deanna. "I can't do this. You don't understand. I don't know her. I don't want to know her."

She turned from petting Halle and said, "Look, Ronni, if anyone in the world can understand your feelings, it's me. But I'm afraid if you don't at least try to reconcile with your mother you'll regret it. Surely you see that."

"No, I don't. She shut me out of her life for over twenty years. She made no attempt to find me. She went her own way happily without her daughter..."

"All of those," she interrupted, "are things I said about Violet before I knew better."

I wished she didn't feel it necessary to fix my life. It was broken enough with the loss of Rick. All I wanted to do was crawl in bed with a good book and a pizza. Instead, I had Florida's preeminent amateur psychiatrist in a polyester pantsuit dragging me out the door to meet with a woman I'd been avoiding, mentally and physically, for years. For good reason. Deanna was the closest thing I had to Violet, though, and I felt like I should listen to her.

She swung open the door to my apartment and waved me through, clutching the address in her hand.

An hour later we drove up to a small, grayish-white cement block house with the thoroughly depressing remains of a flower garden sticking out of three tires in the yard. A shiny Buick SUV sat in the gravel driveway. At least her relationship with the used car dealer had paid off. I glanced at Deanna, who looked every bit as unimpressed as I was.

"We can still leave. It's not too late," I said.

She grabbed my hand and smiled, trying to pat away my fear. "Come on. How bad can it be?" Deanna opened her door and began walking up the narrow footpath to the tiny fake porch. I had no choice but to follow.

The front door opened before we got near it, revealing a very thin woman in faded jeans and—Lord help me—a red halter top. She looked far closer to seventy than forty-six. Jocelyn waved her cigarette-free left hand at us and took a deep hit of nicotine with her right. Her smile revealed yellowed teeth. I guess I should've been glad she had teeth at all. Her hair was a somewhat believable shade of blonde, but frizzy and twelve inches too long by any standard. My first emotion was relief that I looked nothing like her, no matter what Rick thought. My second was intense anger. I tried to stuff it down, but it was like attempting to put a king-sized pillow in a standard case. Anger was overflowing everywhere and I couldn't stop it. I stood back a few feet as Deanna shook Jocelyn's left hand awkwardly. My opening line was, "Remember me, your daughter?"

The frozen smile melted into a layer of sagging skin. I almost felt sorry for her, for whatever illness she might be suffering. I couldn't believe there was enough booze and pills in the world to age anyone this much.

My mother opened her mouth and released a voice that had passed gravelly years ago and conjured barbed wire and shattered glass instead. "Come on in, Ronni and Deanna. I'm glad y'all came." She enveloped me in an awkward hug that felt like a straightjacket.

Jocelyn seemed to feel better than she looked; maybe she was not sick after all. Certainly not sick enough to stop her exaggerated hip sway. I rolled my eyes at her back, watching carefully as she walked to her nubby brown sofa and sat, waving us into mismatched recliners. On my right was the biggest TV screen I'd ever seen, blaring "Wheel of Fortune." She muted it with a flourish and settled into the worn cloth. I spotted two upholstery holes near her knees.

"Do y'all want a Coke or something?" It came out: Do y'all wont a Coke or sumpum?

"No, thank you," I answered for both of us. "I'm here because Deanna thought I should meet with you, Mama." I nearly choked on the word. "I've had a hard time over the years, but I'm grown now and doing fine. I wanted you to see that."

"Baby, I'm so sorry. There's not enough words I can say to tell you how sorry. I was a addict most all my life. Still am, have to remind myself," she paused to locate an ashtray, "but I ain't usin'. Haven't for a long time. Don't drink, neither. I got a six month chip at meetin' last week."

I didn't know what to say, so I just looked at her.

"You know," she began and stopped to reconsider as she stubbed her cigarette. "Ronni, did it ever occur to you I let you go so you could have a decent life? I didn't know anything about takin' care of a kid. I was mostly a kid myself when you was little. You turned out all right. You still workin' in some nursin' home?"

"How do you know where I work?" I looked to Deanna, who shrugged.

"Your boyfriend, that's how. Came by here in his cop car months ago, like he was checking up on me. Like he was seein' if I was worthy of you findin' and talkin' to. I told him to please bring you, but he never did. Anyway, I'm real proud of you, bein' a nurse and all." She looked genuinely impressed.

I started babbling like I always do under the pressure of a compliment. "Well, I'm not an RN. I'm an LPN. I'm good at my job though, and I make a difference in the lives of lots of people." *Sheesh. It's not like she asked you to look at a mole, Ronni.*

She offered me the same crooked yellow smile and a wave of pity washed over me. She was such a sad case, such a loss. And maybe it wasn't my loss; it was her own. I was just fine. I glanced over at Deanna. Was this what she had planned? Not a reunion, but a reminder of the place I'd made for myself in the world despite my mother's absence? I didn't feel angry anymore.

Deanna said, "So, what do you do these days, Jocelyn?"

"Oh, not much. I get my check from the state on accounta my disability. I have a bad back. I worked answering phones at a used car lot for a while, but I couldn't take sittin' in a chair all day. 'Specially without any medicine for it, you know." She nodded as though we needed to sympathize. I didn't have it in me. She looked long and hard at Deanna. "When you called me up, you didn't say, but I'm figurin' you're the one who adopted Ronni."

All I could think was: *You didn't even know. You obviously never tried to find out.*

"No," Deanna said. "I'd be incredibly proud to claim Ronni as mine, but I'm only a friend. I'm visiting from Florida."

This seemed to capture Jocelyn's attention. "Where in Florida? I love Panama City. I love any beach anywhere. I'd rather be bakin' in the sun with the waves lappin' on the shore than anything."

"I live in Palmetto," Deanna answered, "not on the beach. We're about an hour south of Tampa on the west coast."

Jocelyn laughed. "Close enough for me. I'll just have to come visit you, won't I?"

"They died," I said suddenly, grinding her travel fantasy to a halt. "My adoptive parents, the Johnsons, whom I loved very much. Both of them passed away a few years ago."

"I'm sorry, Ronni," she said. "I truly am." There was almost as much sincerity in her voice as when she described her love of the beach.

"And before them, I lived with a family who kept me as cheaply as possible for a state check each month. They treated me like something stuck to the bottoms of their shoes. Then I was finally placed in a nice home, but my new mom died after eighteen months..." Deanna placed a hand very lightly on my arm, which I ignored. "Where were you? Did you not wonder if I was crying myself to sleep every night?"

Jocelyn contemplated her ashtray. "Look, I know you're mad, Ronni..."

"Mad?" I fought the urge to slam my fist on the ratty recliner. "I was devastated. I was a little girl blindly longing for the worst mother in the world. I don't know what I thought I'd accomplish by coming here, Jocelyn. I should have known you'd have no comfort for me."

"I am your mother. You don't call me Jocelyn. And I said I'm sorry. What do you want from me?!"

"Here's one thing I want from you. I want to know who my father is."

Jocelyn brushed at some invisible lint on her jeans. "I have no idea. I was a kid when I started using, Ronni. I'm not proud of it. My friends and I...well, we did what we had to do to get money." She shook her head. "I didn't take names."

"You whored yourself out for drugs." I felt Deanna stiffen next to me.

"I did what I had to do. I was addicted. My body needed heroin or pills or whatever I could get to keep going." She leaned forward. "But when I got pregnant, I stopped, Ronni. My parents checked me into rehab and I stayed clean. I stayed clean for a long time, and you were born healthy and beautiful. You were the most perfect little baby..."

I swiped at my eye, determined not to cry in front of her. "So what happened?"

"My mama and daddy moved off to Mobile. They'd come to visit every month or two when you were tiny. I was doin' good and they knew it. They sure loved you, Ronni."

"And?"

"When they died, I fell apart. I ended up quittin' my job—I was workin' in a dry cleaners—and I started drinkin'. Just a little at first. I was goin' to get another job, but it all got out of control and it was too much for me..."

"I know the rest of the story. I remember the men like Mose who came around. I remember living in a car. I remember waiting for you to come home." I rolled my eyes to the ceiling. "I guess you did the best you could, though it's pitiful to think that."

"You could be more understanding, Veronica Jean," she said quietly. "I tried harder than you think. I loved you. I was always goin' to make things better for you, and then the damn Nazis from the state came and took you and there was nothing I could do."

"The damn Nazis saved my life. That's the part of the story you're too self-centered to realize." I took a deep breath. "Do you know what "obliterated" means? It's a word I discovered when I was about seven. I wrote it down in a little book, and I put a star next to it. It means destroyed completely—and it was how I felt. No one wanted me. And whoever that little girl was who left you at five...well, she's long gone."

She glared at me and lit another cigarette.

We sat in arctic silence for what felt like an hour. I think Deanna was holding her breath.

The nicotine seemed to calm Jocelyn and she tried to change the conversation by assuming the hostess role. "I'm sorry I don't have much food to offer y'all. There's some chips in the kitchen, though." She waved and acted like she was about to get up. "My check runs out way before the month is over. You know how it is." She stared at me meaningfully.

No, I really don't.

"We're not hungry, thank you," I glanced at Deanna, who nodded in agreement. "In fact, we have to be going soon..."

Jocelyn seemed to recall some urgent words. "It's good to see you, Ronni, and I'm glad we cleared the air between us," she smiled, either oblivious to all I'd said or the finest undiscovered actress of her generation. "I was wonderin' if you could maybe spot me a hundred for a week or two. I'll pay you back as soon as I get my check."

"No, I don't think so. I'm sure you'll get by. I couldn't resist a pointed glance at the muted TV, now featuring a soap opera I recognized from Fairfield. I stood up and held out my hand to Deanna, who was clearly flustered. "We have to go now," I announced.

"Jesus, Ronni, not so soon!" Jocelyn trilled. She paused for a beat. "Ronni, wait. I was kiddin' about the money. Y'all just got here."

"Jeez Louise," I smirked. "Yes, and now we have to leave. I'm glad you're doing all right, Jocelyn."

"I am your mama, Ronni. Stop calling me that. And you are welcome to come see me anytime you like."

"You are no more my mama than a stranger on the street. Bye, now. I won't be seeing you again." I pulled Deanna along the path to the car, my heart racing toward a conclusion of how poorly or how well I'd handled our visit. I had no idea. I only knew I had to get away from Jocelyn.

I turned to look at Deanna before starting the car. She smiled Violet's smile at me and reached out with a hug. "You okay?"

I sat with my eyes closed for a few seconds. "Yes, I'm fine. And you're right. I'm glad I came to meet with her, because now I can move on without looking back all the time," I paused, "and I think I can start to forgive her. She's too pitiful for anything else."

"You did good, honey," Deanna patted my arm and fastened her seat belt. "I'm proud of you for saying what you needed to say. I'm sorry you had to hear all she said in return."

"It was pretty much what I'd expected," I replied. "And though this was far from my favorite thirty minutes ever, thank you for arranging it. I needed to face her."

Deanna nodded and put a hand on my cheek. "We passed a Dairy Queen on the way here. I could use some ice cream. Ice cream makes everything better."

"Did I tell you that Violet scooped ice cream in Florida when she was pregnant with you? She said she ate up more in profits than she sold."

"I guess that explains that," Deanna said. "I could happily live on it. Why couldn't she have consumed salads for nine months?"

Late that night I found my email from Jennifer Meyer. She thanked me for my submission and offered to reevaluate my manuscript if I augmented it, but it was at least twenty thousand words too short and "not suitable for the current market." She said I showed promise as a writer and should continue to develop my skills. I was welcome to contact her with any submissions in the future, including, she reiterated, a longer version of Violet's story.

I tried to concentrate on something else. I was feeling one disappointment away from Audrey Ledbetter-level bitterness.

I thought about how Rick helped me with my struggle to write Violet's book for nearly a year. How he'd gone to all the trouble to check on my mother's condition before even thinking of allowing her into my life. The way his arms felt around me, his sandalwood cologne, the sound of his laugh, the spot at the base of his head where his hair was baby soft. I loved the little things he did to show me he cared; the flowers on my windshield and the Starbucks he'd occasionally bring during my shift.

I missed him so much and couldn't be angry with him any longer. He was trying to do the right thing for his sons. I had to appreciate that, even as I hated Professor Lecherous Noxious-Gasbag the Third for creating the situation. Even as I cursed Victoria for running to Rick.

Surely she'd go back to Tuscaloosa. I looked at my phone for the millionth time, willing a text or missed call from Rick. There was nothing.

I walked over to the closet and took Mrs. Noodle out for the first time in years, the closest thing I had to a teddy bear to sleep with. Deanna was softly snoring in the next room. She'd be leaving soon, and I dreaded saying goodbye.

I was working on a patient's chart the next day when Kait summoned me to the phone. "It's someone named Victoria," she hissed, her hand over the receiver.

I took a deep breath. "Hello?"

"Hello, this is Victoria Pratt. I'm Rick's former wife."

"Yes, I know who you are. Has something happened to Rick?" I walked as quickly as possible to the nearest supply closet, closing the door and sinking to the floor.

"No, no, I'm sorry if I frightened you. I called to talk with you for a moment about Rick's and my relationship, Connie."

"Ronni."

"Oh, of course, Ronni. Anyway, my husband and I are working through some difficulties, but I am sure we'll be reconciling soon and the boys and I will leave the lakehouse. I know Rick has brought you here. It's a bit small for the three of us."

I was bewildered. "Well, I hope you, umm, reconcile."

"I want you to know there's nothing going on between Rick and me. He's Joshua and Jeremy's father, but that's it."

"Did Rick ask you to call me?"

"Oh, of course not. He did tell me, though, that you won't speak to him until my situation is worked out. I truly appreciate that. So, I'm simply trying to help you, um, Ronni."

"Okay, thank you." I couldn't wait to hang up. My hands were shaking so hard I thought I might drop the phone.

"Ronni," she hesitated, "you seem like a nice person. There are some things I feel you should know. You're very young and Rick's a man with a lot of history. He's prone to making the same mistakes over and over."

"I don't think this is a conversation we should be having, Victoria."

She sighed dramatically. "I've been where you have. I know all his moves. He put you on a pedestal, right? There's no one in the world like you. He's left sweet notes on your car. Rick O'Shea makes you feel like the center of his universe. He tells you how beautiful you are..."

"Excuse me?"

"Ronni, Rick has a pattern. He pursued me the same way, and he'll continue to pursue you until the precise moment he starts pursuing someone else."

"Victoria, I don't know what you're talking about, or why you're telling me this, but..."

"You deserve to know some things, Ronni. Has he mentioned his first wife?"

"You're his ex-wife." I was shaking my head at a row of disinfectant supplies on a shelf.

"His first wife. Her name is Becca. He left her for me. I'm not surprised he didn't mention it. I'm eight years younger than Rick and I was pretty naïve when I met him. Do you understand what I'm saying, Ronni?"

I wasn't about to admit it. "No, Victoria, I really have to go ..."

"Carrie Douglas," she interrupted. "You should ask Rick about Carrie Douglas, too. When and if you decide to speak with him, make him tell you about his past." She hung up and I stood with my mouth hanging open, staring at the phone.

twenty-eight

VIOLET

Violet was in the middle of drying the shower walls when she heard the truck. Tolly considered one droplet of water a breeding ground for mold and the first step on the road to the hellish vision of spotted bathroom tiles.

She walked to the bedroom window and pulled the gold brocade back to see the Superior Electric logo and Chet walking the stone pavers toward her house. Had he completely lost his mind? She grabbed her robe and turned to the mirror instinctively, smearing heavy makeup on even as she knew she wouldn't answer the door.

He rang the bell three times before resorting to knocking. He was pounding harder each time and Violet wondered if he'd damage the antique wood door. At last he backed up, examining each window for signs of life. She stayed carefully hidden, heart pounding with excitement and fear. Violet swept her eyes down the street; the next house was far away and she knew the Garrisons would likely be out at this hour. Besides, it was perfectly normal to have an electrical service call at one's home, wasn't it?

Maybe not one from two counties away.

She watched him climb into the truck and drive off. Out of sheer habit, Violet did her hair and makeup in full. She was a Southern woman empowered by those rituals; the type who wouldn't walk to the mailbox without making sure she looked her best. Even telephone conversations were easier for her after thirty minutes in front of her vanity. She chose a rose silk dress and paired it with a white cardigan to cover the bruises on her arms, thinking if you'd asked her why she was going to all this effort with no possibility of being seen, she'd have had no reasonable answer.

She made the bed and perched delicately on its edge, wondering if Chet would come back. Just seeing him from her window had plastered a silly grin on her face. She chided herself for acting like a teenager. Violet jumped when the gold princess phone next to her bed rang.

"Hello?"

"Why didn't you answer the door? I drove all the way from Anniston to see you. Well, honestly, I had to pick up some parts in Bessemer. But still."

"I was busy and hadn't even dressed for the day, Chet. You can't simply drop by here."

"I know that. First I called the office and asked to speak with Dr. Thompson, so I could be sure he was there and occupied with patients. I'm not crazy."

That was debatable. Violet had no idea what to say next.

"Well," Violet said, "Thank you for coming by. I'm sorry I didn't get to see you."

"Oh, you're going to see me. I'm at a pay phone a few miles from your house and I'm stopping by with a little present. Don't even protest, Vi. Anyone who sees will think I'm on a service call or soliciting for business. I don't have to come inside, just please open the door."

She glanced at the mirror to see if her bruises showed. She decided she'd risk it to see him, if only for a minute. She was very curious about his "present."

"All right."

"Great," he answered. "I'll see you in a minute. Bye."

She was waiting in the foyer, terrified someone might drive by and determined to dispatch Chet as quickly as possible. She opened the door before he knocked. He beamed at her—Violet couldn't help but remember the way he looked at her when he was a boy—and handed her a gift wrapped in floral paper. It was obviously a book of some sort.

"Should I open it?"

His eyes never left her face. "You truly are the most beautiful woman I've ever seen." He glanced over her shoulder into the house. "Yes, open it. Do you think I could come in for maybe two minutes?"

Violet shrugged and opened the door wide enough for him to pass, carefully scanning the street for people who might be taking malicious notes.

She pulled the paper off and found a book covered in deep purple fabric. "Violet" was embroidered in fancy gold script at the lower right corner.

"Open it," Chet said. "Turn to the very back."

It was a blank journal. At the end he'd handwritten, "You are beautiful."

"Oh, Chet, this is so lovely. I don't know what to say. Thank you." She hugged the book to her chest and fought tears. One or two escaped and traced her cheeks.

"Well, you said you like to write, remember? I figure this would be good to put your first novel in. And I wrote at the back like I did..."

"When you were ten and sneaked "You are pretty" into my notebook," she finished. "This is so sweet, Chet." Violet forgot that her tears would destroy her makeup until she saw him staring.

"What happened to you?" he demanded.

"Oh," she put her hand to her face, "I ran into a door facing. I am such a klutz." Violet started pushing him toward the door, loving the warmth of his solid chest on her hands even as she hurried to get rid of him. "Thank you, Chet, for the beautiful gift, but you have to go now."

He grabbed her arm and pulled up a sleeve. His eyes met hers. Violet tried to think of an explanation and her mind went blank.

Chet shook his head and ran his thumb along her jawline without a word.

"Please, Chet, it's not what you think. I'm fine." Violet found herself following him to his truck, fighting to appear calm and cheerful. She had lots of practice.

"If it's not what I think, what is it?" He opened the door with his back to her and waited for an answer.

"I told you. I ran into..."

"You didn't run into anything, Violet. Please don't lie to me." His hands were clutching the steering wheel like it was all that held him together. "Does he even have a Corvette? Did you make that up, too?"

"Of course he does, Chet." Violet's mind raced through all the horror Tolly had promised would rain down on her if anyone ever found out. She was putting her daughter at risk. "Look, it wasn't my husband. It was my friend's husband. I tried to intervene when he hit her and he attacked me. Tolly and I are not pressing charges because Genny doesn't want anyone to know..."

Chet's eyes were full of pain. "All right, Violet. What's his name?" He was still clutching the steering wheel, twitching his thumbs up and down.

"I can't tell you. Let it go, Chet."

"Use that pretty book to write some fiction, Violet. You're very good at it." He started the truck and rolled away slowly without another look.

twenty-nine

RONNI

Deanna accompanied me to Mel's office in Birmingham to bid her cousin goodbye before returning to Florida. Her eyes grew round as we entered the elegant lobby, just as mine had months ago.

Laura came from behind her desk, hand extended. "So you're Mr. Sobel's Cousin Deanna! It's so nice to meet you." She turned to me. "Ronni, you look wonderful. I'm guessing you've met a charming prince, if not Prince Charming. Am I right? No one glows like that without romance in her life." She waved her hand from my head to my toes. "You are transformed."

I was glad my size six Tahari suit, half-off at Nordstrom, had the desired effect on elegant Laura. I resisted the urge to kick out my cute Kate Spade pumps with their tiny bows for inspection. "Well, a lot has happened since I met you, Laura. I've learned I can write a book. I'm much more comfortable in my skin these days. And yes, there is someone special." *There was someone special. You'll be better off when you admit it to yourself, Ronni. No one just forgets to mention an ex-wife and an affair. And he's gone, anyway.*

I hadn't even told Deanna. I didn't want to ruin her glowing admiration for Rick, and my stomach wrenched up every time I thought of Victoria's phone call. Rick was still avoiding me, and I sure wasn't trying to find him.

"Do either of you want to freshen up or have a drink of water before you see Mr. Sobel?"

I glanced at Deanna, who was looking overwhelmed. She shook her head gently from side to side.

"We're ready to go in when he's available," I told her.

"Follow me, then." Laura's Christian Louboutin sandals flashed red at us as we walked behind.

Mel stood to greet us and offered Deanna a brief hug. His eyes were locked on mine as we seated ourselves across from his desk. I nodded, and he slid a piece of paper to me.

"This is for you," I said, handing it to Deanna. "Thank you for letting me see a glimpse of Violet again. I loved her so much."

Deanna smiled and nodded at me, looking to Mel as though waiting for him to continue.

"Look at it, Deanna," I prompted.

"Oh," she said. "Just a minute." Deanna dug in her purse and retrieved a pair of wire reading glasses. She held out the paper and I watched her scan down to the detachable cashier's check made out to her for one hundred thousand dollars. I heard her inhale sharply. "I...I don't understand."

Mel answered her, "Your mother's will stipulated this amount would go to Ronni upon completion of her book. Ronni has decided you should have it."

Deanna's eyes were wide. "Ronni, this is yours. You earned it. You worked hard for a year. You risked your job."

"Well," I said, "if my manuscript's any good, I'll be paid by the publisher. In the meantime, this money could be helping Violet's daughter, granddaughter, and great-grandchildren. I can't imagine any better use for it."

Mel held my gaze. I knew Jennifer had told him I didn't have enough of a book to get into print. It didn't matter. I was doing what Violet would've wanted.

thirty

VIOLET

The beautiful journal, the color of violets, lay unused in a vanity drawer under a pile of innocuous paperwork. She hadn't written a word in the past two weeks; hadn't the heart or the concentration. Tolly came and went, oblivious to her moods. He pecked her cheek perfunctorily every morning before he left the house. He was sleeping in a guest bedroom.

She drove to a pay phone one afternoon, armed with enough dimes to stay for hours. Violet managed to locate a private detective in Tampa with an operator's help. His name was Benny Carlock, and he'd promised to have a report when she called again at the end of the month.

"I will do my very best, Mrs. Thompson, but please understand the adoption process in Florida protects the minor child first and foremost." Violet listened to him light a cigarette and waited impatiently for something she hadn't already heard over and over. "If you have the resources to cover my time, though, I may be able to...shall we say...open a few locked doors?"

"I understand, Mr. Carlock. How much money will you need to get started?"

"For the next two weeks, I'll need eight hundred dollars."

Violet nearly dropped the phone. She would have to use some of the money she'd saved to travel. "All right, Mr. Carlock, I'll wire it today. I expect answers the next time we speak. Thank you."

She'd been counting the days, fantasizing about the news he'd give her. She tried to keep her expectations reasonable; tried to tell herself that simply knowing Alicia was well and happy would keep her going. Maybe Mr. Carlock could provide her photographs of her daughter. That, alone, would be worth eight hundred dollars and more.

Violet had not heard another word from Chet since his visit. She suspected he was disgusted with her, either for lying or for allowing herself to be abused by her husband. She could relate to that; she was disgusted with herself.

Most days she found plenty of soul-crushing housework to fill the time and provide distraction until she could expect Mr. Carlock's report. She was well enough now to go out in public, but didn't feel like lunching with her friends or shopping. Either one required too much acting skill.

Violet had arrayed her late mother-in-law's silver all over the dining room table to polish. She despised every piece and wondered why anyone would choose to own so much troublesome metal. She was halfway through some unknown variety of fork when the doorbell rang. Two uniformed officers stood there, hats in hand.

"Mrs. Thompson?"

"Yes?" Violet wished they would sell her their fundraiser tickets and move on. She had two hours until Tolly came home and tried to resist the twin temptations of bourbon and wife beating. She sighed and pushed a lock of hair into place.

"Mrs. Thompson, may we come inside for a moment to talk with you?"

"Yes, officer, of course." Violet swung the door wide and wondered what she could offer them to eat and drink. She led them to an informal den and sat on the sofa, indicating the chairs opposite her.

"Ma'am, there's been an accident and I'm afraid your husband's been injured," the older one said. She noticed he had a tiny smear of mustard in his white mustache. "Mrs. Thompson?"

"Oh, yes, I'm sorry. Well, is he all right? Is he in the hospital? I don't understand."

"He's at the hospital, ma'am." The policeman turned his gaze to his partner, who cleared his throat and added, "I'm sorry, Mrs. Thompson, but we have to tell you he's deceased." Both men looked so uncomfortable Violet felt sorry for them.

"There must be some mistake," she said. "My husband works in that hospital. They would have called me right away. I believe you have the wrong Mrs. Thompson." She smiled sweetly and waited for them to comprehend.

"Yes, ma'am, we know Dr. Thompson works there." White Mustache took over. "Dr. Thompson was coming down the stairs from the roof, ma'am. People at the hospital told us he liked to go up there for a cigarette sometimes."

Violet felt ice forming in her veins. Suddenly she knew what they were going to say next, and she couldn't let them. She tried to stand, but the younger policeman gently eased her back down.

White Mustache glanced at his partner before continuing. "It appears Dr. Thompson was drinking, ma'am. He fell down a flight of concrete stairs. There was nothing they could do to help him."

"He fell?" That was all she could say.

"We're going to take you to the hospital, Mrs. Thompson, all right?"

"Yes, let me get my purse." Violet's head swam. It was hard to see or hear anything. The younger officer took her arm and helped her up.

"Mrs. Thompson? Can you tell us if you've been home all day?"

"Yes, I haven't left the house."

"Did anyone visit you?"

"No, I've been alone. Wait, you don't..."

"No, of course not, ma'am. We have to ask." White Mustache looked apologetic. "I'm so sorry we had to tell you this. We'll wait here while you get your purse."

thirty-one

RONNI

Kait's eyes were wide as a horse's in a barn fire. "She left you all that money, and you gave it away. She set you up to write a book about her, and you've given up because it's too short? You exasperate me, Ronni. How many people get a chance like that?"

"There's nothing else to add, Kait," I said. "I'm out of information about Violet's life. I don't have an interesting ending. It's a mess. A mess I worked on for a year. I'm over it." I shrugged and turned to chart meds.

"Wait a minute," she grabbed my arm, "you're missing the obvious solution, Ronni. This journey has been yours as much as Violet's. You're not the same woman I knew a year ago, and it's not only because of Rick."

My stomach clenched at the mention of his name. I couldn't bring myself to open up to Kait or anyone about my situation with Rick.

"What do you mean, Kait? I should write a book about the life and times of Veronica Jean Johnson? For the New York Times Best Boring List?"

She bit her lower lip in excitement, eyes blazing. "You could alternate chapters between your life and Violet's. You'd start where you found out the way her will was set up. I mean, you're the only person I've ever heard of in that situation, Ronni. It's a neat story."

I considered for a minute. "It does have possibilities." I shook my head. "The problem is, even if I do that I don't know enough about Violet to fill out her part. No one who's familiar with her past is still around to help me. Except Herb, maybe, and I can't interview him for obvious reasons."

"Are you sure there's no one else?" Kait studied my face like a kindergarten teacher coaxing the next letter in the alphabet.

"I need someone who knew Chet. Certainly not his wife." I watched Audrey Ledbetter grab the hand of our newest resident, the tiny and taciturn Mrs. Gates. She looked like a terrified urchin being dragged down the hall by Audrey's wheelchair, a bedraggled five-year-old in a much older body. A lot, I realized, like Violet's description of a young CeeCee Wilson. "Oh my gosh. His sister might be able to help, if I can find her. Have I told you lately that I love you?" I hugged Kait and turned back to work, just in time to avoid Donna's hourly spy stroll down the hall.

It was depressing to see the dark, rain-streaked windows when I got home that night. Deanna had given me a reason to look forward to the end of the day, and Halle was a terrible conversationalist. I hoisted the bag of groceries from the passenger seat and prepared to dodge raindrops, then I lost my grip on the bag and spilled its contents all over the pavement. I scrambled to gather bruised apples and soggy ice cream sandwiches. I had to get on my knees in an inch-deep puddle to retrieve a can of soup under the car. I stayed there, unable to summon the energy to laugh at myself or cry. I lifted my face to the ink-swirled sky and muttered, "I give up."

"Don't do that just yet. Hang in there long enough to talk to me." Rick appeared from nowhere, holding a runaway apple. Water dripped from the brim of his trooper hat. "I know you don't want to, but you need to talk to me, Ronni."

He pulled me to my feet and added, "Please." I nodded.

Rick grabbed the groceries and threw them in the general direction of the grass strip in front of my apartment. He drew me to his chest and we stood in the rain for a minute, oblivious to anything but our heartbeats.

He held me at arms' length and wiped tears and rain from my face. "I love you," he said. "I can't stop thinking about you, Ronni."

"What about Victoria?"

"She and the boys are still at the lakehouse."

I sighed and shook my head. "The next thing you'll say is 'it's complicated'. I can't be with you when I'm constantly guilty because you aren't together as a family, Rick."

"You never gave me a chance to explain, Ronni, but I don't have any intention of going back to Vicky. The boys know that. I think they understand we're better off apart. Vicky and I fight constantly."

She sounded so much less threatening as "Vicky." I liked that. But her words kept echoing in my head, like little splinters of glass. "You're right. We do need to talk."

"Come on," he said. "I'm not going to stand in the rain for this conversation." He tugged at my left hand and I fished for the door key with my right.

I got a few bath towels for us to mop our faces with and threw them on the couch. We sat awkwardly, Halle watching from the kitchen and swishing her tail like she was reminding me to be angry.

"Okay," I began, "Tell me everything."

He threw up his hands and I saw water drip from his sleeves, but I refused to mention the possibility of anyone removing wet clothes. "She's still deciding whether or not to go back to him, even though the boys miss their friends in Tuscaloosa and Vicky knows it. There's a rumor that the girl who accused Professor Gasbag did it because of a failing grade in his class. The university has an official inquiry in progress. And with all that going on, the biggest consideration for her is that his agent is courting a movie deal for Noxious Gasbag's third book, and it's liable to drag on for a year or two. I'm sure Victoria has mentally spent all but a hundred dollars or so already."

"And she wouldn't get any of the movie deal money if they

divorced."

"Correct. Apparently we're talking about a massive amount. Bigger than the professor's circumference, even surpassing his ego. And that's visible from outer space."

"You know what? I'm really not in the mood for jokes right now."

He turned to fully face me. "She'll go back to him, and I've known that for a while. But I thought you should have some time to consider whether you'd be better off with someone else. That's the truth. You're very young, Ronni. You and I are at different points in our lives. And this thing with Victoria reminded me that she and I will always be connected. I don't know if that's fair to you."

Where was this going? I stared at him and raised my eyebrows, determined to wait until he finished his little speech before telling him the things that had torn me apart for days.

"Ronni, you're going to want children of your own someday," he said, searching my face for a reaction. "I have the boys to consider..."

"Stop. Please stop. I don't want to talk about this right now. Why the hell did you turn up on my doorstep if you were determined to break up with me? Are you already chasing someone else?"

"What the hell are you talking about? Where did that come from?"

"Victoria called me, Rick. She said she wanted me to know there's nothing between the two of you..."

"There's not," he interrupted.

"Let me finish. She also said you have a pattern of chasing woman after woman. She said you'd put me on a pedestal, just like her, and then it would be on to the next one."

I watched his jaw clench. "That's ridiculous, Ronni, it's not true. It's typical manipulative, dramatic Vicky bullshit. I can't believe she had the gall to...don't you see what she's trying to do?" He shook his head. "Vindictive bitch. After I let her and the boys stay there all this time while her idiot husband..."

"And you were married before Victoria."

I watched his face rearrange itself from outrage to shock.

"Oh my God. Did Vicky leave anything out?" He was yelling now, and I glanced involuntarily at my neighbor's wall. Rick took a breath and continued quietly, "Look, I was going to tell you. That was so long ago. Becca and I screwed up. We were married for less than a year and a half, and we both knew it was wrong two months in."

"And you left her for Victoria, didn't you?"

"No, I left her because we couldn't stand each other anymore. We argued about my patrol buddies, who she hated. Becca liked the idea of my uniform and service, but she hated having me on the road all the time. She worried constantly and spent hours on the phone with her mother, who helped her worry even more." He shook his head, remembering. "We argued about her parents a lot, because they were right about everything. We argued about money, which she was fine with taking from them. We didn't agree on anything except she belonged with her Mommy and Daddy, not me." I glared at him. "Okay, yeah, I'd met Vicky. But I told you, my marriage was a mess and Becca didn't care about me. That's the truth. And I thought the sun rose and set on Vicky, I admit that."

I let that thump around in my stomach for a minute, wondering how and when the sun stopped rising and setting on Vicky.

"Where is Becca now? Do you still hear from her?"

"Of course not. She moved to Atlanta with a new husband years ago," he laughed softly, "and her parents, I swear to God. I never think of her, Ronni, maybe that's why I didn't bring it up."

"You have to admit, Rick, it was a pretty important thing to 'bring up'."

"I'm sorry. I should have told you." He held my eyes. "None of it compares to the way I feel about you, Ronni. That's the past, and we should be talking about now."

"There's something else. Who is Carrie Douglas?"

Rick shook his head and was on his feet in a flash. "She

mentioned Carrie to you? I don't believe this. Damn Vicky, she's gone way too far. I have to go. I'll be back, but I have to leave for a while."

"Just tell me who she is, Rick."

He was almost at the door already. "She's a girl I knew." Rick read my face. "No, not like that. She's an innocent girl who died, and Vicky isn't going to use her this way. She's not going to use me anymore, either, that's for damn sure."

He slammed the door and it reopened a few seconds later. Rick dropped my drenched cans of soup and bruised apples into the apartment and slammed it again.

thirty-two

VIOLET

Beatrice, newly restored, stood outside Violet's bedroom door. She knocked lightly and announced, "They're here. She brought her husband and little boy, too. Marched in like they own the place."

Violet opened the door with a shaky hand and stood smoothing her black dress. "She probably thinks she does own the place. Tolly hadn't spoken to her in twenty-eight years, and she was surprised to hear he had a wife. I'm sure she's hoping he included her in the will. It's going to be a major shock, traveling from California for nothing. He left almost everything to me."

"Do you know that for a fact?" Beatrice reached to tuck an errant piece of Violet's hair in place, shaking her head with doubt over any good Tolly might've done for his wife.

"His attorney called yesterday. He's a very nice young man named Melvin Sobel, and he assured me," Violet paused to phrase it delicately, "I needn't worry about finances." She turned for a final look in the mirror and turned to join her sister-in-law downstairs. "Please bring us some sweet tea and cookies or muffins, Beatrice. We'll be in the formal dining room."

Beatrice rolled her eyes at the thought of Violet making her visitors as uncomfortable as humanly possible in that rigid setting, when her usual style would be the library or living room. She was delighted, though, because she'd be able to hear every word from the kitchen.

All Violet knew of Charlotte Thompson Andrews was Tolly's description of a woman so embittered by his success investing and managing their parents' money she refused to speak to him. She'd set off for Hollywood at nineteen, weeks after her father followed Mother to heaven, with fifty thousand dollars from her brother and a warning there would be no more. He'd said she was pretty and spoiled then. Now she was a handsome older woman at best, a failure as an actress with a husband who owned a corner drugstore catering to the movie stars she'd dreamed of working and playing with. Tolly had kept tabs on Charlotte; he knew he had a nephew but had never tried to meet him. When Violet walked into her living room she found the three of them picking up vases and figurines like they were casing the house. She cleared her throat and enjoyed the little jump Charlotte made. Violet hugged each of them and asked them to follow her into the dining room, where seven-year-old Herb Andrews grabbed two of Beatrice's cinnamon muffins and asked for a Coke.

The husband, Ron Andrews, looked like a man who'd suffered mightily over the years. He was rail thin and wore the expression of a basset hound. Violet couldn't see any trace of prettiness in her sister-in-law, just a frozen mask of pained politeness.

"The service is at two o'clock, and we'll need to arrive by one," Violet began. "I'm so sorry for the loss of your brother, Charlotte." She held the other woman's eyes and offered her hand. "I know you weren't in touch, but I know he cared about his baby sister." She watched Charlotte's eyes light up at the possibility of inheritance. "I should tell you that Tolly prepared his will years ago, and his attorney has contacted me with its provisions. He left you ten thousand dollars, Charlotte, and five thousand for Herb." Violet watched her sister-in-law's face slowly melt into understanding and acceptance.

"Oh, I see," Charlotte managed. "Well, he was kind to remember us, wasn't he?" She stood abruptly and grabbed a wincing Herb, forcing him to put down the cookies he was pocketing and step away from the table. Her husband joined her with no hint of his feelings. Violet thought she recognized a marriage much like her own, with a Thompson firmly in control. Charlotte dragged her family out of the room. "We'll see you at the church," she tossed over her shoulder. "We want to arrive early and greet some old friends."

"Of course," Violet said. She was pretty certain she was not to be considered a friend from that point on. "There's one more thing, Charlotte. I'm sure you know how Tolly felt about Los Angeles," she watched Charlotte's face twist into a grimace, "and he hoped you'd encourage Herb to return to Alabama for college. If he does, all his expenses will be paid by a trust he set up. It has to be The University of Alabama, though."

"Of course we've been saving for Herb's education. We'll keep that in mind when the time comes. I'm sure he'll prefer an Ivy League school or perhaps something closer to home." She turned on her spiked heel and clicked her way across the parquet floor and out of the house, little Herb in her wake. Her husband offered Violet an apologetic glance and closed the door softly behind them.

thirty-three

RONNI

I was sitting on my bed alone at eight o'clock on a Saturday night, drinking my third glass of wine, numbing my heart at the expense of my liver. Rick hadn't texted or called since he stormed out of my apartment the night before. I was hurt, angry, and puzzled about Carrie Douglas. Google searches told me nothing. I'd tried to read, to watch TV, to sleep. I was incapable of anything except paying attention at work. I almost wished I'd scheduled a shift.

My phone rang and I grabbed it, recognizing the landline at the lakehouse and expecting Rick's voice.

It was Victoria, on the cell phone number Rick must have furnished her.

"Ronni," she began, "I should explain about Carrie Douglas. She worked in a bank where Rick used to provide security, a pretty young blond thing. She flirted with him incessantly and even called our house."

"And this was when you were still married?" I took a hearty swallow of Moscato.

"Yes, it was. And Rick wrote her little notes and took her to lunch, though I found all this out much later. I didn't really suspect anything until he rushed off to the hospital in the middle of the night. The phone rang and he was gone. No explanation."

"Were they having an affair?"

"I don't know if you'd call it that, but he encouraged her and things obviously went too far. Carrie thought she was in love with my husband. She took a handful of Xanax and Percocet. She died before reaching the hospital, but she left behind a note detailing all the many failures in her life. Not having Rick was one of them."

"That must have been horrible for him." I couldn't help it. I felt defensive, whether from wine or love or both.

"It was horrible for a lot of people," Victoria answered. "But it didn't happen in a vacuum. Rick loves attention. He loves the chase. I told you that."

"That may be, Victoria. Are you saying he was responsible for her death? It sounds like there's a lot more to the story."

"I never said he was directly responsible. He can tell you the rest. Rick's on his way there now, and the boys and I are moving to a hotel tomorrow. Good luck, Ronni."

She hung up without another word.

A few hours later he knocked at my door.

"I'm sorry. I couldn't believe she told you about Carrie, and I was too shocked to know what to say. It was the worst thing I've ever experienced, Ronni. So I told Vicky she had to set things right, though I'm sure she still made me look horrible. Maybe even responsible. But I wasn't, Ronni, I swear." He had tears in his eyes, standing there helpless in his official uniform, twisting his hat in his hands. "She was a beautiful girl, but she was disturbed, I guess you'd call it, and I tried to help her. I did compliment her a lot. I did tell her she'd find the right person, who would adore her. I wrote her encouraging little notes. I took her to lunch once or twice, but I swear...even her parents didn't blame me. Her note talked about an ex-boyfriend and bullies in high school and the bank manager and on and on. The reference to me was that she loved me and could never have me. She never said a word, Ronni, I had no idea. I never cheated on Vicky, even though she'll move heaven and earth to try to make you think I did. You're supposed to believe I'm a liar and a cheat and incapable of commitment. She's trying to ruin what we have together. I love you, Ronni. I'd never hurt you. I never meant for Carrie to get hurt. My God, I thought I was helping that girl." He was crying now. I took the hat and set it down, then wrapped my arms around him.

"We don't ever have to mention Carrie again," I whispered. "As for the rest of this, I'm exhausted, Rick. I'm not saying it's all settled, but let's end it for tonight." I took his hand and led him to my bedroom, closing the door against the world.

Afterward I lay with my head on Rick's chest and talked about anything but our pasts or our future together.

"I need to tell you a few things." I traced a path through his soft chest hair. "First, I gave Deanna the book money."

"Good. I was hoping you'd do that." He hugged me and kissed the top of my head. "You have a beautiful heart, Ronni."

"And she made me go and talk to Jocelyn. In person."

"I thought she might. How did it go?"

"Pretty much as I expected, and it dredged up a lot of painful memories, but I'm glad I did it. I'm definitely able to see her the way I should see her now. I'm not afraid of her. She's pathetic."

"I'm sorry, Ronni. Maybe I should never have told you about her." He clasped his hands behind his head and studied my face.

"Sometimes you have to confront the rattlesnake or the airplane or the building's rooftop or the mother," I said. "I can move on now."

"Good," he stroked some hair back behind my ear and kissed my forehead.

"Oh, and the book was rejected because it's too short. I'm allowed to resubmit it, though."

"Then we will fix it. I have five hours until I have to be on patrol, babe. Good thing I left a fresh uniform in your closet. Let's get some sleep."

I watched his profile in the darkness and waited until his breathing was deep and regular. "God, I love this man," I whispered.

Rick's mouth tilted ever so slightly upward. "He loves you, too," he mumbled and threw an arm over his eyes.

The next morning I rolled over and inhaled the pillow where Rick's head had rested, hugging it to me and trying to remember what time he said he'd be back. I had twenty-four glorious hours until I had to return to Fairfield Springs.

I found myself concentrating on Violet's life instead of mine, an old habit.

I closed my eyes and tried to picture the Cool Kids' Table of several years ago. Mr. Perkins had his wheelchair next to Violet, paying rapt attention to her every word. Rose Perkins didn't live in the nursing home, and if she joined Mr. Perkins for a meal they sat at a small table near the kitchen. If she and Violet knew each other, they never showed it.

Mr. Davidson was usually laughing and making the rest of them join in. I could clearly remember his knitted sweater vests and bright bow ties. He was easily the most dapper dresser among Fairfield's male population, and I saw more than one old woman try to divert his attention from Violet.

I wished I'd known Mr. Perkins was Johnny and Mr. Davidson was Sam. Violet never told me anything about their relationships to her until they'd both passed away. So much history, invisible to all but those three. It must have felt like there were six of them, present and former selves side by side in that place, day after day.

It was beautiful outside. The skies really are so blue in Alabama most of the time, and the weather was just cool enough to make me feel energetic. I threw on some yoga pants and a t-shirt and set out for a long walk to the nearby park. It had trails through the woods and I'd discovered nothing helped inspire me more than a silent, solitary hike. I came home pleasantly tired and feeling accomplished. The inspiration turned out to be cooking for Rick instead of writing, so I was heading to the grocery store for spaghetti ingredients and garlic bread after I got cleaned up.

Halle watched me through the shower door and tried to paw her way in. I was almost tempted to let her experience it once and for all and cure her fascination.

When Rick opened the door at six, the apartment was perfumed with garlic and tomatoes simmering on the stove. I'd lit candles on the kitchen table and offered him a kiss with a glass of wine.

"This is perfect, Ronni. I'm tired and hungry and you are an angel. Thank you."

"Why don't you go shower and relax? I'll have dinner ready in about thirty minutes." I grinned and turned him toward the bathroom, feeling all wife-y and proud of myself. I measured spaghetti noodles and tasted the sauce for the tenth time. It was delicious. By the time Rick plopped onto the couch I had everything set for a romantic evening.

Again: very proud of myself.

I snuggled up next to him and inhaled deeply. "Mmmm. I love your freesia shampoo."

"Yeah. I really need to bring some manly stuff over here."

"You're manly enough to counterbalance Strawberry Shortcake shampoo, Mr. O'Shea." I took a deep gulp of wine. "I love having you to myself and..."

I was interrupted by the smoke alarm shrieking and smoke billowing from the oven. "Oh, no, no, the garlic bread!" It was fully on fire and I grabbed a glass of water and threw it on as Rick stabbed the detector over and over before finally shutting it off. I was removing a soggy black mess from the oven as someone banged on the door. Rick answered it to find my neighbor, Mr. Eldredge, anxiously peering into my apartment. "Is there a fire? Do I need to call 911? Are you all right?"

"Everything's fine, Mr. Eldredge," I smoothed my sweaty hands down my sides and walked to the door. "Just a little kitchen mishap. I'm sorry."

"Well, as long as you're okay." He looked Rick up and down suspiciously.

"This is my boyfriend, Rick O'Shea."

He stuck out his hand. "Frank Eldredge. Ricochet. Is that a nickname?"

"No, sir, it's a curse. My first name is Rick. My last name ..."

"Oh, I get it. Well, as long as you're all right, Ronni." He turned to leave. "Take good care of her, O'Shea. She's a nice girl."

"I know it and I sure will, Frank. Thanks for checking on her."

"Sometimes paper thin walls are a good thing, I reckon." He eyeballed Rick one last time and left.

"Well, I hope you've enjoyed your first episode of Domesticity with Ronni," I laughed. "There's still spaghetti." At that moment I heard the sizzle of water boiling out of the pot and running all over the stove.

"I'll get it," Rick grinned and wiped a smear of spaghetti sauce off my cheek. "You sit down and finish your wine. You cooked, I'll serve. Protect and serve is what I do."

I rolled my eyes and headed for the table.

Rick spent a month trying to locate CeeCee Wilson with no luck. He held me in his arms one night and told me maybe I wasn't meant to know the missing parts of Violet's story, not meant to finish the book. "Maybe," he said, "you're supposed to keep taking care of the people at Fairfield Springs. It's something you were born to do, with the kindest heart I've ever known." He kissed my forehead.

"I feel like I'm supposed to know more, Rick. It's almost like Violet is whispering to me sometimes, telling me to keep looking." I rubbed my temples. "I know she left me a lot to write about, but something big is missing. I just know it. Do you think CeeCee died?"

"No, that would've made her easier to locate. All I have is Mary Cecelia Wilson, born in Anniston in 1943. Some files were destroyed in a courthouse fire years ago. There's no record of her marriage, and if she's out there she's not a Wilson." He sighed. "I'm not giving up, babe. I know how important this is to you. And I will keep using my keen police brain until we get an answer, okay?"

I kissed him and turned on my side to sleep. "I'm counting on you, Rick O'Shea. You are my knight in shining khaki."

Two days later Rick pulled up in his cruiser as I dove into my car after work, drenched by an afternoon thunderstorm. He flipped his lights on and drove closer, decorating the parking lot a celebratory flashing blue. He knocked on my window with a big grin, water dripping from the brim of his hat, and pulled the door open. Rick leaned into the car, all official, and announced, "Ma'am, I'm going to have to take you to Atlanta. You're needed for the questioning of CeeCee Wilson, and you're not going to believe who she turned out to be."

A few days later we were led through a warren of offices and cubicles, a few occupied by people we recognized immediately. CNN's headquarters hummed with activity and excitement. A secretary in her mid-fifties rose to greet Rick and me, indicating a sofa and saying, "Bettina will be just a moment. Please make yourself at home."

The woman who emerged and waved us into her plush office looked as though she couldn't possibly be more than forty-five years old though we knew she was over seventy. Her chestnut hair was swept into an elegant chignon, a few careless tendrils framing her ivory skin and amber eyes. She wore a perfectly tailored suit of deep brown silk shantung. I suspected it cost more than I made in six months. Bettina Hughes, the face of CNN's breaking news, settled into her leather throne and clasped her hands on her desk. "I was very surprised to get your call, Mr. O'Shea. No one knows anything of my background in Alabama, and for obvious reasons I intend to keep it that way." She glanced nervously at the closed door. "If you're not here to extort me, why in the world would you want a meeting?"

"Ma'am, I'm an officer of the law," Rick drawled. "I would never think of anything like that. My friend Ronni needs to ask you a few questions about your late brother, Chet."

Bettina stiffened and inhaled sharply, her manicured hands twisting and turning before her. "I don't know much about my brother. My mother took me from our home when I was very young. Chet grew up with my father, and I hardly knew either of them."

"Did you ever hear from Chet as an adult?" I asked.

"He knew who I was, and he respected my privacy. He understood the last thing I'd want is for anyone to know the sad and sordid story of bedraggled CeeCee Wilson. I left CeeCee behind long ago. I have never looked back. My name is Bettina Hughes now." She looked to the ceiling. "So yes, I had an occasional letter from Chet, but he kept my secret. I appreciated that, and communicated my gratitude via annual checks."

"If you don't mind my asking, Miss Hughes, how did you end up as one of the most famous news anchors in the country?" I glanced at Rick and hoped he hadn't just gotten us kicked out.

Bettina smiled and said, "I came to Atlanta with nothing. Absolutely nothing, except a great body and a pretty face, plus a fierce determination to be somebody. It was through sheer luck I met a very powerful man who owned a television station and found me irresistible. He sent me to school, he paid my way, and he set me on a path that worked out rather well. Classic love story." She paused for us to appreciate her sarcasm and met my eyes. "What is it you want to know about Chet?"

"I was wondering if you could tell me about his relationship with Violet Glenn Thompson," I answered.

Bettina crossed her arms over her chest. "I have nothing to say about that woman. She destroyed my brother's life. He was obsessed with her from a very young age, and she did everything she could to string him along, right up until his death." She glared at me. "Yes, I know all about her dying in his bed, the old...bitch. You won't get that story from me. My secretary will show you out, and I trust I can count on your discretion. This is a waste of your time and mine." She started to rise, nodding at Rick and turning to me.

I leaned forward. "Miss Hughes, I am so sorry we've upset you. If you have anything of your brother's, or could share any memory that might tell me more about Violet's life, I'd be very grateful. You see, I'm writing a book about her."

"Why would you do that?" Bettina said. "She was about as

interesting as a bathtub ring."

I detected, for the first time, a trace of CeeCee's erased Alabama accent. She picked up a pen and flipped it over and over on the desk between her thumb and index finger, staring at it.

Rick put his hand atop mine and pressed down. He offered Bettina his knee-melting smile and said, "Of course she was nothing like you, Bettina. You're one of the most beautiful and successful women in the world, and all of America loves you. Ronni became very attached to poor old Violet when she took care of her in the nursing home, that's all. She likes writing about her patients and the lives they led."

I fought the urge to roll my eyes at Rick's "poor old Violet."

"You're a nurse?" Bettina smiled, but coated the word to drip with condescension.

"Yes," I said. "I've worked in a nursing home for years. I love my patients."

Rick sought Bettina's eyes and announced, "We didn't mean to trouble you, Bettina. I am sure you've forgotten about most of this. It was long ago." He waited until she softened in the chair under his gaze. "We are sorry to take up your valuable time." He held out a business card. "Please let us know if there's anything you can remember to tell us about Chet."

My mouth hung open. Was he really giving up this easily?

"It's not that I've forgotten anything, Mr. O'Shea. I remember it all in perfect detail. I am a reporter at heart, you know." Bettina looked indignant at the suggestion her recall might be questioned. "Tell me, though, why I would help you write a book associating me with a past I've carefully hidden for my entire career?"

"I'd never use your name in print, Miss Hughes," I assured her. "No one would have any way of knowing your identity as CeeCee or Bettina." I meant it. I'd make up a new name for the manuscript. I'd identify her with another network in Atlanta. "If you will help me," I added after a beat. I held her gaze and tried to look like someone threatening to expose her.

Bettina bit her lower lip with perfect veneers. "Chet made a choice—a stupid, childish choice—to stay with my father when we left. He did it so he could be near Violet. I never forgave him for that." She took a deep breath, considering her pink nail polish. "I'm disgusted by my brother's lifelong infatuation with that woman. Violet thought she was so much better than we were..." She caught herself and stopped midsentence. "Even after he married Loretta he'd talk to me about her, asking me to use my resources to update him with news of Violet, whether she had children or was helping with some fundraising event or bought a new car. It was ridiculous. He knew she was married to a successful doctor in Birmingham. He'd even sneaked into their wedding somehow, though he wasn't old enough to drive." She threw her eyes to the ceiling at the memory. "I don't know what more I could tell you. There's only one thing. It's no doubt a syrupy, nauseating declaration of eternal love. Chet gave it to me years ago, sealed in an envelope, with the request I get it to Violet after his death. Of course, she was gone, too, so I put it away somewhere." She walked to a filing cabinet in the corner of her office and unlocked the bottom drawer. Bettina stood and shrugged after digging for a minute. "It's not here. Maybe I have it at home."

"Please, please, Miss Hughes," I said, "if you could find it and mail it to me I'd be so grateful." I handed her a piece of paper with my address and cell number.

Bettina Hughes reached for Rick's hand and then mine, giving us a firm and dismissive shake. "I really must get back to work now. I will look when I get home later, and I'll mail the letter to you if I find it. Please excuse me." She swept gracefully back to her chair and began reading some sort of paperwork without another glance.

thirty-four

VIOLET

Violet traded Tolly's beloved Corvette and Coupe deVille in on a shiny new white Cadillac Eldorado convertible and spent most of her days shopping and lunching while Beatrice cleaned. She was a bird with new wings, tossed into a clear blue sky. She hired another investigator to find her daughter and planned the wonderful reunion they'd have. She allowed herself a new diamond brooch and a mink stole. She glowed as soon as it was decent to do so in public, her heels higher and skirts tailored to show off her legs. Every few days she joined Genny and Bitsy and Theresa for cards and a cocktail or two at the club.

Men swarmed like bees around honey wherever she went, but Violet didn't pay them much attention. She thought about Chet all the time, especially in her lonely bed. She wondered where he was, what he was doing, and most of all if he ever thought of her.

The attendant was filling her car with gasoline and checking the oil level while Violet filed her nails. She had no particular plans for the afternoon and thought maybe she'd enjoy a drive to Cheaha Mountain to admire the fall colors. It was crisp and cool, her favorite kind of weather. Then she spotted the Superior Electric truck parked across the street, obviously servicing a dentist's office. Her heart lodged in her throat and Violet found herself checking her hair and makeup before she realized what she was doing. The attendant knocked at her window for the money she owed, startling her with his cheerful, "Everything looks good, ma'am!" She paid him and drove off slowly, uncertain how to find Chet. Surely he'd want her to stop and say hello?

She parked within view of the office and waited for over an hour. Men came and went for supplies from the truck, but Chet wasn't among them. She gave up and drove home, suddenly too tired to go anywhere or do anything.

"Beatrice," she called. "I'm going to lie down for a bit. You take the afternoon off and I'll see you tomorrow." She heard the heavy front door close and lock a few minutes later. Violet tossed her clothes onto a chair and slipped into a satin nightgown. If she could just nap for a little while, she was sure she'd feel better. If she could only stop crying.

She woke, wild-haired and red-eyed, to a dark sky. It was about six o'clock, and Violet was stunned she'd slept so long. She made her way to the kitchen and found leftover chicken casserole. She ate it from the dish, in her peach negligee, sitting in front of the television. Violet caught her reflection in the window of the den and thought she looked like a finely-dressed lunatic. Tomorrow she would do better. Tomorrow she would actually take a step forward instead of killing time.

She arrived at the dentist's office by eight o'clock, wearing her best red silk dress and perfectly made up. There was no sign of Chet's company truck by ten, and Violet concluded he'd finished work yesterday and wouldn't be back. She pounded her fist on the steering wheel and cursed herself for chasing after a man she had no right to. She should go home and write. She should call Genny and meet for lunch. She should check with her private detective in Florida.

Violet put her car in gear and drove an hour to reach Anniston instead. She stopped at a phone booth and located the number for Superior Electric. She dialed with a shaking finger and asked for Mr. Wilson when the receptionist answered.

"I'm sorry, ma'am, Mr. Wilson isn't in. Could someone else help you?"

She sounded young and pretty. Violet hated her. "Is he expected soon?"

"No, ma'am, he's on a job site in Birmingham. Would you like to leave a message?"

Violet tapped her fingers on the phone booth's glass. "Oh, he's still working at the dentist's office?" she tried. "I was hoping to schedule an appointment when they finished there."

"No," the girl replied cheerfully, "He's done with that job. Today the crew is at a private home. I'll be happy to have him telephone you, ma'am, if you'll leave your number."

"No, thanks," Violet fumbled, "I'll call another company. I need help today." She hung up the phone feeling like an utter fool. She drove to surprise her parents with a visit and spent the afternoon hearing about the various illnesses and surgeries their friends had been experiencing. Violet left full of relief at her parents' good health, kissing them both and promising to return soon.

She arrived at her dark and empty house at seven o'clock to find a note jammed between the front door handles.

I'm sorry I missed you. Been doing several jobs in Birmingham lately and stopped by to say hello. Will try tomorrow after work. C.

Violet ensured Beatrice's absence by offering to pay for her family's dinner at their favorite barbecue place, ushering her out the door by three thirty since she had no idea what "after work" meant. She arranged herself prettily in a bay window seat downstairs, watching and waiting. He drove up a few minutes later. Violet was sorry to see Chet had a passenger in the truck until she noticed the other man slide over and drive away as she opened the front door.

"That's pretty presumptuous of you," she smiled despite herself, nodding at the retreating truck.

"Oh, Jerry Lee needed to run some errands. He's picking me up in two hours, at the end of our official work day." Chet winked and brushed past her into the house. He sauntered to an antique divan and settled on it, arms open to Violet.

She ignored the offer and sat in a chair a few feet away, no matter how strongly his presence pulled at her. His hair was a little long-ish in a nod to sixties style. He wore a black tee shirt and jeans though it was barely sixty degrees outside. Violet had never seen a man so beautiful, still tanned from summer and all taut muscle from head to toe. She bit her lower lip and saw him grin in response. "I haven't heard from you in a long time, Chet. How have you been?"

"I guess you didn't notice me at your husband's funeral. I sat in the back row. I'm not gonna lie, Violet, I was happy for you to be free of that monster." He held up her hand to stop any protest. "Don't think I don't know how he treated you. Those bruises didn't come from any Corvette steering wheel, and it probably happened more than once, didn't it?"

Violet looked at the Persian rug and blinked, willing herself not to cry. She nodded slowly.

"Why," Chet demanded, "didn't you come to me? I'd have had you out of here and safe, Vi. You should have told me. You could've..."

"Tolly had other ways to punish me, Chet, things you could never have protected me from. And you're not exactly in a position to take in wayward wives. I'm not going to talk about it any more." She crossed to the elaborate bar and reached for a highball glass. "Whiskey sour?" Chet nodded and she mixed their drinks. He brushed her fingers and stroked them with his as he reached for the glass. Violet shivered and sat back down, gulping courage and willing her body to stop shaking.

"All right, then. No more about the son of a bitch, may he rest in hell. Look, you may not have seen me, Violet, but don't think I haven't kept up with you and how you're doing. Don't think," he flashed white teeth at her, "I didn't see you sitting outside Dr. Lehman's office, either."

"Why didn't you..."

"Because the time wasn't right. I've been waiting to see you, and it wasn't going to be in a parking lot with my guys watching. Nice Cadillac, by the way." He set his drink down and smoothed his black hair out of his face. "I left Loretta five weeks ago. I'm living in an apartment near Fort McClellan. And no, not because of you. Because we have nothing in common except Eric. All she wants to do is listen to hippie music and I'm afraid she may start smoking pot, too. She has a whole new set of friends hanging out and burning incense and talking about their female rights. They're weird, Vi, most of them from California and places like that, followed their men to Fort McClellan." Chet picked up his drink and swallowed the rest. "She takes good care of my son. She's always there after school and on weekends, so I'm thankful for that. She's not another Betty." Violet watched him transform, just for a few seconds, into the little boy abandoned by his mother night after night.

"I'm sorry," she said, though she'd never been less sorry about anything in her life. "I'm sure you two will work things out." Violet smiled sweetly and hated herself for buying the line every married man offered several times per minute all over the world. Poor Chet, faced with a wife with whom he had nothing in common. If she were a better woman, she'd march him to the door right then to wait for his ride. Instead, she walked to the divan without a word and kissed him. He groaned softly and stood to pull her close, his arms around her waist. Violet was oblivious to anything but the sheer joy of his body against hers. Nothing else mattered. Nothing at all.

thirty-five

RONNI

As Rick started the car he said, "Well, do you think she'll find it?"

"I hope so. Even if she does, there may be nothing in it I can use." I watched the crazy array of downtown Atlanta pedestrians fighting their way across the street, among them an old man wearing a billowing rose-print caftan and a girl with bright blue hair and a teacup poodle dyed to match.

"We really don't know all that much about Chet," Rick said.

Something tugged at my memory. "He was mine, even when he was with someone else."

"What?" Rick asked.

"It's something I remember Violet saying about Chet. I didn't think much about it at the time, but he was married to another woman. He had a son." I looked at Rick's blank face. "Maybe she encouraged him from the very beginning. Violet did have a big ego, and Chet fed it. He made her feel special and glamorous, even at the darkest times in her life. He was great at that. He also had the perfect opportunity to make her fall in love with him."

"Huh? How does that work? Please tell me, Oracle." Rick rested his hands on the steering wheel, eyebrows raised.

"Violet suffered abuse from Tolly for years. He beat her down mentally as much as physically, to the point where I think he destroyed the Violet everyone else had known. So, she comes back to the comfort of her parents' house and maybe begins to recover a little bit. And there Chet is. He adores her, he's warm and safe and familiar and gorgeous..."

"He was gorgeous, huh?"

"The most beautiful man she'd ever laid eyes on. And she saw the child in him, the one she tried to help and protect. It's like their roles were reversed. She always told me she felt safe with him, even in her eighties."

"What a man. I'm warm and safe and usually presentable in public. You're the gorgeous one in this relationship. I love you, you brilliant woman." He started the car and grabbed my hand.

"And I love you."

"Why are you staring at me? Is it my great beauty?" Rick asked.

"Yeah, that's it. Let's get something to eat before we head home."

"Deal. Since we're in Atlanta, is Mary Mac's okay with you?"

"Always," I laughed. I could taste the Georgia Peach cocktail already, and needed it after twenty minutes of pure haughtiness from Bettina Hughes, the former CeeCee, Urchin of Alabama.

"You know," Rick mused, "I've been thinking a lot about Dr. Tolliver Thompson's death. It seems so strange to me that he'd fall down the same stairs he used almost daily for over thirty years."

I turned to look at him. "What are you saying?"

"Nah, it's crazy."

"What? What's crazy?"

"The whole drunk falling down stairs thing doesn't add up to me. Maybe it was a freak accident, but Tolly was a heavy drinker for so long, he had to have a pretty high tolerance. And honestly, Chet had every reason to hate him for abusing Violet."

"You don't seriously think Chet murdered him?" My mind was racing, and I didn't like the destination.

"Probably not. But I'm going to call an old friend with the Birmingham PD and see if I can get a look at the case file."

The following Monday I was off work so I went with Rick to meet with his Birmingham police friend. Rick was in uniform, and insisted we go in his patrol car.

I was surprised to find we were meeting in an Olive Garden instead of police headquarters. Corporal Jenkins came to our booth ten minutes late, apologizing and waving a server down for sweet tea. He was a tall man without a hair on his head, muscled like a bull. Rick introduced me.

"Nice to meetcha," he said, shaking my hand over the table. He offered Rick a manila envelope of typewritten paperwork, which Rick immediately buried himself in and ignored us. I made small talk with Jeff Jenkins and occasionally glanced at Rick, trying to read his expression. He only looked up once, to agree on pizza toppings, and then re-read everything from the beginning. He handed the file back and shook his head.

"Pretty much like I told you," Jeff said. "No one's going to re-open this as a cold case. I talked to BPD's crime analyst, just to be sure."

"Yeah. We'll never know for sure," Rick answered. "I'll always wonder if he did it, though."

"Want to fill me in?" I asked, annoyed.

"Oh, sorry," Rick said. "There were no witnesses and there's no way to know if Chet Wilson was in the area when Dr. Thompson fell down those stairs. His death was ruled accidental almost immediately. The autopsy showed a history of alcohol abuse, and there was definitely a lot of alcohol in his system when he died, officially of head trauma from the fall. The hospital seems to have been in a big hurry to close the case and keep things quiet, for obvious reasons." He sighed and crossed his arms. "No one had any reason to suspect foul play. The investigators knew nothing about Wilson, and certainly not about his relationship with Violet."

"So we know nothing," I said.

"We know that Chet was aware Violet was being abused. We know Chet's company worked in Birmingham a lot, including commercial electrical service. We know Chet was obsessed with Violet. And we know Tolly liked his afternoon whiskey on the rooftop, but always managed to walk down those concrete stairs without cracking his skull. But yes, we know nothing." Rick shook his head.

"What if we could get Superior Electric's records from that time?" I asked.

Jeff Jenkins spoke up. "Tried that. It seems they were destroyed in the nineties."

"I wonder if anyone who worked with Chet is still around," Rick said.

"That was a dead end, too, without the records," Jenkins answered. "I think we have a better chance of finding the real Jack the Ripper. Sorry, y'all."

I smacked my hand on the table, startling the girl who approached with our pizza. "Wait a minute! I know the name of one man who worked with Chet back then. He dropped Chet off at Violet's one day after Tolly died. His name was Jerry Lee, like Jerry Lee Lewis. Or maybe Lee was his last name. It's all written in her fancy purple journal, the one Chet gave her."

"I'll look into it and see if I can get you a full name," Jeff smiled and reached for a slice of double pepperoni.

A week later Rick told me Jerry Lee was eighty-three-year-old Jerry Lee Urban and he lived with his son in a dilapidated old house in Anniston. He'd spoken to the man earlier, which involved lots of yelling as he was nearly deaf.

"The first thing I asked him," Rick began, "was if he'd worked on the hospital's roof years ago. The guy squirms in his nasty old recliner and lights a cigarette. I wish I'd worn my uniform, Ronni, because he would've spontaneously combusted. Anyway, he tells me yeah, you had to be on the roof to access the electrical back then and he remembers the job. So I stared at the guy and told him a doctor was killed on the concrete steps there and I think his old boss Chet may have known him."

"Oh my gosh, Rick, what did he say?"

"He laughs, Ronni, and says yeah, he was the husband of that woman Chet nearly drove himself crazy over, I know that much. But Chet's dead and gone. Why are you askin' me 'bout this? So I went on and said he must've been there that day. Of course, he says he wasn't and he knows nothin' about it. Then he starts coughing hard and tells me all he remembers is that it was a terrible accident. He keeps hacking and shaking his head. Says he's not well and needs to rest. I knew he wasn't going to tell me anything else, so I thanked him and left."

"Do you think . . .?" I started.

Rick cut in. "Yeah, I do. At the very least he knows something. I heard him laugh himself into another coughing fit as I walked to my car."

thirty-six

VIOLET

Two weeks after he came to her house, Chet and Violet boarded an American Airlines flight to San Francisco. Genny had told her over and over about her glorious honeymoon traveling down California's Pacific Coast Highway. Violet thought it a perfect beginning for her life with Chet, whom she'd held to caressing her body and no more. She felt like a teenager again, giddy at the thought of their first time. She literally trembled with desire every time he stood close to her. It was delicious and daring to run away with him, the most outrageous thing she'd ever done.

Chet told Loretta he was attending a conference in San Francisco; he'd telephone when he returned.

They looked at the city lights from the tenth floor of the Mark Hopkins Hotel, registered as Mr. and Mrs. Chester Wilkins. Close enough. Violet was paying for most of the trip, though Chet insisted on contributing. It didn't matter to her. She saw all the brilliance of downtown San Francisco and all the stars in the heavens in Chet's brown eyes. She took his hand and led him to the bed, where they stayed for three days.

Violet and Chet spent the next week and a half driving a rented Mustang convertible down California's coastline, stopping over and over to marvel at the beauty of the majestic cliffs and ocean surf. They explored Monterey and then Carmel, where they found a charming inn overlooking the Pacific. Their room had a blazing fireplace and a little balcony where they could watch the seals frolic.

"There will never be a place more beautiful to me than this," she told him.

"There will never be a woman more beautiful to me than you," he said.

In a dimly lit Mexican restaurant in Santa Cruz, Violet returned from the ladies' room to find Chet staring at a wallet photo of his son. He shoved it into his pocket quickly, but she'd seen the pain in his eyes. Violet felt a subtle shift inside her, the first piece of a wall pressed firmly into place.

The night before their flight back to Alabama, she rolled over and put her arms around Chet. "Please listen to me," she began. "Your place is with your wife and son. I'll treasure the memories we made here for the rest of my life, Chet, but I can't be with you knowing you belong to Loretta. Go home and do everything you can to be a good husband to her. I will be fine as long as I know your heart is still beating in this world. That is all I need."

He turned to face her, propping his head on one hand. "That's a lovely and brave speech, Violet, but we both know it's not going to happen. I love you. I have always been in love with you. And it's not your decision to make for me."

"Actually, it is. I'll have nothing to do with you if you leave your family, Chet, I swear it. The guilt is too overwhelming. It would destroy me. I saw you looking at that picture of your son. I can't live with it. I won't."

"I can still be in Eric's life, Violet. This is ridiculous." He shook his head and looked to the ceiling.

"Being in his life and raising him as a full time father are two very different things, Chet. You know that better than anyone."

"I have waited for years to be with you. You can't just..."

"You waited?" Violet arched an eyebrow. "Maybe you didn't notice, but while you were 'waiting' you married and had a son."

"Some of us didn't have the world at our feet, Violet," he spat. "I did what I had to do. I told you about Mr. Harris. He offered me a future, and it included his daughter. He made that clear."

"So what does that make you?" She glared at him.

"What did marrying Tolly make *you*? Is marrying for money any different than marrying for a career? Are you going to tell me you loved him? Some worn out old man with a mansion and a country club membership?"

"You know nothing about Tolly and me. Nothing. You don't know what I went through, Chet. There are things I never told anyone." Violet threw her hands up. "You have no idea what you're talking about."

He closed his eyes and took a deep breath, exhaling slowly. "I know he's gone and we have a chance to be happy together. I know you love me. I also know you want me with every cell in your body. You gonna deny that? Violet?" He traced his hand along her cheek. "You and I are meant for each other."

Violet shook her head and bit her lip. "I'm sorry, Chet. I thought I could. I can't. We have to end this."

"Why the hell are we here, Violet?" He jumped up and began dressing. "Why the *fuck* did we take this trip?" He waved his hands around the room. "Look around! We're in an elegant hotel room paid for by your late husband's generosity. Thanks, Tolly, sure appreciate your dying so we could frolic in California for a week or two and make some memories..."

Violet flinched and covered her ears. "Shut up! That's the most vile, hateful thing for you to say, Chet. You know I love you. I can't help it if I have a conscience. Obviously it's different for you."

"I'll tell you what's different for me, Violet," he said. "I never once stopped thinking of you. No matter what was going on in my life, you were there. You always will be. And someday you'll realize I'd do anything for you."

She sobbed into her hands as she heard him gather his things and slam the door. Twenty minutes later the Mustang's lights came on and he roared out of the parking lot.

Violet waited by the window, listening and watching for him to return. Hour after hour she tracked headlights on the Pacific Coast Highway, expecting them to turn toward her. As the sun bathed the ocean in pink, she knew he'd left her there alone and there was no way she'd make their ten o'clock flight from San Francisco. The phone rang and she jumped to answer it.

"This is your wake-up call, ma'am. It's seven forty-five. The gentleman said to tell you he had to leave early and he's arranged a rental car for you to take to the airport for a later flight. We have the keys here at the desk."

"Thank you." Violet gently replaced the receiver and finished packing her things, numb and defeated.

The young man in the hotel lobby handed her a map and the keys to a small green Ford sitting by the front door. "Just drop it off with Hertz at the airport, ma'am. It's all paid for, and the room is, too. He left you this note."

Violet waited until she closed the driver's door before opening the envelope.

I'm sorry, Violet. I can't spend another minute with you ripping my heart out. There's a flight on Eastern Airlines you should be able to get on at four this afternoon. I'll do what you asked. I'll go back to Loretta and Eric. I'll try to stay away from you.

But I'll never, ever stop loving you.

Chet

Violet wiped away her tears and pointed the car north. All she wanted to do was get home and try to start forgetting. She'd have hours to kill in the airport. She'd find a nice dark bar and settle in. She'd watch the Hare Krishnas and hippies from behind her sunglasses.

She'd cry in peace.

Violet was on her second whiskey sour when a twenty-something girl with stringy brown hair and patched bell bottom jeans asked if she could sit next to her. The bar was crowded and she couldn't be rude, no matter how horrible she felt.

"I'm Sunshine Rainbow," the girl announced. She placed her backpack carefully on the floor and settled into a chair, pulling it slightly toward Violet. "You have beautiful hair." She reached out and touched Violet's arm, resting her hand at the wrist.

"Thank you," Violet said, sliding her arm away and stirring her drink. "Sunshine Rainbow is an interesting name." She took her sunglasses off and swiped at her eyes.

"It's really Karen Reynolds. I'm from Iowa." The girl stared at a waitress until she approached the table. "I'd like a Coke, please, thank you." She nodded at the server and returned her attention to Violet. "Sunshine Rainbow is my old man's name for me."

"Your old man?"

"My, umm, boyfriend, I guess you'd call him. Is this the beginning of your journey or the end?"

"The end." Violet swallowed the last of her drink and wished desperately for another. "And you?"

"This is my detour. Back to Des Moines for a couple of weeks, then I'll be here permanently." The waitress placed Sunshine's Coke before her and nodded when Violet pointed to her own glass.

"So why are you so sad?"

"I'm not sure it's any of your business, Sunshine, but I just broke up with my old man."

"Of course it's my business. What hurts you hurts me. It hurts all of us."

"Uh huh. Well, that's very nice of you, Sunshine."

"There is power in sharing your story. What's your name?"

"Violet."

"No, what's your real name?"

She laughed despite herself. "It really is Violet."

"That's beautiful, man. Like the flower. You should wear some in your hair."

"I probably should." Violet accepted her whiskey sour and decided Sunshine could be entertaining for a while. "How long until your flight leaves?"

"I only have about twenty minutes. We'll have to tell each other everything really fast. Like, I live with six people, including River, in the Haight. River's my old man. What's your old man's name?"

"Chet. He's not mine anymore, though, remember?"

Sunshine appeared to consider this for a minute. "He will always be yours. He is in you, Violet. Your paths may have separated for a time, but we all come together again in this life. Or the next one." She nodded sagely. "River says we all drink from the same stream, you know? There is not one drop of water on our planet that is new."

"Uh huh. I guess that's true."

"This sadness will transform you. All sadness does. It will help you understand yourself. Let it guide you."

"I sure will." Violet signaled the waitress for her check, draining every ounce of whiskey as she did. She'd escape to another bar nearby. There must be one.

"Violet, are you going home? Is there someone waiting for you? Children?"

"Yes, I'm going home, and no, only me."

"Then why are you going home? You should explore and learn. You could probably go anywhere. Where would you really like to go?"

It took about three seconds before she heard herself say, "Ireland. I've always wanted to travel there."

Sunshine grinned. "Cool. That's the airplane you should get on. Right now. Your path is calling you."

Violet reached her hand to shake Sunshine's. "It's been fun talking with you. Thank you. I have to run now."

"I should get to my gate, too. I am richer because I met you today, Violet. Peace." Violet stood and watched as the girl hurried away, then sat back down and ordered another drink. Twenty minutes later she found a pay phone and called Beatrice to tell her she'd be later than expected tonight.

Violet hugged Beatrice and thanked her for watching the house. She sent her home with a bonus and sat down to make some rules for herself. Number One: she wouldn't answer her phone. If Beatrice was there, she told people Violet was busy and took messages. Violet called her parents back immediately, but everyone else was ignored, including Chet.

Two weeks later she flew from Atlanta to Dublin, driving all over Ireland in a tiny rental car and listening to music in pubs. She danced and laughed and flirted with charming men. She made friends in hotels and country bed and breakfasts. She learned not to care if people stared at a woman traveling alone. She was truly free for the first time in her life, and came home restored and determined to enjoy it.

Beatrice house-sat for her and told her the same gentleman had telephoned several times, but he wouldn't leave a name. Violet wasn't surprised when her phone rang late that night. Chet spoke as though he was hiding under a blanket, and she supposed he probably was. "Where have you been? Are you all right?"

"I'm better than ever, Chet. Don't call again." She hung up the phone and smiled, knowing she'd be fine.

She heard about him from time to time; he'd send an occasional Christmas or birthday card. Violet never went anywhere without looking for him. Once or twice she spotted a truck like his driving away from her house.

Being without him never grew easier, but Violet had the satisfaction of knowing Chet had rebuilt his marriage and was reasonably happy with Loretta.

Chet mailed Violet a photo of Eric when he graduated high school. She cried that night, clutching a picture of a boy who looked so like the man she loved, grateful he'd grown up with his father by his side. The note accompanying it said:

I'm very proud of him. He's a bright kid and has worked hard. The gold tassel means he's in the top ten percent of his class. Glad Vietnam is over and we don't have to worry about that. He's going to learn the business beside me and take over someday.

I never stop thinking about you.

Love,

Chet

The next year her mother, now an elderly widow, called to ask if Violet knew Chet was in the hospital. He'd suffered a major heart attack. Violet rushed to his side without thinking. She was greeted by a sobbing Loretta and Eric, white as a snowdrift and staring out the window. Eric moved to place a protective arm around his mother. Violet noticed he'd grown several inches taller than his dad.

Chet was hooked up to a bunch of machines, all beeping and flashing steadily. She introduced herself as an old friend of Chet's family.

"I know who you are," Loretta replied, swiping tears from her face. She said it without a trace of venom. Violet wondered what, exactly, Chet's wife did know. "You used to babysit him."

"Yes," Violet smiled. "I did. How is he?"

"His doctor told us his chances of recovering are not good. His heart was badly damaged." Loretta started crying again, and Eric tightened his grip.

"Hello, Mrs. Thompson," he said. "I'm Chet's son Eric. I'll take Mom to get a cup of coffee and give you a few minutes with Dad. He's asleep, but they think he can hear us." He smiled Chet's own smile at Violet and she nodded gratefully.

As soon as the door closed, she grasped Chet's hand and bent her mouth to his ear. "Chet, it's Violet. You have to get better. You have to be strong for Eric and Loretta and for me. I can't bear to be in this world without you. Remember what I said? If your heart stops, mine does, too." She tried to brush her tears off the pillow. The monitor beeped steadily, but Chet didn't move. "Please, please Chet. Come back to your family. Come back to me, because there will be no light in the world if you're gone." She leaned back, never releasing his hand until she heard the door open.

Eric and Loretta found her sitting beside the bed, smiling strangely. She stood and told them, "Thank you for letting me spend a few minutes with him. I feel like he's going to be all right. I'll be praying for him. Loretta, will you please call me at this number and let me know something tomorrow?" She slipped a calling card to Chet's wife and hugged her briefly. "It was good to meet y'all."

The next day, Loretta telephoned and said Chet was awake and had amazed his doctor with his recovery. They would discharge him within a week. He would, however, have to be careful and take a variety of medications. Surgery would be scheduled if possible. "His heart is badly damaged," she said.

Violet thought: yes, mine is, too. "Thank you, Loretta." She hung up the phone and said a small prayer of thanks. Part of that prayer was to see Chet again someday, if only for a little while.

Violet invented a full life. She took friends on trips to Europe and Asia, trips they never could've afforded otherwise. She did charity work at a local women's shelter and made large financial contributions as well, though always anonymously.

She gained nothing through the various investigators she hired, but never lost hope that her daughter would seek her birth mother. Violet even ran personal advertisements, discreetly worded, in the Tampa and St. Petersburg newspapers. She was sure her daughter would come to her if she could find her way.

Many of her Birmingham friends passed on or moved away. In 2003 she sold Tolly's massive house and moved to a renovated Victorian in Anniston, near her parents' former home. She walked by their old place daily and saw herself playing hopscotch on the driveway; heard her mother calling her to dinner. She was lonely at times, but content.

It was by accident she learned that Johnny Perkins had moved into Fairfield Springs. She'd gone there to visit a church acquaintance who bought an apartment in their new, elegant assisted living section. As she wound her way out through the dining room, she saw Johnny in his wheelchair. His hair was pure white; he wore huge, thick glasses—but his name tag clearly read "Mr. Perkins." He was talking to another old man, this one in a dapper suit and bowtie. She grabbed a chair to steady herself. Sam Davidson's blue eyes twinkled as he waved his hands, then mimed a basketball throw for a laughing Johnny.

A week later Violet nodded slowly as the cheerful young woman showed her around the largest apartment Fairfield Springs offered. She couldn't imagine paring her furnishings down to suit fourteen hundred square feet. "Are the buildings all finished?" she asked.

"No, ma'am, they are working on the final phase of construction. Does this not suit you?" Violet thought she looked a little resentful, a sudden cloud passing over her plain features. Maybe she worked on commission.

"It's lovely, dear, just a lot smaller than I'd wanted. Tell me, do you think y'all could combine two units into one?"

The girl's eyes widened and she shook her head. "No one's ever asked that before, Mrs. Thompson. I'm sure the cost would be prohibitive."

"Don't worry about the cost," Violet glanced at the name tag, "Misty. It's very important to me to live my final years here. It's such a pretty place, and I know I'd enjoy all the activities you offer. I heard the food in the dining room is excellent, too." She scanned the small living room and nodded to herself. "If y'all combined two apartments for me, it would be just about right."

"But ma'am, we can't change..."

"Oh, I'm sure you can," Violet answered. "If you don't know how, Misty, have the owner of this complex call me. Tell him it's Mrs. Tolliver Thompson, formerly of Birmingham. I'll bet he finds a way." She smiled warmly and walked toward the door, calling over her shoulder, "I'd like to move in within two months, Misty. This will be the perfect new home for me."

Of course, she got her way. In a little over two months, Violet sold the largest and most uncomfortable pieces of Tolly's mother's furniture and moved into a twenty-eight hundred square foot apartment that cost more than the sprawling Victorian home she left behind. She sat before the same vanity mirror she'd known as a young bride in Birmingham and regarded her reflection. She'd had her hair freshly done and her makeup was flawless. The thing that made her feel beautiful, though, was the excitement shining in her eyes. Today at lunch she'd join two of her favorite men for the first time in sixty years, but she was sure they'd recognize her. She was sure they'd adore her, too.

At noon Violet swept into the dining room in an ivory silk suit, trailing Chanel No. 5 and attitude. Heads turned, both men's and women's, to size up the new girl. Violet found an empty table and sat to survey the room. Johnny was nowhere in sight, nor was Sam. She'd been back to spy at Fairfield more than once, though, and knew they'd turn up.

She hadn't counted on Rose, Johnny's wife, following his electric wheelchair by a few paces. Violet watched as they settled across the room, realizing at once Mrs. Johnny Perkins didn't reside in Fairfield Springs. She was dressed the way a visitor would, cheerful and manicured and coiffed for the special occasion of a visit with her husband. She was much younger than Johnny, Violet noted with the tiniest wince. She took in the Hermés Kelly bag and Rose's Ferragamo flats with grudging respect. This woman, at least, had taste.

Sam Davidson entered the room alone from the opposite side. Violet saw him deliberately avoid the Perkins' table and look around for a place to sit. She gathered her courage and stood to offer a tentative beauty queen wave. Sam seemed to think it was intended for someone behind him, checking and then turning back to face Violet from twenty feet away. She could tell the very instant he realized who she was; the skies parted and glorious sunshine lit his expression. He was by her side as soon as he could make his way through the crowd. Sam took her hand and made a big show of gallantly kissing it as Violet rose to throw her arms around him. He swiped an old-man tear from his eye and said, "I didn't think I'd ever see you again. I can't believe what my eyes are seeing, my beautiful Violet." He hugged her tighter and asked, "How can you ever forgive me?"

"Shh," she whispered in his ear. "We're not going to talk about the past. You're here and I'm here, and that is enough, Sam." She held his hand and pulled him to sit beside her.

There was no one else in the busy dining room for Sam. His

eyes were fixed on Violet's face, his mouth slightly open. "I just can't believe it. First Johnny...did you know Johnny's living here, too?"

"Yes, I saw him with his wife. She's lovely." Violet offered her most sincere smile and lowered her head slightly, gazing up at Sam through extra-length mascara.

"Not as lovely as you, Violet. No one ever has been." Sam leaned back as a server placed salad before him. "Wait...are you visiting, or have you moved in?"

"No, I bought an apartment in Independent Living, which sounds hopeful and depressing at the same time. This place is unlike any I've seen, so pretty and welcoming."

"It oughtta be, for the price," Sam replied. "Is your husband here with you?"

"No, he passed away years ago. And you? What about Debbie?" Violet knew she'd always despised the nickname.

"Deborah passed away a few years ago, too. I've had some health problems and the kids wanted me in a tiny assisted living cubbyhole. This was an elegant solution since our only store is in Anniston now, and they think the winters will be easier for me. You have kids?"

She'd imagined this scene a thousand times. She would collapse into Sam's arms and say, "How could you let your parents leave me sobbing in a train station, carrying your child? How could you leave me? I was ready to marry you, no matter what obstacles we'd face. *We had a daughter, Sam.*"

Sam waited, his head cocked to one side. Violet saw the years of hard work, the wrinkles and gray hair of late nights worrying about sick toddlers and teenagers getting home after curfew. The utter joy of his holding his first grandchild. She saw the map of his lifetime's happiness and sorrows with a family he probably treasured.

She shook her head. "No. No, I wasn't able to have children." A permanent decision was made in that split second: he would never know.

"I'm sorry, Vi. You'd be a wonderful mother." Sam put his

napkin on the table with a flourish. "You know, I don't feel like eating right now. Want to take a walk outside and get something later?" He stared at her like he'd stumbled onto a huge diamond in a cow pasture.

"I'd love to go for a walk," she smiled. "Maybe you can give me the grand tour. I'm learning my way around this place."

She noticed, for the first time, that Sam's hands shook as he grasped the chair to rise. He moved so slowly and unsteadily to a standing position, Violet knew she'd been right to keep the truth from him. He was far more fragile than she'd realized.

Johnny was expecting Violet the next day at lunch because Sam had told him all about her. He wasn't prepared, however, for Harvey, James and Clifton following Violet to the table. By the time Sam took his place of honor on the other side of Vi, theirs was a solid six and that number wouldn't change until one of them passed away a year later. Violet was surrounded by courtiers and found it more fun than her tenure as Homecoming Queen.

Any hint of discussion about Johnny's accident or any of the sadder parts of their shared history were immediately waved away by Violet, dismissed with a few succinct words about enjoying their good memories and creating new ones. She lectured them on appreciating the glorious "chance" that had brought them together again. They should treasure each moment.

All the men but Johnny let her know they'd prefer a more romantic relationship. She'd briefly dated Harvey, a lifelong bachelor, before Tolly came into her life. James and Clifton were retired military men like Harvey, brought to the area by Ft. McClellan and charmed by the local hospitality.

Violet blossomed like her namesake in the adoration, drinking in flirtatious flattery and teasing each man like she was Scarlett with Tarleton twins at the barbecue. She pretended to enjoy chatting with the women around her, but they knew she watched over their shoulders for one of her male admirers. Soon they retreated from Violet and offered an occasional glare in her direction.

The tenth annual Fairest of Fairfield pageant was held a few months after she moved in. Violet blew kisses to her men as she modeled her evening gown, a deep aubergine satin that set off her brown eyes and slightly lavender hair. They cheered loudly as she bent to accept her crown, especially since they'd made her agree to wear it to lunch each day for a week if she won.

Earlier in life, she'd have been thoroughly embarrassed. Instead she strolled into the dining room like Marie Antoinette, and was a little wistful when the week was over.

Afternoons now included a regular bridge game with Johnny, Sam and Harvey. Violet carried a dainty flask of rum and added a bit to her Coke now and then, though she didn't share it with anyone but Harvey, whose medication didn't forbid him occasional alcohol.

She woke each morning eager to greet the day, thanking God for the happiness she'd found in her old age. The only thing she found unpleasant was her nephew Herb's visits, which she regarded as necessary for his mental health, not hers. Herb was hoping for a share of her estate, she knew, and she allowed him to bore her with twenty minutes of frantic minutiae every month or two because it seemed to reassure him. He never asked her for money outright, but let her know the health club he owned was not doing well. He'd introduced a California fitness franchise in Birmingham after his year and a half at The University of Alabama. Now Violet had no hope he'd leave the state.

In her second year at Fairfield Springs the most wonderful thing happened: she met a young nurse named Ronni who reminded her of her younger self. Ronni spent hours listening to Violet, captivated by her stories and, Violet thought, in need of a mother's love and guidance. And she found the daughter's love she needed just as much.

Ronni helped her through losing Harvey, who succumbed to pneumonia, and then James two months later when he died instantly from a stroke. Violet discovered how much strength it took for Ronni to work with patients she loved and lost, over and over again. "The truth is," Ronni told her, "I am no better at grief and loss than anyone. I get through it by remembering these people I love are still with me. I carry them in my heart, always, the smiles and especially the things I learned from them. I learn something, no matter how small, from everyone I come to know."

Violet nodded and told her, "I wish I'd understood that at your age. I also hope I'll remember it when I listen to people talk, no matter who they are." She smiled at two old ladies working on a jigsaw puzzle, women she'd avoided as "vexations" and made fun of for their silliness. She surprised Ronni by joining them and asking if she could work on the puzzle, too.

Sam loved to walk through Fairfield's gardens and around its lake with Violet. Almost every day after lunch they'd set off, usually settling on a bench next to a towering weeping willow to talk. Sam told her his mother had made him fetch switches for his own spankings from an identical tree in his childhood backyard.

One day he sat heavily on the bench and gazed at the willow, distant and preoccupied, so Violet asked what was on his mind.

"You won't let me talk about it," he said. "No bad memories, enjoy today, grateful we reconnected, blah blah blah."

Violet laughed and said, "Okay, for this afternoon only you have my permission. Go ahead, Mr. Davidson."

He cleared his throat and leaned forward, elbows on knees, staring straight ahead. "I want you to know I'm sorry, deeply sorry, for what my parents and I did to you. They convinced me you'd be miserable married to me, and I knew my mother well enough to believe it. That was pretty much a guarantee from her. Plus they told me we'd be forced to find some other way to earn a living, because I'd have no ownership or hope of ownership in the stores, ever. Not even a job, and that was what I'd been trained for all my life. I was too scared to argue. I let myself be led onto a plane and into a new life, and I didn't have the courage to call you. Not once. I hated myself for years because of that."

Violet said, "Oh, Sam..."

"Wait," he interrupted. "There's more. I resented Deborah, I missed you, and I wanted to leave a thousand times for the first year or two. But over time," he shook his head and let it fall to his chest, "over time I grew to love her. And I came to understand you'd never have been happy, especially not if they'd made you convert. I convinced myself that everything turned out for the best. I need to believe that, Violet." He looked up at her, eyes brimming. "I need very much to believe that everything turned out best for us both."

She rested her forehead against his and held her palm to his cheek. "Of course everything turned out for the best, dear Sam," she lied. Violet stood and offered him her hand. "Come on. We're back to enjoying every moment, blah blah blah."

Years passed and Violet grew more content, enjoying her shopping trips with Fairfield's chauffeur even though she had a perfectly usable car. Her hair appointments and other stops were built around a busy social life. She never doubted her decision to move into her overpriced, extra large apartment once.

Violet was busy restocking books in the facility's library, the former study in the Queen Anne Victorian that served as Fairfield Springs' core. She volunteered a couple of days a week and often bought new novels for the collection. She hummed softly, unaware anyone was nearby. Ronni walked in and smiled at Violet's long ivory chiffon skirt and matching blouse, the last thing most women would choose for shelving books.

Ronni hesitated, unsure how Violet would react to her news. She'd heard all about the dark-haired, "beautiful" man named Chet she still missed. It was a topic Violet loved, and it seemed to soothe her to tell Ronni about "the true love of my life."

That morning she'd discovered Chet Wilson was a new patient in the medical wing of Fairfield Springs. He was there for cardiac rehabilitation after bypass surgery, but Ronni had read his chart and didn't think he was recovering well. The man's wife and son were probably at his bedside for visiting hours right now. She bit her lower lip, wondering if she should tell Violet at all. She drew her friend to a wing chair and sat opposite her, Violet tapping her fingers on "Pride and Prejudice" impatiently and smiling in expectation. "What is it, Ronni? You're supposed to be dispensing meds about now, aren't you?"

"In a few minutes. I came to tell you something, Violet. An old...friend...of yours is in the medical wing, and..."

"It's Chet," Violet interrupted, standing and dropping the book. Ronni pulled her back down.

"He's not doing very well," she told her gently, squeezing Violet's hand. "He's recovering from a heart surgery. I think his wife is with him, and will be until at least eight o'clock."

Violet looked puzzled.

"Visiting hours," Ronni explained.

Violet asked quietly, "What do you mean by not doing well? Is he dying?"

"No, I don't think so," Ronni said. "But he's very weak."

"I have to see him, Ronni. I have to go to him."

"The doors to that area are locked at eight fifteen every night," Ronni said. "You can't just walk in there, Violet, you'll have to wait for visiting hours."

"With his wife clutching his hand?" Violet answered. "No, you have to get me past that door, Ronni. You have to take me to Chet tonight." She gathered the dropped book and delivered it to the proper shelf, then started on a new stack without looking up. "I'll knock on the door at eight fifteen, Ronni."

Ronni hesitated and said, "Don't use the main doors. I'll meet you at the one by the garden, where we won't be seen. If I'm not there, give me a few minutes. I might be with a patient." She walked away cursing herself for not insisting Violet visit like everyone else. There would be days, surely, when Chet's family wouldn't come. No matter how much she loved Violet, she needed to keep her job. She would put an end to this tonight.

Ronni stayed in the doorway as Violet walked to Chet and took his hand. His eyes opened and fixed on her.

"Am I dreaming?" he blinked. Ronni saw a tear trace its way to his smile. Chet's hair was gunmetal gray and he lay weak in a hospital bed, but she could easily see the beauty of his face when he looked at Violet. He was still a handsome man by any measure.

"No, darling, I'm close by. I always will be. I'll visit you every chance I get." Violet sat on the bed and put her hands on either side of his face. She leaned to kiss him and then reached into her handbag and produced something small. "I have a present for you," she told him, and placed a glittery gold rock into Chet's outstretched palm.

He shook his head slowly. "Better than gold," he whispered.

Violet laughed and leaned to kiss him again. "No more born too late stuff, Mister. You're looking pretty mature these days."

"And you look like the same girl I met all those years ago. Lovely as always," Chet gazed into Violet's eyes as if they held the answers to every question he'd ever had.

Ronni went out into the hall, hurrying from the sensation she was not needed or wanted in the bubble of their little world.

She walked in an hour later to get Violet to leave, which she did with much fanfare and dramatic promises to return soon. Afterward she checked Chet's vitals and was astounded at the improvement in his heart rate and blood pressure. There was no doubt time with Violet was good for her patient. "Thank you," Chet told her. "She told me you're like the daughter she never had. It means a lot to me that you arranged for her to visit, and that you care so much about her."

"I do," Ronni replied. "I love Violet."

"Everybody loves Violet," he said, closing his eyes with a smile.

That was how it began. Ronni used her key to let Violet steal a few minutes with Chet, holding his hand, reading to him, eventually making him laugh as he got stronger. Chet never was able to leave his bed, but Violet came to him as often as Ronni worked a night shift and could help. Ronni made sure she had charge of Chet's care and kept everyone else away. It worked perfectly until she walked in near midnight, long after Violet was to have left, and found her curled against Chet, sound asleep.

She woke Violet gently and whispered, "You can't be here, Violet. You know this is against policy. I could lose my job. Please go home now and be careful you're not seen on camera." She and Violet had scoped out a route that avoided all the security cameras Ronni knew of. They used a back door that was largely ignored except by nurses sneaking out for cigarette breaks.

Violet stretched sleepily and nodded. "I'm sorry, Ronni. I won't do it again." She kissed Chet's sleeping face and left without a backward glance.

Violet was true to her word for weeks. Her days were filled with the men at her Cool Kids' Table and she looked forward to the nights she could visit Chet. They'd reminisce and laugh for an hour, then Violet would tenderly kiss him goodnight and return to her apartment. But Ronni found her and Chet asleep in each other's arms early one morning and began to fear for her job all over again.

Ronni went to Violet's apartment after work one day and asked to come in.

"Come sit down, honey," Violet waved her to the living room sofa. "Would you like a Coke or something? I think I have some cookies." She started for the kitchen and Ronni grabbed her arm gently and eased her back to sit.

"No, no thank you, Violet. I'm going to eat dinner soon."

"I hope it's with someone good looking."

"Oh, yes." Ronni thought Halle was an exceptionally good looking cat. "Anyway, I stopped by to tell you that our Director of Nursing is paying more and more attention to every detail in the medical wing, Violet, and you can't..."

"No," Violet interrupted. "I have to see him."

"I understand, but you can't spend the night anymore. I'd lose my job if anyone knew I let you in there, Violet, please understand." She held Violet's cool hand in hers.

"No one will ever know you let me in, Ronni. And I have to be in his arms whenever I can. It's the only place I feel safe. It's the only place I've ever felt safe." She began to cry.

"Violet, after an hour you have to leave. You have to promise me, because I can't always get to Chet's room and make sure you're out of there. I have other patients and they need my attention, sometimes for hours."

Violet stared at her, tears rolling down her cheeks. "You have to understand. I need him and he needs me. You know how much better he's doing since I've been staying with him."

Ronni steeled herself. "I can't let you in the door anymore unless I know you'll leave in an hour or two. It's risky enough for you to be there in the first place without spending the night. Promise me."

Violet nodded yes and Ronni reached out to hold her, knowing she'd keep her promise for a week or two at most. Violet would do as she wanted, no matter what. And she had to hope no one would find out how badly she'd been breaking the rules for months.

Johnny came down with a flu-like sickness one day and didn't improve. He was taken by ambulance to St. Vincent's Hospital. Violet waited anxiously for news and when she heard nothing she drove to Birmingham to see him, just like almost seventy years before. She arrived to find Rose Perkins crying quietly in the hallway, her children gathered close. Rose stood to greet her, shaking her head. Violet held her and cried, whispering, "I'm very sorry, Rose. He loved you so much."

She told Sam as gently as she could, watching the life drain from him before her eyes. She spent as much time as she could with him now, at a small table for two in the corner of the dining room, on her sofa watching television, walking slowly through the gardens. One day at lunch Sam asked her to please visit him in his room, which she'd never seen. "I don't feel like getting out much," he said simply. "Don't have a whole lot of energy these days." She walked in and found herself surrounded by photos of Deborah; in her twenties on a beach wearing a modest black bathing suit, gray-haired and heavyset in Paris, leaning to kiss a red-haired baby, riding a carousel horse with a laughing boy beside her. She picked up each one and asked Sam about it, seeing his face light up as he talked about his wife. She sat by his bed and listened to him tell her about Deborah and their life together, and she learned. Just as Ronni said, she learned from Sam. She learned what a good husband was like.

When he died, she cried for him and even more for herself. Chet was all that remained, and she went to him every time she could. Violet was so heartbroken Ronni began to pretend she didn't know she slept with her arms around Chet Wilson and sneaked out in the early morning.

One night a fierce Alabama thunderstorm rolled in. Ronni ran from room to room answering call buttons, reassuring frightened patients. Some were like toddlers, pitifully begging to sleep with their parents. The hallway lights flickered and an emergency generator kicked on.

As rain pounded the roof and lightning cleaved the weeping willow in half, Chet's heart stopped beating. And as she'd promised him long ago, Violet's did, too.

thirty-seven

RONNI

Rick sat on the edge of my bed, his back outlined in the soft dawn light. I raked my fingernails down his spine and he turned to kiss me.

"Why are you up so early? I whispered.

"I'm going to visit the boys today. Jeremy's in some kind of play at school this morning."

"Will you stay in Tuscaloosa for supper?" I was grateful Victoria had returned to her wealthy gasbag husband, and even more grateful to know they were expecting a little gasbag.

"Probably," he answered. "But I'll be back by bedtime." Rick threw my t-shirt upward and cupped my breast in his hand, trailing kisses up toward my neck.

"You're not getting away with that." I pulled him on top of me. "This will just take a minute or two."

"Hey, I resent your implication, lady," he said.

Kait was in the tiny break room when I arrived for work and her eyes were red. I knew immediately a patient had died. "Who?" was all I said. We had a shorthand after years together in this place.

"Audrey. I can't believe I'm crying over the hateful, nasty-tater-growing, bossy old plantation queen who made our lives miserable," Kait covered her face with her hands and I hugged her, tears of my own falling fast. Any time we lost a patient was hard, but Audrey was a special combination of venom and honey. I realized I'd miss her a lot. We allowed ourselves another minute and headed off to fix our makeup and start rounds.

"We should go to the funeral," I told Kait, pushing the med cart to the end of the hall as she reviewed the tablet computer for instructions.

"I'm just going to send some sort of vine," she answered.

We walked over to check on Violet's activity room just before lunch. Construction was almost finished, and I loved seeing her vision come to life. Here was a big red soda fountain counter where we'd hand out ice cream, and the jukebox was already playing some fifties song I didn't recognize. There were small tables and booths for residents to gather and an area at the end of the room with leather couches and a big open space in front of three TV screens. There would be virtual bowling and tennis. Fairfield Springs couldn't have had a nicer gift. I wished Violet could've had some time in that room, the perfect place to have fun with her friends.

Rick and I spent our Saturday afternoon at an old country church thirty miles away, Rick clasping my hand as we sat to honor Audrey Marie Haynes Ledbetter. I hadn't fully believed her tales of inherited fortune but the Haynes nieces and nephews decorated the tiny gravel parking lot with incongruous new Range Rovers, BMWs and Mercedes. They decorated the church pews with expensive custom suits and antique diamond jewelry.

I had never seen one of them at Fairfield Springs.

Kristin, my banker, arrived with her husband and sat next to me. "What a crowd, huh?" she whispered. "I should tell you right now, I'm related through the far more humble Ledbetters. My car is out there crying in embarrassment between a Jaguar and a Cadillac."

I snickered and patted her arm. "I hear you. I'd wait until they're all gone before walking to mine, except we're in Rick's car today. Although it *is* a few years too old for this crowd." Rick smirked at me for a few seconds, then waved at Kris with a smile and reached across to take her hand for a quick shake.

The church was tiny. Its hardwood floors were carefully polished to a bright gleam, and the old-fashioned windows were a swirl of pale purple. Huge bronze stained glass lamps of green and deep purple dangled at the front of the sanctuary while the rest of it glowed with harsh modern fluorescence. The pews were padded with deep green velvet cushions. A green runner ran the length of the center aisle. The worn hymnals were purple.

Audrey's family might not spend a lot of time in this, their ancestral church, but they knew the color scheme well. Almost all the massive floral arrangements were made of purple flowers, from gladiolas to tulips. Audrey's casket was blanketed in green roses.

The service was a typical Southern Baptist one, with several hymns sung by the congregation. Most stood and sang along with no need to consult the lyrics. The preacher, who'd never met Audrey, praised her strong faith. He told us of a husband who'd left her widowed at forty-two and son and daughter who'd preceded her to Heaven.

I understood Audrey better after listening to this man who never laid eyes on her.

He preached a sermon full of Bible verses warning against the wages of sin and the promise of rewards for the faithful and virtuous. Then, as all Southern Baptist preachers do with rare results, he called all the sinners among those present to the altar for a chance to repent. After a one hour and thirty minute service, it would've taken a very brave person to go forward. When no one did, we all breathed a sigh of relief and slowly followed the crowd behind Audrey's pallbearers down the steep front stairs.

Kristin waited until we four walked alone to speak. "Hey, Ronni," she said. "How is your book coming along?"

"It's been written and rewritten and rewritten. I think I'm pretty close to finishing it," I said. "Thank you for asking. I still don't know if it will be published."

"Of course it will. I'm looking forward to it!" she called,

turning toward her car.

"So am I, Kristin. So am I."

"It has more twists and turns than Chubby Checker in a maze," Rick added. We stared at him blankly. "Children," he muttered. "Y'all are *children.*"

The letter was waiting when we got to my apartment, addressed in Bettina's perfect script with no return address. I hurried to the kitchen to open it as Rick tapped a drumroll.

"Well," I said, "this is it." I slit the envelope with a sharp knife as Rick watched from across the kitchen table. The smaller envelope within was the color of weak tea, taped twice with flaking cellophane. The back flap read "CeeCee, please give this to Violet only after I'm gone."

The seal was undisturbed and I had to open it very carefully. I pulled out the typewritten pages and gasped as I scanned them.

"What? What is it?" Rick jumped up and came around to read over my shoulder.

March 23, 1958

Dearest Violet,

You are always on my mind, no matter where I go or what I do.

The thought of you brings light into the darkest day.

There is something I have to tell you. Nothing happened the way it was supposed to, Violet. I was a stupid, heartsick kid at the time.

Please understand. I was ten years old, longing to go home with you every time you left. I only wanted to look at your face and stroke your blonde hair. I would've done anything, given anything, to hear you laugh at my jokes. To notice me. To need me for something. For anything.

You were the only world I wanted to live in.

Over and over I watched you get into Johnny Perkins' shiny black car, the one that cost more than my family's house. I saw Johnny kiss your lips. I saw the light beaming from your eyes when you talked about him.

One Friday after school I walked the half mile to Uncle Chunk's garage.

"Hey, kiddo," he said. "You wanna Coke?"

"Sure," I told him. I sat down on a stack of tires. "I was wonderin' if you could teach me about cars."

"What is it you want to know, boy?" Uncle Chunk let loose a river of tobacco juice onto the cement floor, smacking his wrench against his greasy hand. "You gonna grow up like your favorite uncle and fix cars? There's good money in it. You could do worse."

I nodded at the Pontiac hovering on a hydraulic lift. "Could I get under there, and you maybe show me what's what?"

Uncle Chunk grinned with teeth the color of my baseball mitt. I think he was pleased to see his nephew admiring his career instead of my dad's at the train station window, apologizing for a living. "You got it. Man's gotta know about engines and what makes 'em work." He waved, inviting me into the cool cave under the car.

For the next thirty minutes I asked questions about the snake's nest of hoses and belts. My uncle answered patiently, and even drew a diagram for me to take home and study. He handed it to me with an extra Coke to take home for later. "Don't tell your mama or CeeCee. That's just for you, now."

I smiled and thanked Uncle Chunk.

Late that night, I pulled the warm bottle from my bottom dresser drawer and crept into the kitchen to open it and grab a stale sausage biscuit from the counter. My parents and sister were sound asleep. I could hear Dad's snoring all through the house. I went back to my room and eased the window open, sliding my legs out and falling to the soft red clay with a thud. I threw the empty Coke bottle into the woods and set out for the Perkins' house. I tossed little bits of sausage at the dogs along the way to keep them quiet.

I stared at my target shining in the driveway for a long time. Then, I slid under Johnny's DeSoto and pulled a flashlight and pocketknife from my jacket. The brake line was easy to locate, and I made a tiny puncture in it.

Violet, I never meant for Johnny to get hurt. I somehow thought if I took away his flashy car you might not want to be with him. Maybe he'd get in trouble with his dad if he tore up the fender. Maybe he'd have to stay away from you.

When our neighbor lady came to tell Mama about the wreck, and about Kimmie, I ran to my room in tears. I remember Mama telling her, "Oh, Chet has a big crush on his babysitter, Johnny's girlfriend. I'd better see about him."

My mother sat on my bed with her arms folded and demanded to know why I was crying. I panicked and blurted out everything. She stood up and slapped me hard. She told me the police would be coming for me soon.

Mama didn't cry. She didn't yell. It was almost as if she'd wanted me to give her a reason to leave.

She walked over to the door and just before she closed it she said she and CeeCee were going somewhere else to live and my father could take charge of me. She promised me one thing: if I'd stay away from her and my sister, if I'd live with Dad and behave, she wouldn't tell anyone what I'd done.

I dug a hole in the back yard and buried the pocketknife that afternoon. Mama and CeeCee were gone by suppertime. She left a note on the kitchen table, and my father fell to pieces when he read it.

When he said I had to go live with my aunt, I ran to your house. I wanted to explain. I wanted to confess what I'd done. All I could do was cry, especially when I saw the pain Johnny's accident had caused you.

I destroyed so much in a few seconds of my life, Violet. I'd give anything if I could take it back. I am so very, very sorry.

I still wake up shaking in the middle of the night, sure my secret is about to be discovered. Maybe it will be. Maybe I deserve it.

The last time I saw you—that night at the train station—you looked so beautiful, even crying about your canceled trip. You even cry pretty, Violet. Everything you do, you do pretty.

It hurt me so bad to see you that way. I knew you would never be happy with Sam Davidson and his mother always harping after you. When I saw the reservation he'd made at the station, I asked my daddy about it. He said you two were taking a trip alone and it was a secret. So I tried to help the only way I could. I called Mrs. Davidson and told her my daddy asked me to confirm Sam's reservation for him and you. I figured they would try to stop you from making a big mistake you'd regret for the rest of your life, Violet. I only want you to be happy. Someday you'll know it's me that is meant for you.

You used to laugh when you said it, but it's true, you know—everybody loves you. But I love you more than anyone, and I believe you know that. I believe I am going to see you again someday, and I hope you can somehow forgive me in your heart. If I never get the courage to tell you what I did out of love for you, well, you'll know after I'm gone.

Yours forever,
Chet

"This is unbelievable," I put the letter down and picked it up again immediately, as though the words might have changed. "All that time, and she had no idea. She was in love with a man who destroyed her life, Rick."

"Makes you wonder what else he kept from her." Rick drummed his fingers on the table, a sure sign he was in deep thought.

"We'll never know for sure what happened with Tolly, Rick. We're not going to find out if Chet had anything to do with his death, but if he did he was trying to protect Violet from him, and I understand that. Tolly might have killed Violet if he'd lived." I grabbed Rick's arm. "Oh my gosh. There wouldn't have *been* a Tolly if Chet hadn't done this. Maybe she'd have stayed with Johnny. Maybe she'd have married Sam and raised a beautiful daughter with him. Maybe several children."

Rick took the letter from my hands and said, "He killed Johnny's sister and nearly killed Johnny. He caused her to marry a cruel man who beat and tortured her, then she fell in love with him. I've never heard of anything like it, and I've seen a lot. Son of a bitch should've been in jail."

"I don't know, Rick. He was a child when he did all that." I pictured the neglected little boy Chet had been; the lunch money Violet gave him and the nights he spent wondering where his mother had gone. No one understood him as well as I did.

"You have got to be kidding me. He was a psychopath. At least a sociopath." He swept an arm toward the window. "There are bad people in this world, Ronni. They smile at you in the grocery store and help old ladies cross the street and charm the hell out of strangers and make proclamations of love. Don't be naïve."

"Maybe your job shows you the worst of humanity, but mine doesn't, Rick."

"Oh my God. You live in an idealistic world, Ronni. I'm a realist. And the truth is, someone you loved with all your heart had her life wrecked by a criminal. What do you think Violet would have said if she knew any of this? You think her precious Chet would still have been precious?" He threw Chet's letter down on the table, exasperated.

"He didn't mean for anyone to get hurt in that car. He didn't know how much she loved Sam, and he certainly didn't know Violet was pregnant..."

"And that makes it all fine? Ronni, I love your sweetness and kindness, but you have a lot to learn."

"What the hell is that supposed to mean?"

"People like Chet Wilson will stop at nothing to get what they want. There's no telling what else he did."

"I don't know." I put my head in my hands. "I don't know what to think about all this, except it makes me sick. I'm not even sure if I'd have shattered Violet's heart with the truth if I'd found out." I started to cry, picturing Violet and Chet in his little room at Fairfield, the two of them oblivious to anyone but each other.

Rick pulled me to my feet and held me close, brushing tears away and smoothing my hair.

"I'm sorry, baby. I'm sorry," he muttered. "I wish we'd never seen that letter."

"I was expecting a syrupy love note, like CeeCee suggested. Rick, you don't think CeeCee knew?"

"No. I'd bet anything she had no idea. That stuff about ruining Chet's life had to do with his obsession with Violet and his unhappy marriage. I didn't see any sign she knew what he'd done. This letter would've been burned in CeeCee's fireplace years ago if she had. Well, I should probably say *Bettina's marble fireplace*. CeeCee would've burned it in a backyard bonfire."

"That's true," I said, collapsing back into the chair. I traced Chet's words with my finger: *There is something I have to tell you. Nothing happened the way it was supposed to, Violet. I was a stupid, heartsick kid at the time.*

"Wow." I shook my head. "I guess I have the rest of my book."

He tipped my chin up with his finger. "Give yourself a little time to digest all this, huh? You don't have to start right now."

"Yes, I do. Writing about it will help me," I said. I kissed him and pulled away. "I'll be fine. Just give me a few hours to work on it." I nodded at the front door, knowing he understood my need to be alone.

He paused and turned around before he left. "Ronni," he said, "have you thought about the implications of the story, when the book is printed? Johnny and Sam and Chet may be gone, but their children and grandchildren and Deanna..."

"All deserve to know the truth," I answered. "As horrible as it is."

I sat at the table for the longest time, reeling from shock. I read Chet's letter over and over until every word was familiar.

When I met Violet I was a scared kid, untethered, insecure, and unsure about anything in my life. She'd loved me and encouraged me and somehow I'd turned into what she'd thought I was all along.

I *was* the person who could tell her story like no other.

I walked to my bedroom and took Violet's angel bracelet out, turning it over and over in my hand. I hung it on the corner of the photos I'd framed side by side and placed on my dresser. Violet beamed at me from her school's entry arches in the one on the left.

She shined even more brightly on the right, next to a grinning Johnny, pretending to dance in her "perfect" world.

I sat down and started to type. The first thing I did was change the opening sentence of Violet's first chapter to: "Johnny pulled his daddy's shiny new black DeSoto to the curb in front of Violet's house."

epilogue

RONNI

Six Months Later

"You're not getting white or silver. Too hard to see on the road." Rick pulled his head out of a green Honda Accord, the thousandth car we'd looked at today.

I rolled my eyes. "Maybe bright red with lime green stripes?"

"Laugh all you like. I want you safe. How do you feel about school bus yellow?"

"Fortunately, Honda wouldn't do that to me. Not even an option. Maybe another deep red like Ruby." I nodded wistfully at my beloved car across the lot, who was suffering from transmission problems and needed new brakes, too.

In the end we chose a shiny black Acura TL and I named him Melvin.

Two weeks after I sent my revised and expanded manuscript, Jennifer Meyer had called and given me the name of a literary agent, Mark Forbes. Mark and Jennifer had negotiated a $110,000 advance on my book, plus a generous royalty deal on future sales. Melvin was the first major purchase I made.

"You realize," Jennifer told me, "you're going to go on a cross-country tour to launch your book. That will mean a leave of absence from your job, or quitting altogether. We'll schedule it for spring of next year so you'll have plenty of time to make arrangements."

I'd called Deanna at our usual three o'clock that Saturday, when I knew she wouldn't be babysitting Lacey, The Center of the Universe.

"I can't believe it! I am so proud of you, Ronni, and I know my mother would be, too. You've worked so hard. I can't wait to read it."

I felt a little stab at the things Deanna would discover. "I hope you like it," was the best I could manage.

"I have some big news, too, Ronni."

"What? Are you coming to visit?"

Deanna was silent for a few seconds. "Actually, I'm coming to stay. I've been in touch with a realtor in Anniston and we've found the perfect house for me, Sarah and the kids."

"All of you!" I shrieked. "I can't wait, Deanna. I need you here. And you're going to love it. Can you imagine seeing the leaves change every year? And we even get snow sometimes, not too much, but enough to have fun. And..."

"I know," she laughed. "I don't need the chamber of commerce spiel. Besides, I've already bought ten new sweaters. I have Alabama red clay in my blood, Ronni. I love it there. The truth is, I also want to be near you, honey." She paused. "Sarah is doing well, and we've found a twelve-step program meeting she can attend a few times a week. Charlotte will be going to college next year, and she likes Auburn. We'll have in-state tuition after a year of residence. And," she sighed, "Kevin will be enrolled at Oxford High School. He thinks he'll become a football star there and Nick Saban will chase after him. Not that he's ever been off the bench for Palmetto High."

"I am positive the Alabama air will give him mad skills," I said. "Anyway, Rick's on his way here. We're going to celebrate tonight at Classic On Noble in Anniston. It's a gorgeous restaurant, Deanna. You'll love it..."

"I'm sold already, Ronni. You can stop. We'll see you in a couple of months. I love you."

"I love you, too." I grinned at my cell phone, dying to tell Rick.

He'd been with the boys all morning and was driving back from Tuscaloosa.

Mr. and Mrs. Gasbag had a new baby boy named Gaston, which Rick claimed would ensure the kid regularly scheduled playground beatings if they didn't give him a less pretentious nickname. Jeremy and Joshua were as revolted by the name as their dad, but good big brothers by all accounts. So far. Victoria was giving Rick all the time he wanted with his sons, busy with the baby.

He walked in a few minutes later. "You won't believe what Vicky did to that child. There's a portrait of his little three month old blob self propped next to Daddy's best-selling book. A professional portrait, hanging in the foyer." He laughed and picked me up in a hug, swinging around me before setting me down. "If they only knew we call them the Gasbags, Gaston would be even more hilarious," Rick said, "Little Gaston Gasbag, destined for a life of bowties and seersucker shorts. Roll, Le Tide."

I giggled. "I guess there are worse names, but I can't imagine one. I need you to sneak a pic of that portrait for me."

"Oh, I will. I thought Rick O'Shea was the cruelest thing parents could perpetrate namewise. I was so wrong. Speaking of parents, mine want us to join them at the lakehouse next weekend."

"Fine," I said. I'd grown to like Mr. and Mrs. O'Shea a lot, and they seemed to be relieved I was nothing like Victoria.

Rick produced a bottle of French champagne and handed it to me. "For my favorite author. Let's chill it and get an early start on tonight's celebration. I love you, babe, and I am so proud of you."

"There's one more thing to celebrate," I said. "Deanna and her family are moving to Anniston. In two months!"

Rick's grin was ear to ear. "I know," he admitted. "She made me keep it a secret."

I parked Melvin in front of Fairfield Springs and took a deep breath. It would be my last day there for several reasons. When my book was published, Donna would not be happy with its portrayal of her, to say the least. I doubted Fairfield would keep me employed after finding out my role in Violet and Chet's meetings. Herb would probably bring another lawsuit. I was paying a much bigger price than I'd considered by telling Violet's secrets. The thought of giving up my patients broke my heart, but Kait and Rick both promised me I'd be able to find a job at another facility later on if I wanted, if not back at Fairfield.

I had, at least, changed all the characters' names in the book. "Chet's" family would be spared embarrassment, though I really hoped "Loretta" never read it. Even "Fairfield Springs" wasn't the real name of my employer.

I wrote it for Violet. I loved her, and I'd live with the consequences. I was terrified of the book tour coming up, but Rick had promised to fly out and join me as often as he could. My notice had been given to Donna with the excuse I was going back to school for my RN degree. Maybe I'd actually do it if the writing thing didn't work out.

My biggest concern, the one that kept me awake at night, was Deanna. I'd tried to prepare her for what she'd learn, to tell her that her mother's life had been far more difficult and painful than anyone had known. I'd offered to tell her everything months ago, sitting on my couch, and she refused.

"Let me read the book, Ronni, and experience it like everyone else. Then we'll talk. I think it will be easier for me that way." She'd looked at my face and smiled. "Honey, if it weren't for you, I wouldn't know my mother at all. Nothing I find out can take that away from me."

I'd smiled back and gulped my wine, hoping she'd feel the same way after learning about Chet and all he'd set in motion.

Kait, the only person at Fairfield who knew the real reason I was leaving, was crying with me in the break room after I'd kissed the last of my favorite patients and residents goodbye. Donna stuck her head in to tell me she'd be gone, too, in three more weeks. "Paul got a big promotion at Petsmart. They're moving him to the corporate headquarters in Phoenix. I'm going to try to find a less stressful job there, like air traffic control." I laughed and held out my arms to her for a hug. "You'll be missed around here, Ronni. Come back and reapply when you get your degree. By then they'll have a permanent director of nursing. It's gonna be hard to replace moi."

"I probably will, Donna. You know how much I love this place. I hope you're happy in Arizona."

We watched Donna walk out to the parking lot. Kait smiled and held me by my upper arms, wide-eyed. "Guess who's interim director? And who's determined to make it permanent?"

"No!" I gasped. "Really? Oh, gosh, Kait, you'd be perfect."

"Perfect if you decide to come back, too," she smiled and shook me a little. "You're the best nurse we've ever had, Ronni. Well, when you're working with *me*. And you changed all the names in the book, so I don't think there'd be a problem. Even if old Herb decides to sue again, Fairfield will probably settle. You were trying to do what was best for your patient, and it *was* good for Chet."

"That's true. I hope you're right. In the meantime, I am going to miss you more than I can say." I hugged her tight and stepped back, afraid I'd break into sobs if I said any more.

"One more thing," Kait said. "I want you to see something in Violet's Activity Room Malt Shop Diner Bowling Alley Love Shack."

I laughed and grabbed my purse, following her down the hall.

The first thing I noticed was that the jukebox music wasn't right. I heard Bruno Mars singing "Just The Way You Are" before we got near the room. All the lights were dimmed and candles blazed on each table, surrounded by glasses of champagne and trays of appetizers. And there, in the center of a crowd of people—Deanna, Sarah, Mel Sobel, most of the Fairfield residents I'd kissed goodbye thirty minutes ago—was Rick O'Shea coming to lead me to the tiny dance floor.

He kissed my forehead and pulled me close. "They wanted a little goodbye party. I wanted to dance with you. It worked out."

"Well, I am truly surprised," I whispered as Mrs. Shaddix patted my passing elbow. Across the room a few old men surrounded Deanna, who was laughing and lapping up attention as the younger temptress. "This was very sweet of y'all."

"I have ulterior motives," he grinned and winked. "I intend to seduce you later and defile Violet's entertainment room." He twirled me around twice as the song changed to The Righteous Brothers' "Unchained Melody", then dipped me dramatically to applause from the entire room. "All the songs from here on are from these people's courtin' days," he whispered. "We'll dance to all of 'em if you want to."

"No," I giggled, "I need to talk to my guests. Most of them have an early bedtime."

When the song ended, Rick settled at a table in the middle of the room while I hugged and kissed everyone in sight.

"We're so proud of you, Ronni," they told me. "You have to come back and see us, even after you're famous. Send us postcards from your book tour." I cried each time I said goodbye.

By seven thirty most of my party had retired early to settle in and watch TV. Deanna and Sarah kissed my cheek and followed soon after. Mel Sobel asked me to walk him to his car. Rick nodded and said he'd wait.

Mel opened the passenger door of his Mercedes and extracted a small package. It was beautifully wrapped in floral print and fabric ribbon, topped with an ornate bow. "They said no gifts, but I want you to have this," he said. "Go ahead, open it." His eyes were twinkling.

Inside was a gold pendant necklace bearing a small book with an amethyst set in the center. The box bore the name of Birmingham's fanciest jeweler.

"It's so beautiful!" I was crying as I held it up to the fading daylight. "You shouldn't have."

"I wanted you to have it for the book tour. It's a locket, so we'll pick your favorite photo and have it placed inside. Here, let me put it on you." I turned my back and felt him fasten the necklace, patting it into place.

"I can't thank you enough, Mel. I will treasure this."

"Good, Ronni. I treasure our friendship." He clasped both my hands in his. "Listen, umm, could you take another minute or two and sit down with me? There's something I'd like to talk to you about."

I nodded and he led me to a bench near the entrance to Fairfield's lobby. We settled and Mel turned to face me.

"I've gone around and around for months with this, Ronni, not knowing if I should tell you. Violet didn't really want me to, but she didn't forbid it."

My heart thudded. "Okay."

"Tolly Thompson was not a good man, Ronni, as you know," Mel began. "But when he died, he left Violet a wealthy woman. At first, she played with her money; she traveled and bought a new car and jewelry and other expensive stuff. It didn't make her happy, though." He stopped to smile at me. "So, she came to see me about setting up a foundation to fund shelters for battered women, which we did. Soon after, we formed another charity called All God's Children. Its purpose is to assist families in adopting children out of foster care, getting them out of the system. I still serve on the board after all these years."

"Oh my gosh." I thought I knew what was coming, but waited for him to say the words.

"The Johnsons weren't very well off, Ronni, and they depended on the monthly checks they received to care for you. But they loved you and very much wanted to adopt you permanently. They approached Violet, and she approved the funding for your adoption."

Memories of my parents brought tears to my eyes. I sat quietly for a minute, thinking about them, before it occurred to me and I blurted, "So she knew who I was when we met *here*?" I shook my head in disbelief.

"Not at first. She pieced it together after a while. Violet didn't tell you because she didn't want to diminish the love your Mom and Dad had for you and all the sacrifices they made. They adored you, Ronni, and dedicated themselves to raising you and securing your future. Violet said all she did was write a check with her dead husband's money."

"It was much more than that," I palmed away a tear. "When Mom and Dad told me they wanted to adopt me, that I was going to be Ronni Johnson...well, it was the first time the ground under my feet felt solid. It's the point where I started looking forward instead of back."

"Maybe I should have kept quiet, Ronni. Like I said, I've debated whether to share this with you for a long time." Mel stared at something in the distance.

"No, you did the right thing, and I thank you so much. I'm grateful to know Violet helped me all those years ago. She changed my whole life."

Mel smiled and patted my hand. "She changed a lot of lives, Ronni. Everybody loved her."

I laughed softly. "So she mentioned."

Mel stood and said, "I have to get on the road. Have a wonderful book tour, Ronni. You'll be great."

"Thank you." I hugged him goodbye and watched him walk to his car, lingering until his lights faded into the distance.

Rick was waiting alone near the corner booth. "Beautiful necklace," he told me as I walked up. "That was so nice of Mel."

"Yes, it was." I reached to touch the locket, then chastised myself for getting fingerprints on it. "But you won't believe what he told me..."

Rick smiled and kissed me into silence. "We'll talk later. Right now we're going to dance real slow and then I have a little gift for you and this..." he looked around, "romance emporium of Violet's." He pressed a remote button and the oldies jukebox came back to life. I recognized the opening chords of Elvis Presley's "Can't Help Falling in Love."

"Take my hand, take my whole life too," Rick whispered. We were barely moving in the middle of the tiny dance floor. When the song ended, he held my face in his hands and said, "I love you, Ronni Johnson."

I smiled into his eyes and said, "I love you, too. Where's my present?"

"I see the Romance Emporium Effect is wearing off." Rick laughed softly and went behind a booth to retrieve a large package wrapped in brown paper.

It was a poster-sized enlargement of the photo of Johnny and Violet laughing and holding hands in the school's archway, beautifully matted and framed.

"Oh, Rick, this is wonderful," I said. "Thank you."

"It's to hang behind the soda fountain." He took it from my hands and hung it on a hook he'd obviously sneaked onto the wall earlier. "I even had the mat matched to the countertop."

"Yes, you did. Thank you so much, Rick. They belong there." I looked at Violet, so full of beauty and love and happiness, on the brink of beginning her grown-up life. I couldn't help thinking that I was beginning a new chapter, too. I closed my eyes and just for a second I saw the blonde and brown-eyed little girl I'd have someday.

I already knew her name.

—The End—

A word about this story:

**I've said it before: authors are thieves.
Though this is a work of fiction, some of the most incredible scenes are based on actual events.
The crazy vine thing in the first chapter, for instance.
I couldn't have made that up if I tried.**

**Writing about the abuse Violet suffered was dark and painful, particularly as she lived in a time when help wasn't readily available.
It is now.
Please support your local shelter for victims of domestic violence.**

Acknowledgments

I am the most fortunate writer in the world to depend on a discerning and lovable group of advance readers. My heartfelt thanks go to Lucinda Hathaway, Beth Monette, Marianne Barnebey, Robert Gebhardt, David Boyd, Dan Brown, and Lillian Pizzo.

Debbie Tuckerman deserves a title far more special than advance reader. She has been by my side through every revision as well as the entire publishing industry roller coaster, offering steadfast encouragement, inspiration, ideas, and support. She's lived with Ronni and Violet only a fraction of time less than I have, and there are no adequate words to express my thanks. Debbie, you made this a much better story. I am so grateful to you.

My beautiful daughter Savannah read the manuscript while pursuing a master's degree, which is above and beyond any call of duty. Thank you, baby!

I am very thankful also to my original advance reader, my mother, Patricia Poucher. Everything I write, I write for my mom. I joke that I'm still trying to make things she'll hang on the refrigerator—*and she actually asked for this book's author photo page to hang on her refrigerator,* which made my heart sing all day.

My cousin, Amanda Winfield, is a completely dedicated nurse to her elderly patients. She shared fascinating (often hilarious) stories and even allowed me to shadow her at work, where I learned a lot and witnessed the beauty of her kindness. Mandy and so many nurses like her are love and compassion personified.

Thank you to my dad, Bob Poucher, for expert answers to questions on a variety of topics I researched for this book, from automobiles to telephones.

Kristin Gause is not only a dear friend, she's a fabulous banking consultant. She has a namesake character in this book, like the real Kris, but not as cool.

Thank you to many wonderful residents of Anniston, Alabama for helping me bring the 1940s and 1950s to life. I love my hometown and her gracious people.

I am grateful to John Ferrell, owner of Mary Mac's Tea Room, for his story guidance and for serving the best soul food in Atlanta. It's a real and delightful place, folks. You should eat there at least once in your life! The same is true of the elegant and much-loved Classic On Noble in Anniston. Both restaurants are fabulous, and if you visit, please tell them I sent you with my highest recommendation.

Finally, thank you Jay, Jason, and Savannah for your endless patience, support, love and understanding. Writers can be slightly irritable, self-absorbed, preoccupied, and diva-ish. Not me, of course.

And thank you, cherished reader. Always.

Other books by Beth Duke:

Delaney's People: A Novel in Small Stories
Don't Shoot Your Mule

Please visit www.bethduke.com

Beth Duke is the recipient of short story awards on two continents and is eyeing the other five. Her work has been published in numerous magazines and literary digests.
IT ALL COMES BACK TO YOU is her third novel.
She lives in the mountains of her native Alabama with her husband, one real dog, one ornamental dog, and a flock of fluffy pet chickens.
She loves reading, writing, and not arithmetic.
Baking is a hobby, with semi-pro cupcakes and amateur macarons a specialty.
And puns—the worse, the better.
Travel is her other favorite thing, along with joining book clubs for discussion.

Author photo by Savannah Duke
Florence, Italy, New Year's Eve 2017

Made in USA - North Chelmsford, MA
1248307_9780578448831
05.25.2021 0954